PROSPICE

A NOVEL

PROSPICE

A NOVEL

Karen Kelly

LEGITUR BOOKS

FIRST EDITION
All rights reserved, including the right of
reproduction in whole or in part in any form.

Copyright © 2013 by Karen Kelly

Published by Legitur Books
New York, New York

Manufactured in the United States of America

ISBN 978-0-9893200-0-9 (hardcover)
ISBN 978-0-9893200-1-6 (paperback)

0 9 8 7 6 5 4 3 2 1

Cover and interior design by Sheila Hart Design, Inc.

For more about this book and author, visit www.prospiceanovel.com

To the girls who lived down the hall—

Leigh, Tate, and Nina.

To Will—the lone brave.

And to Bill, for everything.

I'd like to thank Betsy Cussler for her encouraging support and critical approbation, which meant so much; Daniel Slager of Milkweed Editions for his affirmation; Sally Maenner for her generous resourcefulness; Susan, Dave, Janet, Marianne, my grandmother Ethel (still reading thoughtfully at 97), and especially Nina— my most enthusiastic audience; my editor, Laura Ross for her keen eye and dab hand; Sheila Hart for her artistry and guidance; and finally, my mother, Mary, whose unorthodox childhood inspired this story.

CONTENTS

Part One: Family

Part Two: Damage

Part Three: Look Ahead

O soul of my soul!
I shall clasp thee again.

— Robert Browning
"Prospice"

PROSPICE: (Latin) Look ahead

FAMILY

CHAPTER ONE
Others Will, Too

THE MAN IN THE GREEN COVERALLS had only one hand. While the other movers labored in twosomes to haul a three-drawer bureau or a slender tallboy up the limestone steps, this man single-handedly (quite literally) hoisted one of the more cumbersome pieces—a heavy hickory chiffarobe—onto his shoulder, gripping the top edge with his good hand and balancing the outer weight with the stump at the end of his wrist.

From her vantage point on a large cardboard box, Dinah thought about the strange incongruity of his occupation, watching him disappear through the classic Georgian Revival doorway. The house was situated close to the street, as most homes in Salem were. She had visited her grandparents here as a young child, but had only vague recollections. It had an aura that few homes have, which can only be acquired over time—an indefinable quality of grace. It basked in the assurance of its own dignity. The façade had a columned portico, and the roof held a balustrade that gave the impression of a widow's walk—an actual feature of many homes in the area, where in centuries past anxious wives and daughters had watched for the distant outlines of returning sails.

Her ancestors were not the first family to live in the house, but they had been there for generations. Her great-great-grandfather had been a Salem ship builder and founded the Seaward Company, which became one of the preeminent boat builders in the country. Some years before, the Seaward Company had been sold to Latcher Industries, a conglomerate, which continued to build boats, but during and since World War II found its main source of revenue manufacturing munitions. Her mother had explained this to her, adding with a wink, "Latcher now does a booming business," which made Dinah laugh.

Inside the house the wear of a century and a half had taken its toll, but the grand curving staircase and the massive fireplace over-mantels maintained an elegance and beauty that neither time nor neglect could diminish. Wandering through the wide center hall to the library, Dinah found the ponderous form of Bel, their basset hound. Her father had surprised them with the puppy when he won his first big commission—for a library in Charleston. The dog's name was actually Beleaguered, a suggestion submitted by Caroline, who said it suited the puppy's demeanor. Gideon's proposal—Ichabod—had been roundly rejected by the women of the family, as Dinah pointed out that the dog was a female, and Aunt Bat declared that she had hoped *she* would be the last victim in a long line of misguided monikers: "I swear, I refuse to allow another single soul in the power of my bein' to bear a cross as heavy as mine has been," she drawled. "You wanna talk about beleaguered. . ."

"Batty, you couldn't possibly have been named anything else," Gideon had teased, sliding his arm around his aunt and giving her a kiss on the cheek. "You are the battiest woman I know." The Hunt family had a long-established tradition of using names from the Old Testament. In fact, it was an unspoken rule, as Caroline had explained to Dinah, and although Gideon had been the first to break with the tradition that had called generations of Hunt men to the clergy, he was unwilling to break with that particular custom. Her mother confided that she was relieved, when Dinah was born, that she could agree with her husband on a name. She had been prepared to defend her baby girl from the burden of a clunker like Dorcas or Hagar, although she worried that Dinah would be mispronounced.

"People will be confused . . . maybe it should be spelled Deenah," she suggested. But taking liberties with the spelling didn't follow the Hunt family tradition; thus Dinah became yet another in the long-suffering line of Hunts who would spend much of their lives explaining their names.

"Consider her lucky," Gideon had told Caroline, and she knew what he meant—in addition to Batty, short for Bathsheba, his other aunt was Bilah, known as Bee.

Bel's arrival these days was heralded by a soft scuffing sound—her squat legs overwhelmed by her pendulous belly, which had acquired a shiny, leathery patch from its contact with the floor. It reminded Dinah of the elbows of her father's hound's-tooth jacket. It was the jacket he always wore when they walked by the river in the late autumn evenings. He would make up spontaneous scavenger hunts, giving the girls impossible challenges, such as finding a bluebird's feather, or a four-leaf clover, but they never gave up hope of finding these magical objects. Rather, Dinah never gave up hope; Jemima simply toddled along behind her, looking in exactly the same places, mimicking every action. It kept them busy as their parents strolled along, sharing the simple details of the day. One time Dinah did find a four-leaf clover—she simply looked down and there it was. Gideon said it was an event to be commemorated, and they all went to the Tasty Treat and celebrated. She still had the clover—pressed inside Numbers 1:11, the first mention of Gideon in the bible.

As Caroline directed the movers, she noticed her daughter's distant expression. "Why don't you come on up and show me where you'd like to put your bed?" she asked.

Dinah looked up, and Caroline could see a look of determined optimism replace that of ineffable sadness. Dinah's concern for her mother was heartbreaking in its generosity. There was a sweet, selfless valor in the way that she tried to mask her sorrow to protect Caroline—as though she felt responsible for keeping her mother buoyant through the cold, deep channel in which they'd found themselves drifting.

"Sure," she answered brightly. "Where's Jemima?"

"I sent her up to start on her boxes—she'll have my old room, so we don't need her little trundle bed anymore," Caroline replied. "Back me up on this, Dinah—you know how attached she gets to her things."

Dinah was quiet, thinking about their house in Beaufort. She felt ambivalent about the remnants of their old life. It was almost a relief to start fresh—a convenient remedy to the strong grip of nostalgic longing that had continually pulled at her since her father's death.

Predictably, they found Jemima, not upstairs tackling her unpacking chores, but face-down on the kitchen floor, intently peering into the heating register in the floorboards. "Momma, come and see this," she insisted. "There's a hole in the floor. I think there's something in there. I saw it move. Something really small. Like a leopardcon." Jemima's fantastical beliefs were accepted as a matter of course by Caroline and Dinah, and though she was getting to be an age to outgrow her fanciful notions, neither of them was particularly eager to dispel them.

"Sugar, I am sorry to disappoint you, but what you've got there is a furnace grate, and I'm fairly certain that no leprechauns have ever been sighted in this old house. Mice, yes. Leprechauns, no." In Beaufort, their home had been heated, when heat was required, by an old pot-bellied stove. "Come on upstairs and be the boss—you're in charge of the movers."

Jemima's chirpy prattle trailed through the house as Dinah lagged back, quietly studying the details that surrounded her. She noted the worn mahogany of the banister and the elegant coffered ceilings. The walls of the stairway had vague outlines of absent frames—her grandfather had once been acknowledged as a leading collector of nineteenth-century American artists, but his collection was long since auctioned away. Dinah absorbed all this with a remote detachment. Since her father's death, everything seemed just a little out of focus, as though there were a cloud surrounding her. She noticed a small painting that had managed to retain its place on the landing—a sailboat carried along in the breeze. An image suddenly replaced the sailboat, and she was watching a paddleboat, festive with red and gold trim, moving gently down the river. Their house on Bay Street had faced the Beaufort River, just visible through the live oak and crepe myrtle as it bent toward the sea. As a little girl, she could often hear the melancholy moans of barges and tugs, but it was rare to see a paddleboat, and that was what she had seen as her father wrapped her in his arms to say goodbye. The association was indelible—she would forever think of that paddleboat as a symbol of loss. Once, when she had the flu, her mother made fried chicken, and it had turned her stomach. She hated fried chicken now, and that's how she felt about the poor, benign paddleboat. The idea of it turned her stomach.

After the moving van pulled away, Caroline absently wandered through the house, pausing briefly here and there to look at boxes labeled "Linens" or "Good China." She couldn't seem to think of what to do next—a strange lethargy was settling in. A ray of sunlight reflected off a silver pitcher on the sideboard in the dining room, momentarily shining into her eyes, summoning a memory: the image of a brass button on a Marine's uniform, similarly reflecting the sun, so that she hadn't been able to see his face when she opened the door. Once again, Caroline saw the soldier standing on the threshold. His hands were behind his back, and he was rhythmically swaying forward and back again, heel to toe. It was a nervous motion that rang out his purpose like a bell. She had stared at the button, willing it to blind her, to obliterate all of her senses, but when he spoke she could still hear. "Mrs. Hunt, may I come in?" She wanted to shut the door. She wanted, with every particle of her being, to scream *No! No! You may not come in!* Instead, she simply stepped back to let him pass.

Now she sat on the worn satin of a Chippendale dining chair, tracing her finger over one of the small golden bumblebees in the "French Bee" pattern. *A war widow.* She had never even considered the possibility. Her husband was an architect, not a soldier. But a sense of patriotic duty had impelled him to sign up for the Reserves, and now, here she was, in her childhood home again, still not quite believing it was real.

It had been almost two years since the officer had clasped her hand, offering his deepest sympathy and a letter from the United States Marine Corps. Not long after the officer's visit, her mother, who had occupied the house as a widow for nearly a decade, had died. The old place sat empty for over a year, and then one morning, lying alone in her bed in Beaufort, staring at the empty pillow beside her, Caroline felt an urgent need to escape—to move away from the ghost who sat in Gideon's chair, who kept his shirts hanging in a neat row in the closet. She had intended to put the old house in Salem up for sale, but in an impulsive moment of decision, she listed the Beaufort house instead.

Looking around, Caroline marveled at how little things had changed since she had left, with the exception of the disappearance of some of the more valuable antiques, sold as the family business crumbled. She remembered an ormolu commode that once stood majestically in the foyer and the elaborate French Rococo clock that used to sit on the living room mantel but had never kept accurate time. She wondered what price it had brought. A lot, she supposed, functional or not. The bottomless human capacity to revere beauty was a wonder that often gave her solace. In the months immediately after Gideon died, one of the few comforts she could find was in the works of Chopin or Beethoven, the exquisite genius of the music transporting her like a spiritual experience, filling her with an aching hope. She had wanted to bow her head in gratitude for the faith and grace that such beauty could bestow. It was the hope of human possibility—of something good in the world.

"Momma!" Jemima's small voice had an amazingly projective quality that sometimes—Caroline had to admit—felt a bit assailing. Her shoulders jerked upward slightly at the intrusion, but she summoned a smiling patience.

"What is it, Mimer?" she called up the stairs.

"I can't remember my poem." The normally bright little voice was tired and cranky.

"All right, Sweepea, I'm coming." Caroline made her way up the staircase. She closed her eyes briefly as she reached the upstairs hall. It broke her heart that Jemima clung so tightly to one of the few things she had from her father. Gideon had loved the name Jemima, which meant dove, and he often called her his little dove. At bedtime, he would frequently recite Tennyson's "Come into the Garden," not only because he loved Tennyson, but because Jemima liked to hear the poet call his beloved Maud "my dove," just as her father called her. Also, by the eleventh and final stanza she was usually fast asleep.

Caroline had taken over the duty when Gideon had been shipped out, intent on maintaining the traditions and rituals that the girls had established with their father, particularly for Jemima, who was only three. But after she learned that Gideon's ship had been hit—that he would never come home—she could no longer bring herself to say the words. Numbly, she kissed her daughters at night, not trusting herself with anything more than a choked "Goodnight." Then one day she heard Jemima in the garden, playing with Bibby, her small muslin doll. Her baby voice piped quietly over the patch of lily-of-the-valley where she sat:

"Come into da gawden, Maud. A bwack bat night has fwown." She repeated the phrase over and again, tenderly looking down at the doll that she cradled in her arms. Suddenly Caroline found herself next to Jemima in the lilies, holding her little girl as the words welled up in her own chest and escaped, released from their grief-locked vault.

Now, she found her younger daughter slumped by a long window in the bedroom that once had been her own. The soft floral draperies were the same. Jemima had unpacked only one of her boxes—unpacked being an optimistic description. Dumped out was more like it. She appeared to have collapsed onto the floor in utter exhaustion, like a puppy, with her beloved Fuzz Monkey draped around her neck.

"Come on up here—and bring that atrocious creature with you," Caroline patted the bed. Fortunately Gussie, her mother's long-standing housekeeper, had left the bedding fresh before shutting up the house; Caroline was in no mind to hunt through boxes of linens. Jemima crawled up onto the delicate mahogany four-poster bed and gazed up at the lace canopy.

"This is a funny bed," she mumbled. It was clear that the foreign formality of her surroundings was testing her sense of security; Caroline could see that she would need to work hard to compensate for the loss of the familiar.

"Well, let's see now . . . you and Fuzz could pretend you're camping out in our old back yard, and this is your tent. You know that old pup tent that Daddy used to put up for you and Dinah?" Jemima looked up doubtfully at the dainty lace, but fatigue won out over complaint, and she snuggled into the curve of Caroline's arm and closed her eyes. Softly, Caroline began to recite:

Come into the garden, Maud,
For the black bat, night, has flown,
Come into the garden, Maud,
I am here at the gate, alone;
And the woodbine spices are wafted abroad,
And the musk of the rose is blown . . .

Jemima barely stirred, and Caroline was certain her little girl had drifted off after several stanzas, but as she quietly and carefully abbreviated the poem Jemima shifted and murmured, "I didn't hear my name." So Caroline picked up at the tenth stanza:

There has fallen a splendid tear
From the passion-flower at the gate.
She is coming, my dove, my dear;
She is coming, my life, my fate.
The red rose cries, "She is near, She is near";
And the white rose weeps, "She is late";
The larkspur listens, "I hear, I hear";
And the lily whispers, "I wait."

Caroline had been gazing at the window, and she now looked down at small rosy lips, faintly open in a child's dreamless slumber. She tenderly traced her finger along the top of Jemima's brow as a tear rolled down her cheek, and her own voice became Gideon's as she whispered the final verse:

She is coming, my own, my sweet;
Were it ever so airy a tread,
My heart would hear her and beat,
Were it earth in an earthy bed;
My dust would hear her and beat,
Had I lain for a century dead,
Would start and tremble under her feet,
And blossom in purple and red.

The next evening, Caroline announced to the girls that they would be treated to dinner at one of Salem's finest restaurants, as she hadn't yet had time to get the kitchen in order.

"You two may think that you've experienced fine dining before, but you are in for a treat tonight!" she said playfully. The early evening air had a trace of the crispness that comes with autumn in the Northeast. In Beaufort, the summer lasted well into fall, with the languor of the humid nights casting a veil of somnolence over the town. Here in Salem, an alert energy attached itself to the diners at Melville's. As they slid into a booth, Jemima delightedly moved her hands over the tiny sparkles in the red vinyl upholstery. She looked around expectantly, as if waiting for a genie to appear. Each new experience was dazzling to her—she opened her whole self to life's surprises.

A buxom waitress in a brown and orange apron with a pen stuck behind her ear took the place of the expected genie. "Meatloaf and mashed on special tonight, choice of corn or peas," was all she said as she laid down the menus and hurried away. Dinah and Jemima looked bewilderedly at their mother. In their young lives, they had never experienced the curt abruptness of a Massachusetts Yankee; back at the Cotton Café, Wanda Jane would talk an ear off before you even got water.

"It's straight to business around these parts," Caroline said with an amused smile. "But it's all right, you just have to get used to getting to the point."

They ordered hamburgers and fries, their mother's powers of persuasion failing when it came to convincing the girls to try the meatloaf. They also had milkshakes, and Jemima kept blowing bubbles through her straw.

"Mimer, please stop that." It was evident in Caroline's voice that they were at the end of a very long day, but Jemima couldn't resist one last gurgling puff. Her mother's attempt at scolding had a weary, half-hearted quality—she was resting her chin on her hand as she murmured, "Jemima Hunt, that barbaric behavior is so far beneath dignity that I can hardly see you." This choice of words served to inspire Jemima to grab another straw from the tall stainless steel cup on the table and proceed to put the two of them in her nose, crossing her eyes and growling her lowest, fiercest roar, in her best impression of a barbarian. Dinah nearly spit out a French fry in a failed attempt to contain a laugh.

"That's it!" Caroline shook her napkin and tossed it on the table in exasperation. "Let's go. You two are an embarrassment." The expression in her eyes didn't quite match the tone of her words, and the girls understood that this stern reproof was partially to cover her amusement. They had finished eating, at any rate, and Caroline left payment on the tab as she stood up and gathered her sweater and handbag.

As the girls trailed behind her, they passed a booth with a single occupant—a man with lightly graying temples and warm, amused eyes. He smiled at them, and Caroline said, "I hope you aren't put off your dinner by the revolting antics of my, um, children . . ." She gave them a disgusted look as though she weren't entirely sure what species they were. And then she looked quickly back at the man. His expression had changed from anonymous benevolence to alert recognition.

"Tom?" Caroline's voice was incredulous.

"Hello, Caroline."

Something in his tone captured Dinah's attention—the words sounded somehow fraught, holding private, undue familiarity. She looked at her mother, who was suddenly wearing a wide, easy smile.

"Tom Stuart! I don't believe it! It's been, what? Twenty years?"

"That's about right, I'd say," he leaned forward over his crossed arms on the table. There was a wry smile playing on his lips. "It was May of '26, to be exact."

Caroline was at Smith, and Tom was in his senior year at Amherst, when they had met at a mixer. They dated for almost six months, but although the relationship had all the makings of a serious romance, Caroline still had two more years at school when Tom graduated and accepted a job offer in Pennsylvania with Bethlehem Steel. Ultimately, they had to admit that the timing was wrong, and they sadly parted ways.

Seeing him so suddenly after all this time caused a strange, phenomenal transportation, and for an instant Caroline could feel the regret and confusion of the weeks following the break-up. The visceral immediacy of this sudden memory was disorienting. It took a moment to find her balance, and she turned to the girls to steady herself.

"Let me introduce my daughters. Dinah, Jemima, please say hello to Mr. Stuart." As the girls said hello, Caroline regained some composure. "Tom was my beau in college—until he went off to make his mark on the world." Her words were teasing, and she turned to Tom with a smile. "What are you doing in Salem?" she asked. "The last I knew, you had become a man of steel in Bethlehem."

Tom laughed. "Well, the corporate ladder is long and steep, and the climbing feels awfully shaky. I thought it might be best to build my own tower and sit in the guard station." He grinned, and elaborated: "I have a lumber company here in town—with the unlikely name of Stuart Lumber." He shrugged in mock dismay at the immodesty of the self-reference.

"Is that the giant hammer place, Momma?" They had passed Stuart Lumber driving into town, and the sign bearing an enormous fist and hammer had captured Jemima's attention.

"It never occurred to me that that was you!" Caroline said.

"It's a little disheartening, when you think about it," Tom continued. "From 'Man of Steel' to poor lumberjack . . ."

"I'll bet," Caroline laughed. She knew that Stuart Lumber was the biggest lumber company in the area, operating several mills throughout the Northeast. "You must be exhausted at night from all that wood-chopping."

Jemima was looking at Tom with new respect, surreptitiously trying to check out his arm muscles, but Dinah understood the teasing sarcasm, and she studied her mother intently. She had not had the opportunity to see Caroline in a social exchange with another man who wasn't somehow in their employ—whether it was their lawyer, or the pediatrician, or the movers, or a gas station attendant . . . at least not since her father had died. Caroline had been unable to bring herself to accept any social invitations in Beaufort after Gideon died, and those had dwindled away, as casual friendships do when they're not nurtured. Dinah had come to expect a distant, business-like demeanor in her mother's interactions with the opposite sex. Now Caroline's eyes were bright, and she actually seemed to be aware of this man as an individual, and not just an associate. This was somehow unnerving to Dinah. She felt a little tug of apprehension, made manifest by a curt impatience: "I think Bel should be let out, Mom. We should go."

Caroline looked at her, surprised at this uncharacteristic interruption from her normally polite firstborn. "I suppose you're right—we'd better get home." She turned back to Tom. "It was nice bumping into you like this. Perhaps we'll be making a call on your mill someday to shore up that old pile of lumber that we live in, before it falls down around us!"

Tom tilted his head inquisitively. "Are you talking about the house on Chestnut Street?" he asked. During the time they had dated he had been invited to meet Caroline's parents at home, and they had driven from Northampton for Easter Sunday dinner.

"I'm afraid so," Caroline replied. "Right back where I started from." She paused and gave a weighty glance toward her daughters, communicating her reluctance to say anything more. She was suddenly tired and overwhelmed. It occurred to her that this awkward moment was to be repeated over and over again as she found herself in a position to explain the tragedy of her loss, not only to new acquaintances, but to ghosts from her past as well.

Tom astutely read the signs, and she was relieved that he didn't pursue the topic, but simply took her hand in both of his and said, "It's wonderful to see you again, Caroline. Feel free to call me about any lumber needs you may have."

"Thanks, Tom." She gave him a wide smile. It was spontaneous and real, and she couldn't help but note it—more marvelous by virtue of its long absence. She ushered the girls out the door and into the car, and drove home with the windows down and the radio on, whistling along with Frank Sinatra to "All or Nothing at All." Jemima waved her arms out the window, and for the first time in a long while the girls felt the reassuring contagion of their mother's light-heartedness.

Salem Junior High was just a few blocks away, and Dinah walked to school, stopping first at Bentley Elementary School to deposit Jemima in her first-grade class. It was a beautiful, sunny September day, with a soft breeze coming in over the harbor that covered Salem in a warm caress. Jemima was fairly bouncing with excitement at the prospect of an entire room full of new friends; she was chattering about the superior style of her green plastic pencil pouch when her attention jumped to the next shiny thing that caught her eye, which happened to be a gleaming black Armstrong-Siddeley convertible with whitewall tires. Jemima wasn't the only one who noticed, although Dinah's attention was captured not by the car but by the boy in the passenger seat. She was still gazing at him as the car disappeared around the corner, and she nearly walked into the low brick wall surrounding the school.

Mrs. Lifson's first grade class rang with the cacophony of first-day hubbub. Several small bodies were glued to adult legs—crying and begging to be taken back home—while others gathered in happy little groups, proudly displaying the latest fashion in lunch boxes. Jemima lost no time inserting herself into the second category, creating quite a stir with her flashy new pouch.

"Don't be naughty, Mimer," Dinah teased as she kissed her little sister on the cheek. "Remember what Mom always says: 'Watch and learn.'"

Dinah walked the final block to the old, brick junior high on Essex Street by herself. A bell tower stood sentry over the entrance, and just as she mounted the wide marble steps it rang a sonorous sequence of deep chimes. She felt a shiver run up her spine and a momentary nervousness at the prospect of being new. Then she breathed deeply and heard her father's voice: *If you know who you are, Dinah, others will too.* Propelled through the doors by a throng of students, she managed to find her way to the school office, where she tapped her heel anxiously while waiting for the secretary to double-check the paperwork.

"Let's see now . . . yes . . . I believe we have it all here." The woman's movements were aggravatingly slow as she leafed through a file. Finally she looked up, beaming in apparent oblivion to the ticking clock on the wall. "I think we're all set. You'll have Mrs. Booth for homeroom—that's room 209."

The words had no sooner left her mouth than the first bell rang, and Dinah had to dash down the unfamiliar halls, giving an unintentional vaudevillian performance as she slid past the door to room 209 and wheeled backward. The only seats left were in the front row of desks. Taking her place, she had the uncomfortable feeling of being examined from behind her back. She smiled to herself as she thought of Jemima's furious accusation that people were talking about her "around her back." Dinah and her mother often found themselves sharing a laugh about what they called "Mimerisms": Jemima had a bounty of misinterpreted phrasing that never failed to provide amusement. This small, cheerful reverie was interrupted by the roll call, as she heard her own name mispronounced by Mrs. Booth. "It's *Deenah*," she offered.

A low voice in the back of the room snickered and echoed "It's Dayna, y'all."

A rising heat crept up her neck; Dinah had been quite aware that most people in Salem spoke with a clipped, nasal-sounding accent, but it hadn't occurred to her that her own would be noticeable.

"I'm sorry, dear," said Mrs. Booth. Her dour, pinched face was trying to arrange itself into a semblance of sincerity. "Such an unusual pronunciation. Your parents must be very . . . avant-garde."

Feeling defensive, Dinah tried to explain. "It's from the Old Testament. That's how it's supposed to be pronounced."

Mrs. Booth looked over her glasses. "I'm quite familiar with the story of Dinah and Shechem, but unless you have it on the authority of King James, I believe that biblical pronunciation is open to interpretation."

There was more snickering, this time even a loud laugh. Dinah sank low in her seat, wishing she could somehow disappear. She was dangerously close to wallowing in her new-school misery—something her mother had been vigilant about: "To wallow is to secretly relish," she would warn. But she was saved from herself by the sudden image the one-handed mover, carrying such a heavy load on his back for his living, putting a shameful perspective on her prickly, self-conscious sensitivity.

When the school day finally ended, she and Jemima walked home, making a detour to stroll through the commons in the mellow Salem sunlight. They held hands as Jemima chatted about her first-grade experience. "And Peter Cannon Ball is my best friend," she said, which finally got Dinah's attention.

"Did you say Peter Cannon Ball?" she asked.

"Yep, and he's short like me and he has a African Fur Turtle at his house."

At this, Dinah just shook her head and decided to continue in a state of suspended comprehension, as was often the case with the stories Jemima told. "Short like *I*," was all she said, and they found themselves at home, even though it didn't feel like home.

The fall passed slowly for Dinah. Aside from getting off on the wrong foot in homeroom, she had a harder time making friends than Jemima, who had the advantage of starting at the beginning. There was a girl named Betsy who was funny and nice, and Dinah sat with her at lunch. Betsy MacEvoy had moved from Ann Arbor, Michigan, just the year before—her father was a professor at Salem State College. Dinah had managed to befriend a few of the other girls, but most of the kids had known each other all their lives. "You're too pretty, that's the problem," Betsy had said authoritatively.

Dinah had occasionally overheard remarks about her appearance—her parents' friends had commented on the unusual, sea-green shade of her eyes and the luminous gold in her hair—but asceticism ran deep in Hunt heritage, and neither Gideon nor Caroline encouraged an awareness of physical gifts. In fact, they had determinedly set out to deliver their daughters from vanity, and Dinah was still surprised when someone mentioned the way she looked. What gave her pleasure when she looked in the mirror these days was that she saw a little of her father looking back at her. In truth, she suspected her own solitary nature as the more likely cause of her meager social life. She simply preferred the company of dead authors.

Jemima was another story. She drew people to her like fire draws air. Peter Campbell, whom Dinah still liked to call Peter Cannonball, had become Jemima's best friend. On a rainy Saturday afternoon Jemima and Peter played in the garage attic, which had once been the carriage house. They had dragged several old blankets up the rickety pull-down stairs and were building a tent village in a make-believe land.

Dinah was in the kitchen, trying to figure out how to light the old gas oven to make cookies. Most of the old appliances had been replaced by her grandmother over the years, but the antiquated cast-iron stove and ovens were still solidly functional; Caroline told Dinah it was the best way to cook in the world, and she would just have to get used to lighting the gas. The kitchen had been designed for domestic staff and had the "downstairs utilitarian" aspect of an English country manor. Worn black and white marble tiles covered the floor, and there was a long, scarred oak trestle table running through the center of the room. There was also a more formal butler's pantry in the passage to the dining room, with polished walnut cabinetry to house silver and china.

As Dinah started to turn an ancient pewter knob, squinting into the small match hole on the side of the oven, Jemima suddenly charged through the back door. It was rare for Jemima to appear anything but happy, because her sherry-brown eyes had a slightly elliptical shape that gave the impression that she was laughing even when she wasn't. She had curly, soft, brown hair, deep dimples, and from some unknown ancestor had inherited a slightly olive tint to her complexion, which gave her skin an incredibly soft quality that compelled total strangers to want to stroke her face.

"I want Peter to go home now. Call his mother!" Her expression was stormy, and Dinah could see that she was trying not to cry.

"What happened?" A sudden, fierce protective urge flared as Dinah started toward the door.

Jemima's bottom lip quivered. "He called me a pygmy." Her little shoulders shuddered as she bravely confessed her worries: "I'm like a ganome or something. I'm smaller than everyone in my class." She looked sorrowfully at her dainty feet. "I'm only as big as I was last year. I think I'm all done."

Dinah remembered that Jemima had a reading primer that stressed phonetics, and a picture book of fairy tale creatures. Evidently the combination yielded questionable results. "Oh, Mimer . . ." She was trying not to smile, and she felt her heart contract a little at the pitiful expression on her sister's face. "You aren't all done. You're just getting started. Peter's hardly any taller than you are—he must be the second-shortest kid in the class. He's just trying to make himself feel bigger."

Jemima drew back indignantly. "Do you think he's *using me?*"

This time she couldn't squelch it—Dinah laughed out loud. "Where did you hear that phrase? What a kook!" She took Jemima's hand and led her out the door. "I think he's using you as his best friend, and sometimes friends hurt your feelings by accident. I'll bet Peter feels worse about this than you do."

At the top of the attic stairs they looked around at any empty room. Dinah imagined Peter skulking home in shame and remorse, but Jemima went straight across the floor to a pile of old blankets and gave a little kick. In an effort to become invisible, Peter had rolled up in one of the blankets and refused to respond, but Dinah neatly pulled one end, sending him rotating out like an anthropoid rolling pin, making Jemima laugh. Dinah told them that they were giants in the land of Lilliputians, a word which made both children howl, and Dinah could see that the pygmy incident was behind them as they ran around shouting "Pew, pew, I smell a Lilliputian!"

Back in the kitchen, Dinah finally figured out how to put the match into the little hole without blowing up the house, and continued to mix ingredients into an old, chipped ceramic bowl. She found herself once again smiling at her little sister's inimitable interpretations. Dinah had been almost eight when Jemima was born; until then, she had largely lived in a world of adults, with Aunt Batty—who lived just down the street—her preferred companion. But when Jemima came along, a natural tendency to nurture presented itself, and Dinah adored her little sister. She pictured the long glider swing on their porch in Beaufort, where she would hold Jemima on her lap, making up stories until the sun set and the cricket chorus nearly drowned out her words. An image of a sweet, chubby face with a mysterious brown chip clinging to a rosebud lip flashed through her mind. "Mimer, what's on your face?" she had asked.

A baby voice, unable to pronounce certain consonants, explained: "Pineappo."

Dinah noticed then that Jemima was clutching a wet pinecone, with the top gnawed off. After a long moment of consideration, the little girl generously handed it to her big sister: "You can have the rest."

CHAPTER TWO
Grace

AS CHRISTMAS APPROACHED, Caroline was inspired to deck the halls as festively as possible. Although the girls had taken over their bedrooms with hurricane-like assimilation, she knew they were still having a hard time calling Salem home. She wanted to establish a new set of traditions, beginning with Christmas. Cold weather and snow seemed so much more apropos the holiday. Their decorations in Beaufort had been lovely, but minimal—it had just never felt real to Caroline with palm trees growing outside the door. She understood the irony, knowing full well that there were plenty of palm trees around in Bethlehem, but her childhood Christmases had been all about sleigh rides and Santa in his red flannel suit. She wanted the fresh experience of a wintery Christmas to give Dinah and Jemima an appreciation for their new home, something on which to build a new life.

After the girls left for school, Caroline drove to the old YMCA on Essex Street. The beautiful old limestone and brick building held fond memories; while she was growing up she had accompanied her father there to pick out a Christmas tree almost every year. She found a lovely, aromatic balsam pine, and after the young attendant strapped it onto the roof of her old Nash Ajax she paid him a couple of dollars to stop over when his shift ended to help her get it into the house. She tried not to think of the myriad instances that would require a new resourcefulness in order to accomplish tasks that had been Gideon's domain. She was certainly not the only widow in the world—in fact she could number herself in good company right here in Salem, with the wretched tolls of war—but flying solo was terrifying without a single lesson. With determined resolve she decided to head to the lumber yard for some pieces of wood to make a small stand for her tree. What could it take? A hammer and a few nails—voila!

Humming a jazzy version of "Winter Wonderland," she pulled into the parking lot beneath the giant fist and hammer. She hadn't run into Tom

Stuart since their meeting at Melville's, and she didn't really expect that he would be at the lumber yard that day. After all, he ran mills in several different locations—what were the odds that he would happen to be at this one today? As she wandered through the piles of lumber, it occurred to her that perhaps she was looking for a penny in a copper mine. She probably should have just gone to the hardware store—one didn't need an entire sawmill to find a few small sections of two-by-four. But how would she know these things? She had never even been to the hardware store in Beaufort. She started to leave, embarrassed by her novice mistake. As she rounded the corner to the parking lot she almost stepped into the path of a dark green pick-up truck bearing the fist and hammer logo on the side doors. The truck slammed on its brakes, and she gave a feeble wave to the driver, meekly contrite. The driver leaned over and rolled down the passenger-side window. "You really know how to get a guy's attention."

Caroline was momentarily at a loss for words. She felt a fluttering in her stomach, which she attributed to the adrenaline of having nearly been run over, but she also had a niggling, unformed suspicion that made her wonder if the flutter had anything to do with the fact that Tom Stuart was smiling at her from the driver's seat. Flustered, she found her voice: "Well," she replied coyly, "I've never had to risk my life before." She had no idea where this flirtatiousness had come from. "Beware the pedestrian," she added teasingly, "we're hazardous."

He looked at her for what seemed like a very long moment, and then, with a nod at the door, simply said "Get in." The authority of this command had an alarming effect—she felt an electric tingle that she hadn't experienced for a long time. When she hesitated, he continued, "I'll give you a ride to your car. I'm assuming you do have a car here? And I would never call you pedestrian."

Caroline had almost forgotten Tom's cleverness. She recalled a facility with language that—combined with his wit—produced an urbane charm that belied his construction hardhat. He leaned over again to open the door, and she stepped off the curb and into the truck.

Forty-five minutes later they were still in the truck, idling in the parking space next to Caroline's car. She had explained her situation, telling him all about Gideon and their life together in Beaufort. Tom was uniquely sympathetic—he had lost his wife when his son, Tru, was only nine. If possible, his story was sadder still: Margaret Stuart had killed herself by asphyxiation from a gas oven in 1940. As a single father, Tom had been exempted from active military duty, and he had raised Tru by himself, albeit with the questionable help of his sister, Coco. He underscored questionable with one raised eyebrow as he described his home situation. They laughingly recalled what Caroline remembered of Coco from college.

"Is she still as intimidating as she was that night at Charlie's Tavern?" Caroline asked, referring to an evening long ago, when Tom had taken her to dinner to meet his sister. Constance Cordelia Stuart was something of a legend in the more rarefied circles of the Northeast—she had been pronounced "Debutante of the Year" in the *Boston Herald* social pages. Coco had chiseled features, with sleek, dark brown hair cut in a sharp angled bob at her chin. Her expression was perpetually superior; she had perfected the art of the withering glance. Dinner had passed in a blur, Caroline practically mum with insecurity and Tom talking too much to make up the difference. Afterward, she had begged Tom never to subject her to dinner with his sister again, and Tom had readily agreed.

"She's still the same, ah, piranha she's always been, but since moving to the provinces she seems to have lost some of her bite."

"It seems contrary to her nature to give up her life in Boston to help you raise Tru," Caroline said. "I don't remember Coco as being all that altruistic . . ."

Tom let out a short laugh. "You've got that right. It was 'mutually convenient,' which means convenient for her. After Margaret died, I felt like I needed a change of scenery, and I wanted Tru to have a fresh start, too, so I decided to leave Boston. I had just opened the mill here, so we packed up and moved. It didn't really matter which city I lived in—the mills are all over the region, and I have to do a fair amount of driving anyway. It didn't take long for Coco to follow. I think she was seeking refuge, or maybe even asylum," he added dryly. "Her husband Whit was killed in a sailing accident just before Margaret died. She was spending a lot of time with Harley, and I think she wanted to avoid the scrutiny and gossip of greater Boston. There were a lot of ugly rumors. Her social clout was also slipping, and I think she wanted to find new territory to conquer."

Caroline looked at him strangely. She wondered what the rumors were, but didn't want to dwell on the implications. "Who is Harley?"

"Harley O'Grady was Whit Wells's best friend. The three of them used to sail together all the time. They'd take Whit's sloop out nearly every Friday afternoon, after the stock market closed. Sometimes Harley brought a date, but usually it was just the three of them. From what I understand, Whit was mixing drinks while Harley took the helm. As Whit stood up to hand Coco her gin fizz, the boom smashed him on the side of the head, and he fell right into her lap. Harley told me once that Coco's first reaction was to swear at Whit for spilling the drink on her white linen trousers." He shook his head a little and sighed. "It didn't surprise me a bit."

"That's terrible," Caroline mused. "I can't imagine a worse thing than to have the person you love most die right in your lap."

Tom didn't reply immediately—the look on his face was inscrutable. "Listen, let's change the subject. We've wasted enough time talking about Coco. How would you like to have dinner sometime?" Tom asked.

"Well . . . let me think about it—yes." Grinning at her obvious lack of reserve, Caroline tried to gain back a little ground by adding, "I should check with the girls. Why don't you call me tomorrow? The number is Parker 9-4807."

Tom got out of the truck and went around to open her door. As she got into her own car, Caroline smiled up at him. "That was nice—it felt like old times. Will you call me tomorrow?"

He gazed at her for a moment and said, "You still look exactly like Hedy Lamarr—and I'll call you tonight."

They were married six months later, on a beautiful afternoon in June. The wedding was small, with Dinah as maid of honor and Jemima as flower girl. Caroline had asked her to be a bridesmaid, but Jemima had insisted that she wanted to be the "flowers" girl. Tom's son Tru stood up for him as best man.

Caroline had worried a little about Dinah. She knew that her daughter's sorrow for her father was still fresh, and she didn't want her to believe that her own love for Gideon was in any way diminished by her love for Tom. But she had noticed Dinah quietly observing the relationship over the course of the preceding months, and it appeared that she was genuinely pleased that her mother was happy.

Jemima was thrilled by any new excitement—she considered the wedding plans to be mostly about her. She spun around in the dresses at Nolan's Prom Shop, adamant that she should wear the one with the brightest pattern of pink peonies.

"How about this pretty yellow chiffon with the lace?" Dinah had suggested hopefully.

"Dinah, I'm a *flowers* girl," Jemima said, impatient with her sister's obtuseness. "That one doesn't even *have* flowers."

Fortunately, their mother reassured them their dresses didn't have to match, and Dinah chose a soft lilac crêpe de Chine with a handkerchief hem and an organza overlay at the collar. Studying her reflection in the dressing room mirror, Dinah thought about life's twists and turns. Everything had happened so fast, and she often felt like she was going through the motions of some strange dream; she couldn't shake the feeling of waiting to wake up to her old life.

She thought about the moment when she had realized that her life was about to change yet again: Her mother had been seeing Tom for a couple of months, and both of the girls had warmed to him quickly. He was kind and funny, and it was nice to see their mother laughing again. He always brought something for the girls when he came to pick up Caroline—it started with trick playing cards, and then each time the gift grew in size, though not necessarily in value. It had become a much-anticipated joke; he insisted that each successive token had to be bigger than the last. A painted fan was followed by large book entitled *Across the Sea*, full of photos of exotic travel destinations. Recently he had shown up with a large tin sign from the mill that read: "Beware Shifting Piles." Caroline had commented that it was perfect for Jemima's bedroom, and the little girl delightedly propped it against her wall amid the scattered toys and clothes. The girls knew, of course, about his son Tru—Tom talked about him all the time. Then one day their mother announced that Tru would be coming for dinner with his father that Sunday, and Dinah sensed something in the air.

Jemima had answered the door, conveniently close to it from her vantage at the window, where she had been watching for at least half an hour. Dinah was in her room, pretending to study, although she had an ironic awareness that the only audience she was pretending for was herself. She came down the stairs slowly when her mother called, feeling slightly foolish about her grand entrance. Tru stood in the foyer, looking sideways through the living room, apparently searching for an escape route.

"Here she is," chimed Caroline. "Dinah, this is Tru Stuart. Tru, this is Dinah.

He wasn't really paying attention, and it was only as Dinah reached the bottom stair that Tru distractedly pulled his gaze away from the bay window at the far end of the room. As he turned to her, she felt an odd little thump in her chest. It was the boy she had seen on the first day of school, riding in the convertible. She was struck by the surprising contrast of his features. He had light, sandy hair that carried streaky brushstrokes from the sun, but his eyes were the deepest brown—like two pools of dark coffee. As their eyes met there seemed to be a wrinkle in time—a fractional vacuum that suspended animation for an instant.

At that moment Jemima marched up and ceremoniously shook Tru's hand. "It's very nice to meet you, Truce." She gave him her most official smile.

"And this is Jemima. That's Tru, honey," Caroline hurried to correct her. "It's short for Truman, just like the president.

"Nice to meet you, too, Jemimace," he said with an oblique grin.

Jemima looked appalled, saying, "It's Jemima. It means dove," as she turned away and sat down on the stairs with her arms crossed and her face to the wall.

He turned to Dinah. He was wearing a shirt and tie, with pressed chinos, and she noticed he wasn't wearing any socks inside his loafers. "Hi, how are you?"

"Fine, thanks." As she took his extended hand, a small shock crackled through her body, and his eyes widened slightly. He released her hand quickly, and she stared at him dumbly.

When neither of them spoke, Tom stepped in to alleviate the absurd awkwardness of the moment. "What do you say we all sit down—get to know each other a bit?"

Caroline gave him a sympathetic look—it was something they'd just have to get through.

At dinner, Tom related some stories of Tru's football and sailing successes, while Tru related mostly to the napkin on his lap. It was easy to see that Tom doted on his only child—each reference to Tru was accompanied by a proud, cherishing smile. Caroline chimed in with accounts of Dinah's academic awards, and when she revealed that her daughter had written her own epic version of *Gone with the Wind* when she was ten years old, Dinah had the sensation of sinking slowly into a slurping swamp.

Never bashful, Jemima piped in with an accounting of her own accomplishments, citing last week's spelling test and her ability to do a backward somersault. At this proud announcement, Tru laughed and seemed genuinely impressed. "Way to go, pipsqueak," he offered. Jemima beamed, and after that she addressed her conversation to Tru alone.

It was at the end of dinner that Caroline and Tom announced their intentions. Tom made the gesture of actually asking Dinah and Jemima for permission to marry their mother, and Dinah couldn't help wondering what they would do if she actually withheld her consent. But the thought was merely rhetorical—her appreciation for her mother's happiness was genuine.

Tru was quiet. He had been without a mother for eight years, but the sad circumstances had produced a special, privileged bond with his father. Although his aunt Coco had provided a female presence in the house, she had never provided anything in the way of maternal instinct, and Tom had raised his son without much outside influence. Tru's expression was unreadable, and Dinah noticed Tom watching him intently. His son's approval was so clearly paramount; she liked him more than ever.

The elephant in the room was illuminated by Jemima, in her typically blunt fashion: "Where will we live? Do I get to share my room with Tru?" She was clearly enchanted with the idea of a big brother and all the exciting things that would come with having a boy in the house.

A complicit look passed between Tom and Caroline. She spoke first: "We've given that some thought, and if it's all right with Tru, we think it might be nice for us all to live here. And no, Jemima, you will continue to share your room with Fuzz alone. There are plenty of bedrooms to go around." Everyone's eyes were on Tru.

He turned quickly to his father with an affronted, quizzical look. "What?"

Tom stepped in, putting both palms out in front of him, in a *slow down* motion. "We can talk about it, of course. Nothing has been set in stone. We were thinking that it may be the best option, considering the space, and your aunt Coco." The Stuart home was spacious, but Caroline's house was bigger, and more important, did not have the additional feature of Coco Wells living in it.

Coco's presence had not imposed on her relationship with Tom so far, but Caroline was wary of the effect she would have once they all became part of the same family. They had intentionally avoided her company, which wasn't difficult because she was wrapped up completely in her own world of society events. "My sister is a virtual saint," Tom had remarked ironically one day after seeing Coco's name once again in the social pages for a charity function.

Tru looked back down at his napkin, saying nothing more. Tom looked distressed, and Caroline tried to smooth things over by saying: "Let's give all of this a chance to settle in. Everything will be fine—we've all just got a little adjusting to do. Who would like dessert? I picked up apple turnovers from Madsen's, and speaking for the girls, I know we have at least a couple of takers." The party turned their attention to the pastries with welcome relief; the weight of the announcement had taken a toll on everyone's nerves, and they all seemed content to put the subject on the shelf.

As the men were getting ready to leave, Dinah noticed Tru gazing around the house, as if taking measure of the surroundings. A chord of empathy rang through her as she recognized the look on his face; it was a look of wary uncertainty, and she knew where she had seen it before. It was what she often saw when she looked into the mirror.

A few days before the wedding, the aunts Batty and Bilah arrived with a flourish. Caroline had insisted that they stay at the house, and the sisters had moved into a third-floor guest room with all the flurry and twittering of a pair of wrens building a nest. "My goodness, Bee," Batty said to her sister, "it appears we have been assigned the garret. We'll have to tip this nice porter who has been kind enough to carry our bags up all these stairs." She gave a wink to Tom, who was trailing behind with their luggage.

The girls had never had the opportunity to get to know Gideon's aunt Bilah very well—she had married a man in the Army Corps of Engineers, and during their long marriage they had been posted all over the world—"from Dover to Dubai," as Batty was fond of saying. But Bee was a widow now, and the two sisters had taken up lovingly contentious housekeeping together in Beaufort.

"Batty, do tell: who is this enchanting creature hovering by the door?" Bilah teased as they were settling into their room. "I remember Gid and Caroline having two little girls, but the youngest is still a baby, is she not?"

Jemima thrust her shoulders back and stood as tall as she could.

"Well I'm not sure now, Bee. I do remember a child with dimples, but this couldn't be the same girl. This must be the chamber maid," Aunt Batty played along.

"It's me! It's Jemima!" She proudly presented the information with the *Eureka!* tone of one who has solved a mystery.

"Well I'll be a gator's bride. You must be nearly twenty! Come on in here and give your old aunties a hug." Aunt Bee extended her arms.

Delighted by the misapprehension, Jemima gave a brilliant gap-toothed smile and skipped into the room, saying "I'm only seven, but I'll be twenty pretty soon!"

At this hopeful declaration the sisters exchanged a bittersweet look, and Batty murmured, "Ain't it the truth, darlin'—ain't it the truth."

Dinah had been thrilled to see her dear Aunt Bat, and she was eager to spend time with Aunt Bee, too. It provided a tangible connection to her father, wrapping her in a cocoon of warmth and familiarity. Batty's deep Southern drawl was music to her ears, and though Bee had lost most of her accent over the years of foreign travel, it came back like a boomerang when she returned to her roots. On the night before the wedding Dinah found herself lingering in their bedroom, cozily listening to the soothing susurration of their chatter, reluctant to leave, even when they pointed out that they should all get some rest before the big day tomorrow.

"Goodnight, Babydoll," Batty kissed her forehead. "You are the image of your daddy." She held Dinah's face in her hands, and they both felt tears start to well. "I know those eyes," she said softly, "I can see him here," she touched Dinah's nose, "and here," she brushed her cheekbones, "and here," she laid her finger gently on Dinah's lips. "You have been given a gift, my love. You inherited not only that beautiful face, but a beautiful soul to match. Gideon would be so proud."

Feeling a serene contentment, Dinah made her way down to her bedroom on the second floor, careful to avoid running into her mother's cousin, May Carroll, and her husband Roger. Dinah and Jemima found May's husband vaguely creepy; he was much older than May and rarely said anything. Caroline had overheard Dinah refer to him as "Roger the Codger," and scolded her, saying, "You have to walk in a person's shoes before you can understand what they might see in someone." At the thought of wearing May's large mules, Dinah cringed.

With the arrival of the Carrolls, the house was almost fully occupied for the first time in years. Tom would move in after the honeymoon, and Tru had opted to stay at the Stuart house until his father returned. Caroline had made a special effort to make his room welcoming; it was decorated in tones of maroon and white—the Salem High School colors. He hadn't yet moved any of his things over, and Tom had carefully refrained from suggesting it— he wanted to give his son plenty of time to make the transition.

The wedding took place on the neatly manicured back lawn of the house on Chestnut Street. The azaleas and rhododendron were in full bloom, and the lovely symmetry of the clipped boxwood parterre garden that Caroline's mother, Cecelia Croston, had so lovingly maintained lent a stately formality to the surroundings. It was an intimate gathering; in addition to the aunts and May and Roger Carroll, there were a group of Tom's old friends, a few couples that Caroline had maintained contact with over the years since she was in school, and, of course, Coco, who brought Harley O'Grady. The girls were each allowed to invite two friends, but Dinah opted to ask just Betsy. She had made a small venture into the deeper end of the social pool, but there wasn't anyone else to whom she felt close enough to include in such a personal affair. Jemima invited Peter Campbell and Sammy Taylor. The fact that she had chosen two boys on which to bestow such an honor seemed to tickle the adults at the party. They couldn't decide if Jemima was a tomboy, or if she simply preferred the company of men. Either way, they all found her singularly charming as she ushered her little dates around, introducing them with exuberant panache.

Tru was solemn in his grey morning coat and tie. The effect made him appear much older—looking more like a member of the nobility than a seventeen-year-old schoolboy. Although it was only June, he had already spent many afternoons on the water, sailing his catamaran in regattas or by himself. He was an accomplished sailor, and his reputation had garnered quite a bit of local attention. The hours spent on the bay had given his skin a warm tan, which contrasted arrestingly with the golden streaks in his hair.

He had invited two of his best friends, but it had been a hard decision for him. Tru collected friends like some people collect marbles; he had Jemima's knack for drawing others to him.

The ceremony was brief and lovely, with the strains of a single violin hovering sweetly in the air. Caroline wore an elegant cut-away suit made of ivory silk shantung, and looked hardly older than she had been on the day she walked down the aisle at St. Peter's Church, only blocks away from where she now stood. She couldn't help thinking of the impossible turns that life could take. Never in her imagination could she have considered the idea that she would be married to someone other than Gideon. To have found love again, after experiencing such harrowing grief, was an incredible gift. She felt tempered and mellow. She felt evolved. She felt the grace that allowed her once again to look ahead.

"With this ring, I thee wed," Tom's words interrupted her thoughts, bringing her back to the moment. He was looking at her with the steady, embracing love that so captured the quality of his nature. His look also conveyed the delighted adoration that he had for his new bride. Caroline couldn't help being flattered by his playful attraction to her—he seemed to believe she was some kind of delicious treat, and his eyes held a mischievous gleam that never failed to make her knees a little weak. As she repeated the vows, her own eyes suddenly brimmed with tears. She hadn't expected the onslaught of emotion, and she knew that it sprang from a well of gratitude. She was, above all, grateful. Tom gently wiped a lone tear that slipped down her cheek as he slid the ring onto her finger. He then leaned down to kiss the spot where the tear had been, and there was an audible sigh from the guests seated on the lawn. Caroline turned to Dinah, who stood to her right, and took her hand. With her other hand firmly enclosed in Tom's, the minister pronounced them man and wife. Tom's left arm was around Tru's shoulders, and Dinah was clasping Jemima's hand, so that the new little family had unconsciously formed a chain; the photographer standing at the back snapped a picture.

A four-piece combo played from a raised podium in the shade of the house and a small dance floor had been installed over the lawn. As the musicians struck up a soft and slow version of "Time After Time," Tom pulled Caroline into his arms. "You are a goddess." His voice was low and he gave her slow smile. "When do we start the honeymoon?"

Caroline laughed. "Be good—we have guests," she reprimanded, and her eyes widened a little as she felt the weight of his hand on her lower back pull her close. Before long, others joined them on the dance floor, swaying to the combo's adroit rendition of "String of Pearls." Jemima tried to navigate dancing with both of her dates at once; the trio held hands and moved in a circle, in what looked more like ring-around-the-rosy than any traditional foxtrot.

Tru stood with his friends in the shade of the porte-cochere on the driveway, coat slung over his shoulder. They had somehow acquired a baseball, which they were tossing around in a preface to the inevitable sports-related diversion. Dinah and Betsy were trying hard to look like they weren't aware of the boys while they milled around among the guests, eating canapés from passed trays and pretending to be occupied. "There's Coco Wells—turn around!" Dinah ordered Betsy.

"Who's that?"

"Tom's sister. She's scary. I've met her three times and I'll bet she doesn't even know who I am."

"I'll take the bet!" Betsy was patently a bit bored and looking for amusement. "Let's go up and say hello—you can introduce me, and we'll see if she knows your name."

Dinah gave her a skeptical look—an encounter with the dreaded Coco was not something to which she would normally subject herself. Feeling responsible for her friend's entertainment, she reluctantly agreed. She turned to make her way to the refreshments table that was set up on the flagstone terrace. "She's over by the punch bowl, probably poisoning it. A dollar," she added, with a confident look.

The girls moved across the lawn, weaving around a few of the guests. As they passed her mother's cousin May, Dinah overheard a snippet of conversation: "That Tom Stuart bears an uncanny resemblance to that new congressman in the eleventh district—what's his name again . . . that's right—Kennedy . . . don't you think?" Dinah agreed. She hadn't realized that anyone else had noticed the resemblance, but she had seen a picture of Congressman Kennedy in a magazine at the library and was struck by the similarity of their features. The coincidence pleased her. She felt pride and a kind of reflected glory in the fact that her new stepfather was considered handsome like the young congressman.

As they approached the terrace, Dinah was having second thoughts. Coco was standing with one hand on a slender hip and one hand holding a cup of punch. Ostensibly talking to Harley O'Grady, it looked to Dinah more like she was surveying the crowd for her own derisive amusement. She had retained the distinctive sleek hairstyle and was wearing a deep scarlet shade of lipstick that Dinah would come to recognize as her signature shade, Copacabana. Her dress was a pale green silk Christian Dior that draped off the back of her shoulders. Dinah took a deep breath and walked up to her. "Hello, um. . . hello there," her words came out hesitantly. It hadn't occurred to her to think about what she should call Coco. Mrs. Wells sounded too formal, but she certainly wasn't about to call her Aunt Coco.

Coco looked startled to see this young person standing there next to her, and slightly irritated at the intrusion. "Oh—hello . . . ah . . . Tina!" She was clearly impressed with herself at this surprising feat of observation.

A wide smile spread over Dinah's face, at which Coco seemed taken aback. She wasn't accustomed to such a sincerely glad reception. Dinah sneaked a sideways glance at Betsy, who wasn't even trying to mask her disappointment. "It's Dinah," she corrected, making a subtle hand movement, palm up and fingers wiggling.

Coco gave a bored glance at Harley, raising one brow slightly, as if to say *"Whatever."*

"And this is my friend, Betsy MacEvoy," Dinah continued. "Betsy, meet Coco Wells, and . . ." She knew who Mr. O'Grady was, but they had never been introduced. She looked expectantly at the slightly paunchy, sunburned man with the thinning blonde hair standing at Coco's side, and waited for an introduction.

Coco made a half-hearted attempt by waving her hand in Dinah's direction, saying "Yes, this is Tom's, ah, *stepdaughter*." The last word rolled off her tongue with sour twist.

Harley looked at Dinah with what felt like an appraisal, and then just nodded and said "Hmmm."

"Well, be a good little hostess and go ask that Chinaman over there if a person can get a real drink around here," Coco ordered. "Gin, to be specific—on the rocks. Just a splash of tonic." She tossed her head at Harley. "Make it two," she added.

Betsy's eyes were wide as Dinah steered her along toward the nearest waiter, a young Japanese man in a white serving coat. Dinah gave the order, and as the waiter moved away, she noticed a commotion near the dance floor. The boys had found their ballgame, which consisted of throwing the baseball onto the roof of the house and then shoving each other out of the way to catch it as it rolled back off. Unfortunately, one of them put a little too much muscle into the last throw and the ball had curved across the roof and rolled onto the bandstand, narrowly missing the shiny bald head of the bass player. Since none of the boys would confirm who had actually thrown the ball, Tom had decided they could all atone for their reckless behavior by taking to the dance floor with some of the ladies. Tru was escorting Caroline onto the floor, while his friend Bill Lange shuffled around with Cousin May, who had been swaying by herself, clutching a cup of sloshing punch and sporadically offering up slurry vocal impressions of Peggy Lee. The shorter boy with the red hair—Dinah couldn't think of his name—had opted for Jemima.

Over the strains of the music they heard an indignantly outraged voice. "What kind of service are you running here? This isn't a drink, it's a vapor! Listen here, Chop Suey, you take this right back where it came from and tell whoever's behind the bar to find the bottle labeled gin—that's G-I-N, do you understand me? And get back here pronto. P-R-O-N-T-O."

Betsy turned to Dinah. "You really should have warned him."

"Maybe I should have suggested strychnine," Dinah replied.

Turning back to the dance floor, she watched her mother dancing with Tru. He was a surprisingly confident dancer, leading Caroline in a better-than-passable Lindy, and Caroline looked like she was having a ball. Dinah wondered where Tru had learned to dance. As she looked on, he suddenly looked up, as though sensing her gaze. She immediately focused her attention on Jemima, now perched on the shoulders of her latest conquest, but not before noticing that her new stepbrother missed a step.

CHAPTER THREE
Fearful Truth

AFTER TOM AND CAROLINE LEFT for their honeymoon, Dinah found herself drifting around the big house, looking at a long summer with nothing to do. Tru had enrolled in a six-week sailing camp in Maine, so she didn't even have the anticipated diversion of having a new stepbrother in the house. The honeymooners would be gone for four weeks themselves, having booked passage on the *Queen Elizabeth* for Europe, with an extended stay in Venice. Tom had done some careful planning, and he was thrilled to announce that they would hear Maria Callas sing *Aida* at the Fenice Opera House. He was passionate about opera, an art form that baffled Dinah. She could not see the logic in listening to music without understanding the words, and the idea of adults going around singing about everything that happened seemed silly to her. Tom had brought some of his favorite recordings over to play for Caroline, and he laughed when Dinah took him aside and said, "This is what you're planning to do on your honeymoon? Does my mother know about this?" He asked her to sit down as he put on a recording of the "Sull'aria" duet from *The Marriage of Figaro*, and when the exquisite, soaring harmony of the sopranos actually made her skin tingle she began to understand.

Tom noticed her rubbing the goosebumps on her arms and gave her a conspiratorial wink. "That's what Mozart can do to you," he said with a satisfied smile.

It was Aunt Batty, staying to watch the girls until Tom and Caroline returned, who suggested that Dinah put her library addiction to use. "Sugar, you spend so much time at that library they should make you the librarian," she had remarked one day, as Dinah came home with another armload of books. She did spend a lot of time there, and not only searching for titles. She loved the beautiful old rooms, with their warm mahogany shelves, and the smell of leather bindings and old paper. The Italianate brick and brownstone mansion was originally the home of a successful merchant and ship owner who was once considered one of the richest men in Massachusetts. It had become Dinah's refuge, and her long hours in the stacks and the reading rooms had fostered a new friendship with none other than Betsy's mother, Jane MacEvoy, who happened to be the head librarian.

It was Betsy who had introduced Dinah to the library, pulling her along as they walked home from school one day early in the school year. "I have to stop in and see my mom," she had explained, and Dinah felt like she had come home. And so, on a sunny afternoon in June, she made the familiar stroll down Essex Street and approached Mrs. MacEvoy at the front desk. "I was wondering if there might be something I could do here," she ventured. "You know . . . on a regular basis."

"You mean, apart from what you already do here on a regular basis?" Jane looked perplexed.

"Well, yes, I mean something that would be considered official, like . . . work?"

"Oh, work!" Jane smiled at the idea, and then she sighed. "I would love to say that we have an opening for an apprentice librarian on the payroll, but unfortunately there isn't such a thing." She looked apologetic, but then her face brightened. "I have an idea. If you'd like to help out as a volunteer for a while, I could try to submit a proposal to the library board for an on-the-job training policy, and maybe after a while we could figure something out in the way of pay." Her voice trailed off a little at the end, signifying that the chances might be slim, but Dinah liked the idea anyway. It would provide some structure to the summer—a purpose to her days. "I'll figure out what I need you to do, and you can start tomorrow, all right? There's just one thing," the librarian added. "It's a policy of mine that anyone who works in my employ is required to call me by my first name, so no more Mrs. MacEvoy, is that clear?"

Dinah smiled and looked around at her new place of employment. "Sure." She wasn't actually sure she was comfortable with the first-name status—it didn't really feel appropriate to her, and she knew her mother would be appalled, but she figured she could probably go a while without using any title whatsoever. She waved as she was leaving, calling "Thank you so much—I'll see you in the morning."

"Thank you so much, *Jane*," she heard as she went out the door.

As the summer wore on, Dinah became immersed in the tasks Jane gave her. Back from the honeymoon, her mother remarked that Dinah spent more time at the library than she did at home. She had become a wiz at cataloguing, and she was particularly helpful in the children's room, discovering a natural ability to hone in on a child's interests and personality to find just the right book. Jemima often came along, but Dinah had to be careful to keep an eye on her.

Apparently Jemima was under the impression that she, too, was an official volunteer. Whenever she noticed anyone in the juvenile section choosing a book, she would hurry over to share her opinion. This didn't always bode well for the noise level of the reading room. "That book is boring," was her usual critique, and she often forgot her quiet voice if she didn't think her patrons were paying attention. Toward the end of the summer Jemima had come to think of herself as indispensable. One afternoon she approached an unsuspecting visitor with an especially authoritarian zeal: "You shouldn't read that one," she insisted to the hapless child. "It's too old for you and doesn't even have good pictures."

The little boy looked alarmed, as though he had been caught doing something wrong. He turned to find his mother, a look of panic beginning to spread over his face.

"Just a minute, didn't you hear me?" Jemima's voice grew louder as she trailed after him. "I'm telling you something, now stop right there young man!" In her determination to make her point, she had somehow transmuted into a diminutive Dickensian schoolmaster.

The boy looked wildly around the room. Hesitantly, he started to call for his mother, but within moments his voice was a full-blown wail: "MOMMY!"

"Shhhh!" Jemima put her finger to her lips. "Don't you know this is a quiet place?" she demanded loudly. She was attempting to pry the offending book out of his chubby little hands when an outraged woman appeared and pulled the book away. The mother gathered up her now-sobbing son and headed to the check-out desk, where she indignantly filed a complaint about "a pig-tailed little bully" in the children's section.

As they walked home, Dinah rather irritatedly told Jemima that she would not be able to come with her to the library if she didn't learn to leave people alone. Jemima was quiet for a while, deep in thought. As they turned the corner to their house, she finally spoke: "It's not nice to leave people alone."

Dinah was turning this strange pronouncement over in her mind as she struggled to open the door, arms full of books. Jane MacEvoy had introduced her to Nathaniel Hawthorne, whom she described as "a local boy who made good." Dinah had already finished *The House of Seven Gables* and *The Scarlet Letter* and was eager to start *Twice-Told Tales*. She was particularly interested in a short story that Jane had recommended called "The Gentle Boy," about the persecution of Quakers in Massachusetts. The history of persecution was an accepted part of everyday life in Salem. The spooky fascination with the Witch Hysteria had endured over the centuries, evolving into a familiar and even cherished legend. Its macabre distinction lent a quirky sort of character to the town, which residents seemed to enjoy. Just a few years earlier Coco Wells had been actively involved in establishing a historic preservation foundation to preserve "The Witch House," home to Jonathan Corwin, the renowned witch-trial judge. As they passed it one day, Caroline noted that tourism in Salem had become a thriving industry. "At least those poor girls didn't sacrifice their souls for nothing," she remarked drolly.

Entering the foyer, Dinah almost tripped over a large army-green trunk with rope tied around it. Beyond the trunk an off-white canvas windbreaker was slung over the newel post of the banister, and there were voices coming from the back of the house. She looked at Jemima, who registered the implication with delight as she ran to the kitchen.

Tom and Caroline were seated at the table sipping iced tea while Tru rummaged around in the refrigerator, reporting on his camp experience. "We rigged out the big ketch," he was saying, "and the weather looked like it would hold, but out of the blue a twenty-foot swell slammed us starboard and she started to roll, so I told Stan to grab the helm, and I leaned out over the . . ." his voice trailed off as he noticed Dinah in the doorway.

"Hello girls—look who's home!" Caroline announced.

Jemima ran to Tru and threw her arms around his waist.

"Hey there pipsqueak—how's shakes?" he pulled on one of her pigtails.

"We've been waiting for you! It's been so boring here—we wanted you to come home so we could have a brother to play with!" The words tumbled out of her mouth as she looked up and swayed around him, arms still encircling his waist. Dinah was mortified. She had never admitted to Jemima that she was eager for Tru to return, but there her crazy little sister was, implicating her in this unbridled enthusiasm. She felt her face turning red as Tru looked at her with an amused expression.

"Were you waiting for me to come home and play with you?" he said with mock seriousness. Speechless, Dinah just stared at him. She was completely humiliated, certain that he considered her and Jemima to be roughly the same age. Tru continued to look at her, until Tom saved her from her mute embarrassment by brusquely standing up and lifting Jemima out of the way.

"Move over, Mimer," he said heartily. "Tru has some unpacking to do." He threw his arm over Tru's shoulders, saying "Let's get your stuff up to your room. I've taken the liberty of bringing over the rest of your things." As they moved down the hall, Dinah heard Tom start to explain to Tru that he had decided to sell their old house, and she gladly hurried off to her own room, thankful for handy distractions, however sticky they may be. Remembering Jemima's statement earlier, she couldn't help thinking that, in some cases, it was very nice to leave people alone.

That night Caroline tapped lightly on Dinah's door.

"Come in." Dinah was lying on the bed, making good progress on *Twice-Told Tales*. Caroline crossed the room and lay down next to her, stretching out with her arms behind her head and her ankles crossed.

"How's my little bibliophile doing?" she asked. "What do you have, about thirty or forty titles to go?"

"That's about right. I'm all the way through the Ts, and there aren't many authors whose names start with U or X, so I should be finished by next week." It was a standing joke that the library would run out of books that Dinah hadn't read before the end of summer.

Caroline asked her about her day, and they both had a laugh about Jemima's debacle. "So . . . how do you like having a brother in the house?" Caroline rather clumsily moved to the point of her visit.

"He's not really my brother." Suddenly Dinah felt defensive and annoyed.

Caroline was surprised by her daughter's reaction. "Well, no, not technically," she replied in a conciliatory tone. "But he is your stepbrother.

I thought that you might like having another member in the family, and it will be nice to have a boy around, don't you think?" It was such tricky business, she thought, trying to read the thoughts of a teen-aged girl. Her older daughter didn't reveal much in the way of personal feelings, and Caroline found herself constantly wondering what went on behind those very private eyes.

"I don't know. I guess so."

That was as much as Caroline was going to get. "Well, as it turns out we won't get to have him around all that much after all. He has decided to go to St. Paul's."

There had been discussion in the past about sending Tru to his father's alma mater, but Tom had preferred having his son home with him and hadn't really encouraged him. Earlier that day, Tru informed his father that he had filled out the application in June. Tom had been taken aback by this unexpected turn of events. He was ambivalent about his son's decision to transfer for his senior year, but he couldn't deny that the change in their circumstances put a different perspective on things, and he reluctantly agreed to let him go.

Dinah absorbed this news with apparent disinterest. "Are you going to redecorate his room?" was her only response, and Caroline decided to leave her to her reading, resigned to the fact that she would never have access to full disclosure of her daughter's thoughts.

For the next two weeks, Jemima followed Tru around like a puppy, fascinated by his every move. Dinah could tell that he was really warming up to her little sister, maybe even getting a little attached. Her own interactions with Tru were stilted and brief. She didn't know how to act around him and could never think of what to say. For his part, he was busy getting ready to leave again, and when he wasn't horsing around with his friends at the ballpark, he was out on the cove in his sailboat. One clear blue morning, as Tru was finishing a bowl of cereal, Jemima asked him what he was going to do all day.

"Take the cat out for awhile," he told her. "There's a regatta tomorrow, and I want to be ready." By this time even Jemima knew that "the cat" was his fifteen-foot catamaran, his favorite type of racing boat. "I may need a little ballast, short stuff," he offered. "Want to come along?"

Jemima lit up like a Christmas tree. She ran to change her clothes, hollering "Momma I'm going to be ballis on the boat! I'm going to be ballis on the boat!"

Caroline met her in the upstairs hall, smiling and holding out her hand. "Well, come on then, skipper—let's get you set to go!"

Jemima grabbed her mother's hand and pulled her along to the bedroom, stopping abruptly at the door. She looked up, a question forming on her face. "What's ballis?"

Dinah could hear her mother's laughter as she went down to the kitchen. She was buttering her toast when Jemima came swirling back in.

"Dinah, did you hear? I'm going sailing!" she sang out.

Tru was out in the yard; as Jemima made her announcement he passed by the window, carrying a coil of rope over one shoulder. Dinah's heart dropped. She couldn't help feeling excluded, and she was surprised by an unsummoned resentment for her sister. She gave Jemima a wan smile.

"Congratulations. Be careful not to fall overboard." That was mean and she knew it. Jemima was prone to anxiety. Dinah and her mother had always been careful not to even joke about possible dangers, lest they set off an avalanche of obsessive worry.

"It's okay, I'm ballis," Jemima brightly reassured her. "Tru said he can tie me right on." Dinah had to smile, and she was glad that her comment hadn't found its mark.

Spending most of the day at the library, Dinah was relegated to organizing the periodicals. There were a couple of old men who were regulars, arriving most days mid-morning to page through the daily paper and check out the latest editions of *Life* and *Look*. Mr. Remarcik was always friendly and talkative, but Mr. Veness was reserved to the point of rudeness, and she had come to consider him a real grouch. That day, Mr. Veness appeared by himself, and Dinah attempted polite conversation.

"Where's Mr. Remarcik today?"

The craggy-faced old man stared at her in silence for what felt like an eternity. Finally he responded. "Fell."

"He fell? Is he all right?" She felt a real concern for nice old Mr. Remarcik.

"Nope," was the answer, and he turned back to his newspaper.

Baffled, Dinah moved to another section, and when Jane passed by she relayed the news.

"That's a shame. He must have broken a hip or something," Jane said. "If he's laid-up, we can send over the papers at the end of the day—I'll see if I can find out where he lives."

Dinah thought she might try again to ask Mr. Veness for the information, but when she checked back in the periodicals room he was gone.

That evening Caroline had prepared a special meal, using the excuse that it would be one of Tru's last nights at home. She loved to cook, and would find any reason to pull out all the stops. She had grown up with Gussie, her mother's beloved live-in housekeeper/cook, but she preferred to do her own cooking, ambitiously trying any new recipe that fired her imagination. Gloria, Gussie's daughter, only came in twice a week, unless they needed her for a special occasion, and once in a while to look after Jemima. As they ate their veal tournedos Jemima was an incessant chatterbox, detailing every tiny detail of her day on the water, but Dinah only half listened as she absent-mindedly pushed her food around, thinking about the strange, terse answer given by Mr. Veness. When it seemed that her little sister had finally run out of steam, Dinah related the incident about Mr. Remarcik.

"Did you say Remarcik?" Her mother sounded vaguely disturbed.

Dinah nodded.

Caroline had a strange look on her face. "Dinah, I don't think it's a good idea to fraternize with strangers like that."

"Well, he's not exactly a stranger, Mom. I mean, he comes in to the library almost every day. What's wrong with being nice to an old man?" Dinah was confused. Her mother had always encouraged her to be polite to her elders.

"Dinah, I want you to do as I say, without any questions. I'm not asking you to be disrespectful, I just ask that you keep a distance in this circumstance, and that's all I'm going to say about it." Caroline looked upset. Dinah was bewildered. Sensing she shouldn't pursue the topic, she put all of her concentration into carefully picking the chopped asparagus out of the rice pilaf.

Diplomatic as always, Tom changed the subject, turning to his son.

"Are you all set to go on Sunday?" The St. Paul's football team started practice on Monday, and they planned to drive to New Hampshire on Sunday afternoon.

"I think so. I'm packed." He hesitated. "I still have to do that English thing, though." St. Paul's had notified all rising seniors of a summer book report on any work by a nineteenth-century American novelist. Tru's voice had trailed off as he found a sudden urgent interest in his food.

Tom looked at him, exasperated. "You've been home for almost two weeks. Don't you think it's a little late?" He rarely lost patience with his son, but Tru generally didn't provoke him.

Flashing a disarming smile, Tru looked at Dinah. "I'm pretty sure there's someone at this table who could give me a hand with this."

Tom rolled his eyes. "Dinah, if you can forgive this acute short-sightedness, perhaps you could see your way to offering a reading suggestion. It seems we have a case of severe procrastination on our hands." He gave his son a look of mild disgust.

Dinah was completely caught off guard. This was the first time Tru had ever really addressed her with any actual purpose, and she wasn't expecting it. She stammered slightly as she said, "Sure, I guess. I mean, I have a bunch of books upstairs, and I could give you some ideas . . ."

Jemima had run out of her own patience with all of the boring talk that had nothing to do with her, and she took the opportunity to jump back in with further description of her new life as a sailor. "Tru said maybe I could be on his crew someday, and I'm going to go to Camp Genoa so I can sail my own boat—it's called a cat of Moran . . ."

Dinah was in her bedroom wondering what she should suggest when Tru swung in, knocking on the door as it opened.

The bold entry surprised her. "Come right in," she said, with faint sarcasm.

"Weren't you expecting me?" The question hung in the air for a moment. His words held a curious weight. Or maybe it was the way he said them—measured, familiar, and looking straight at her.

Dinah was rattled. Her words came out unintentionally curt: "I was expecting you to knock."

He shrugged with a contrived innocence, and his tone lightened. "I knocked."

Dinah found firm footing in the task at hand. "I have a bunch of Hawthorne, and some Poe, and some old Mark Twain. I assumed you wouldn't want Alcott or Kate Chopin. If you want something else, you should come to the library tomorrow," she offered.

"I'm racing tomorrow," Tru said as he picked up Dinah's copy of *Twice-Told Tales.*

"Haven't you read that yet?" she asked. "I mean, you grew up here, I would think you would have been assigned a lot of Hawthorne."

"We only had to read *The Scarlet Letter* and *Seven Gables.*" He sat down on the bed, examining the cover. "Any good?"

"So far. I haven't read the stories all yet. Some are sort of . . . creepy, if you like that kind of thing. There are a lot of them, though. Aren't you supposed to choose a novel?"

He started thumbing through the pages. "This will be perfect," he said. "I'll just pick out a couple, compare and contrast . . . bingo—mission accomplished."

Dinah felt a conflicted admiration for this efficient solution. She would have been up all night slogging through some heavy thing, diligently following instructions. Tru simply changed the rules.

Standing up, he glanced around the room. He seemed curious, as if he'd never been in a girl's bedroom before. It crossed Dinah's mind that maybe he hadn't. He walked over to her desk and picked up a picture of Gideon. "This must be your dad," he said. Dinah nodded. He gazed at it for a moment. "He looks like you." Abruptly, he put the picture down. His eyes moved to the bulletin board over the desk, and he briefly studied her library schedule, tacked among the bric-a-brac, before noticing the piles of books in the corner.

"Do you do anything besides read?" His brow was raised in an expression of mild disbelief.

Dinah wasn't sure how to respond. She felt the color rise in her cheeks, but she looked at him evenly. "Are you mocking me?" Even to her own ears she could hear that her indignation had deepened her accent, and the words came out sounding more like "Ah you mahkin' me?"

Something caught him short, and he just stared at her.

"Maybe it isn't as . . . fascinating . . . as drifting around on the water, but it's not such a bad hobby," she said defensively. "After all, I didn't come to you for help."

He shook his head a little and looked around the room. "True enough." Tapping the book against his palm, he moved to the door. "I'll let you get back to it. Thanks for the help."

She stood in the middle of the room, feeling strangely disoriented. Looking down at the rug, she tried to regain her composure. Her voice was subdued. "You're welcome."

"Hey," he turned from the door, and she looked up. "Why don't you bring Jemima and come and watch me drift around on the water tomorrow?"

"I . . . um . . . I'll have to check my schedule."

"I already did," he said, nodding his head in the direction of the bulletin board. "The race starts at eight. Tell Mimer to bring me some luck."

He closed the door gently behind him, and Dinah sat down on the bed.

Later, as she lay waiting for sleep, she wondered why she had felt so defensive. She didn't think it was just because of he had made fun of her reading propensity. There was just something . . . unsettling about having a brother. She couldn't figure out how it was supposed to feel.

Her last thought came unbidden, as she remembered her mother's strange behavior at dinner, and wondered with a vague and sleepy curiosity how Mr. Remarcik was doing.

In the morning, everyone in the family decided to go to the regatta. Tru had left well before the rest of the family was awake, and they had to hurry to get to Marblehead before the gun went off. As they rounded the boardwalk entrance to the yacht club they found Coco and Harley sipping Bloody Marys on the deck.

"Hello Sis." Tom's voice held a question. "Harley," he nodded. Although Harley held a partner position in a large Boston law firm, Tom couldn't help feeling sorry for him—he was reduced to the role of lap dog where Coco was concerned. In Tom's opinion, Harley had become rather pathetic in a dissolute, gin-soaked way. "We didn't expect to find you here today!" he said with forced joviality.

Harley made a half-hearted military salute by way of greeting, and Coco gave a brittle smile. "I don't suppose you did," she said dryly. "We thought we'd come and watch my nephew, if it's all the same to you." Coco had resented having to find a new place to live when Tom told her that he was selling the house. He assumed she would want to go back to Boston, anyway, now that she no longer had the excuse of helping to look after Tru. Besides, Harley lived in Boston, and he had to be getting tired of the drive.

Caroline regarded the couple, noticing their formal wear. "I think it's nice that you dressed up like this for the regatta—I'm sure Tru will be flattered by your efforts," she said with a knowing smile.

Harley sat back with a stretch and rubbed a hand over his jaw, which had acquired a telling shadow. "Yes, well, the party went a little late, and we just decided to keep up the spirit, you know . . ." he trailed off with a bored yawn. Coco and Harley were famous for prolonging any fete until the sun came up.

Coco twisted a long strand of pearls around her fingers, and said, "Tom, a word please," in a tone that was less a request than a command. She looked pointedly at Caroline and the girls, who had been observing the glamorous couple as if they were animals in a zoo.

Caroline took Jemima by the hand, placing her other hand on Dinah's back. "We'll be down by the shore, Tom. We'll save you a spot on the blanket."

They sat on a small knoll in the shade, watching the sailors tack back and forth as they lined up for the start. Dinah and Jemima had never seen a regatta before, although Jemima now seemed to consider herself an expert on all things nautical. "You have to go by the lee," she informed them officiously. "And see that line—that's the downhaul," she pointed into the distance. "If you want to turn, it's called jibe."

Caroline winked at Dinah, attempting to put a harness on Jemima's newfound authority. "We'll just have to pay attention. Let's watch and learn, all right?"

Jemima made a face, exaggeratedly mouthing "Watch and learn!" to Dinah.

Tom joined them several minutes later, with a wry smile and a small shake of his head. "The winds are a little unstable this morning—probably about a force three or four." He looked out at the catamarans lining up as he took stock of the conditions. Caroline understood that it wasn't the right time to ask about his conversation with his sister.

The boats lined up, and the gun went off. Tru's boat shot off the starting line. His pal Bill Lange was crewing for him—they were seasoned mates. The morning passed quickly, with Tru and Bill winning two of three races. They were leading at the windward mark in the third race, expertly playing the shifts and gusts of the winds, but in the last beat a knot holding the trapeze hook slipped and as Bill dove to grab for it he flew off the boat. Tru laughed so hard he couldn't recover. They were both laughing as they accepted trophies for the first two races, and Dinah couldn't help noticing that their attitude was slightly cavalier. The regatta had been for participants ages eighteen and under, and Tru had been a little dismissive, saying that he had bigger fish to fry.

Afterward, Tom suggested that they take the girls to the amusement park. Caroline had not been back to The Willows since returning to Salem—it was the place where she and Gideon had first met. He had been working on a commission for a new park pavilion, and she had been babysitting a seven-year-old who had wanted to ride on the carousel. She had noticed him watching as she rotated by, and couldn't help laughing when he tripped over a low iron fence surrounding the periphery. As she came around again, he looked at her so mournfully that she felt horrible and heartless. She didn't wait for the ride to end, temporarily abandoning the child on the horse to begin her new life, via penitent apology.

Now, overcoming a tender hesitance, she determinedly embraced the idea on behalf of the girls. Strolling down the promenade of the beautiful old park, they enjoyed the end-of-summer poignancy of late August. They all seemed to share the desire to drink in the day, conscious of a subtle sense of impending loss that comes with the first scent of autumn.

As they neared the magnificent carousel, Dinah was quiet, watching her mother's face. They stood off to the side together as Tom bought a ticket for Jemima. After walking around the entire circuit twice, Jemima finally settled on an astoundingly beautiful black stallion adorned with turquoise and gold. Tom hoisted her onto the intricately carved and painted saddle, and hopped off the ride as it started to turn.

Caroline looked down at Dinah as Tom approached, giving her a smile that held an implicit reassurance, and Dinah understood that her mother would be fine. It amazed her that so much language could be transmitted by a single smile. She read an entire text in it—the acknowledgement of loss, the place that would always be held in their hearts, the relief of moving beyond pain, and the joy of finding contentment again. She suddenly felt a lightness that she hadn't even known she was missing—a feeling that she recognized from before her father had died.

The ride slowly spun to a stop, and Jemima insisted on trying a camel, and then a lion, while Tom, Caroline, and Dinah waited patiently for her to have her fill; to experience the exquisite beauty of the carousel as it went around on a lovely summer's day was reward in itself. When Jemima was satisfied they moved on, trying out the roller coaster and the Tilt-A-Whirl, ending up taking turns at the games on the arcade. Tom revealed a hidden talent for Skee-Ball, winning an enormous panda bear for Jemima, and for Dinah a floppy-eared basset hound that looked a lot like Bel.

After gorging on salt water taffy, homemade ice cream, and caramel popcorn, they finally headed for the car. Jemima had a mélange of unrecognizable smudges painted on her face, and they all felt sticky and tired, but it was the happy, sun-kissed fatigue that comes with spending the day outdoors.

They returned home to find Tru sequestered in his room, intently working on his reading assignment. Everyone wanted to clean up, and Caroline announced that dinner would be served later than usual. As Dinah passed Tru's door, she had an urge to poke her head in to see how the assignment was coming, but as her hand touched the doorknob she hesitated and moved away toward her own room.

At dinnertime, Jemima was fully in charge of reporting on the day: "And the horses have real hair for their manes and tails, and there's a whole village carved in the center, and even a circus parade . . . "

Her prattle was interrupted by the doorbell. Tom excused himself and went to the door. Dinah could hear several voices, and recognized one of them as belonging to Bill Lange. She thought one of the others could be Hayes Swanson, another friend of Tru's, but there were a couple of female voices that she didn't recognize.

After a brief, unintelligible exchange, she heard Tom say, "I'll let him know you were here." He returned to the table with his chin set firmly, addressing Tru: "Missed opportunity comes to those who wait." He raised an eyebrow in warning: "Don't even think about it."

Tru just shrugged, and with a grimace of acceptance, excused himself to his room.

The house was quiet earlier than usual that evening; everyone was tired, and Jemima fell asleep while her mother combed through her freshly washed hair. Caroline gently pulled a soft flannel nightgown over the child's head, who sleepily slipped her arms into the sleeves. She tucked her in with their usual routine—a kiss on each cheek, one on the nose, butterfly eyelashes, and the last on the lips. It was something on which Jemima always insisted, a ritual that Caroline wished her little girl would never outgrow.

Luxuriating in the reward of her own clean, crisp sheets, Caroline snuggled into the crook of Tom's arm. "What do you have there?" she asked. Tom took off his glasses and looked down at his wife.

"It just won the Pulitzer Prize—a really fascinating story. It's a *roman à clef* about southern politics called *All the King's Men*. What a cast of characters! This Warren guy can really write."

"Speaking of characters, what was it that Coco wanted to speak to you about today?"

Tom sighed and looked at the ceiling. "You won't believe this one. It seems that my high-living sister has run through her funds. Let me rephrase that: My high-living sister and her high-living paramour have jointly run through all of their combined capital, and they have also managed to exhaust several loans, tapping out the good will of all of their banking relationships. Evidently Mr. O'Grady has a small issue with the ponies."

"Do you mean he spent all of his money, and Coco's too, at the track?" Caroline asked disbelievingly.

"No, I mean they both did. Actually, it goes a little deeper than that. Apparently they made significant investments in some racehorses, and, much to their dismay, the investments didn't prove to be sound."

Caroline thought for a moment. "What do they propose to do about it?" she asked.

"Well, for one thing, they got married last night."

"What?"

"I believe that was my response exactly. I have to give old Harley credit." His tone was ironic as he shook his head.

"I don't think I understand."

"It's complicated. I'm the executor of a trust that my father set up years ago. It's to be distributed in parcels at ten-year intervals. Harley knows this, because his firm did the work when my father put it into place. He also knows that, as Coco's brother, I am unlikely to let them sink when I have the means to keep them afloat. It is definitely in his best interest to be a legitimate member of the family. As far as Coco's reasoning, I'm not as sure. If I know Coco, it was a whim. She has never been one to bother with the reality of life's little problems. Frankly, I never understood why they didn't get married years ago. After Whit died, I assumed they would make it legal." He turned onto his side and drew Caroline close. "Let's not talk about it anymore," he murmured as he lightly grazed her earlobe with his teeth. "I don't want to risk the nightmare of having Coco and Harley in my dreams," he began to kiss her neck, "when I could have you."

In her own room, Dinah wished she had the Hawthorne back. She had finished the pile stacked in the corner, and she wasn't accustomed to going to bed without a book. She walked into the hallway and looked at Tru's door. It was so strange that this boy was now part of her life. She had absolutely no idea how to relate to him. She wondered if it would ever feel like Tru was her brother. For some reason, she simply couldn't imagine it. A subconscious voice suggested that perhaps she could make a better effort. On impulse, she knocked on the door. There was no reply. She tried again, tapping lightly several times. Still nothing. Surprising herself, she turned the handle.

The lamp on the desk was burning, but Tru wasn't there. She crossed the room and picked up some papers: He had started a comparative analysis of two of the Hawthorne stories, but Dinah could see that it wasn't finished. She put the papers down abruptly, suddenly afraid of being caught red-handed. The copy of *Twice-Told Tales* was sitting on the desk. She had a strong inclination to take it back to her room, but she knew he would need it to finish; he had probably just gone downstairs for something from the kitchen. She left, making sure to put everything back just as she found it. She had a slightly ridiculous feeling of guilt, as though she were some kind of cat burglar. Closing the door, she went downstairs, telling herself that she needed a glass of water.

The kitchen was empty. Curious, she made a cursory patrol of the other rooms on the main floor; it confirmed what she had known all along—Tru wasn't home.

The next morning Caroline took the girls to church while Tom worked in the yard. Tru hadn't come down yet when they left, and Caroline remarked that he must have been up very late studying. Dinah was silent, and when the minister's sermon included a parable about a sin of omission, she looked up in wonder, sighing at the inescapable scrutiny of God's omniscience.

After the service, Caroline stopped to visit with several old friends in the congregation, trying Dinah's patience. She was anxious to get home, but she didn't want to dwell on the reason. Suddenly she realized that her mother was addressing her with exasperation.

"Dinah, did you hear me? I'd like you to meet an old friend—Martha Koening. I haven't seen her in years." Caroline smiled apologetically at a tall woman in a navy blue dress, indicating the she had no idea where her daughter's manners were.

Dinah smiled politely. "It's nice to meet you, Mrs. Koening." After enduring several more minutes of small talk, she finally led the way back to the car, with Jemima babbling away about her Sunday-school lesson: Joseph and the Coat of Many Colors. Jemima loved going to church, not only because in Sunday school they put on plays and had doughnuts and punch, but also because she could wear delicate cotton gloves and one of her flowery hats. She carried her white leather Bible under her arm like a prim little bookkeeper, prancing along in patent-leather Mary Janes. Dinah had never liked church. She always came away with a heaviness in her heart, brought on by a guilty feeling that she wasn't doing enough, or she was doing it all wrong. It was her nature to feel responsible for everything anyway, and the presumption of sin added to her burden. And she hated wearing hats.

When they finally arrived back home, they found that Tom and Tru had decided to leave early and have lunch on the road. Tom left a note explaining that he wanted to get there in time to say hello to the football coach—an old teammate from Tom's St. Paul days—before he left campus to go home for his Sunday dinner.

Dinah felt inordinately deflated. At lunchtime Jemima put Dinah's thoughts into words when she looked forlornly at their mother and said, "He didn't even say goodbye." Dinah picked at her chicken salad and then excused herself.

She went upstairs and passed Tru's bedroom, gazing in from the doorway. The bed was made, and all the clothes were gone, as though the last two weeks of having a "brother" had been a dream. She found herself mentally cringing at the word. She looked for the book, but it was no longer on the desk. When she went into her own room, she saw it on the bed. Feeling tired, she took off her Sunday dress and slipped on some old clothes, curling up under a quilt with the copy of Hawthorne.

As she picked up the book, she noticed a bookmark holding a place toward the center. The book fell open to the mark, which was a story called "Fancy's Show Box." Dinah assumed that Tru had forgotten to remove the bookmark when he had finished. When she glanced at the page she saw that he had underlined parts of a passage in blue ink. Tru had underlined a library book! Would anyone notice? But her momentary ire, fueled by the fact that it was her name on the check-out card, was forgotten when she began to read the lines:

> *What is Guilt? A stain upon the soul. And it is a point of vast interest, whether the soul may contract such stains, in all their depth and flagrancy, from deeds which may have been plotted and resolved upon, but which, physically, have never had existence.*

Here he skipped a few lines, but resumed again on the same page:

> *In the solitude of a midnight chamber . . . the soul may pollute itself even with those crimes, which we are accustomed to deem altogether carnal. If this be true, it is a fearful truth.*

She quickly rifled through the rest of the book, scanning the pages to see if he had underlined anything else, wondering if this passage was part of a larger theme for his comparative analysis, but there was nothing; only the one page, where the bookmark had been.

CHAPTER FOUR

A More Terrible Thing

DINAH AND BETSY DECIDED to walk together to their first day of high school. They had spent most of the previous week consulting each other about what to wear. Caroline had taken them both shopping in Boston, where they splurged on cashmere twin sets at Filene's, but the day was warm and they decided on sleeveless camp blouses with plaid skirts—Dinah in a new pair of saddle oxfords and Betsy in loafers, complete with shiny pennies. Dinah was waiting at the door when Betsy arrived.

"Do you have Gustafson for civics?" Betsy asked, unable to hide a nervous excitement. "I've heard he's the worst—he gives mounds of homework on the very first day."

"No, I have Schaffer," Dinah replied. They compared schedules as they walked along. When they got to the school, they were welcomed with squeals by a group of fellow sophomore girls, who were gathering for strength in numbers. There was a squirrelly giddiness in their purported fear; the intimidation by upper classman was a rite of passage they had been looking forward to all summer.

Marlys James gave Dinah a hug, nattering away with barely a pause. "I've heard that the senior girls corner sophomores in the bathroom and take their lipstick . . . it's considered paying dues, and you have to watch the door for them while they smoke . . . " She was rising up and down on her toes, looking around for more first-years to bolster the *esprit de corps*. "Oh my God, there's Lana Gervais," she said in a stage whisper. "I heard she's dating Jimmy Wright. She is the spitting image of Elizabeth Taylor, don't you think?"

"Did you see *National Velvet?*" added a pudgy girl named Joan Marconi. "Lana could have been her understudy."

The girls clung nervously together until the first bell broke them up for homeroom. Dinah didn't have any morning classes with Betsy, but they met up in the cafeteria for lunch, finding a table with some of their friends in the corner. The noise in the shiny lunchroom was deafening, as pitched voices caromed off the tile walls and travertine floors in the frantic scramble to reestablish connections after the long summer break. Suddenly Marlys grabbed the arm of the person sitting next to her, a rabbity-looking girl in heavy glasses, and squeezed. "Uh oh! Look who's coming!"

Dinah looked up and saw a small group of older girls making their way toward the table. She recognized Lana Gervais from the conversation that morning, but she didn't know the others. There was suddenly a palpable tension at the table, substantiated when a tall redhead put her tray down on the table.

"Well what do we have here? Look, Janet—it seems there are some strays that have mistaken our table for their kennel." She looked around at her friends for favor, their laughter spurring her on. "Don't you think you should get back to the pound? The dog catcher may be out looking for you." The redhead was clearly enjoying her performance.

Joan, Marlys, and the three other girls at the table hastily picked up their trays, but Dinah was strangely immobile, as a sudden bold indignation settled in her chest. The senior clique started to sit down, arranging their trays on the table, before realizing that two of the sophomores remained. "You must be a little dense," the redhead continued. "I'll speak slowly. This is *our* table."

This presumed superiority—not to mention rudeness—offended Dinah on such a primordial level that she reacted instinctively: "We were here first," she heard herself saying, although her voice sounded strangely far away. Betsy had been half out of her chair, nudging Dinah's shoulder, but with this she loyally sat down. Dinah could feel her face hot with adrenaline, but she maintained a level gaze and braced herself.

The older girls were temporarily stymied at this unexpected display of nerve, but it didn't take long for their ringleader to slowly slide her tray across the table until it made contact with Dinah's. She paused only for the briefest moment, keeping her eyes leveled on Dinah's face, and then continued to push, silently daring Dinah to stop her.

Dinah was frozen, not quite processing what was happening until it was too late. She grabbed for her tray just as it tipped into her lap. Jumping up quickly, she couldn't avoid a lapful of mashed potatoes and gravy. The older girls laughed nervously. Betsy stared at her friend in horror.

Standing there dumbly, watching the creamy potatoes slide down her skirt, Dinah heard a familiar voice:

"Hey Dinah—it looks like some clod must have spilled all over you." Bill Lange was standing next to her, holding his lunch tray in one hand. "It's really too bad some people are so clumsy," he continued. He shot a disparaging look at the other girls. They were suddenly regarding Dinah with a wary curiosity. He turned toward the redhead. "I don't think Tru will be very happy to hear that you've gone and spoiled the very first day of school for his new sister," he said.

This news was met with stunned silence. Every eye in the group turned expectantly toward Lana Gervais. Finally, a small brunette with a pony tail and short bangs spoke up. "Lana? Did you know that Tru had a new sister?"

"I haven't spoken to Tru since last spring—you know that." Lana's voice was dismissive, but her expression revealed shock. She looked at Dinah with narrowed eyes. "I knew his father was getting remarried. He didn't mention any stepsiblings." Her caustic delivery reminded Dinah of Coco Wells.

Bill picked up a napkin from the nearest tray and handed it to Dinah. "Why don't you come over and sit with us. We have a couple of spots at our table. You don't want to stay here—Sally made a big mess."

It was true that the floor was covered in spilled milk, peas, two large meatballs, and the rest of the potatoes and gravy. Dinah wiped a glob of potatoes off her skirt and tried to blot up most of the gravy. Bill took the soiled napkin from her hand and dropped it onto Sally's tray, where it covered the peas. The table was silent as he led Dinah across the room. Betsy, clutching her own tray, followed close behind.

As they approached the table Bill gallantly made introductions: "Guys, do you know Tru's new sister? This is Dinah Hunt, and . . ." he looked questioningly at Betsy.

"Betsy MacEvoy." Her voice came out in an apologetic squeak.

"Slide over, Stan. Make room," Bill pulled up an extra chair.

Stan obligingly shifted, while keeping his eyes on Dinah. "Mmmmm—she looks delicious," he teased. "Have you guys tried the gravy?" He reached out a finger and swiped her left hip, then put it is his mouth. "Superb! They've done something new with the recipe. It's a big improvement!"

Joey Fetzer, the short red-haired boy who had danced with Jemima at the wedding, jumped into the act: "It's sweeter than usual," he said, running his finger across her knee and making a show of tasting it. "And a little spicy . . ."

"I don't know—I'm afraid I'll burn my tongue. It looks like it might be too hot." Hayes Swanson pantomimed a burned finger. Dinah had the fleeting thought that she might actually burst into flames from embarrassment.

A tall, dark-haired boy paused on his way past the table, observing the commotion. Without putting down his tray, he leaned over and drew his finger up the side of her leg. Licking the tip of it, he offered his bystander assessment: "Honey from the hive," he said slowly, and winked at her.

It took Dinah a second to realize that Bill had asked her a question. "I'm sorry, what did you say?" She dabbed at her skirt again while one of the guys passed her a new tray of food.

"I was just asking how our old pal is doing at St. Paul's," Bill said.

"Oh, Tru. Um, I guess OK. I know he got the quarterback position; my family is going to a game this weekend." She hadn't talked to Tru since he had left for school, and by the time her mother had mentioned going to see him play, Dinah was already scheduled to work at the library. Once again, she felt an obscure disappointment.

While the rest of the table moved on to talk of their own upcoming football game, Dinah excused herself to find the nearest bathroom to finish the clean-up job, with Betsy scurrying behind her. No sooner was the water running in the sink than the bathroom door flew open and they were surrounded by their friends.

"Oh my God, do you know who that was? That was Jimmy Wright, and you should have seen the expression on Lana's face. Oh, I wouldn't want to be you for all the tea in China . . ." Marlys was running on again. The girls flocked around Dinah as though she were a celebrity.

Dinah was wrestling with the towel dispenser, trying to pull out enough of the fabric loop to reach the sink, while Betsy wrangled a fistful of toilet paper to dab at the remaining stains. "Who's Jimmy Wright again?" Dinah tentatively revealed her ignorance.

"He's a senior, and he's the captain of the football and basketball teams. He's dating Lana Gervais, and everyone knows he hates Tru Stuart. Tru had the quarterback spot all locked up until he transferred, and he had

Lana locked up, too." Joan Marconi rattled off this information with the authority of a bona fide private eye.

Dinah looked at her with amazement. "How do you know all this?" She felt like she must have been living on the moon.

"Joan is our very own Hedda Hopper," answered Marlys. "If you want to know anything about anyone—unless they're younger, of course—just ask Joan. She should have her own gossip column in the school paper: *Just Ask Joan.*" A chorus of agreement and laughter was drowned out by the second bell. The girls scattered as they dashed off to class.

After school, Dinah managed to sneak into the house and out of her stained skirt before her mother noticed—she wasn't in the mood to explain the incident at lunch. It had been hard enough getting through the rest of the day—not only because of the unsightly gravy stains across her lap, but also because she had attracted the whispering buzz of most of the student body. She ran a tub and threw her skirt into the hamper, thankful that Gloria would be in the next day to do the laundry.

Halloween in Salem was an extraordinary experience. In a town that celebrated a history rife with tales of witchcraft, the event was treated with a reverence usually reserved for major Christian holidays. Pranks and practical jokes were the duty-bound obligation of all teenage residents, and people had recently begun to hand out candy or treats to buy insurance against being victimized. Dressed in identity-disguising masks and costumes, the kids had free reign to terrorize the town.

Jemima deliberated for several weeks about her costume for the school party, finally deciding to be a ghost. She wanted to be the ghost of Dorcas Good—the youngest girl accused during the Witch Hysteria. Her mother obligingly fashioned an eerily ethereal gown out of gauze that floated around her diaphanously. At night, in just the right light, it gave the unnerving impression of intangibility.

On Halloween morning, Dinah and Caroline painted Jemima's face with a pale whitewash and smudged delicate shadows beneath her eyes. The effect was perfectly spooky, and gave both Caroline and Dinah a moment of shivery discomfort.

"My lord, Mimer, you do look like a corpse," Caroline shuddered.

Jemima held her arms out straight in front of her and walked with a stiff and swaying gait, eyes stretched open wide. Dinah was surprised by a sudden sick thud in her stomach at the sight of her ghostly little sister, which she shook off with impatience at her own melodramatic superstition.

On the way to school, the girls could already feel a strange and exciting vibration in the air. Small children were dressed like vampires, witches, and goblins. There was also a more benign assortment of cowboys and Indians, clowns, and ballerinas. Dinah said goodbye to Jemima at her classroom, peeking inside to see the decorations for the party—the tub for apple bobbing, the black and orange crepe paper streamers, the dancing skeletons and huge paper jack-o'-lanterns on the walls. She wished for a moment that she were Jemima's age again.

The past two months had been laced with a vague, hovering dread. Her famous first day had mostly been forgotten by her classmates, but she had to tread lightly in the presence of the older girls. She had managed to avoid Sally Vecchi for the most part, keeping close to Tru's friends during lunchtime. Bill Lange frequently appeared just as the final bell rang and fell into step with her as she left school, walking part of the way with her. She had also noticed that they often crossed paths in the halls between classes, which she chalked up to the lucky coincidence of proximity. She had seen Lana Gervais, often walking with her hand on the arm of Jimmy Wright, but Lana acted as though she had no idea who Dinah was and looked right through her. This was perfectly fine with Dinah—she preferred invisibility to the alternative. The library became her refuge, and she spent most of her after-school time there, keeping a low profile.

The day passed quickly, with the thrilling spark of anticipated mischief jumping through the air like an electrical current. There were no costumes allowed at the high school, but a few of the boys had sneaked in some masks, which they put on during lunchtime. To Dinah many of them were virtually indistinguishable with their heads covered. They made the rounds of tables, stopping to tease the girls with outrageous comments, cloaked by protective anonymity. A shorter version of John Wayne approached Dinah's table, laying his hands on Joan Marconi's shoulders. "Well hey there, little lady," he drawled. "Would you like to go for a ride on my horse?"

Joan giggled and said "Susan loves to ride," indicating the girl to her left. "Why don't you ask her?" There was loud laughter, and the girl named Susan made an exaggerated show of offense.

Dinah missed the innuendo. "I didn't know you rode, Susan," she offered. The whole table looked at her and laughed.

"Dinah, you are so naïve." Marlys indicated her friend's hopelessness with a raised eyebrow and a resigned grimace.

John Wayne sauntered around the table. "Any time you want free riding lessons, Princess, you just come right to the Duke, you hear? My stallion is gentle and reliable—"

He was abruptly cut off by Bill Lange, who grabbed him by the arm, pulling him along to another table: "OK, cowboy, that's enough. Your stallion stays in the barn."

After school, the girls and Caroline started to carve the jack-o'-lanterns. Tom came home from work early to join them, taking the prize for the most original face: He chiseled an outline of a strong, square jaw, managing to achieve an uncanny resemblance to Dick Tracy.

"Who knew that a common lumberjack could be so artistic?" Caroline teased.

"I have talents you've only begun to discover," he said slyly, and Caroline was suddenly very busy cleaning up the piles of seeds and pulp on the spread-out newspaper.

Dinah had offered to take Jemima trick-or-treating. For their part, Caroline and Tom were planning to put on costumes and greet anyone who came to the door with caramel apples, which Gloria had spent the entire previous day dipping. Tom came down in a very elegant Count Dracula ensemble, wearing his evening tails and a bright red sash, with a medal dangling on a wide ribbon from his neck. With his hair Brylcreemed back, face whitened with powder, and a rather unconvincing dribble of lipstick blood trickling from the corner of his mouth, he looked more dashing than menacing. He swept Jemima up and buried his face in her neck, declaring, "I vant to drrrink your blood." She squealed and wriggled free as Caroline descended in her Bride of Frankenstein get-up, wild fright-wig standing straight in the air.

"Exquisite, my dear," Tom intoned in his best impression of a Transylvanian accent. "You are even lovelier than I remembered. I'm feeling rather weak—I fear I need sustenance . . ." He took her arm and kissed the inside of her elbow, moving upward to the tender skin of her inner arm.

"Sir, unhand me, I beg," Caroline swooned dramatically. "What would my husband say?"

Jemima's eyes danced at their playfulness. "Yeah, you lousy old count!" She jumped gleefully into the act. "Her husband is Frankenstein, and he could take you with one arm tied behind his back!"

Tom gave her a narrowed-eyed look of exaggerated evil, swooping her up again as she screamed in mock terror. He tossed her into the air, and Dinah was amazed at the effect of the flowing costume—Jemima seemed to float into the air, defying gravity as she hovered for a moment in space before landing back in Tom's arms. It was an astounding illusion, and again Dinah felt a shivery apprehension, as though her sister were liable to float away like a ghost.

They stationed the jack-o'-lanterns on the front stoop, letting Jemima light the candles. Dinah breathed in and closed her eyes. She loved the smell of Halloween—a combination of dry leaves, cool autumn air, and burning pumpkin. It was a sense memory that never failed to evoke a happy, vaguely nostalgic feeling. She took Jemima by the hand and they started off toward the common. Caroline and Tom had given Dinah explicit instructions to visit only homes of people they knew and to stay away from the wharf area, which hooligans traditionally ransacked with graffiti, smashed pumpkins, and other forms of vandalism. Dinah and Jemima wanted go to Salem Common first, because there was always a bonfire, with hot cider and popcorn balls provided by the Salem Historic Society.

They walked down Chestnut Street and up Washington to Brown. There were glowing jack-o'-lanterns on almost every doorstep. Many houses had ghosts suspended from trees, and small graveyards had sprouted in several yards. When they arrived at the Common, Dinah found several of her friends among the crowd, nonchalantly hovering around the bonfire, attempting to look blasé. Dinah and Jemima stayed long enough to hear the Warlocks (formerly Al's Barbershop Quartet) sing a hauntingly harmonic version of "Sentimental Journey" transposed to a minor key. Jemima had a popcorn ball and a caramel apple, but before long, she was tugging on Dinah's jacket, insistently impatient to move on.

As they wandered down Essex Street they passed the elementary school, and Jemima launched into a recounting of her class party that day, unintentionally hilarious when describing her determination to win the apple bobbing contest:

"And I was winning, because I had bit the most apples because I have my new teeth, and Sheldon Smith didn't even have one of his teeth and he said that I must really be a carp, because I was coming back to life, and I didn't know what he meant, so I tried to push his head in the water, but Mrs. Lifson got mad and said I had to sit in the corner. Then we had a little talk, and I told her what Sheldon said, and she said that's because the water washed off all my white and I didn't look dead anymore. So I said I'm sorry to Sheldon, and we tied."

She seemed very pleased with the outcome, which made Dinah smile. How simple to be seven, she thought. She looked fondly at Jemima. Caroline had reapplied the whitewash and shadow, and in the dark of evening she looked more unearthly than ever.

They worked their way down the streets, ringing the doorbells of houses where they knew kids from school lived. As they approached Derby Street, Dinah realized they were getting close to the wharf, so they changed course, turning up an unfamiliar avenue. It was a street like many others, lined with wood-framed Victorian homes situated close to the street, many with little or no front yard. The jack-o'-lanterns virtually lined the road, so close were the doorsteps. Dinah was trying to recall whether she knew anyone who lived there when Jemima scooted up to the nearest door and rang the bell. There were candles glowing in both of two front windows, but no jack-o'-lanterns on the doorstep.

"Wait, Mimer—you're not supposed to go to strange houses."

But the door was already swinging open, and as Dinah joined her sister she was surprised to see Mr. Remarcik smiling down at them. He hadn't been back to the library since Dinah heard that he had fallen. When she asked Jane MacEvoy if she had found out what happened, a very strange expression took the place of her ordinarily open countenance—it was a look Dinah had never seen on Jane's face before—as if shutters had been drawn closed. "Did you find out about his fall?" Dinah had asked.

"Yes, well . . ." Jane paused, as though she wasn't sure what to say. "I guess that's the truth," she ventured. "He certainly did fall. Yes, you could surely say he fell."

"Is he going to be all right?" Dinah felt confused, registering Jane's reluctance.

"Let's just say that Mr. Remarcik is a very sick man, and he won't be coming into the library anymore." Jane turned away, leaving Dinah with the alienated feeling of being left out of a secret. She wondered what the illness could be, but had the distinct impression that she shouldn't ask anymore about it. Since then, she had been so wrapped up with school and friends that she had almost forgotten about poor Mr. Remarcik. And now here he was, with the same nice smile, looking perfectly fine, except that he was wearing his bathrobe and slippers, which confirmed that he must not be well.

"Well hello there, young ladies!" He opened the door wider. "Come right in!" His voice quavered with age, but he seemed delighted to see them, and Dinah couldn't bring herself to refuse his invitation. She ushered Jemima into the dimly lit foyer, noticing the smell of mothballs and something else . . . a strong odor of ammonia. She couldn't place it at first, and then she remembered the cat box at Aunt Bat's house when it hadn't been changed for a few days. On cue, a mangy-looking grey cat slinked around Mr. Remarcik's ankles. Jemima was staring up at the old man with a quizzical look on her face, like she was trying to remember where she had seen him before.

"Jemima, you remember Mr. Remarcik from the library, don't you?" Dinah nudged her sister to remind her of her manners.

"Oh yes, hello," Jemima said in her best company voice. "Do you live here with your crabby friend?" she asked innocently. Dinah was mortified, but Mr. Remarcik just laughed.

"No, I live here with Esmeralda and Aloysius." He looked down at the grey cat, adding "This is Esmeralda."

Jemima leaned down and reached a hand out to the scruffy creature. It arched its back and hissed.

"Now, now, kitty, that's no way to welcome guests." His voice creaked a little, and Dinah found herself trying not to stare at the blue veins on his hairless, knobby ankles. There were a scattering of crusty, red patches visible on his lower legs, and she quickly looked at the nearest diversion, which was a fringed lampshade on an old porcelain lamp painted with faded and chipped cabbage roses. Mr. Remarcik had turned and was walking toward the old-fashioned parlor, beckoning them to follow. Dinah hesitated, but she didn't want to be impolite. She felt confused. The house gave her a creepy feeling, and it seemed inappropriate to be visiting with an old man in a bathrobe. She wished he were fully dressed, but she felt sorry for what she imagined must be a lonely life. The awkwardness of the situation made her feel a little queasy. Jemima trailed after him with blatant curiosity, looking around at the dusty old pictures on the walls, stopping to examine the ship in a bottle that rested on an old Victrola cabinet. "Have a seat, ladies," he gestured to a worn horsehair sofa.

Dinah sat on the edge of the scratchy cushion, skeptically eyeing the stains on the worn fabric. Jemima was riveted by the tiny ship, speechless for once at the marvel of it.

"That's a model of the *Santa Maria*," creaked Mr. Remarcik. "I put it together myself." Jemima looked at him with awe, as though she had found herself in the presence of a wizard. She had always loved tiny things, and she accepted the miracle of the perfect miniature ship somehow residing inside a bottle with the absolute faith of a religious postulate.

"I think I've got a little something to offer my guests." The old man shuffled to the kitchen, calling over his shoulder, "I'll just be a jiffy, now don't go away." Dinah thought he sounded sadly pathetic, as though he was afraid they would run off and he'd be left alone again.

He returned with a plate of thin cookies, holding it out to Dinah, hopefully expectant. She picked up a ginger snap and took a small nibble. It tasted like a combination of dust and old wood, and she wondered how long it had been in the cupboard. She held the cookie on her lap, hoping Mr. Remarcik wouldn't notice she wasn't making any progress. Her main concern was Jemima, who had no sense of diplomacy, and would undoubtedly spit the cookie right out on the rug.

"Mimer, you're not allowed to have any cookies tonight. Remember, you've already had a popcorn ball and a caramel apple."

Jemima gave a disinterested shrug and moved on to look through a stereopticon at an old photograph of some people in a boat. Mr. Remarcik set the plate down on a scratched side table and settled into a wingback chair adjacent to the sofa. He crossed his legs, revealing more psoriasis. Dinah looked around the room in a determined attempt to avoid looking at Mr. Remarcik's bare skin.

"You have a very nice home," she said.

"Thank you. I've been here a long time," he chuckled softly. "This was the house I was born in, you know. Say, little miss, why don't you bring that contraption over here and I'll show you how to use it," he addressed Jemima. She trotted over and handed him the apparatus, along with a small stack of cardboard-mounted photographs. "This is what you call a Vista-Vision. What you have to do is slide the lens forward or backward along this track to get focus." He turned to Dinah. "Come over here and take a look." He patted the arm of his chair, indicating that she should perch on it next to him. Jemima was standing on one side, and Dinah obligingly sat on the other arm of the chair. Mr. Remarcik pulled out the photograph that was in the slot, and rustled through the stack. "Here's one that's a beauty," he mused as he replaced the picture. He grasped the handle and held it to Dinah's face. She looked into what would have been an amazing realistic alpine scene, except that it was in black and white.

"Let me see," demanded Jemima, and he moved toward her with the Vista-Vision.

It took Dinah a few moments to realize that as he shifted in the chair, his bathrobe had pulled open below the belt, revealing an unobstructed view of his private parts. She was horrified, but mostly on behalf of poor old Mr. Remarcik; she had no idea how to let him know about the offending gap. She quickly looked at Jemima to see if the little girl had noticed, but Jemima had the Vista-Vision to her face. The seed of a thought was trying to germinate and signal a warning, planted by the disturbing realization that he had nothing on beneath the robe, but before she could process it, he shifted back toward her, causing the robe to fall even further agape. She had never before seen what her girlfriends referred to as "manhood," and she was shocked and revolted at the tuberous, swollen appendage. He shuffled through the cards again, silently this time, and placed a new photo in the slot. Dinah felt sick, desperately trying to keep her eyes away from the horrible brown tube of flesh that was protruding from the robe. She also felt terrible for Mr. Remarcik. She knew that he would be mortified to know that he was exposed like that. She was relieved to see that Jemima had turned to wander back to the ship in the bottle, and she grabbed the Vista-Vision from the old man, stuttering something about needing to adjust the focus for herself. She thrust the lens to her eyes, frantic for the diversion. It took several moments for her to register what she was looking at through the three-dimensional lens: There were several bodies, and what Dinah noticed first was that they had no clothes on. She felt stunned—unable to take the apparatus away from her face. As she numbly gazed at the photo, she began to register the details of the two women and two men, engaging in unfathomable acts. She couldn't even begin to comprehend the meaning, but she knew that it was vile and depraved. She dropped the Vista-Vision as though it had burned her, and jumped off the arm of the chair. Mr. Remarcik was looking at her with an odd, glazed stare. His face was red, and his hand had moved to his lap. Dinah thought with relief that he had finally realized the hideously embarrassing situation, but then she noticed that his arm was moving, and he seemed to be caressing himself. She stumbled backwards, tripping into the sofa. He was mumbling something unintelligible, and his arm moved with increasing vigor. Dinah felt as if she had fallen down a deep well, dizzy and nauseous, with an overwhelming thrumming noise in her head.

She instinctively looked around for Jemima. She didn't see her at first, but just as she noticed a bright flash out of the corner of her eye, a high-pitched scream broke through the wall of static in her ears.

Jemima had picked up the bottle with the ship inside, and, dissatisfied with the dim light provided by the weak overhead bulb, she had crouched near a candle in the front window to better see the tiny masts and sails. As she leaned into the light, the edge of her gauzy gown brushed the flickering flame. In an instant it jumped up from the wick, devouring the fabric with the voracious appetite of a Hydra.

Dinah rolled off of the sofa where she had fallen and stumbled forward, pitching headlong to reach her sister. Within seconds the flames were gorging on the inviting chemicals of the fabric, wrapping Jemima in a cloak of furious orange. Terrified screams became agonized. As Dinah reached her sister she was pushed back by the fiery fists of the flames. It was as though an invisible wall had suddenly slammed down between them, and she couldn't reach through it. She was aware of another voice screaming, but didn't know it was her own as she fell into a deep, dark void.

The next thing she saw were the scaly, scab-pocked legs of Mr. Remarcik, which were aligned with her face. After taking in the wider panorama, she realized that he was kneeling on the floor next to her, stark naked but for his slippers. His pale, nearly hairless body was blotched and sagging, and Dinah jumped up as it all came rushing back. Jemima was lying on the floor, wrapped in the old man's plaid flannel bathrobe, eyelids fluttering and breath coming in quick, shallow puffs. There were wisps of smoke drifting up from under the robe, and a strong, acrid smell filled the room. Mr. Remarcik looked stunned, staring at Jemima with the empty expression of a hypnotic. Dinah fell to Jemima's face, her voice teetering on the shaky, shrill edge of hysteria.

"Mimer? Are you all right? Jemima! Can you hear me?" Jemima moaned a soft, airy gasp. Dinah felt like she was going to faint again, and she looked desperately at the frozen face of the old man. As if feeling the impetus of her pleading eyes, he blinked, and in a weak, croaking voice uttered, "The phone is in the kitchen."

Dinah managed to propel herself to the kitchen, nearly pulling the phone off the wall in her frenzied effort to reach the operator. She had no idea what address to give, but in a moment of supernal clarity she remembered that it was the first house on the right, just above Derby Street on Clark.

Somehow she found herself back in the parlor, with no memory of going there. Mr. Remarcik was gone, and Dinah gently lay down on the worn carpet next to Jemima, pressing her body as close as possible without actually touching the burned shell encasing the small body. Jemima had started to tremble, her whole body quivering like a captured sparrow. Her eyes were closed. Dinah put her hand to her sister's face, softly resting her palm on an impossibly cold cheek. She listened for her breath, barely discernable in faint but steady reassurance. Her lips were as pale as the make-up on her face, and it was now hard to tell where the whitewash left off. Dinah closed her own eyes, vaguely aware that the room had started to spin, slowly at first, and then faster, like a ride at The Willows, and then she was gone.

Caroline and Tom arrived at the hospital still dressed in their costumes, oblivious to the stares from the nurses at the station as they rushed into the emergency room. Dinah was sitting on a hard plastic chair in the hallway, wrapped in a white flannel hospital blanket. She looked blankly at her parents, too dazed to recognize the bizarre characters standing before her.

"Where is she?" Caroline's voice was cracked and quavering, and the strident tenor, combined with the wild fright wig, was surreally terrifying. Dinah was momentarily relieved by the thought that this must all be a horrible nightmare.

Tom dropped to his knees in front of Dinah, grasping both of her arms. "Dinah—where is Jemima?" He emphasized the words distinctly, as if speaking to a foreigner. She drifted back into reality with sad reluctance, unwilling to relinquish the possibility that she had been dreaming. As she looked again at the anguished face of her mother, reality slammed into her like a sledgehammer, and she burst into shuddering sobs, unable to speak a word. Tom stood and barked out a demand to the nurse walking by with a clipboard. "Where is the doctor? We're here for Jemima Hunt— she's seven years old, and she's been badly burned. We need to see her immediately."

The nurse looked at him with disapproval, implying her resentment, not only of his tone, but of his costume as well—as though he had intentionally dressed up like a vampire to make an emergency trip to the hospital. "Wait here a moment, I'll page Dr. Downey." Curtly dismissive, she walked away at a determinedly measured pace. Tom couldn't take the apathy in her bearing; he strode forward and grabbed her by the arm, literally spinning her around to face him.

"We will *not* wait here. Tell us where we can find our daughter."

The nurse looked pointedly at Caroline's wig and then back at Tom. "I believe she's in the intensive care unit. That's one floor up. You won't be able to go in. No one can," she said archly, "not even a count. You'll have to sit in the upstairs waiting room, and the doctor will see you when he can."

Caroline was tearing off the wig, the nurse's snide glance reminding her of its existence. She now took a turn kneeling in front of Dinah, wrapping her daughter in her arms. "Oh, Dinah, what happened?" She was trying to keep a pressing hysteria out of her voice, but it was useless. Dinah had begun to rock slightly forward and back, trying to catch her breath through the convulsive sobs. "I should have thought about that damned gauzy fabric when I made the costume. It isn't your fault. Please, please Dinah, calm down. We need to go upstairs." She was torn by her oldest daughter's clear need for the comfort of her mother, and her own deep, primal need to go to Jemima.

Tom came and pulled both of them up, supporting an elbow in each of his hands.

"It will be OK. Let's go upstairs, we don't have to talk about it now . . ." He murmured soothing words as he ushered them down the hall to the elevator.

Through the haze of worry and despair, Caroline had registered his reference to "our daughter," and she was nearly overcome with love for her new husband. The extraordinary relief of having someone to lean on, to share the nightmare of this horror—combined with her raw anguish for Jemima—had the effect of knocking the wind out of her. She stumbled, and couldn't contain a low, keening whimper.

Tom stopped walking and wrapped her in his arms. "Shhhh, it's all right. Everything will be fine." He held her for a few moments.

As they stepped into the elevator, an instinctive response to Caroline's need summoned a frail composure, and Dinah took her mother's hand.

They sat on vinyl-cushioned, stainless-steel furniture in the antiseptically spare waiting room, all eyes fixed on the swinging door to the ICU. Tom had visited the men's room to wash his face, and he had removed the red sash and medal from his neck.

Without her wig, Caroline's costume consisted of an elaborately baroque evening gown, so she and Tom now looked like they must have come from The Queen's Ball. Dinah was nestled under her mother's arm, head on her shoulder. She felt drowsy, intermittently closing her eyes, only to snap them open whenever the door swung back and forth. Finally, a white-coated young doctor came through the door and approached them. "You must be the family of our little burn victim," he said, looking sympathetic.

"It's Jemima. Jemima Hunt." Caroline's voice was hoarse.

Tom stood. "I'm Tom Stuart, Jemima's father. Her mother, Caroline," he nodded at his wife, "and Dinah, Jemima's sister," another nod. He and the doctor shook hands.

"Sit down, please. I'll just pull up a chair here so I can explain the situation to you all." He settled into a chair and leaned forward, elbows on knees, hands clasped. "First of all, let me say that Jemima is going to be all right. She has suffered third-degree burns over much of her back, but she was very lucky that there is no damage to the skin on her face, and only a bit of first- and second-degree injury to her arms and her left hip. Those burns should heal on their own just fine. We need to harvest some skin from her inner thighs to graft onto her back, but we've had great success with this procedure in the past, and I have every expectation of smooth sailing. Whoever saved her acted quickly, and should be commended." He looked at Dinah, but she looked away. "We have the bathrobe, but I don't think you'll want it back—it's pretty well seared." Caroline and Tom looked at Dinah questioningly. She continued to stare at the linoleum, and the doctor cleared his throat. "Do you have any questions?"

Caroline spoke immediately. "Is she conscious? Is she in pain? Does she know what happened?"

"Of course; I'm sorry, I have clearly omitted some important details. No, she isn't conscious at the moment, but that's because we have anesthetized her for the surgery. She will have some pain from the grafts and from the first- and second-degree burns, but the severe burns don't cause much pain at all, because the nerve endings are destroyed. We will medicate to control any pain that she does have, and we should be able to keep her quite comfortable. I don't know how much she'll remember—she was in a state of shock when the ambulance arrived, which is the body's natural way of dealing with trauma like this. Physically, shock lowers the body temperature, but we've stabilized her vitals and she's doing just fine. Beneath that fragile-looking body is a strong little girl, and I'm confident she'll come through this like a champ."

Although meant to reassure, the imagery of his words hit Caroline in the gut, and she began weeping silently. Dr. Downey squatted next to her, resting his hand on hers. "You're in a bit of shock yourself." He gave her a sympathetic smile and a couple of pats on the arm. "Well, I have some work to do, so I'll check in with you as we progress." He started to walk away, and then turned. "She gave us quite a scare," he added, smiling at the irony: "That make-up job was fairly convincing."

As the night wore on, the trio nodded off at various intervals. At around three in the morning Tom stretched and offered to get coffee. He came back with three steaming cups, and a plateful of doughnuts. "The nurses here aren't so bad after all," he admitted. "They bring in a stash of these every night for people like us."

Energized, they shared a counterfeit alertness—their bodies signaling a new day. Caroline got up and started pacing in a slow circle. They had avoided asking Dinah anything further about the incident, afraid to upset her fragile composure. Now she seemed stronger, and Caroline couldn't wait any longer.

"Honey, do you think you can tell us what happened?" she asked tentatively.

The question caught Dinah off-guard. She hadn't allowed herself to think about it—letting her mind drift aimlessly to childhood memories, school assignments, speculation about the age of the doctor . . . anything to avoid replaying the scenario. Now she was suddenly confronted with a simple question, one to which she knew she owed an answer, and she had no idea what to say.

"I was just letting Mimer go to houses that we knew," she started slowly, "but we ended up on an unfamiliar street, and she went up to a strange house. I didn't have time to stop her. It turned out to be Mr. Remarcik's house." She glossed over his name quickly, hoping that her mother wouldn't remember it from their dinner conversation several months ago. Dinah had not forgotten her mother's reaction at the time, and she was beginning to put the pieces together. She couldn't look at Caroline—she didn't want to see the process of recognition. Staring at the floor, she continued in a muted voice: "He invited us in, and I thought it would be rude to say no, so we went in. He wanted to give us a treat . . ." She paused, wondering why she couldn't bring herself to tell the whole truth. "And then Mimer got too close to the candle and she was on fire, and I couldn't get to her . . ." Her voice broke and she tried to continue. "I . . . I don't know what happened next." She was choking back a sob. "I think Mr. Remarcik put the fire out with a bathrobe . . . it was on the chair . . ." Now she had told them an outright lie—something she had never done before. It was as if she was physically incapable of repeating what had really happened. She had a foggy memory of being taken into the ambulance with Jemima, and of the medics talking to Mr. Remarcik, who was fully dressed. That was the story he had given them.

She finally looked up at her mother, whose eyes held a painful question.

Exhibiting hard-won restraint, Caroline calmly said "Dinah, I'm going to ask you something, and I want you to give me a straight answer: Did Mr. Remarcik behave improperly in any way to you or Jemima?" She continued to level her gaze directly at her daughter's eyes, and Dinah couldn't bear it. Pretending to have heard a noise from the nurse's station, she quickly turned her head.

"What?" She said, looking distractedly at one of the nurses. "What do you mean? I told you, he just wanted to give us a Halloween treat, that's all." But she couldn't look at her mother, and didn't seem to wonder about the reason for the question.

Caroline closed her eyes.

The rest of the night passed slowly, with Dr. Downey's nurse appearing at intervals to give them updates. Finally, the doctor reappeared, wearing a weary smile. "It went well. We won't know immediately how the grafts will take—it's a difficult process, and it will take several weeks until we can see the results. But the good news is that she will have no visible scarring when she's dressed. Most of the damage was to her back, and, of course, there will be some scarring where we harvested the tissue from her inner thighs, but it won't be noticeable unless you look closely. Her hair was singed, by the way, so you'll want to give her a nice trim. As I said before, she was very lucky that it wasn't worse." He gave a congratulatory smile to Dinah, which had the effect of making her feel sick again.

He told them it would be a while until Jemima was awake, encouraging them to go home and rest. Caroline refused to leave until she could see her baby, a feeling shared by Tom and Dinah. The hours dragged by, broken up by visits to the cafeteria. Despite the pervasive odor of canned spaghetti mixed with the unmistakable hospital smell, they welcomed the diversion of mealtimes. At four o'clock in the afternoon, a new nurse came to tell them that Jemima was waking up and they could go in for a brief time.

Dinah hung back as they entered the room, suddenly reluctant to face her little sister. She was terrified of what she would find. She knew what the doctor had told them, but she was helpless against exaggerated visions of disfigurement—a tormenting self-punishment born from regret.

Caroline and Tom rushed into the room, forgetting about Dinah behind them. Jemima was groggy and dazed, barely able to open her eyes. Tenderly, Caroline took a small, warm hand into her own. She kissed her daughter on the brow, murmuring gentle phrases and trying to hold back her tears. "Hello sweet baby . . . Momma's here. Everything's going to be all right . . ." She struggled to keep her voice steady through the enormous lump in her throat.

Jemima blinked drowsily and found a vague focus on her mother's face. Her voice came out in a croaky whisper: "I saw a ship in a bottle."

Caroline assumed this was part of a dream, and she stroked her daughter's head. Dinah hovered in the doorway, watching from a distance. Tom noticed and signaled her in with a tilt of his head. She slowly walked forward, forcing herself to look at her sister. Jemima looked tiny in the hospital bed; there were tubes and wires hooked up all over. Dinah's stomach clenched, and for a moment she thought she would lose the egg salad sandwich she had eaten for lunch. She closed her eyes and felt Tom's arm around her.

A faint voice steadied her. "Dinah, do you have my treats?"

"Um . . . yes . . . yes, Mimer—I have them." Dinah had no idea what had happened to Jemima's little trick-or-treating sack. She assumed it was still in Mr. Remarcik's parlor, but there was no way that she could make herself explain that to Jemima; she would just have to replace it. Another lie.

The nurse didn't let them stay long. Jemima drifted in and out of sleep until the administration of another dose of pain medication put her solidly out. Finally, they went home. It was dark by the time they pulled into the driveway, but the windows were still lit from the night before. The jack-o'-lanterns had long since burned out—their charred shells a disturbing reminder of what had happened. Caroline shuddered as she climbed the front steps, instinctively pulling away from the now-offensive icons. Without a word, Tom scooped them up, piling all four at once into his arms, and walked to the trash can.

Exhausted, they all just wanted to clean up and go to bed. Caroline felt like she needed a long, hot bath. As she soaked in the tub, she thought about Dinah's reaction to her question about Mr. Remarcik. She was furious with herself for being so opaque when Dinah first mentioned his name. Caroline had remembered it from her own adolescence—he was considered an old man even then. She had heard whispers amongst several of her friends, admitting that he had "revealed" himself to them. The stories had repulsed her, but having had no contact with the old man herself, she eventually forgot him. When Dinah mentioned the name, Caroline had to comb her memory for the association. She wasn't absolutely certain that her misgivings were accurate, so she held her tongue. But her daughter's reaction to the question and conspicuous lack of curiosity about Caroline's reason for asking it confirmed her suspicions.

Tom was already asleep when she climbed into bed, which wasn't surprising, but Caroline was disappointed nonetheless. She felt a need to talk about the incident. She was worried about what had really happened. She didn't believe the girls had been interfered with, but she thought that something had transpired, and she could guess what it was. She just didn't know how to approach Dinah about the subject without making it worse.

She sighed and closed her eyes. In the scheme of things, her concern for Jemima trumped everything else. Sadly, she contemplated the strange, mitigating effects of perspective—the frightening truth that what was once considered an unthinkable situation could so easily be subordinated in light of a more terrible thing. She started to drift away, but not before offering a final, silent prayer: *Please, please . . . let this be our most terrible thing.*

Dinah didn't go to school the next day, barely able to force herself out of bed. She spent most of Saturday at the hospital; she wanted to keep Jemima company. A memory from a summer day had been hovering in her mind—it was her little sister's response when Dinah had reprimanded her for bothering children in the library: *"It's not nice to leave people alone."*

The little girl drifted in and out of sleep. By late afternoon, Dinah was drained and Tom took her home. Caroline insisted on staying until she was certain Jemima would be asleep for the night. At home, Tom fixed sandwiches, but when Dinah noticed him looking blankly around the kitchen, she sensed that he needed to be with his wife.

"I'm OK here, you know. You can go back to the hospital if you want."

He gave her a slightly surprised look, like he had been caught napping. He seemed hesitant—torn by a protective sense of responsibility that would ideally have him in two places at once. Dinah assured him that she just wanted to go to bed, so he packed up a couple of the sandwiches and a thermos of coffee and headed back to the hospital.

The big house felt lonely, and Dinah decided to take her sandwich to her bedroom. She carried a tray upstairs, with Bel laboring along behind her, the pooch's poor, abbreviated legs scaling each riser with valiant, heaving leaps. She reminded Dinah of a toppled penguin. Passing Jemima's door, Dinah paused. Without any conscious purpose she found herself entering the room. Absently, she set the tray down next to the ballerina music box on the dresser. There was a shelf of books on the wall—a collection of children's selections that mapped Jemima's life. Wedged at the end with the titles from her younger years was *A Giant Treasury of Beatrix Potter*. Dinah had forgotten about this little gem. She pulled it out and opened to the table of contents, running her finger down the list until she found *The Tale of Two Bad Mice*. This had been their favorite story; the first time she read it to Jemima, Dinah had been delighted to discover that her baby sister had a sense of humor. She hadn't expected her to absorb the facetious subtleties of the action, and when Jemima had giggled at Tom Thumb's reprobate vandalism, and then laughed outright at the concept of a dolly policeman standing guard, Dinah was impressed. Now, as she scanned the pages of the clever tale, even the droll wit of Miss Potter couldn't raise a smile.

Forlornly, she put the book away and gazed around the room at her little sister's world. She noticed Fuzz Monkey sitting alone in the corner. Sinking down against the wall, she hugged the stuffed animal to her. Bel flopped down next to her, resting her nose on Dinah's thigh. Dinah absently stroked her head, wondering if dogs could sense sadness. Surrounded by the stuff of Jemima's life, she couldn't keep from wandering to a place she had been carefully avoiding. In her mind's eye, she saw the image of the scars her sister would have on her beautiful, velvety skin. She pictured her on the beach in her blue gingham bathing suit with the ruffle around the bottom. As she envisioned the corrugated, red, shiny patches of scarred and grafted skin on Jemima's back, a tidal wave of guilt surged over her. The thought that had hovered just below the surface—the one that she had been struggling to suppress—rose up and swallowed her: While her little sister was moving toward certain danger, she had been looking at the disgusting photograph. If she had only kept her eye on Jemima, if she hadn't been riveted to the image in the Vista View, her sister would have been safe. She not only felt responsible for the tragedy, but dirty and defiled. Her head sank to her knees as the regret poured out in heaving gasps—the effort of holding her emotions at bay collapsing like a sandcastle in a storm.

Somewhere in the fog of her misery she sensed a presence. Lifting her head, she found herself looking straight into deep, ebony eyes. Tru was standing in the doorway, his jacket stuffed under an arm, hands in pockets. For a moment he looked hesitant, and then silently he crossed the room and sat down beside her. He didn't say a word, and Dinah felt strangely unsurprised. His presence felt preordained—almost expected—like remembering the words to a song. They sat for a while in commiserative silence, and then Dinah asked quietly, "How did you get here?"

"Hitchhiked," he replied in an equally subdued tone. "My dad called yesterday morning, but I had to finish exams."

"Does he know you're here?"

"No, he told me not to come home—to wait a while."

Dinah smiled, discerning a subtle pattern in what was revealing itself to be a rather defiant nature. "Mimer will be asleep for the night; you'll have to wait until morning to see her." She felt calm—as if she were drawing a current of quiescence from the warmth of his body.

"That's all right. I wanted to be here." There was a slight emphasis on the last word, and Dinah felt a small catch just below her breastbone. He wanted to be *here?* She wondered if she had understood correctly. What exactly did he mean by *here?*

"I brought up a sandwich, if you want some." She indicated the tray on the dresser with a nod of her head.

"What kind?"

"Chicken salad—Gloria brought over a bowl of it."

"Sounds good." They continued to sit on the floor against the wall, neither of them showing any inclination to move. "How's she doing?" Tru finally asked.

Dinah told him Jemima's prognosis, keeping the details clinical and straightforward. As she was explaining the grafting procedure they heard the front door open and Caroline's voice:

"Dinah? We're home."

At the moment Dinah lifted her face toward him, Tru looked down at her. Inches apart, their eyes locked. For an instant, Dinah felt transported to another place—a parallel universe where nothing else existed. It was as though she were falling into his gaze. A heavy tread ascending the staircase pulled her back to reality.

Tru drew a deep breath and blinked, quickly pushing himself up from the floor. "Would your monkey like a hand up?" He indicated Fuzz, who was still clenched in Dinah's arms. He reached down and held out his hand, pulling Dinah to her feet as Tom appeared in the doorway.

"Would you look what the cat dragged in!" Tom couldn't contain an enormous grin at the sight of his son. "How did you get here?" It was clear that he was anything but disappointed in Tru's decision to disregard his instructions.

"I hitched a ride." Tru looked steadily at his father—he didn't need to offer any further explanation. Tom didn't seem surprised that they were standing in Jemima's room. He noticed the tray on the dresser.

"Why don't we go down to the kitchen? It doesn't look like you two have had any dinner yet. By the time I got back to the hospital, Mimer was already down for the night, so we came back. Let's skip the sandwiches and I'll see if I can whip up something more substantial."

They ate spaghetti in the kitchen, with Tru giving wicked impersonations of his teachers—his trenchant humor working a magic that lifted everyone's spirits. After dinner, Tom offered to take them all out to Brickman's for ice cream.

As she slid onto the upholstery of the big Buick, Dinah felt the exhausted relief of a kitten rescued from a river. She leaned into the soft cushion of the roomy backseat. The evening was unseasonably warm for early November; the windows were rolled down part-way. Caroline swiveled around to face Dinah and Tru from the front seat. "The doctor said that Jemima may be able to come home in a few weeks," she said hopefully. Dinah could tell that her mother was making an effort to sound positive, and knew it was mostly for her benefit. Wearily, she closed her eyes and let the salty breeze blow across her skin.

The next morning, they all went together to the hospital. Caroline didn't even mention church, and Dinah suspected she had forgotten what day it was. Jemima was awake when they arrived, surrounded by several nurses who appeared to be there for social, rather than medical, purposes. They greeted the family with a warm reception, clearly captivated by their small charge. "You have quite a little charmer here," said a rotund, fiftyish matron with a jolly expression. The others agreed that Jemima was indeed a singularly beguiling patient, and they moved away to make room around the bed. Jemima still looked drowsy—her normal sparkle more a low shimmer—but she smiled with sweet delight when she saw Tru.

"Hey, Smidgen, how are you feeling?" He looked down at her with a tender smile.

"My costume got on fire," she explained in a pathetically sorrowful tone, as though losing the gown was the tragedy.

"So I heard," he responded. "Next year, we'll make sure to put you in a coat of armor, like Sir Galahad, or maybe you could be the Tin Man from *The Wizard of Oz.*" His teasing was a tonic, and her eyes flickered brightly at the reference to her favorite movie.

"I'd rather be Dorothy, but Bel can't fit in a basket. Maybe I won't go trick-or-treating anymore . . ." Her doubtful hesitancy was heartbreaking.

Tru picked up her hand and kissed it. "I'm going to personally take you around in Hayes's convertible, and you can dress up like the Homecoming Queen and sit up on the back of the seat, waving to everyone. People will line up to watch you go by."

Jemima was beaming. "I have a crown already," her voice was still weak, but her enthusiasm was fighting to stay afloat. "I got it for being a wise man in the nativity play."

"Wise man? Hmmm . . . I'd say you were miscast. You should have been the Star of Bethlehem, shining up in the sky and telling everyone where to go."

Dinah watched the interaction, relieved that Jemima had perked up so much at Tru's visit, but also still struggling with the sick feeling of remorse for the permanent scars that her sister would carry. As she tried to shake the persistent picture of imagined damage, a sudden image of a man in green coveralls offered what had become a totem of sorts—the pitiable reassurance that things could be worse. But this time Dinah couldn't help thinking that in the balance of things, this was getting close.

Tuesday, November 5 was Election Day. Tom and Caroline went separately to the voting booth, taking turns staying with Jemima. To their gleeful satisfaction, President Truman won, holding onto the office that no one had expected him to keep. On Wednesday, as they shared the newspaper in the hospital room, Tom made the mistake of remarking in front of Jemima that the Dixiecrats hadn't abandoned all their principles after all, and she insisted on knowing why anyone would abandon their principal, and what was a Dixiecrat? Tom shook his head—he had forgotten about little pitchers—and he had to scramble to come up with an explanation she could digest:

"President Truman wants to give people of all colors equal rights, and some people who live in other places of the country aren't accustomed to that idea. But he took a train all over the country and explained his ideas to everyone, and people saw reason, so he was elected for another term."

"Gloria is brown, and she always says she is right, even when I say I don't have to eat broccoli. But I'm equal, so I can tell her I'm right too, right?"

Tom and Caroline looked at Jemima in wonder: How perfectly marvelous that she did not know which side of the equation she was on.

"No, sweetheart," Caroline replied. "In some cases seniority, and not color, is the distinguishing factor. When Gloria tells you to do something, you should follow her suggestion."

They spent the morning quietly triumphant, lauding the Marshall Plan and the Truman Committee, and scoffing at the phone polls that failed to consider all the Democrats who didn't have telephones. "You know that Humphrey fellow from Minnesota is really to thank for pushing the civil rights plank into the platform," Tom mused idly as he paged through the final sections of the newspaper, searching for any last article to pass the time.

"Well, let's just be thankful that Strom Thurmond didn't get his way—we might have had another Civil War on our hands." Caroline was contentedly knitting, using yarn of the finest lamb's wool to fashion a sweater for the little girl in the bed. She knew Jemima wouldn't be able to wear it for a while, but she wanted her to have something very soft to the touch when she was finally able to get dressed again.

Jemima had fallen asleep, her pain medication having a narcotic effect. Caroline stretched and looked at the clock on the wall, and then at Tom. "You should go back to work. I know you had plans to get up to the Vermont mill this week, and Lord knows what else you've had to neglect. I'll be all right here with Mimer."

She tilted her face up as he leaned down to kiss her goodbye, fondly laying her hand on his cheek. "Thank you," she said with a solemn significance, and she knew he understood the full extent of her meaning.

Dinah reluctantly returned to school. Tom had driven Tru back to St. Paul's on Sunday evening, and she knew that she, too, would have to get back to everyday routine. The first day felt like an inquisition. Dinah had always hated being the center of attention—it made her feel exposed and vulnerable. She fielded the questions from her friends with terse answers and minimal explanation, diving into her schoolwork; her studies were suddenly a crucial diversion—a crutch to hold up her wobbly psyche. Her English teacher, Mrs. Crawford, had assigned the class an in-depth biography on an author of their choosing, and Dinah had eagerly picked Nathaniel Hawthorne, flush with the ready resource of her summer reading.

After school she stopped at the library, explaining to Jane that she wasn't there to work, but to do research for her biography. Jane heartily approved of her subject, showing Dinah to a room in the back of the building. Dinah had been unaware of its existence, but there were several rooms in the old mansion that weren't open to the public and she wasn't surprised. "This is not something I would offer to just anyone," Jane said conspiratorially. "We received some boxes from the Peabody Essex Museum when they added the Phillips Library—evidently they had ample documentation on Hawthorne and decided to share the wealth. We now have a treasure trove of material on Hawthorne's life, but haven't had time to go through it all, so we haven't released the materials for public access yet. You should be able to find more information than you bargained for . . . and if you could begin to organize a little, it would help us as well!" She was clearly pleased with the complementary nature of the two projects. Dinah looked around the room, which must have been a bedroom in its former capacity. It was situated at the rear of the house on the top floor. Probably a maid's room at one time, it wasn't very big, and had two dormer windows overlooking what was once a back garden but now held a scattering of cars in its new incarnation as a parking lot.

After Jane left her to begin her research, Dinah looked at the stack of boxes warily, daunted by the prospect of weeding through the disorganization. She hoisted a box off the top of the stack and deposited it next to a metal office chair, the only piece of furniture in the room. Opening the lid, a plume of dust wafted evidence of years of dark, undisturbed hibernation. The papers had been stuffed into the cartons in no apparent order. On the top were several ledgers documenting Hawthorne's work as a surveyor at the Custom House. Dinah made a cursory examination of one, scanning the columns of imported items listed by quantity and value. She set the ledgers aside, establishing the first of many organizational piles. Next were several old periodicals that included publications of some of his short stories and sketches. For her own purposes she could see no practical use for these, and she set them aside in another pile. The afternoon crawled by as she diligently perused the contents, creating small categorical mounds all around her.

It was nearly six o'clock when she neared the bottom of the box, and she decided to call it a day. She was hungry, and there were a couple of assignments from other classes waiting for her. She picked up one more sheaf of papers, which turned out to be legal documents detailing some publishing contracts and fees, and was about to put the lid back on the box when she saw what appeared to be a letter. She picked it up, her interest piqued. It was the first example of anything truly personal that she had run across, and she had to squint to make out the faded cursive writing.

Dated September 23, 1839 and labeled "Letter 17," it was a letter to Hawthorne's wife, Sophia. Dinah sat back, propping her feet on the box, and labored to make out the scratchy handwriting.

"*Beloved little Sophie,*" it began, and, in a tone of scarcely-banked passion, continued for several pages. There was a section that had been inked out, as though someone knew that other eyes would someday fall upon it and had taken the precaution of covering up the most personal of sentiments. The letter was romantic, illustrating Hawthorne's deep and abiding love for his wife, not to mention a physical ardor that was almost embarrassing to read. Dinah felt slightly voyeuristic, though touched by his devotion. It was toward the end of the letter that she made out a passage beginning with a very familiar endearment: "*My little Dove,*" he continued, and went on to describe the butterflies that had appeared on the salt ship on which he was working. He imagined they must have been sent to him by the fantasies of his beloved's thoughts. Signing off, Hawthorne once again addressed his dear wife as *"Dove."* Dinah closed her eyes and breathed deeply—she could hear her father's voice as he came to kiss them goodnight: *"And the moon watches over the ones that I love—Dinah, my angel; Jemima, my dove."* She folded up the letter and put it in her coat pocket.

CHAPTER FIVE

There's Your Trouble

JUST BEFORE THANKSGIVING Jemima came home. Her classmates had been working on get-well cards and letters for weeks, and Peter Campbell and his mother came to deliver them after school that day. Peter clasped his mother's skirt, uncommonly shy as Caroline ushered them into the foyer, calling for Jemima: "Peter is here. I think he has something for you!"

In addition to Mrs. Campbell's skirt, Peter was also holding a small nosegay of paper flowers, which he thrust at Jemima as she came in from the kitchen. "We made flowers for you, because we couldn't get any from outside. Mrs. Lifson said in the spring we can pick real ones."

Jemima was enthralled. Delicately fingering the layers of folded tissue that formed intricate petals, she looked up at Caroline. "Can we put them in a vase? But not with water, Momma, because these are paper!" It was clear that she considered them far superior to the lowly earth-grown type. Caroline assured her that she had just the thing, and invited Peter and his mother into the living room to sit down. She arranged the pink and purple flowers in a Chinese porcelain cachepot that sat on a small table by the window. The women settled into a pair of gilded carver chairs to visit, while Jemima and Peter sat on the floor, looking through the pile of well-wishes they had dumped out of a decorated shoe box.

Jemima's hair had been cut short, framing her face in tousled curls. She was buoyant—happy for the return to normal daily living. She seemed unfazed by the experience of her trauma, but Caroline knew this was because her little girl had not had been subject to the jarring visual evidence on her back. She wanted to delay the harsh realization as long as possible, hoping the angry pink patches would fade before summer.

"I'm coming to school next week," Jemima proudly informed her friend. "After Thanksgiving. We're having a giant turkey, because the pilgrims only had turkeys for food, and they were giant, and the Indians came over for dinner and brought some corn. So I think Coco and Mr. O'Grady will probably bring some corn."

It had been Caroline's idea to invite Coco and Harley to spend Thanksgiving with them. Initially, Tom had laughed when she mentioned it: "Let's see . . . last year I believe they were in St. Tropez, and the year before that must have been skiing in Banff . . . November is high season, you know. I haven't known Coco to spend Thanksgiving at home since . . . well, ever, really. But now that you mention it, I don't see how they'll swing it this year. I suppose it would be the charitable thing to provide a face-saving explanation for their clipped wings . . ."

"That's the spirit," Caroline said playfully. "We need to share the bountiful harvest."

"I'm not sharing my bounty with another single soul. Come here, Pocahontas," he replied, pulling her onto his lap.

"Not so fast, Captain Smith." She put a hand lightly on his chest, smiling down at him. "While we're at it, I was thinking it would be nice to include May and Roger as well. It's just the two of them, and I don't think they have anyone to break bread with."

Tom made a small groan. His limited exposure to Caroline's bibulous cousin and her husband had been too much, in his opinion. He had remarked after the wedding that a small amount of May Carroll went a long way. It wasn't that he didn't like her, exactly—it was just that eccentric, loud personalities were not really his type. Roger, on the other hand, didn't contribute anything at all, but sat meekly by while May sniped at him.

"Come on, Mr. Stuart. Thanksgiving is supposed to be about family, and she's really the only family I have here." Caroline had often wished she had a bigger family, especially at holidays. This year, she felt an extra impetus to give thanks and celebrate with an extension of their new, combined families. "And don't forget, Tru is bringing a friend from school—that boy from Alabama . . . Carleton or Clayton . . . something like that . . ." She trailed off, hoping that the spirit of community would possess her husband as it had her.

Like a schoolboy with a new toy, Tom's attention had wandered to the buttons on her cotton dress, and he was trying now to nip at the top one, with no sign of having heard what she was saying.

"Stop it!" Caroline swatted him lightly on the top of his head, laughing. "You didn't hear a word I said."

"I heard you, Mrs. Stuart," his voice was slightly muffled as he pressed his face closer to her dress. "Your wish is my command. Set as many places as you like. Invite the whole town if you want. Just move your arm a little, please . . ."

After Peter and Mrs. Campbell left, Caroline began thinking about preparations for the dinner. It was only Monday, but with Tru and his friend coming home on Wednesday she wanted to be ready in advance. She recalled a pair of Staffordshire pilgrims that her mother had placed at center table for the Thanksgivings of her childhood. Wondering what became of them, she made her way to the basement to search among the shelves, starting in the old canning cellar, where the rows of jams and sauces had been replaced by boxes of Christmas decorations and memorabilia from her childhood. She had to restrain herself from delving into the miscellany of her youth, the picturesque bordered edges of memory lane threatening to draw her off the main route.

After determining that the antique figurines were not in the cellar, she moved into a larger, stone-walled storeroom that held some furniture and rolled-up carpets, as well as quite a few boxes, some inspiringly labeled with words like "China," and "Decorative Items." She found quite a few things she had forgotten existed, but not the pilgrims. She put a couple of the more worthy pieces aside to take upstairs. In a box of dishes, there was an entire set of Johnson Brothers *Historic America* china, with the *View of Boston, Massachusetts* pattern. The rich brown oak-leaf and acorn border was a perfect complement for a Thanksgiving table, and she carefully moved the box to the stairway.

As she turned back to investigate the shelves on the south wall, she noticed a stack of boxes that looked unfamiliar. They were recent additions to the storeroom, deposited there haphazardly after Tom sold his house. She hadn't even realized they were there, and she suspected that Tom had forgotten about them. Most of them were unlabeled, which didn't surprise her. Living as a bachelor for so many years, Tom had established a fairly casual approach to organization. As she peeked into the top one, she had to smile at the predictable disarray of the contents.

Jumbled into a mix of documents, hardware, and even a couple of leather-bound diplomas were several framed photos. She picked up one of them; it was a picture of Tru as a tow-headed toddler, angelic in a sailor suit, holding a toy sailboat. The sunlight glinted off the water behind him, and he was squinting at the camera with a solemn expression, clutching the wooden boat to his chest. She gently put it on the pile of winners that had passed "upstairs" scrutiny. The next photo was of Tom and Margaret, or a woman she assumed must have been Margaret Stuart. Caroline hadn't realized until that moment that she had never seen a picture of Tom's first wife. Tom was reticent about her, and Caroline thought she understood. She imagined losing someone that way had to leave an enormous wound, undoubtedly painful to probe.

She studied the photo intently: The couple were in evening dress, and they were each holding party favors. Tom had some kind of paper horn in his hand, and Margaret was dangling a festive little crown from her wrist. Looking at the background, Caroline could guess that it was New Year's Eve. Margaret's blond hair was pulled up in an elegant twist, and she had a beautiful, wide smile. Caroline recognized traces of Tru in the smile, and in her high, patrician cheekbones. As she laid the photo back in the box, she noticed one more frame. This one was also of Tom and Margaret, but there was another couple as well. They were on a large sailboat. Tom was standing on the left, with Margaret seated beside him. Seated next to her was another man, and standing at his side, to the right of frame, was Coco. This had to be Whit Wells, Caroline thought. She was struck by a familiar sense of déjà vu, certain that she had seen this man somewhere before. But she had never met Whit, and didn't think she would have seen his photo anywhere. She looked at the picture for a long moment and then put it back, shaking her head slightly, like she was shaking off a persistently buzzing insect.

Wednesday the sky darkened, and the forecast was for snow on Thanksgiving. Jemima was ecstatic—snow was still a novelty for her. The previous winter had been dry, the brown grass poking through a frozen dusting that yielded nary a snowman. She sat at the kitchen table all morning, cutting and pasting brightly colored construction-paper turkeys for place cards. Caroline had asked her to help with the table arrangement, and Jemima took the request as an imperative duty. She was carefully placing her turkeys around the table, each labeled in crayon with the seat-occupant's name, when Dinah came in.

Dinah was lighthearted as she admired her little sister's handiwork. School had been fun that day—everyone was in high spirits about the impending holiday, lending a boisterous, celebratory ring to the atmosphere. The students had finished midterm exams the week before, so the shortened week had been a breeze, with no major tests or assignments. She was still working on her biography, but it wasn't due until just before Christmas.

Bill Lange had caught up with her as she started home, ostensibly to ask what time Tru would be getting back from school. Dinah didn't think it would be until later that evening, and as she elaborated the Concord-Salem bus schedule, he abruptly changed the subject to what the student council was planning for the Winter Formal.

"This year we're getting The Retreads. They're the best. It's a good thing Linda and Pam didn't get their way, or we'd be listening to Merlin Hughes and the Hi-Tones again."

Dinah hadn't known that Bill was on the student council. "When is the Winter Formal?"

"It's the Friday before Christmas break." There was a mounting enthusiasm in his voice. "We had to start planning early to get the band," he continued. "Some of the guys have dates already." He left it hanging there, like a jig in a trout stream, and Dinah blindly took the bait.

"Who are you taking?" she asked innocently.

"Um, well, I haven't asked anyone yet. I thought maybe, you know, we could go together—I mean, if you aren't already going, and you feel like it, because I have to be there anyway . . ." He rambled to a stop, looking a little panicked, like his mouth had just taken him on an unexpectedly wild ride.

It took her a moment to process what he was asking. "So...you're asking me to the dance?"

Bill looked down at his shoes, suddenly quiet as the specter of rejection rose before him. "Yeah, I guess that's what I said."

"Well, sure." She recovered her footing. "It sounds like fun. Thanks." Dinah smiled at him. She suspected that Bill felt a kind of duty to look out for her and she appreciated it. Not only did her status as Tru's stepsister provide protection from the practical animus of the older girls, but evidently it afforded dates to dances as well.

He was grinning now, the bounce back in his step. "Great. Super. You're welcome—I mean, thank *you* for . . . um . . . yeah, well, thanks. It will be fun—have you heard The Retreads?" He steered out of the murky depths, back to shallow waters.

Dinah said that she hadn't, and he was still talking about the talent of the bass player when they reached the house. Bill seemed to have forgotten about Tru as he kept on walking. "Don't forget to put it on the calendar—December 20!" he called, looking back with a little wave.

Dinah waved back as she opened the door. "Got it," she called back, and she was smiling as she found her little sister intently arranging her turkeys.

The bus from Concord got in at 7:10, and Tom had offered to swing by Wong's on the way home for Chinese food. Jemima was waiting at the window again, just as she had been on the first night Tru had come for dinner. She jumped up and down when she saw the Buick pull into the driveway. "Tru and his friend are here!" she called.

Caroline came into the foyer, wiping her hands on her apron as Tom made a grand entrance with the Chinese food, waving the bags in front of him, announcing, "I come bearing gifts—young men and food! Who's hungry?" Jemima was still bouncing on her toes, trying to peer around Tom's legs.

Caroline smiled at her husband and took the bags, kissing him on the cheek and whispering in his ear "I am." He gave her a salacious grin and took off his coat as Tru and his school friend came up the steps.

"Welcome home, boys," Caroline greeted them warmly.

Bags were slung and jackets shucked as Tru made introductions: "This is Carson Hewitt. Carson, this is my mom, and this is my little sister, Jemima."

Caroline was astonished. She hadn't expected that kind of ease in their relationship after less than a year. In fact, she had told Tru that he could call her Caroline if he wanted. But the words had come out naturally, and she wanted to hug him.

Instead, she held out her hand to Carson as he said, "It's nice to meet you, Mrs. Stuart. Thank you so much for having me."

His southern drawl momentarily threw her—she couldn't help being reminded of Gideon. "We're so glad to have you. Please make yourself at home."

Jemima was halfway hiding behind her mother, peeking her head out with a rhythmic sway, clearly waiting to be noticed. Carson Hewitt leaned sideways a little, extending his hand. "Hello Tru's little sister; how are you?" He shook her hand with mock formality.

She practically curtseyed as she replied, "I'm fine; thank you," suddenly shy as she examined the inlaid marble pattern on the floor. Just then, Dinah came in from the library where she had been reading. Carson was still leaning down toward Jemima, and as he turned toward Dinah he straightened up quickly, almost backing into Tru.

Tru stepped around him, saying, "This is my, um . . . this is Dinah." He abruptly moved his attention to the rucksack on the floor.

Carson stared at Dinah for a prolonged beat, and then, remembering his manners, he put out his hand and said, "Carson Hewitt. Nice to meet you."

Dinah had the same fleeting reaction as her mother had had—he sounded something like her father. She shook his hand, smiling a welcome. "Nice to meet you, too."

Tom picked up Carson's bag, saying, "You'll be in the second-floor guest room, next to Tru. If you fellows want to wash up, dinner will be ready when you are." The boys moved up the stairs, and Caroline and the girls set the table and laid out the Chinese spread.

Because the dining room table was already set for Thanksgiving, they ate at the long refectory table in the kitchen. There was a cozy, intimate ambience that brought a relaxed ease to the conversation, despite the newcomer at the table. Caroline set the tone, saying "Carson, you'll have to tell us about all of Tru's misdeeds at school. And don't leave anything out!"

Carson was a natural entertainer, regaling them with funny anecdotes, though careful not to reveal anything too incriminating. "Did Tru ever mention that he had pneumonia?" he asked, looking at Tru with a glint in his eye.

Tom and Caroline looked at him in surprise. "Tru—you never mentioned that! When was this?" Caroline sounded alarmed.

"It was no big deal. Walking pneumonia. It felt like a cold. Coach made me go to the infirmary."

"Ah, but that's where the story gets interesting," Carson intoned.

Tru looked sideways at his friend, raising one eyebrow. "Watch where you're going," he warned.

"It seemed that Nurse Harris took a liking to old Tru here." Carson started to chuckle. Tru stared at him with narrowed eyes. "She started showing up at the dorm, just to 'check on' poor Tru. Oh yeah, he got the star treatment all right. Some of the guys were taking bets on how long it would be before Nurse Harris—ow!" Carson looked down and rubbed his shin.

Tom sat backed and grinned. "Nothing new there," he said. "When Tru was about eleven, I had to have a meeting with his teacher." He squinted, trying to recall. "I believe her name was Miss Becker. She wanted to see me regarding a little problem he was having getting assignments turned in on time. After about an hour of rhapsodizing about his 'unusual maturity,' she finally got around to the issue at hand."

"I really liked Miss Becker," Tru said, deadpan, and Carson made a choking noise as he swallowed his food.

After dinner they played Parcheesi in the library, where Tom had built a roaring fire. The mahogany paneled walls glowed with the reflection of the flames, while the lead-paned windows framed the cold night sky, contrasting the warmth of the cozy room and giving it a cocoon-like quality. Jemima won twice, and they all decided to call it a night. Caroline reminded the girls that she needed their help preparing food in the morning, and Tom offered to take the boys to the YMCA to play basketball.

Dinah woke to the smell of the turkey roasting, which she thought had to be one of the finer smells in life. She stretched and snuggled into her pillow, prolonging the dreamy, half-woken limbo, letting her thoughts drift randomly. She thought about Tru's friend Carson, and how nice he had been last night. He sat next to her during the Parcheesi game, making scattered references to their shared Southern bond. Carson had a Southerner's ability to differentiate regional nuances, and he could do a spot-on impression of Dinah. "Pass the dahce please, Cahson," he mimicked, the aristocratic, non-rhotic softness of her accent contrasting with his Alabama twang. Tru had been unusually quiet, focusing on the game and giving encouragement to Jemima. When Carson tried to draw him into the fray with an impression his buddy's clipped Northeastern patois, Tru had given a weak smile and turned his attention to the board.

Finally roused from her downy nest, Dinah found her mother in the kitchen, organizing prep stations. Caroline lost no time directing the girls to their respective tasks, with the efficiency of a professional chef. Jemima peeled potatoes, Dinah diced carrots and rutabagas. The pies had been made the day before by Gloria, who had offered to come back and help with the rest of the meal, but Caroline had refused, assuring her they would be fine and insisting that Gloria spend the day with her own family.

Most of the dishes were prepared and waiting for the oven when May and Roger arrived at about three o'clock. It had been snowing lightly all day, but it was starting to come down harder, and the flakes were growing in size. They stomped their feet in the foyer, bustling with the business of overcoats and galoshes and handing off a corn casserole to Caroline.

"You're the Indians!" Jemima crowed. "Then what will Coco and Mr. O'Grady bring?"

"I can't see Coco making a casserole," Caroline laughed as she took the covered dish into the kitchen. "I'm sure they'll bring the sauce," she added dryly, without elaboration.

"Speaking of sauce . . ." May said, the words sliding out the side of her mouth.

Tom mixed drinks for the adults, with the exception of his wife, who declined on the grounds of keeping a clear eye on the meal.

It was close to four o'clock when Coco and Harley arrived. Coco swept through the front door like an empress, with Harley trailing behind, carrying a brown paper bag. She handed her fur coat to Tom and stood rubbing her hands together, looking around expectantly. "Where is the help?" She had a slightly annoyed expression.

"You're looking at it," Tom replied. "Gloria has the day off, but we are privileged to have one of the finest chefs on the Eastern seaboard preparing our feast today." He put his arm around Caroline as she came into the hall, kissing her lightly on the cheek.

Coco looked toward the kitchen. "Do you mean to tell me you got Arthur Salisbury from Donovan's?"

"Even better," Tom replied.

"I did the cooking, Coco" Caroline smiled modestly. "I can't agree about my culinary talents, but it's hard to ruin a turkey."

Coco looked like she had just found a toad in the punchbowl. "How perfectly marvelous," she said flatly.

While the younger set maneuvered for landlord status on the Monopoly board in the library, the adults moved to the living room for cocktails. May was at the bottom of her second bourbon, moving toward the butler's tray in the corner of the room. Roger sat by the massive marble fireplace, nursing his drink with his legs crossed; the dangling foot swiveled around in lazy circles. His pants leg rode up to expose a short brown sock, revealing at least three inches of bare leg. Coco was staring at him like he was a stray mongrel who had hopped up onto the furniture.

"What is it that you do, Roger?" She pronounced his name as if it were a joke.

He answered her with a bit of a lisp. "I'm an accountant with Whistler, Stanton, and Massey. I'm also an amateur ornithologist," he added.

"Ah, ha!" Coco suddenly looked interested, and her eyebrows shot up. "An ornithologist—how divine!" She stood up and walked over to the window, grasping a side chair and pulling it over to sit next to him. Tom and Caroline exchanged dumbfounded looks, while May obliviously helped herself to the decanter on the tray. Harley stood by a painting of Lord Baltimore, drink in one hand and cigarette in the other, looking bored.

Coco lit her own cigarette and leaned toward Roger, offering the pack. "So tell me Roger, what kind of . . . *birds* . . . interest you the most?" There was a predatory gleam in her eye.

Roger took a cigarette, becoming newly animated. "Oh, I love all birds," he enthused, the unlit Gauloises waving in his hand. "But I suppose, if I had to choose a favorite, I might be partial to the yellow-rumped warbler."

Coco looked like she was choking on her drink.

"It has such a sweet song," he continued. As his reticence fell away, his lisp became more apparent. "It can winter up here, you know, because it digests waxes from bayberries." He paused, giving it some thought. "Some people consider it too common, but they are mistaken. The male form, especially, is so beautiful. The females are a little duller." He shifted, re-crossing his legs and lighting the cigarette. He leaned toward Coco, who was smiling like the cat who ate the canary. "They usually breed in coniferous forests"—his tone sounded almost conspiratorial—"but you can easily find them in residential areas."

"I'll bet you can," Coco replied.

Caroline stood up and excused herself, saying she had work to do in the kitchen. "We have a bird of our own to attend to," she said, giving Tom a pointed look.

"I'm the surgeon," Tom acknowledged, and he followed his wife to do the carving.

The seating arrangement had been determined by Jemima, with the only stipulation being to put Tom and Caroline at either end. The others were randomly scattered. Jemima, not surprisingly, had placed herself next to Tru. Without compunction, Coco picked up her paper turkey and switched it with Carson's, who was seated next to Roger. "I'm sure you won't mind sitting between those two lovely ladies," she indicated the chair flanked by Dinah and May, stating it as a foregone conclusion. "Everyone knows that one doesn't seat three females in a row." Jemima looked hurt, and a furtive disappointment flashed across Roger's face as he watched Carson obligingly trade seats.

May, seated next to Harley, was already going full throttle about her travails with the legal profession. Harley wore a pained expression as he grabbed the claret decanter and filled his glass to the brim. Tom cleared his throat and asked everyone to clasp hands for the grace. Bowing her head, Dinah felt Carson's grasp becoming a gentle squeeze, and she opened her eyes in surprise. She saw that the others at the table were all looking down in obeisance, except for Tru, who was staring at the point where her arm met Carson's. As she looked up, he met her eyes briefly, and then bowed his head.

The dinner conversation was animated, and Caroline was pleased to have achieved her goal of a real family Thanksgiving. She had never seen Coco so accessible; she was downright friendly to Roger, encouraging him with all sorts of questions. Caroline thought she would never understand her new sister-in-law. Roger was among the last people on earth that she would have predicted would interest Tom's sister, but there she was, asking him to tell her all about his opinion of Dior's "New Look." What a surprise that quiet old Roger would have such a sophisticated knowledge of fashion! Looking at May, in her loudly-striped jersey caftan, Caroline was baffled. She noted that Harley was thawing as well, settling into his role of captive audience. He looked almost as if he were starting to enjoy himself; she actually heard him chuckle at one of May's rambling anecdotes. It must be the wine at work, Caroline thought, and silently sent a prayer of gratitude to St. Vincent.

Carson was describing his own family's Thanksgiving tradition, spent at their quail-and-pheasant-hunting plantation in Georgia. Dinah was fascinated, visions of Tara parading through her mind. He went on to explain that they usually spent the Christmas holidays at their chalet in Sun Valley, and invited Tru to join him that year.

"Isn't that the place that Averell Harriman developed, so his railroad would have a destination?" Caroline asked.

"Yes," he laughed, "I guess that is probably the truth of it. My family were initial investors in the resort, and I've been going there most of my life."

"I read that they have a device to lift people up the mountain on chairs! Isn't that something?"

They continued to discuss the remarkable qualities of the resort, but Tom looked skeptical, unhappy with the idea of Tru being absent at Christmas. He privately leaned over, *sotto voce*, to tell his son that they would discuss it later.

The snow had been steadily falling throughout the evening, and by the end of dinner the winds had picked up, blowing white sheets past the windows like whipping sails. The group retired to the living room for coffee and dessert— Gloria's famous pecan pie. Caroline asked the girls for help with the dishes, and they left the others to games of pinochle and cribbage, safe from the howling winds.

By the time the girls had finished cleaning up, Harley and Coco were donning their coats. "You can't possibly be thinking of driving in this!" Caroline exclaimed.

Harley was slurring a little as he responded: "I've seen much worse. This is nothing—we'll be just fine." He reached around to help Coco into her sable, stumbling a little as he leaned to the side.

"Now hang on a second, Harley." Tom tried to intervene. "I think it would be best if you bunked down here for the night—we've got plenty of room for everyone. I'll just turn up the heat on the third floor . . ."

He was interrupted by Coco, declaring, "Harley is an excellent driver. I prefer to sleep in my own bed, thank you very much. We'll be on our way. Thank you for your hospitality." Her voice had the obligingly formal tone of a restaurant patron.

Tom and Caroline watched from the window as Coco and Harley made their way to the DeSoto, now completely covered in snow. It took quite a while for Harley to clear the windows, as Coco sat smoking in the passenger seat. Finally, he backed down the driveway, only to get stuck at the bottom, gunning the engine as the tires spun. In a final burst of acceleration, the Chrysler grabbed purchase and shot into the street. Harley hit the brakes and the car swerved straight into the linden tree on the boulevard, smashing the right tail light and popping open the trunk.

When the couple reappeared in the foyer—steaming through the frost on their coats—Caroline and Tom had rearranged themselves in the living room, feigning ignorance of the spectacle in the street. "It appears that we will be staying after all," Coco said icily. Harley looked at the floor, not bothering with an explanation.

"That's a fine idea," Tom concurred. "Why don't you come back in and relax—it's a good night for Puccini." He took their coats once again and went into the library to put on a recording of *Gianni Schicchi*.

As the traditional post-Thanksgiving lethargy settled in, Caroline took Jemima by the hand, claiming exhaustion. "I think Mimer and I will turn in," she announced. "The rooms are all ready—just make yourselves at home."

Tru and Carson were engaged in a pitched battle on the library chessboard, and May was leaning on the bookcase by the record player, accompanying Callas on "O Mio Babbino Caro." Harley was now reclined in a large, leather wingback chair, hands folded in his lap, eyes closed, a fresh snifter of brandy at hand. Tom lit his pipe and settled into the worn club chair behind his desk. He contentedly watched the boys make their moves on the chessboard, trying to block out May's voice as he listened to the recording.

Dinah surveyed the situation and decided to find a book to take to her room. She scanned the titles on one of the bookshelves, picking out *A Tale of Two Cities*. Tucking it under her arm, she said goodnight. Carson looked up with a mildly disappointed expression.

"See you tomorrow," he said in a hopeful tone.

Tru kept his eyes on the board.

Tom stood and gave her a hug. "Good night, my dear. Enjoy the Dickens."

In the living room, Coco and Roger were engaged in a tête-à-tête on the sofa, and as Dinah passed she was astounded to see that Coco appeared to be crying. Roger's arm was wrapped around her shoulders, and Coco was holding a glass of sherry, which was sloshing dangerously close to the edge as she gesticulated her meaning.

"And it's not as though I wouldn't have had plenty of money, you know." Her voice was slurry. "I should have been set for life, all right, because old Whit did jus' fine for himself." She wiped her hand across her nose. "But I didn't get it all, did I? No, I didn't. And I'm the only one who knows about it, except for Harley, of course, because he did the will." Her head bobbed emphatically with each statement. "But it's not his fault—he has no idea! And I can't hold it against him." She straightened up and looked Roger in the eye. "Do you know that I really loved my husband?" she asked insistently. "I did! When I found out, it broke my heart. That's what happened. My heart just broke." In a final leap the sherry succeeded in making an escape, and Coco staggered up to blot the stain. She looked hazily at Dinah, who stood riveted in the doorway. "Can I help you?" The words were carefully enunciated.

"No, I was just going to bed . . . I didn't even know anyone was in here . . ." Dinah hurried away, hoping they believed her.

The morning dawned sunny and bright—a winter postcard that was already becoming a memory as the icing from last night's storm dripped from the trees. Coco and Harley were up and gone, fleeing like felons at dawn's first light. Dinah trundled down to the kitchen in her bathrobe, finding the rangy frame of Aunt May slumped over the newspaper with a cup of black coffee, a bottle of aspirin open on the table. The woman made an effort at a smile, but it came across as a grimace.

"Good morning, dear. We're the only two up, so far. I made some coffee." She indicated the pot on the stove.

Dinah didn't like coffee. She was pouring a bowl of cereal when Roger joined them, wearing a silk kimono. He walked over to May and kissed her cheek, stroking her hair lightly.

"Morning, Maysie," he said, and Dinah noticed a slightly sing-song pattern in his speech. Until last night, she hadn't really heard him say much of anything. He poured himself a cup of coffee and settled in next to May, sharing the paper. Dinah couldn't bring herself to look down, for fear of seeing his bare ankles. She felt uncomfortable—she hardly knew him, and the fact that he was in his bathrobe bothered her. At least it wasn't plaid flannel.

She took her bowl of cereal and went to the sunroom, sitting down at the ornate wrought-iron table by the bay window. It was a lovely feeling to look out at all that sparkling white, ensconced in the sunny warmth of the plant-filled room. The green-trellised wallpaper provided a little corner of year-round summer, a welcome haven during the long northern winters. A sudden longing for Beaufort took her by surprise—she hadn't thought about her old home for a long time. When she realized that she still thought of it as home, she felt a sharp pang. It occurred to her that grief had many guises, and that homesickness was one of them—a pianissimo variation of the theme. She dispiritedly thought that she was becoming all too familiar with the entire symphony.

From her bedroom window, Dinah could see Tru and Carson building a snowman for Jemima—or at least Jemima was the excuse they had used. The little girl could barely be persuaded to eat breakfast before pulling on her woolen snow pants. She ran out to the front lawn, flopping down to make slushy angels in the melting snow. Now the snowman was temporarily abandoned for a snowball war, with Tru hoisting Jemima onto his shoulders. From that vantage she ineffectually hurled her ammunition, and Carson made an elaborate show of cringing as the mushy orbs plopped against him. Dinah wished she could join in, but she was scheduled to work at the library. Her diligence as a volunteer had finally paid off, and she was now officially on the payroll.

She left the house quietly, with a feeling of relief. The busy household had worn on her—she had an admittedly low tolerance for commotion. As luck would have it, Jane assigned her to the Hawthorne files that day, and she gladly climbed the stairs to the little back room to work by herself. She had to be vigilant about avoiding any conflict of interest—her job was to organize, not to research her own project. But she had found that she could ferret out possible leads without compromising her efficiency, setting aside items that she thought might be pertinent as she worked on categorizing the boxes.

Hawthorne's life was becoming almost as familiar to Dinah as her own. Over the past few weeks she had made copious notes for her biography, finding the trove of information in the Peabody files both compelling and rewarding. She hadn't realized that the Peabody Essex Museum was actually named for Elizabeth Peabody, who was not only Hawthorne's champion and first publisher, but also the sister of Sophia Hawthorne. The more she read, the more Dinah had become interested in Elizabeth Peabody. She particularly loved the idea that Peabody had instigated "reading parties," where she would arrange lectures for groups of women on literary and philosophical topics. What a perfect concept, Dinah thought, to combine a social gathering with an intellectual pursuit. It would make getting together with other girls so much more interesting! She thought about her own friends from school and the empty chatter that comprised practically all of their conversation. She could hear Joan Marconi voicing her desperate curiosity to know whether Jimmy Wright had given Lana his class ring—the echo of her banality clanging a ridiculously empty knell as it contrasted with the topics that Elizabeth Peabody promoted—the essential importance of social reform and philosophical curiosity. Dinah had even been inspired to do some side research on Transcendentalism, Peabody's trademark philosophy. The idea of inherent human goodness made her feel almost giddy—she thought that she may have finally discovered an aspect of religion that made sense to her.

Weeding through yet another box, she laboriously catalogued the business documents, abstract notes, and journal publications that made up the bulk of the contents. There were several items that she decided to set aside for her own use later, among them a copy of a collection of children's stories that Hawthorne's wife Sophie had illustrated, which Dinah was fairly certain was out of print. Underneath this collection, she saw something different. Lifting out a small cigar box labeled *Panama Gold*, she opened the lid to find a stack of letters. Excitedly, she pulled them out, resting the pile on her lap. These were the only letters she had run across since finding the love letter to Sophia, which Dinah guiltily remembered was still in her desk drawer at home. She wasn't sure why she had taken the letter—it was a strange compulsion that she thought may have had something to do with her need to feel her father's presence in the wake of the Halloween incident. Seeing the private endearment, "*Dove*," that her father had called Jemima was such an uncanny coincidence—she wanted to believe that he was watching over them. She needed to believe it. She needed him.

Riffling through the letters, she saw that most of them were from Sophia, written to her husband. The box must have been Hawthorne's private cache, for there was nothing from his own hand. Dinah opened the top one, scanning it to find a delicately-inferenced letter of love and devotion—not nearly as overtly passionate as the one her husband had written, but tender and sweet. Dinah felt like an intruder, and decided not to read the others. The thought of someone reading her letters after she died horrified her, and she felt a duty to respect the privacy of this nice woman. She was about to put the letters back in the box when she noticed that there were several envelopes on which the handwriting did not match the others. These had no return address, and she curiously opened one of them.

The handwriting was in marked contrast to the small, precise script penned by Sophia Hawthorne. Instead, the words were boldly scrawled, with ink so heavy that it retained its dark imprint even through a century of age. It took a moment for Dinah to discern the author. Ultimately, the body of the text—detailing specific business ventures—revealed the identity of Elizabeth Peabody. It was the first paragraph, however, that revealed even more:

> *My Dear Nathaniel—*
>
> *I haven't the heart to tell you in person, but I cannot let another minute pass without giving you some advice: It is with great sincerity that I bless your union, but let there be no impediment to your true understanding of my sister—she is not well, and will require constant care. Mary has seen to her treatments in the past—I trust you will be willing to continue these efforts. For my part, I am, as I stated, happy for you both. Do not let our own history stand between you and your new wife. I am looking forward—never back . . . I will be honored to call you "brother,'" though it isn't what I once thought . . .*

The letter continued, addressing matters relevant to the professional relationship between Peabody and Hawthorne, but it was clear to Dinah that the poor woman harbored feelings for her brother-in-law that were more than that. Dinah read on, skimming over the parts about publishing issues; these details did not interest her as much as the personal aspects of the letter. She read again Elizabeth's warning about her sister's delicate constitution, her tone of concern failing, in Dinah's opinion, to cover her disappointment at having lost the object of her affection to her youngest sister.

Feeling sorry for this remarkable woman—who had continued to champion the career of the man that she loved, despite the fact that he had chosen her own sister—Dinah was about to open the next of the letters when she heard Jane coming down the hall. A smiling face peeked around the doorway. "I hate to break it to you, but I'm about to lock up. Haven't you had enough of these dusty old documents?"

Dinah quickly stuffed the letter back into the envelope, feeling guilty about reading on company time. Telling Jane she would be right down, she straightened up some of the papers that had scattered on the floor. Before leaving she placed the letters carefully back into the cigar box. And then, for reasons unknown to even herself, she tucked the box behind a tall stack of books in the corner.

Heading out the door she heard her name. Jane was reading something at a table behind the check-out desk as she motioned Dinah over. It was a newspaper, open to the obituaries. Dinah looked at it blankly; she couldn't understand Jane's purpose until she came to the end of the list. At the bottom of the page, with only a few lines of text beneath it, was the name Remarcik. There was nothing but the bare facts: name, age, date of death.

When Jane spoke her voice was quiet, but her contempt resounded. "It doesn't say how he died, but I have my own theory: I think his conscience finally caught up to him." She gave Dinah a meaningful look, and there was no need for elaboration.

That evening, Tru and Carson had plans to meet a few of Tru's buddies at the Red Barn—a roadhouse on Winter Island that had a long and colorful history. Tru asked Tom for the use of the Buick, citing Moss Bodean, the legendary blues singer, as ample reason to loan out the car. Dinah had just come in from her day at the library and was heading toward the kitchen when she heard their voices:

"I didn't think they let kids into that place," Tom remarked in a dubious tone.

"No one pays any attention to that," Tru replied, clearly trying to gloss over the issue. "It's no big deal. We just want to hear Moss play. All the other guys are going," he added, which only drew raised eyebrows and a look of mild disgust.

"You know that line doesn't go anywhere with me," Tom said. He was silent for a moment, and then he gave Tru his most serious, message-of-import look. "Despite your flawed methods of persuasion, I think you have proven your good sense, so I'll give you the keys; but remember—I do so with complete faith in your judgment and maturity." He smiled at his son, adding, "I know you want to show Carson a good time." He handed over the key ring with a pat on the back. "Enjoy yourself, son."

Tru came out of the library, rhythmically tossing the keys in his hand and whistling a surprisingly intricate blues riff. Dinah smiled at him.

"I didn't know you were so musical."

He was clearly caught off-guard, but was saved from a response by Carson bounding down the stairs. "What's the status, Captain?" Carson was buoyant, anticipating good news on the car front.

"We have clearance for take-off," Tru dangled the keys in the air.

Rounding the corner in the hall, Carson drew up as he encountered Dinah. He suddenly looked like he had just won a prize. "Maybe your sister wants to go with us," he said, addressing Tru but keeping his eyes on Dinah. "Hows about it, Dinah—care to come along and hear some mean blues?" He grinned at her in his most persuasive manner.

"I don't . . . I mean, I'm not sure . . ." The idea of going to a roadhouse was a little intimidating, but before she could process an answer she was interrupted by Tom's voice as he came out of the library.

"That might not be a bad idea!"

Dinah could not have been more surprised; at the same time she sensed a thinly veiled purpose to his encouragement.

"This would be a good opportunity for you young folks to have some fun together. What do you say, Dinah? Would you agree to be the chaperone to these two juvenile delinquents?"

Although she felt there might be an ulterior motive in play, she wasn't sure what it was. She was certain that Tom didn't really see her as a chaperone. Tru still hadn't spoken. "I think I should ask my mom," she offered feebly. The idea was quickly growing on her. A real roadhouse! She had never seen a blues band. In fact, aside from the time her mother had taken Jemima and her to the Boston Pops, the only group she had seen play music was the high school marching band.

"Why don't you let me talk to her," Tom said. "Go ahead and get ready—I'll see what I can do."

Dinah looked at Tru—he was studying the floor. She suddenly had the uncomfortable feeling that she was unwanted. But Carson was encouraging: "You don't have to dress up. Just wear what you have on—you look great."

His approval was the bolster she needed. She decided she would definitely go, if her mother consented. "I think I'll change, anyway," she said, moving toward the stairs. She was wearing an old cable-knit cardigan and tweed skirt, with a pair of old, scuffed saddle shoes. She hurried to her bedroom, going through her wardrobe inventory in her mind. At the closet, she pulled out the soft, cream-colored cashmere twin set from Filene's and a heather-green gabardine skirt. She also grabbed her new saddle Oxfords, throwing the others into the corner. She pulled her hair out of its customary pony-tail and brushed it until it shimmered in waves, like moonlight on a lake.

Tom found Caroline in the kitchen, laying out plates of leftovers for dinner. She was initially against the idea, but he presented a thoughtful line of reasoning: "I don't think Tru and Dinah have hit it off very well. I notice a real fondness between Tru and Jemima, but there seems to be a bit of a distance between the older two. I think it would be a good idea to put them together in a social setting and let them get to know each other as friends. Beyond that, it will keep the guys on the straight and narrow if they have a little sister to watch out for."

Caroline felt a poignant little catch in her heart as she watched her daughter walk to the car—a rite of passage she hadn't experienced until now. She unconsciously took a mental snapshot, memorizing the moment. It was a bittersweet feeling to watch her go—another step away from the fold. She was glad her introverted oldest child was going to mix in with Tru and his friends, and she hoped the experience would help Dinah finally see the advantage of having an older brother, but she couldn't squelch the small pang of nostalgic regret that transformed the young woman strolling down the driveway into a shyly smiling six-year-old, skipping to school in her pinafore.

Carson opened the passenger door for Dinah, who stood there uncertainly. She hadn't expected to sit in the front seat. "It's OK, I can sit in the back," she offered. But Carson insisted, his Southern manners on display. She slid in as Tru was fiddling with the radio dial.

"Don't you think Dinah looks nice?" Carson settled into the backseat as Dinah self-consciously pulled her coat close.

Tru put the car in reverse, throwing his arm over the seat as he swiveled around to look out the back window. He didn't look at Dinah. "Yep," he said curtly. "We have to swing by for a buddy of mine." He addressed his comment to Carson, and then turned back around, shifting gears and turning up the volume on Big Joe Turner singing "Cherry Red."

Just a couple of blocks away, on Endicott Street, they pulled up to a small, white clapboard house. Tru honked the horn and Bill Lange trotted out and jumped into the backseat, looking surprised when he noticed Dinah up front. Tru introduced him to Carson, and then said, "You know Dinah."

Bill smiled at her. "Happy to say that I do."

They drove with the radio turned up—now Coleman Hawkins playing "Body and Soul"—discussing the many virtues of the talented Moss Bodean. As they pulled up to the Red Barn, Bill was explaining to Carson that a farmer had converted his old barn to a speakeasy during prohibition, and it had become renowned not only as a venue for musicians from all over the region but for its storied history of wild, lawless, all-night antics.

"It's really the only thing on the island, except for Fort Pickering, so the bands can play as long as they like."

Dinah was surprised to see that the building looked like any old barn, painted a peeling, dull red, with nothing at all to indicate that it was a public establishment. The only evidence was the large gravel parking lot, crowded with cars. The entrance was almost hidden—a small side door near the front corner of the barn without a sign. Upon entering, however, the anonymity fell away. The walls were covered with an eclectic assortment of old billboards and advertisements, and a collection of neon signs cast a dim, red-hued light. The massive interior had a rough, wood-plank floor that was covered in sawdust; a large stage occupied the far end, under the old haymow. Running down the middle of the room was an oblong bar with low, green-glass lamps swinging overhead. Smoke hung in the air; an ample crowd buzzed with electric anticipation. On stage, a saxophonist and a bass player were playing slow jazz riffs, warming up the room for the big draw.

A group of Tru's old friends were already there and they gave him a hero's welcome, as though he had returned not from the privilege of an elite boarding school but from waging a distant war. They bellied up to the bar, arms thrown around shoulders, exchanging jabs and quips, barely able to contain a rising head of collective steam. Dinah felt lost in the boisterous crowd, until she felt a brush on her arm and turned to find Carson standing at her side.

"This is quite a joint." He had to raise his voice to be heard. He was holding two glasses of beer, and he offered one to Dinah.

"Oh . . ." She was dismayed. "No thanks . . . I don't really like beer," she stuttered.

"OK," Carson smiled. "More for yours truly, I guess." He took a swig from each glass, winking at her.

Tru was suddenly upon them. "What do you think you're doing with that beer?" There was a warning in his voice, but Carson didn't seem to notice.

"Being mannerly, offering some refreshment to the lady."

"Well put your manners to use somewhere else. Dinah doesn't drink beer." He took one of the glasses for himself, adding "Thanks," as he moved back to the group.

Carson looked at Dinah and shrugged. Dinah felt a subtle resentment at Tru's presumption. She could make decisions for herself, and she didn't like being told what she did or didn't do. "Maybe I'll just try a sip," she ventured.

Carson grinned and handed her his glass, saying "You'd better do it quick—big brother may be watching."

She put the glass to her mouth and took a tentative sip. It was bitter, and she grimaced, thinking it tasted like something that had fermented. It took her a second to remember that was exactly what beer was.

"The second taste is always better than the first," she heard Carson saying, so she boldly took another drink, this time letting the brew fill up her mouth before choking it down. It was a little too much to swallow and she started to cough. Carson laughed, taking back the glass. "Slow down there, partner. We don't want to alert the sheriff."

The kinetic energy of the room suddenly increased as the popular blues band took the stage. They immediately started into the Buddy Banks favorite, "Ink Spill," the crowd cheering. Those standing near the stage drew back as that part of the room became a dance floor, with several couples already sliding around on the sawdust. Carson and Dinah moved to stand with Tru and his friends near the bar, jockeying for a view of the stage. A group of girls had just come in the door and were making their way toward the bar; Dinah recognized Sally Vecchi, Lana Gervais, Janet White, and several others who traveled in their pack.

The girls approached the bar, sidling up to their fellow classmates with flirtatious commotion. They were particularly attentive to Tru, elaborately fawning over him like a long-lost son. All except Lana Gervais, who was studiously ignoring him, but making an obvious show of noticing Carson. Dinah moved over to stand with Bill, trying to distance herself from the group of girls that Betsy had aptly coined the Sinisters.

She watched the band and the couples on the dance floor, swaying slightly to the beat of the bass guitar. As Moss segued into a red-hot version of "Bessie's Sin," Dinah happened to glance back toward the bar, watching as a girl with pale reddish-brown hair grabbed Tru by the arm and pulled him onto the dance floor. Dinah was trying to think of the girl's name, and had just remembered that she was suitably called Ginger, when she felt a pull on her own arm. She found herself following Bill onto the dance floor, nervously glancing around. She didn't really know how to dance, but it turned out that Bill wasn't so sure of himself, either, and they laughed as they awkwardly tried to improvise the moves. She couldn't help noticing Tru—he moved with a smooth assurance, swinging Ginger in controlled swoops and twirls. Bill followed her gaze.

"You ought to see him dance with Lana," he remarked. "They won a contest last year." For some reason this information gave her a knot in her stomach, like she was digesting something that had turned sour. Suddenly she didn't want to dance anymore, and told Bill she needed to use the restroom.

The bathroom was situated in a makeshift shed that had been tacked onto the outside of the building, with a door cut into the wall to allow access from the inside. It consisted of a wobbly sink with a cracked mirror hanging askew, and one stall with a creaky, swinging door. Dinah waited in line for a few minutes, and was just sliding the small bolt in the stall when she heard the door open and several voices talking:

"Did you know Tru was going to be here tonight?"

"I'll bet Lana did." That sounded like Sally Vecchi.

Another voice piped up: "Did you see Tru and Ginger? Lord, I'd almost forgotten how that boy can dance. Maybe I'll see if I can get him on my card!"

"Get in line, Sister." Sally again. "Everyone knows Tru Stuart has the smoothest moves in Essex County."

This produced hilarious giggles, as one of the girls added, "I think you'd have to ask Lana about that!"

Dinah didn't know what to do. She didn't want to just walk out of the stall, revealing herself as an eavesdropper, but she knew that they would be waiting to use the toilet. She was saved when the door flew open and a dramatically urgent voice hissed, "Tru's dancing with Lana!" The three girls scurried out, leaving Dinah to exit safely. She quickly washed her hands, scarcely bothering with a towel.

The area around the dance floor was crowded, and Dinah had to sidle through a sea of shoulders and beer glasses to get back to where Bill was standing with Hayes Swanson and Joey Fetzer. She looked at the couples on the floor, noticing that Carson was dancing with another one of the Sinisters, a girl she thought was named Peggy something. Carson was a pretty good dancer himself, Dinah thought. And then she saw Tru. He had Lana wrapped in one arm as he moved her around the floor, fluidly controlling her with the slightest pressure of his left hand. Watching him, Dinah understood what Sally had meant: Tru's center of balance seemed to hang on the easy, rolling sway of his lower body. His feet moved agilely in smooth rhythm, but it was the subtly loose movement of his hips that gave him an extraordinary, slinky grace, which was further complemented by Lana's yielding pliancy. She followed him like a river—flowing water slipping along on the current. The effect was almost hypnotic. A shocking jealously squeezed tightly around Dinah's chest. Until this moment, she hadn't permitted herself to think about her feelings for her . . . stepbrother. But watching him with Lana, she felt a suffocating longing to be the one held tightly in his right arm, swaying against his body.

She studied Lana Gervais. It was true that she looked like Liz Taylor—right down to the violet eyes. Dinah could see from where she stood that Lana's eyes were locked on Tru's face, but she also noticed that Tru kept his gaze steadily over Lana's right shoulder as they danced.

There was a stirring on the other side of the room as people parted to make way for a tall figure crossing the floor.

"Holy cats—Tru's in for it now." There was a note of alarm in Bill's voice. Dinah turned and saw Jimmy Wright wend his way through the dancing couples and stride up to Lana and Tru, tapping him on the shoulder. Even from where she stood, Dinah could see a distinct flash of triumph in Lana's eyes. But Tru simply stepped back, appearing neither surprised nor bothered, and literally handed Lana over to Jimmy. If Jimmy wanted trouble, Tru wasn't about to give it to him. Lana's triumph turned to visible disappointment as he casually turned and walked away, leaving Jimmy to finish the dance.

Approaching the bar, Tru smiled and went right back to joking with his friends as he ordered another beer. Dinah looked back at the dance floor, and was amazed to see that Lana dancing with Jimmy was nothing at all like Lana dancing with Tru; Jimmy's clumsy, lurching steps and obvious lack of rhythm had turned her into an awkward, shuffling mannequin.

"I wonder where Tru and Lana learned to dance like that." She tried to sound casual as she turned to Bill.

He seemed to hesitate for a moment, looking over at Tru, and Dinah thought she detected a slight twitch at the corner of his mouth. "I think they used to, um, practice a lot."

A spray of beer shot out of Joey Fetzer's mouth. "Practice! Is that what you call it?" He laughed loudly. "In that case, I wouldn't mind practicing a little with Lana, myself."

Bill shot him a stern look, his foot simultaneously making contact with Joey's shin. Hayes was chuckling as he grabbed Joey's arm. "C'mon, JoJo, let's go for a walk."

She stood with Bill for a bit, listening to the music. Hoping she didn't sound overly curious, she finally asked, "Do you think Tru knew that Jimmy was here when he asked her to dance?"

Bill snorted. "She asked him, and he's too polite to turn a girl down. But knowing Lana, I'd bet she knew Jimmy was just coming in. That girl has always liked to stir things up, especially where Tru's involved. I don't think Tru cares one way or another about Jimmy Wright though—they had their showdown a long time ago."

Dinah wanted to ask what he was talking about, but at that moment she felt someone grab her shoulders, spinning her around. Carson pulled her onto the dance floor, leading her around in a shimmying samba to "Lowdown Dirty Shame." He was fun to dance with and Dinah caught on fast. They stayed on the floor for two more songs and she was starting to perspire by the time the band took a break.

"I think I could use a refreshment break myself," Carson drawled as he led her to the bar, where he ordered two glasses of beer. He grabbed them both and said "Follow me," starting across the room. Dinah trailed behind him until they got to the door, which he nudged open with his shoulder. "Let's sit outside for a while—it's a jungle in here."

The cool night air did feel wonderful, and there was a picnic table over by an old swamp oak. She slid onto one of the benches, which she noticed too late was still a little damp from the snow that had melted. To her surprise, instead of sitting across the table, Carson slid in next to her. He handed her one of the beers. She took a sip and was amazed to discover that it tasted much better now that she was hot and thirsty. "The taste really grows on you," she said, chugging a generous gulp.

Carson laughed. "Easy there, kiddo. You don't want to get me in hot water with your brother."

Dinah was silent, looking down at her beer. Why did people keep calling him that? She felt confused and a little disoriented. As she pictured Tru dancing with Lana, she picked up her beer glass and slugged down a long draft. Carson was looking at her with a mix of surprise and admiration. "Whoa . . . you must have been really thirsty!" He tipped his own cup at her in salute and followed her lead, quaffing most of it.

They both started to laugh. Dinah was still laughing when Carson leaned in and covered her mouth with his own, catching her completely off-guard. She jerked her head back, looking at him wide-eyed. Neither of them said anything for a few moments, and then Carson gently leaned in again. This time she saw the kiss coming, and it felt nice. There was a warm, fuzzy sensation in her head, and her lips reflexively responded, kissing him back. He shifted slightly and slid an arm around her back. Dinah's eyes were closed and she felt a little dizzy. She started to feel like she was drifting away, even as their lips were pressed together. In her mind, she saw deep, coffee-colored eyes. She was lost in this image when they pulled apart, a jolt of dismay running through her as she looked into the pale hazel of Carson's eyes. She took a deep breath, grasping the edge of the table. "I think we should be getting back inside." She had started to shiver from the cold.

"Whatever you say." Carson was obliging, standing to pull her up from the table. Dinah walked quickly to the door, with Carson keeping pace, his hand on the small of her back. As they re-entered the barn, the noise and the heat of the room seemed oppressive. Dinah was still dizzy. She looked around for Tru and Bill, hoping they might be ready to leave. She was moving toward the bar, Carson still at her side, when suddenly Tru materialized out of the smoky haze. Without preamble, he threw a roundhouse swing at Carson's jaw that connected with a resounding smack, laying him flat on the floor. The crowd swarmed around them as Bill and Hayes pushed their way through.

Hayes grabbed Tru by the shoulders. "Hey, buddy, take it easy." He ushered him away from Carson, who was starting to sit up, bewildered by the ambush. Bill reached down to give him a hand.

"What the hell was that about?" Carson, thoroughly baffled, was also righteously steamed.

Bill looked uncomfortable. "Tru's been looking for Dinah," he said. "When he noticed you were both gone, he got a little tense. I think the beer may have had something to do with it," he added feebly. "Tru doesn't usually imbibe. I don't know what's eating him tonight."

"Well he's just a little over-protective, I'd say."

"I don't feel very good," Dinah was swaying a little. Bill grabbed her arm, but Carson already had her by the other one.

"Let's get out of here," Carson said, rubbing his jaw. "Go see if you can get President Truman to call it a night. I'll take Dinah to the car." Dinah had started to giggle at the reference to President Truman, and she stumbled a little as they left the barn.

The clock on the nightstand was ticking more loudly than it usually did, and Dinah's bedroom felt hot. She kicked off the covers, opening her eyes slightly to bright sunshine streaming through the window. Her mind was numbly blank; she had to think for a moment about what day it was, and if she had to get up for school. The hands on the dial read nine o'clock. *That's right, it's Saturday*, she thought—the holiday weekend had upset her inner calendar. She stretched, feeling the odd sensation of an amnesiac. She had never had to wait for awareness to kick-in before. It felt strange, like her brain had a mechanical glitch. Suddenly the cogs engaged, and the events of the night before registered in a tactile rush that swept over her skin. She replayed the evening, lingering on certain aspects. She felt guilty about drinking the beer, but that was overshadowed by the drama of Tru hitting

Carson. It all seemed so surreal. Bill had driven them home, insisting that he could walk back to his own house once he got the car home. Tru sat in the passenger seat, looking silently out the window the whole time. Dinah and Carson sat in the back. When Bill pulled up to the house, Tru made no move to get out, and she and Carson had gone inside by themselves as Bill backed the car out and drove away. Dinah was glad that everyone in the house was asleep. Carson was fuming, and it would have been awkward to try to explain what happened. She said goodnight hastily, feeling awkward and uncomfortable.

Now she wondered what would happen today, and whether Tru had even come home last night. Downstairs, she could hear movement and the sporadic chirping of Jemima's voice. She peeked out the door. Finding the coast clear, she hurried to the bathroom for a shower.

There was a delicious smell coming from the kitchen, and Dinah found Jemima helping their mother bake cookies.

"We're making cookies for Tru and Carson to take back to school," her little sister explained. "We have to hurry, because they're leaving pretty soon."

Dinah looked at her mother questioningly.

"Don't ask me," Caroline said. "Tru has suddenly remembered he has a paper due on Monday and the book is at school."

"Where's Carson?" Dinah asked.

"He didn't want any breakfast." Jemima said. "He went outside for a walk, but don't worry, he's all packed up and ready to go. They're taking the bus in a little while. That's why I'm helping Momma, so we can give them some cookies. I wish I could take a bus. I would go to the Statue of Liberty and the Grand Canyon and Saginawmichigan."

Dinah and her mother exchanged amused glances. "Why Saginaw, honey?" Caroline asked.

"That's where Peter goes to his grandmother's house, and he said Saginawmichigan is better than any place else, except the Statue of Liberty and the Grand Canyon."

"That's quite a bold statement," Caroline laughed. "He sounds like a man of the world. You'll just have to set your sights high, and someday, if you're lucky, maybe you too will get to see Saginaw."

Pouring a bowl of cereal, Dinah smiled. She was idly thinking about Michigan and cookies when Caroline asked, "How was your night?"

The question caught her off-guard. "Oh—fine. It was fun. The band was great, and there were lots of kids there. I had a good time."

"Did you dance with anyone?"

"I danced with Bill and Carson. Carson's a good dancer; Bill's not so great. But that's all right—I wasn't any Ginger Rogers myself."

They chatted as Dinah ate her breakfast, laughing as Caroline recounted some of the bumbling partners she had encountered in her younger years. Dinah decided that her mother had no idea that Tru hadn't come in when she and Carson did, and she was relieved that she wouldn't have to explain what happened. She didn't even know what happened, exactly. She wondered if Tru was mad at Carson about the beer, but she wasn't a child; she was accountable for her own actions. If Tru disapproved, he should have taken it up with her. Poor Carson, he certainly hadn't expected to get punched just for being nice to her. Dinah's mind wandered as her mother and Jemima chattered on, and she once again saw Tru dancing with Lana. She wondered what it would feel like to dance like that . . . with Tru.

"Dinah?" Her mother was looking at her.

"Hmm?"

"If you can find your way back from wherever you just were, could you please put these cookies into that box? I think the boys are getting ready to leave."

Carson was in the foyer, rucksack on his shoulder, when Dinah came in with the cookies. "My mom wanted you to take these back to school with you," she said, holding out the box.

"Thanks. I thought I smelled something good." As he said the words, his eyes ran over Dinah's skirt and blouse, causing her to blush.

"That was fun last night . . ." Dinah felt a little awkward. "I'm sorry about, you know, what happened."

"It's all right. I'm willing to let it go. I'm sure he'll get over . . . whatever it was."

Dinah smiled and shrugged, shaking her head. "Well, it was nice to meet you. I hope you enjoyed your Thanksgiving—at least, most of it."

"All things considered, it was very nice. I can't say I've ever seen snow at Thanksgiving before. In Georgia, we're huntin' quail in shirt sleeves." He paused for a moment, looking furtively up the stairs. "Listen, I was wondering if you would consider going with me to our school dance. It's a Christmas thing. You could stay with the girls from Stanwick, just down the road. They keep spare rooms for visitors, you know, and it would be fun . . ."

Dinah's mind raced. St. Paul's? A dance? Tru would be there. Was he taking someone? Was it a girl from Stanwick? She realized Carson was looking at her, waiting for an answer. "When is it?"

"December 20th, the last Friday of the term."

Her heart fell. "Oh, I'm sorry. I would have loved to, but I'm already going to a dance that night. It's the Salem High Winter Formal. Bill asked me just a few days ago."

Carson's face fell, but he took it in stride. "Lange beat me to it, huh? And here I thought I liked that guy."

Just then there was a movement in the hall, and Dinah saw that Tru was standing in the archway, watching them. His usual friendly, confident expression was gone, and a distant, cool look had taken its place. "My dad's in the car—we'd better get to the station."

Carson went into the kitchen to say goodbye to Caroline and Jemima, leaving Tru and Dinah alone in the foyer. He was staring at a point just in front of her shoes. "You're going to a dance with Bill?" His voice was flat.

"Yes. The Winter Formal."

He nodded his head a couple of times, pressing his lips together. "Have a good time." He didn't look up as he turned and walked out the door, closing it softly behind him.

It wasn't until after second hour that Dinah heard the first of the whispers. Betsy fell into step with her as she passed through the halls, moving from civics to biology. "Do you have something to tell me?" There was an expectant, excited ring to her question.

Dinah knew exactly what she meant—she had expected the word to spread. An incident that involved both the drama of a knock-down punch and Tru Stuart was bound to be the topic of the week at school. "So you heard about the Red Barn?"

"I heard that Lana Gervais is very curious about your relationship with your stepbrother. I can't believe you went to the Barn! Why didn't you call me?"

"It came up at the last minute—Tru had a friend in town and . . . I don't know . . . he just asked me if I wanted to come along. What do you mean my relationship with Tru?"

They were standing at the door of Mr. Calloway's biology class, and the second bell rang.

"I'm gonna be late! I'll see you at lunch!" Betsy dashed down the hall, skidding as she turned a corner.

Hovering over a Bunsen burner, Dinah found it hard to concentrate, as wary speculation crowded her thoughts. What was Lana saying? The thought of being the topic of anyone's idle gossip was unnerving. She didn't know exactly what was going on, but she didn't like what Betsy had implied. Her lab partner glared at her when she dropped the Petri dish for the second time.

At lunch, Betsy and their regular group of friends were already seated, waiting for Dinah when she arrived. As she sat down Marlys gave her a conspiratorial smile. "So what's this we hear about you out carousing with the seniors?"

Dinah was starting to feel defensive. "Like I told Betsy, I just went along with Tru and his friend from school. No big deal."

"According to the word on the street that's not what Lana thinks," Joan contributed. "Is there something you're not telling us?"

Dinah felt a little fluttering in her heart. "What do you mean?" She tried to sound casual.

Betsy looked at her seriously. "Lana is spreading a rumor—making a big deal out of the fact that you and Tru are related." She paused, and the rest of the table nodded, looking at Dinah.

"Where's the news in that?" Dinah had an idea, but she wasn't about to admit it.

"You know, because he's your stepbrother, and for some reason," Betsy looked at Dinah with a questioning, raised brow, "she thinks there's *something going on* between you two." She gave a weighty emphasis to the words.

"That's ridiculous!" Dinah was appalled. "First of all, there is no reason to think that there's anything 'going on' between us, and second, we are not actually related!" The last part came out as a virtual shout, drawing the attention of several of the other tables.

Shaken, she tried to eat her lunch, but nothing was going down very well. She refused to discuss it further, and her friends disappointedly went back to talking about their own inconsequential weekends. She was just getting up to clear her tray when Sally, Lana, and Carol walked by.

"Look, Lana," Sally said loudly, "there's that little hillbilly . . . where did you say she was from? Some place down south, wasn't it?"

"I think it was Appalachia," Carol chimed in.

"Isn't that where they have those kissin' cousins?" Sally and Carol were smirking, but Lana narrowed her violet eyes and looked straight through her, sending a chill down Dinah's spine.

The afternoon crept by, and Dinah distractedly muddled through it. She was glad when Bill caught up with her a block away from school; he was beginning to feel like a brother. The irony didn't escape her. He fell into step without comment.

"I suppose you've heard that Lana and her friends have it in for me," she finally said.

"Well, I did catch a whiff of something rotten, but it's no big deal. Don't worry about those girls. Lana will never be over Tru, and she's threatened by anyone who gets near him."

"But I wasn't even near him on Friday night. What is she talking about?"

Bill hesitated for a moment. "I didn't tell Carson exactly why Tru hit him. I mean, maybe Tru *was* being overly protective as a brother. But I don't know if that was really the case. Some of the guys . . . some of the guys were talking about you at the bar. I mean, you know, in a complimentary way . . ." He was distinctly uncomfortable, and Dinah looked confused. He started over. "A lot of the guys at school think you're really pretty."

She started to feel the flush of embarrassment.

"They were ribbing Tru that they wanted to, you know, go out with his sister. And he was watching you dance with Carson, and he was pretty quiet. And he had another beer, and then the band stopped, and before I knew it he was gone. And then he came back and asked if anyone had seen where you went. So Joey said he saw you go out the door with Carson, and he just sort of snapped. He started pushing through people to get to the door, and Hayes and I were trying to stay with him, and that's when you came back in, and Carson . . . well, I guess poor Carson got a quick lesson in how to tick off his new pal."

Dinah was silent. They walked past the Hawthorne Inn and the Custom House. The flag on the tall pole was flapping gently in the breeze. After a few moments, Bill continued. "After you left, people were talking about what happened, and Hayes made the comment that he'd never seen Tru act like that over a girl before. I guess Lana heard him, and there's your trouble."

He'd never seen Tru act like that over a girl before. The phrase echoed in Dinah's mind. *He'd never seen Tru act like that over a girl before* . . . the shadow of a hollow beneath a cheekbone . . . the slight curving lift at the top of a lip . . .

Her reverie was interrupted by an insistent voice: "I said, I guess you're not too worried about Lana." Bill was looking at her queerly, and Dinah quickly rearranged her features into a semblance of solemnity; she hadn't realized that she had been smiling.

CHAPTER SIX

Most Beloved

THE SNOW WAS FALLING OUTSIDE the window as Caroline found Tom at his desk in the library, absently puffing on his pipe, going over some papers. She curled up in the wingback chair by the fire—the same one that Harley had fallen asleep in on Thanksgiving. It was turning out to be a very snowy winter, and she leaned her head against a wing as she watched the fat flakes drifting down.

"Dinah looked nice tonight, didn't you think?" They had seen their daughter off at the door when Bill came to pick her up for the dance. Caroline had taken her to Nolan's to pick out a pretty dress, and had again been amazed at the adult-looking young woman standing in the foyer. She was proud of the fact that Dinah had never seemed aware of her extraordinary beauty. Even as a little girl Dinah had possessed a unique quality that seemed to defy physical laws. It was as though she shone with an inner light—a soft, mesmerizing radiance. Caroline had tried to discourage people from focusing attention on it. She believed that absorption with one's appearance was the enemy of character development. Not a day went by that she wasn't thankful for the results of her careful rectitude.

"Of course she did," Tom smiled at his wife, "she has the advantage of good genes."

"Well, thank you, but I was thinking more about how suddenly mature she seems. It's like she grew up overnight. I guess that's how it happens . . . one minute they're children and the next they're adults." She studied Tom, reading a pensive look on his face. "What are you thinking about?"

Tom sighed. "I guess I just miss having Tru around. I'm still not used to his being away at school. It's hard to accept that he's doing all the same kinds of things the kids here are doing, but we don't get to be a part of it. And I guess I'm having a little trouble adjusting to the idea that he won't be here at Christmas. Don't get me wrong—I'm glad he has the opportunity; he loves to ski, and Sun Valley is supposed to be phenomenal . . ." His voice tapered off forlornly.

Caroline felt both sympathy and admiration—it had been such a gesture of love for Tom to give his son permission for the ski trip with Carson. Her husband's selfless nature never ceased to amaze her. "I didn't expect him to pursue that invitation," she said. "Not with the frost in the air on the day they left. I was certain something happened between those two the night before—they were hardly speaking to each other."

"Kids get over things fast. I'm sure that whatever it was evaporated by the time they got back to school." Tom sat back, looking up at the ceiling. "Speaking of frost in the air, Coco is coming up tomorrow for a library board meeting. She wants to have lunch. You can probably guess what that's all about."

"I didn't know Coco was still involved with her Salem philanthropies, now that she's back in Boston."

"She still has tenure to fulfill on a couple of boards. I know she's slated to chair the Centennial Celebration for the Friends of the Library foundation, so we'll have the pleasure of Coco's presence in town for a little while longer."

As Tom raised his pipe to his mouth, there was a wobbly tremor in his hand. He looked at the offending appendage curiously, as if it were not attached to his body. With a slight shrug, he continued: "I think I may have to arrange some financial details . . . it's hard to believe, despite the four-legged follies, that she bled through everything Whit had. He was a wealthy man. I think Harley makes enough to support them, but not in the style to which they're accustomed. They've dug their hole pretty deep. I may have to consider extending a loan."

Caroline was touched that Tom was so intent on disclosing all of this to her. She knew he wanted to keep her abreast of his personal business, and she appreciated it, but she really didn't care about the details of Coco and Harley's financial troubles. Whatever he decided to do as Coco's brother and the executor of their father's estate was fine with her. She stretched and got up, crossing a few steps to Tom's desk. Standing behind him, she wrapped her arms around his neck and leaned to kiss his cheek. "I think I'll go to bed. Will you wait up for Dinah?" She knew it was no imposition—her husband was an inveterate night owl.

Tom kissed her hand. "I'll be right here. Bidu Sayao will keep me company." The exquisite virtuosity of the coloratura soprano singing *Manon* quietly emanated from the corner of the room.

She left her husband to his papers and his music, peeking in on Jemima as she passed her bedroom. Caroline had to peer at the tousled blankets, searching for her tiny form. She was grateful that the Halloween accident had already become a dim memory for Jemima, who was now fixated on the imminent arrival of Santa Claus and the hopes of a Bright Star doll. Caroline went over to the bed, patting the blankets. Jemima was barely perceptible, even to the touch. She pulled the bedding away from her daughter's face and kissed her on the forehead, which was slightly damp from the heat of the insulating blankets. As she smoothed back a tawny curl, the sight of her own hand triggered the image of her husband's strong, square one, trembling as he clutched his pipe.

Dinah had to run to get to the library on time for her Saturday-morning shift. She had been up late the night before. After Bill dropped her off she sat in the library and talked to Tom for a long time. He wanted to hear all about the dance—it was clear that he missed his son. She curled up on the sofa, filling him in with as much detail as she could, and he leaned back, puffing on his pipe, smiling at her descriptions of the dresses and the dancers and the band. He raised his eyebrows slightly when she told him that Jimmy Wright and Lana Gervais had been crowned Snow King and Queen, but he didn't comment.

The Winter Formal had been a relief—she hadn't realized that she'd been nervous about being thrown in with the seniors, more specifically the Sinisters, but Betsy, Joan, and Marlys had all been asked, and Bill seemed content to congregate with Dinah's friends and their dates. The Retreads lived up to Bill's expectations, covering all the popular tunes from Ellington to Porter, and by the end of the evening even Bill seemed to be getting the hang of dancing. There was an awkward moment when he walked her to the door—he held her hand for a minute while she thanked him for the nice time, and then he quickly pecked her on the cheek and hurried back to the car.

Saturday mornings were busy at the library; she knew that most of her time would be spent in the children's room. She still enjoyed helping the kids, especially when she happened across a child who shared her wonder at the transporting magic of books, but she was disappointed that she wouldn't be able to work on the Hawthorne cataloguing. Her biography was finished; she had turned it in just the day before. She thought it was good—the back-room boxes had provided access to information that couldn't be found in any of the texts on the shelves. But despite its completion, she was looking forward to reading the letters from Elizabeth Peabody. After reading the first one she had put them away, not allowing herself the distraction until she could find an opportunity to read them on her own time.

The morning dragged by, crowded with children leaving books on the floor, or worse, putting them randomly back on the wrong shelves. Finally, the big Hamilton clock on the wall struck one o'clock, and Dinah told Jane that she wanted to go up to the back room for a little while.

"You want to work on the cataloguing? But you're off the clock, dear. I can't extend your hours, I'm afraid. We have to stick to our payroll budget."

"That's all right; I just want to do a little research for myself."

"I thought your biography was due yesterday." Jane looked puzzled.

"Yes . . . I turned it in. I just . . . I'm just interested in some of the things that I found." Dinah was reluctant to mention the letters.

Jane shook her head disbelievingly. "You are an unusual girl. I can't imagine Betsy choosing to spend her Saturday afternoon poking through old boxes of documents from a hundred years ago. What is it that's so fascinating up there?"

Dinah hesitated. "I'm not sure. I've found a few things that seem a little . . . well, revelatory . . ." The word rolled off her tongue and Jane started to laugh.

"Revelatory! What a lexicon you have! Well, if you run across anything really fascinating, let me know. You might want to show it to Mike—he's something of an authority on nineteenth-century American authors."

Mike MacEvoy, Jane's husband, was an English professor at Salem State University. Sharing the warm demeanor of his wife, he insisted that Dinah call him by his first name. Dinah thought Betsy was lucky to have a professor for a father, but Betsy insisted that she'd rather have a policeman or a veterinarian.

In the small room that had begun to feel like her own private domain, Dinah pulled the cigar box from its hiding place. She felt vaguely guilty, as if she were spying on someone. How strange to have one's life exposed to prying eyes a century after the fact. She made a mental note to carefully consider everything she ever wrote, on the off-chance that it would turn up in a stranger's hands decades in the future.

Instead of sitting on the hard metal chair, she moved to the window, sliding onto the floor to lean against the wall, surrounded by boxes. Taking out the letters, she realized she had no way to determine their chronological order; there were no dates. Randomly she chose one, opening the crumbling envelope carefully. The same bold, distinct writing greeted her. She began reading, hoping it wouldn't be limited to the prosaic. Before she had finished the first line, she knew that she would not be disappointed. It took only moments for Dinah to realize, with a shock, that what she had stumbled upon was much more than the unrequited affections of a woman scorned. In passionate prose, the words revealed an intimacy that was undeniable:

> *Most Beloved—*
>
> *I tremble for what we are doing—you have devoured my very soul—I live only in you. Don't speak to me of our lives apart, for mine does not exist without you. My only course is to stay asleep and dream of our time together.*
>
> *In the dull tedium of your absence, I await your awakening touch*
> *—Libby.*

Stunned, Dinah quickly opened another letter—it was equally impassioned. Holding it on her lap, Dinah stared at the others in the box, afraid to open any more. She was flummoxed. Could it be possible that Nathaniel Hawthorne had a relationship with his sister-in-law that was— improper? Were they having an affair? Or were these letters written before he had married Sophia? The first letter that she had read could have been the last one written, but what if that was not the case? The idea was quite disturbing. Dinah recalled the sweet, tender words that Sophia had written to her husband, and Hawthorne's passionate letter to his wife. Was it possible that the author, renowned for his moral purity, was unfaithful? The mystery inspired her to open another letter . . . and then another. While some were more overtly romantic than others, they were all personal, all private. By the time she had read several more, she was still no closer to the answer. There were no dates, no timely references. And, aside from the first one, there was no further mention of Sophia. But there was something . . . She couldn't put her finger on it, but there was something in the words that hinted at the clandestine—at the illicit. Although there were more letters in the box, her inclination to read them was fading. She was unwilling to look further— afraid to find her suspicions confirmed. Carefully, she put them all away, stashing the trove back in its hiding place for another day.

Lambent candlelight cast a glow on the congregation of St. James Episcopal Church, reflecting the aura of God's grace on a cold and snowy Christmas Eve. The Reverend John Stallworth was bestowing his annual Christmas oblation to the parishioners—a short and simple sermon, abandoning his usual discursive ramblings about moral turpitude for a more benevolent holiday offering. Caroline bowed her head, allowing the hope and wonder of the season to fill her heart. She felt the warm hand of her husband close around hers—it was steady and strong.

That morning, Tom had spilled hot coffee down his shirt front. When she leaned in to blot the stain, she saw something she had never seen before—there was a shadow in her husband's eyes, and it took her a minute to recognize it for what is was: Fear. The thing they had both been trying to ignore, to attribute to fatigue or too much coffee, had asserted its claim in a bold and venomous strike, undeniable and sovereign.

Standing for the final hymn, Tom held the hymnal that they shared. Voices rang out, entreating the joyful and faithful and triumphant to behold and adore the Lord, but the words on the page started to quake, and the book nearly slipped to the floor before Caroline could grasp it. She looked up at her husband. His gaze was locked on the alabaster cross hanging in humble elegance over the altar, his trembling hands now clasped together. As the voice of the choir rose up in all of its reverent glory, he closed his eyes.

It was still dark when Dinah felt a tapping on the back of her shoulder. She was dreaming about Bel. The little dog was chasing through the woods, and Dinah was amazed at its newfound agility: Bel's legs had miraculously grown, so that she leaped gracefully over the landscape like a greyhound.

There was something on Dinah's back—something pawing at her. She wrested her arm out from beneath her, swiping at the offending pest, hoping it wasn't a squirrel fallen out of the trees. But it was bigger than a squirrel, and it knew her name. She rolled over, coming face to face with impish sherry-brown eyes.

"Wake up, Dinah! I think Santa was here . . . hurry! Come downstairs and see!

"Arghh . . ." She reached out and grabbed her sister, pulling her into bed and rolling back and forth.

"Stop, stop!" Jemima was giggling, and Dinah started to tickle her neck. "No . . . stop it!" She was now laughing uncontrollably.

Dinah looked at the clock: five-thirty. "Mimer, do you know what time it is?"

"It's time to see what Santa brought. Get up, get up, get up!"

"OK, but be quiet. Just because you're awake doesn't mean everyone else should be." She got out of bed and put on her bathrobe. Jemima was already scooting down the stairs. As Dinah went into the hall, she met her mother coming out of her bedroom.

"There's no sense trying to keep a child from Christmas morning," Caroline smiled, "whatever time that may be." Tom came down the stairs behind them, yawning in his robe and slippers. When they entered the living room, Jemima was dancing a jig around the tree, anxiously assessing the loot in search of one particular item. She spied it on the far side, sitting primly against a brightly-wrapped package—shining ringlets surrounding its face, velvet dress layered in flounces. The Bright Star doll was the Shirley Temple model, exactly what Jemima had wished for.

Caroline asked that they please wait until she could make some coffee before they started opening gifts, and she brought out a plate of Gloria's Caramel Supreme Coffee Cake on a tray with forks and napkins. When the adults were settled with coffee in hand, they all nibbled on their breakfast as they took turns opening gifts.

Dinah hadn't requested anything particular that year—she couldn't think of anything she really wanted. There was a large, heavy box with her name on it. It was from Tom. When Caroline looked at him questioningly, Dinah could tell that her mother hadn't known about the gift. She opened it curiously, amazed to find an entire leather-bound collection of Dickens.

"I thought you might like your own set," he said. "Mine isn't complete. I have *Great Expectations*, but I'm missing *Hard Times*. He paused with a chuckle. "I guess I should consider myself lucky."

His thoughtfulness was touching. Dinah thanked him with sincerity—it was a perfect gift.

For Caroline, he had found an antique cameo brooch, which he insisted he had to buy because the delicate silhouette looked just like her own. Jemima received a Steiff monkey, dressed in a red felt vest and holding a pair of brass cymbals. "I thought Fuzz could use another friend," he winked at her, "and this one can entertain him."

Climbing onto Tom's lap, Jemima kissed his cheek. "Fuzz wants to be in a band," she said knowingly. "I'm going to get him a drum and they can play together."

They opened more gifts. Caroline gave Tom gold cufflinks and a new recording of *Turandot*. Jemima loved the sweater her mother had knitted for her—it was a soft baby-blue, complementing her olive-toned complexion. Dinah also received a sweater—Caroline had worked on it while the girls were at school. It was a cardigan of the palest pink angora, with small, mother-of-pearl buttons. There was another, smaller box next to it. When her turn came, Dinah opened it and was surprised to find a delicate strand of pearls nestled in the satin lining. She stared at the necklace and then looked wonderingly at her mother.

"Those were my grandmother's pearls." Caroline explained, "They were given to my mother, and then to me, when we each turned sixteen. I could have waited for your birthday, but it's a Christmas tradition." Dinah had seen her mother wear the pearls on special occasions, and she couldn't believe they were now hers. She felt suddenly adult and sophisticated.

When they had finished the gift-giving there were still several boxes under the tree. Jemima wandered over and looked at the tags. "I guess these are for Tru." The disappointment in her voice was not only because the gifts weren't for her. "I wish he could be here," she said gloomily. "I wanted to give him my present—I made it at school. It's a picture of him driving me in the comvertible, and I have on my crown." She had been talking about their plans for driving around in Hayes's convertible ever since she came home from the hospital.

Dinah shared her sister's disappointment. When she heard that Tru was going to take Carson up on the invitation to spend Christmas in Idaho, her heart had fallen. She hadn't seen him since Thanksgiving, but her thoughts were increasingly filled with his image—sailing in the regatta, laughing at the dinner table, dancing at the Red Barn, huddled beside her on the floor of Jemima's room.

"You can give it to him next week," Tom's voice interrupted Dinah's thoughts. "He's coming home for a couple of days before the second term begins." Jemima's face lit up, and Dinah was afraid that her own did too.

The week following Christmas was quiet. The library was operating on a limited holiday schedule, so Dinah only worked one afternoon. Caroline and Tom had been making mysterious trips to Boston. Dinah wondered if they had anything to do with Coco O'Grady. She had overheard a remark her mother made to Tom, referring to "the dreaded luncheon," and Tom had replied something about bearing the burden of relation, but then the voices had become muffled.

She and Jemima drifted aimlessly around the house, reveling in the absence of homework and the fluid timelessness of the days. They slept in, staying in their flannel nightgowns to make pancakes or French toast, sometimes not getting dressed until nearly noon. It was an unnatural state for Dinah—usually she was happiest with a disciplined schedule, but there was something about the collective pause of post-holiday ennui that rolled across her like a sort of anesthetic, and she actually found herself enjoying the lazy, unstructured hours.

On Thursday, Jemima asked Dinah to help her with a project. She and Peter had formed a club: The Secret Society of the Midnight Rider. Peter's mother had taken them to see *Tex Granger*, and they had decided that the garage attic would be the perfect place to recreate Three Buttes. It was a tall order; Jemima wanted Dinah to paint a rugged mountain backdrop on some discarded sheets, while she and Peter moved some old furniture around to resemble a sheriff's office and a saloon.

"Bel can be Duke, Tex Granger's dog," Jemima explained, as she tried to tie a bandana around Bel's sagging throat, losing the ends in the loose flaps of furry skin. Bel sat obediently still, looking true to her full name.

Dinah found some old paint in the back of the garage and was struggling with a rather crude impression of the Grand Tetons when she heard a familiar whistling on the stairs. Bill Lange's buff-colored crew cut appeared over the solid railing.

"I heard there was a Secret Society somewhere in this vicinity, and I was wondering where I could apply for membership."

Dinah wasn't surprised to see him—Bill had taken to showing up on a fairly regular basis, stopping in to visit with the family and accepting Caroline's invitation to stay for lunch or dinner on quite a few occasions. "You'll have to take that up with the membership committee. They've gone down to the cookhouse for some grub."

"I've been rejected by that committee already. I was told I didn't have the proper credentials. Where's a guy supposed to get a horse around here?" He sauntered over to where Dinah was kneeling over the backdrop, standing behind her with his hands in his pockets.

"Well, don't feel too bad—I'm only a hired hand. They wouldn't let me in either. Evidently I failed the entrance exam when I didn't know who Rance Carson was." Dinah leaned back on her heels, brushing stray lock of hair off her face with the back of her hand.

Bill was squinting, making a critical study of her work. "Here—give me the brush. I'll show you how the pros do it." Dinah gladly handed over the paintbrush and stood up, stretching her back. As she watched, Bill made a succession of swift brushstrokes, and Dinah was amazed to see the primitive, amateurish rendering transformed into a realistic range of shadows and light, creating the impression of rugged terrain and snow-topped peaks. He added a few flourishes for effect, and bounced to his feet, sweeping an arm broadly over the work. "Voila!"

"I think you may have found your entry into the very exclusive Secret Society of the Midnight Rider. Mimer will be mighty impressed. Where did you learn how to do that?"

"It's not really something you learn. You just know how to do it." He shrugged, leaning down to put the lid on the paint can.

"Well, you've been hiding your light under a bushel. You should put your talent to use—I bet the Student Council would like to know they have an artist at their disposal. Think of all the school projects they could put you to work on."

He gave her a pained look. "Let's just keep this between us. I have better things to do than log extra hours painting banners for the drama club. Speaking of drama, how'd you like to go to a movie tonight? *Key Largo* is playing at the Odeon."

Dinah hesitated a little. She had just read an article about Lauren Bacall in an issue of *Life* magazine at the library and had been hoping to see the movie, but she had something else on her mind. "We'd have to go to the late show . . . Gloria's cooking up a welcome-home dinner for Tru."

"Tru's coming home?

"My mom and Tom are on their way to Boston right now. They're picking him up at Logan. Dinner's at seven, I think. You could eat here, and we could probably make the nine o'clock."

Dinah wasn't the only one to hesitate. Bill seemed strangely troubled. Looking away, he mumbled something about finding out exactly what time the show started.

"Let's go tell the rangers your masterpiece is ready." Dinah picked up the paintbrush and headed for the stairs. "You can check on the show time and call me later." She made her way to the utility sink in the basement, with Bill trailing silently behind.

Bill was at the house by seven, prompt for his dinner invitation, but by seven-fifteen there was still no sign of Tom's big Buick. Because it was her sister's birthday, Gloria hadn't planned on staying to serve. She asked if Bill wouldn't mind "carrying" her home, so they grabbed Jemima and all piled into Mr. Lange's old green Mercury.

They pulled back up to the house as Tru was lifting a suitcase out of the car. He turned as he closed the trunk, smiling broadly as Bill opened his door. "Couldn't wait to see me, huh?" The last words slowed as he noticed who was in the passenger seat.

Dinah felt a nervous clutch in her stomach. This was the moment she'd been waiting for, ever since Thanksgiving weekend. His eyebrows lifted almost imperceptibly when he saw her, and she waited for a greeting, but he looked quickly away, turning back to Bill. "Grab a bag, will you?" He hoisted his duffle over his shoulder and started to the house.

"Hello there, Bill," Tom called out. "Fancy seeing you here . . . again!" There was an unmistakable note of irony in his voice, and Tru visibly stiffened.

Jemima bounded out of the back seat, throwing herself at Tru like a tiny tidal wave, while Caroline welcomed Bill and cautioned Jemima not to knock Tru down. A cacophony of voices clamored toward the house.

Dinah was confused. He hadn't even said hello. She felt the sting of Tru's indifference like a slap, as she trailed behind the small parade, crossing the threshold with a lurching heart and a dragging step.

Gloria's meal was delicious—stuffed chicken with biscuits and gravy. It was Gussie's recipe. She used to make it for Caroline on her birthday, because it was her favorite. Dinah thought her mother seemed slightly tense, in a distant, distracted way, and Tom's joviality appeared a bit forced, but they both rose to the occasion, industriously nurturing the dinner conversation by drawing out accounts of Tru's visit to Sun Valley. Dinah wondered what had happened with Coco Wells.

Tru recounted the highlights of his trip, with a vivid description of Mrs. Hewitt, who sounded like a southern version of Coco. "She must have had about twenty suitcases and trunks, a different fur coat practically every day. She brought her own porter—Dawson—but she just called him 'Boy.'" He reported this last bit of news with evident disgust, and it was clear that he hadn't cared for the Hewitts. "I don't know. Carson's all right, but the rest of his family are bigots." He looked at Caroline apologetically. "I'm sorry, but I don't know how you could stand to live down there with those kinds of people."

Dinah was outraged. She thought of her sweet aunts, and then of her gentle, compassionate father. "Excuse me?" Her tone bordered on belligerent. "I think you can find 'those kinds of people' in any part of the country. In fact, you wouldn't have to look too far around here to find someone who sounds a lot like Mrs. Hewitt." The rest of the table looked at her, surprised at her outburst. "Well it's true, isn't it? I would stand my father against some of these Northerners any day of the week, if you want to talk about human decency and, and . . ." She couldn't think of the right words, overwhelmed by her own vehemence.

At Dinah's mention of her father, Caroline said quietly, "Of course you're right, Sweetheart. People come in all types wherever you are. Your father was one of God's finest examples of a loving spirit, and I think we are blessed to be surrounded by a continuation of that love here in this home." She smiled softly at Tom, and then at Tru, and the moment was diffused.

Dinah looked down at her plate, wondering where her anger had come

from. It couldn't have been just Tru's blithe stereotype of Southerners—
she had heard that before. The reason for her extreme reaction was just
beyond her acknowledgement, ready and available: Since his arrival, Tru
had been heaping attention on Jemima, ribbing Bill, and directing his
conversation to Tom and Caroline. But he had completely ignored Dinah.

The delayed flight had put a crimp in the schedule, and by the time
dinner was over it was too late for *Key Largo*. Bill didn't even bring it up,
and Dinah didn't really care.

Tom didn't go to work on Friday, and Dinah assumed it was because he
wanted to spend the day with Tru. Although that may have been part
of the reason, the other part was revealed at lunch, when he cleared his
throat, looking first at Caroline and then at the rest of the table.

"There's something we need to tell you kids, and I guess this is as good
a time as any." The reluctance in his voice attested his ambivalence. "As
you know, we've had to make a few trips to Boston over the past week."
He paused for a moment, looking around the table. "I've been seeing a
doctor there—a specialist, in fact. It seems I have a condition known as
Huntington's disease." He looked at his wife again, who gave him a small,
encouraging smile. Tru was staring at his father, his face suddenly pale
under his skier's tan. Tom reached out and placed his hand over his son's,
which was frozen on its path to the water glass. "Evidently there is some
confusion between the signals my brain is sending and the way my muscles
and nerves are interpreting them. Not to worry," he looked reassuringly at
each of them, "it's something I may live with for a long time. The symptoms
come and go, at least for now." He smiled wistfully. "You'll have to put up
with some clumsiness and perhaps a slower pace from me. I would ask for
your patience." His expression was heartbreakingly apologetic.

Tru's voice caught in his throat, but he came directly to the point. "How
long is a long time?"

"It depends. With a little luck, I'll be tottering around spilling coffee
until you are all well tired of me." The little joke fell flat.

Caroline was noticeably silent, and when Dinah looked at her, she saw
that her mother's lips were pressed together in a tight, white line. She was
staring at the corner of the baseboard, eyes blinking rapidly.

"But what else could happen? I mean, what's the worst possible case?"

There was a desperate insistence in Tru's voice.

A slow whistle of air came through Tom's lips, and he looked at his lap. "In severe cases, there is a total loss of muscle control." He left the sentence hanging.

"So you would be, what?" Tru demanded. "Confined to a wheelchair? Would you be able to eat? To breathe?" A hint of hysteria was pushing at his words.

Tom was silent for a moment, lost in thought. Then he met his son's eyes and said evenly, "There is the possibility that those capacities would be affected." Tru took a sharp sniff of breath, as though he had put his hand on a hot stove. "But not necessarily," Tom continued. There have been cases of remission, or at least stabilization. I think we all need to think positively and carry on as before. I'm confident I'll learn to live with the occasional spasmodic symptom, much to the dismay of the laundress." Again, he smiled in an attempt at levity, this time directing his look at Caroline. She dragged her gaze up from the floor and met his smile with a shaky one of her own.

"I don't get it." Jemima's small voice broke through the tension. "You have a coffee-spilling disease?" Nobody could manage a reply. Her voice went quiet as she looked down and said, "I spill my milk sometimes." She got up and walked to Tom's chair, laying a small hand gently on his arm. "It's OK if you make a little spill." Leaning close, she looked calmly into his eyes, her voice tender: "I can help you clean it up."

The day passed in a foggy somnolence. Dinah thought the air in the house seemed thick, almost liquid. Tru stayed in his room, while Tom tried to maintain a hearty, optimistic tenor, and Caroline struggled to keep up with him. The tremors had subsided recently, and it seemed like the symptoms were simply figments of a bad dream.

By dinnertime, some of the heaviness in the atmosphere had evaporated. Tom, Caroline, and the girls were seated around the dining table, joking with Jemima about sending her to charm school to learn which fork to use for salad, when Tru came down and made an announcement: "I'm not going back to St. Paul's." His voice was flat and resolute as he pulled out his chair and sat down.

Tom started to object, but stopped himself. He took a deep breath and said, "Tru, I intend to be around for quite some time. But if you prefer to be here, you know I welcome it." For the first time that day his voice betrayed a quavering emotion, and he looked at his son with manifest love. "But it has to be a decision based on what makes you happy. Don't do this for me—what's good for me is simply what's good for you."

Tru looked steadily at his father, and it was almost possible to see a corporeal link in the space between them. "I prefer to be here."

CHAPTER SEVEN

Tell Your Big Brother...

ON MONDAY MORNING, Dinah was putting her coat on when there was a honk in the driveway. Tru breezed through the foyer, opening the door to wave at a car full of his friends. Then, stiffening a little, he turned back to Dinah and in a polite, obligatory tone said, "Do you want a ride with Hayes?

"I have to walk Jemima to school."

He smiled at Jemima, who was pulling on a bright red stocking cap with large pom-poms attached to the chin straps. "What do you think, Smidge . . . could you persuade Hayes to drop you off?"

"Is it the comvertible?" Jemima's eyes were round.

"Well, yeah, but it's a little too cold to put the top down. You'll have to save your wave for later."

Jemima made for the door. "I'll ask Hayes if it's OK. I can tell him where to go—I know the way!" She skipped ahead, and Dinah grabbed her book bag and Jemima's Howdy Doody lunchbox. Tru held the door open, keeping his gaze directed toward the driveway.

There were already four boys in the car, and Jemima hopped into the backseat next to Stan Thompson. He looked at her with mock surprise. "Tru, old buddy, I feel like there's something different about you. You've changed, somehow. Is this what happens at those fancy boarding schools?"

Jemima laughed delightedly. "It's not Tru! It's me, Jemima. Tru's little sister."

"Well I knew Tru had a couple of new sisters, but I didn't know that one of them was a princess. Joey, did Tru ever mention to you that he had a princess in his family?" He tugged on one of her pom-poms.

Jemima giggled and gazed up at her latest heartthrob. Dinah was afraid her sister might jump right into Stan's lap. She climbed in next to Jemima, feeling dismal. Stan's reference to sisters sat like a large stone in her stomach.

Tru was telling Joey Fetzer to move over as he got into the front seat. "Swing by Bentley, we're dropping Mimer off," he instructed Hayes.

"It's on Essex Street," Jemima offered authoritatively. "You just go up to the corner, then turn that way," she pointed left, "and go down a ways until you see the flag, and then you go that way," she pointed right, "and it's right there!"

"Roger, Wilco!" Hayes gave a little salute into the rearview mirror.

Jemima snuggled in next to Stan, proudly showing him her lunchbox and telling him all about Buffalo Bob and Clarabelle. They debated the gender of Clarabelle, and Stan was explaining that the word Ooragnak was really kangaroo spelled backwards when they pulled up at the elementary school. Tru opened the door and got out, pulling the front seat forward so Dinah could let Jemima pass. She climbed over Dinah and out the door, and as Tru leaned down to push the seatback into place Stan called out: "Goodbye Princess! Tell your big brother he shouldn't be so greedy— keeping his beautiful sister all to himself!"

Tru's face was level with Dinah's, and it seemed to her that the words hung in the air like the echo of a gunshot. She thought she saw him close his eyes as he tilted his face away from her, then he straightened up and got back into the front seat, looking straight ahead. There was a momentary silence in the car, and when Dinah looked to her left she saw Bill quietly watching Tru.

A pane in the window of Principal Dawes' office was broken, and a piece of cardboard had been taped over it. Dinah wondered if someone had thrown a rock through it. Vandalism at the school was rare—she decided that it must have been an errant baseball from the diamond just over the knoll. She looked around, absently noting the framed photos on the desk: one a dated portrait of a woman she presumed to be Mrs. Dawes, posed dramatically in profile with a velvet drape slung low over ample flesh; the other a snapshot of a chubby young girl and a gangly, pimpled, adolescent boy.

She had no idea why Mrs. Crawford had approached her after English class, pulling her aside to tell her the principal would like to see her. She couldn't think of a single reason she should be there. She was starting to worry that maybe something had happened to her mother or Jemima, when the door finally opened and a portly, mustached man in round glasses waddled in. His thighs brushed together as he walked, making an abrasive, squeaky sound. Dinah stood, and he waved his hand in a downward motion, indicating that she could sit down. "Hello there, Miss Hunt! How are you today?"

He was loudly jocular, a style Dinah thought he had probably acquired after years of trying to disarm defensive students who associated him with tribunal. Smiling politely, she responded, "I'm fine, thank you."

"Good, good. Did you have a nice break?

Dinah wished he would get to the point—the idea that something bad must have happened had started to take root, and she felt a growing sense of alarm. "Yes, it was fine."

He raised an eyebrow, looking over the top of his glasses. "Yes, well, you may wonder why you've been called down here today." He looked at her expectantly, but she just waited. Picking up some papers on his desk, he shuffled through them absently. "You have been doing excellent work in your classes." He made a show of scanning one of the papers. "It appears that you are among the students at the top of the class." Setting the papers down, he looked at her gravely. "Your English teacher, Mrs. Crawford, came to see me this morning with a suggestion. Based on your performance, most recently the biography project that you completed at the end of the first term, she believes that it would be in your best interest to advance into Honors English. This is quite a compliment. Honors English, as you may know, is generally open to seniors only, with an occasional exception made for exceptional juniors." The intentional redundancy was delivered with a self-satisfied smile. "We haven't, to the best of my knowledge, had a sophomore in that class before. So that in itself is a great honor."

Dinah felt a wave of relief that there was no emergency, as well as a little swell of pride in her chest. She was processing the idea of Honors English when Mr. Dawes cleared his throat and continued. "There's something else we'd like you to consider. Your overall scholastic performance indicates another option that may be available to you." He paused dramatically. "We believe that, with some extra study, possibly involving taking a math class during the summer, you could graduate a year ahead of time." He beamed at her proudly, as though the accomplishment somehow reflected back on him.

Dinah didn't know what to say. Graduate early? How? Why? She looked at the principal blankly.

"You'll definitely need to take some time to think about it. Talk it over with your parents. In fact, we should schedule a meeting with them to go over the details. But I think when you've had a chance to give it some thought, you'll agree that rising to a challenge like this is the best way to exemplify the policy of educational excellence and personal attention to our students that we have here at Salem High. We would hate to have any of our students find our curriculum . . . insufficiently rigorous. We aim to provide the utmost in education, promoting each student's individual interest. In other words, you are being offered a promotion!"

Dinah wandered back to class, handing her excuse to Mr. Schaffer and taking a seat. Her mind was stuck on a continuous loop, the idea of graduating in less than a year and a half going around and around as it tried to settle in. She didn't hear much of the civics lesson, and at the end of class, she realized that her notes were disjointed and spotty, interrupted by a series of doodles that consisted mostly of figures that looked like question marks.

Walking through the halls, she caught a glimpse of Tru as he turned a corner in front of her. She had noticed that it hadn't taken him long to fall into his regular routine at school. There had been an excited buzz on the first day, as friends surrounded him, eagerly welcoming him back. She had heard him fielding questions about his return with a nonchalant shrug, saying that he just felt like coming home. As far as Dinah knew, he didn't mention anything about his father, but they rarely crossed paths at school. In fact, she felt like she had hardly seen him at all since he had returned. At home, he had asked to move into a bedroom on the third floor. Caroline had immediately agreed, saying she understood the need for privacy and regretting that she hadn't thought of it to begin with. He was home for dinner some nights, but he had been uncharacteristically quiet and usually disappeared soon afterward. He had taken to studying at his friends' houses, and even when he was at home he was often out in the garage with Tom working on their pet project—sanding and refinishing a Crosby catboat. Most mornings the girls continued to ride to school with his friends, but the mere minutes it took to cover the several blocks to school were taken up with Jemima's courtship of Stan, whom she had decided to marry. To Dinah, it seemed there was little difference between Tru being home or away at St. Paul's. It was strange, she thought—having a person living under the same roof didn't necessarily mean that he would be any closer. She felt as though there were a figurative wall between them that was far more solid than the actual walls in the house.

After school, she looked around for Bill to catch up with her so she could tell him her news. Lately she found herself talking more easily to Bill than to her other friends, even Betsy. She waited for a little while near the corner where they usually met, but he was nowhere to be found. She walked home alone.

Upon meeting with the school administration and several of Dinah's teachers, Tom and Caroline agreed that it would be in Dinah's best interest to move ahead. She only needed to take trigonometry during the summer, and she could go right into calculus in the fall. She had already intended to take physics as an elective her junior year, and she could continue with Honors English for another semester, fulfilling a full year. The only other obstacle was history—she would have to double up, starting immediately, adding a period of European history during what was normally her study hall.

"You may have to quit your job at the library, if it gets in the way of your studies," her mother warned.

"I don't think it will be a problem. I don't work that many hours, anyway." Dinah did not want to relinquish her access to Elizabeth Peabody's letters. She had finished reading them all, and though she was still uncertain of the chronology, she was convinced that she—well, the library—was in possession of something of significant historical value. With further research, she thought she might be able to find out when the affair had taken place. In any case, the letters had revealed a facet of the relationship between Hawthorne and Elizabeth Peabody that, to Dinah's knowledge, had never been confirmed.

With Caroline's words still hovering in the air, Dinah kissed her mother goodbye and left to take her shift at work.

CHAPTER EIGHT
Exemption

CAROLINE WATCHED HER HUSBAND SLEEP. The tremors had subsided since Christmas. It was as if, by acknowledgement, the disease had quieted down—subdued by recognition. No more asserting its voracious need for attention, it was now content to hibernate, a ferocious, angry grizzly who slept in their bed. If she felt the constant hovering dread of its awakening, she wondered what Tom must be feeling. Unable to sleep, she restlessly tossed the covers off and flung an arm over her face, once again replaying the scene from earlier that day.

She had answered the doorbell, expecting to see a deliveryman or a door-to-door salesman. Instead, standing there with an expectant look was her sister-in-law, decked out in a pink Dior suit with a sheared mink jacket and a triple strand of pearls. Fortunately, Tom was at the Salem mill that day and not out of town, because he had apparently forgotten that he had asked Coco to come to the house to sign some papers. Without offering a greeting, she ran her eyes over Caroline's simple housedress, which was mostly hidden beneath the rickrack-trimmed apron she was wearing to polish the silver.

Caroline was a little nonplussed. "Oh! Hello, Coco. What brings you to this neck of the woods?" She hadn't seen her sister-in-law since Thanksgiving, although she knew Tom had been meeting with her about her finances.

The woman looked beyond Caroline, sweeping her eyes across the foyer for evidence of a viable human presence. "I have an appointment with Tom," she said brusquely, as she whisked past Caroline into the hall.

"I'm afraid he must have forgotten about it. I can call him at the mill—he's in town today." Caroline reflexively offered coffee or tea—her hospitality grimly declined as her sister-in-law paced around the library, absently drumming her fingers on bookshelves and window sills.

"Well, I'm just giving the silver a little touch-up, so if you'll excuse me,

I'll give Tom a call and then get back to work." This was met with supreme apathy, and Caroline wasted no more time on her reluctant guest.

Tom hurried in ten minutes later, making a quick stop in the kitchen to kiss his wife and apologize for subjecting her to solitary confinement with his sister. "I'm sorry, Sweetheart. I hope she didn't break any skin . . ." He picked up her hands, inspecting them for bite marks.

Caroline laughed. "No harm done. I was saved by the silver . . . thank God for tedious household chores."

Half an hour later, Tom appeared in the kitchen, brushing his hands together. "Well, that's done. You probably won't be seeing much of Coco for a while—she and Harley should be set to reestablish themselves as globetrotters, at least for the time being. I had a word with her about their proclivity for . . . risky investment. The terms of the loan are such that they have to present a full financial statement to my accountant quarterly, so I can keep an eye on their flights of fancy. Once the next distribution of the trust kicks in they will begin repayment. Believe me, the mendicant lifestyle does not suit Coco's ego."

He offered this to his wife reassuringly, and again she was touched by his democratic intent. She knew she was lucky to have a husband who was so committed to sharing everything with his wife, not just the material, but the emotional, the intellectual, and yes, the spiritual as well. Tom wasn't an overtly religious man, but Caroline didn't believe she had ever known a man with as generous a spirit. She kissed him goodbye as he hurried back to the mill, citing a contract dispute at work.

She was almost finished polishing the last of the Francis I dinner forks when, to her utter astonishment, her sister-in-law appeared in the kitchen. Coco had evidently let herself back in, offering no initial explanation as she walked stiffly to the table, pulling out a chair and sitting down heavily. Her expression was remote, but there was something else—something Caroline couldn't define. Something almost . . . haunted.

Finally, Coco spoke: "Tom has told me about his . . . condition." Her voice had a flat quality. She paused, staring at the table.

Caroline drew a long breath, preparing for the sad conversation.

After what seemed like a long time, Coco continued: "I understand that this . . . condition . . . is hereditary." Now she drummed her fingers on the table, her clenched jaw betraying her struggle to maintain her resolve.

"I believe our father had it—he showed many of the symptoms. We just chalked it up to drink, and it was the drink that killed him, but if it hadn't, I think it would have been . . . this." She seemed to be avoiding whatever purpose had brought her to the kitchen.

Finally, she looked directly at Caroline. "I'm not certain this is a good idea." Coco took a deep breath and continued haltingly. "But, here goes: Tom indicated that there is a strong link to heredity for this . . ." she swallowed and finally said the word—". . . disease. He was quite concerned that I should know about the genetic likelihood of its occurrence. I suppose I should be worried myself; I mean, who's to say that I won't start to exhibit symptoms? But that's not the point." She shook her head. "He didn't have to say it, but I think what must be truly torturing him is the possibility that he could pass this . . . thing . . . on to Tru. The thing is . . . I have knowledge that could possibly—no—certainly, bring Tom relief. But it would also break his heart."

She paused again, closing her eyes. "I love my brother very much. He is really the person I love the most in this world." She was momentarily lost in thought, absently biting her bottom lip. "That wasn't always true. There was a time when I loved my husband more than anything in the world." Her voice became sad and almost wistful. "But life isn't always kind." She made a rueful little grimace and went on. "For a very long time, I had no evidence—I had only my suspicions. Well," she sighed, and her shoulders slumped. "I suppose if I am to be brutally honest with myself, I would have to admit that I knew. It was more than a feeling. I think I knew. And after Tru was born, I only had to take one look. But I couldn't allow such . . . such . . . perfidy . . .to exist. It was too humiliating, too degrading." She shook her head. "And so I simply denied it. In fact, I embraced the denial. I employed it. I gave it a job. A big, important job." She enunciated the words slowly and then was quiet for a moment.

Caroline stared at her sister-in-law as the words began to make sense. She had a sudden vision of a framed photo in a box in the basement. She understood now why she had thought Whit Wells seemed so familiar. She sat down weakly, clasping her hands on the table, and remained silent.

Coco looked back at her with resignation. "You do understand what I'm saying?" When Caroline couldn't answer, she went on: "I have to give Whit credit—he never demanded acknowledgement, he never asserted his right. Whatever sins he may have committed, he couldn't allow himself to rob my brother of his fatherhood. Life continued as it had before, and we were all complicit: Whit, Margaret, myself . . . we all took part in a grand charade. Everyone but Tom. And of course, Tru."

She shook her head sadly. "But Whit left one clue—one sure piece of evidence that he never intended to bequeath so soon." She drew another deep breath, exhaling slowly. "When Harley read the will to me, I was strangely unsurprised. I wasn't bitter. I wasn't even resentful." She looked a little perplexed by this fact. "It wasn't Tru's fault. And the fact that Whit had provided for him, that he had taken this ultimate responsibility, seemed somehow honorable." Her voice became reflective. "After Whit died, and then . . . Margaret . . . I felt drawn to Tru. I had lost Whit, but part of him lived on. Of course, I couldn't let the secret out then. It was difficult, at times, to look at Tru. For years I thought about how I would explain it when he came of age. I could have said that a nephew was the nearest thing Whit had to a son . . . that it was only natural that he would want to leave something. Or I could have said that I had insisted, as Tru's aunt, that part of whatever was mine should go to him. I had prepared for the day. I was going to be convincing." Her words resonated with intent.

A resigned, pragmatic expression settled over her features, and she looked directly at Caroline. "So what do you suggest? Will it bring Tom more comfort to know that Tru is exempt from this hideous . . . curse that runs in our family, or should my brother be allowed to keep the innocence that he deserves?"

Caroline closed her eyes. She was staggered by the force of this terrible truth. Her heart had twisted into a painful knot for her husband—her dear, innocent husband. And layered beneath her heart-wrenching concern for Tom was her astonishment at the revelation of Coco's humanity. The bas relief of the woman sitting across from her had cracked and crumbled to reveal a flesh-and-blood human being, and Caroline was shamed by the indecency of her own preconceptions. It was almost as hard to absorb the tragic masquerade that had been her sister-in-law's life as it was to come to grips with the shattering knowledge that Tom had no idea Tru wasn't his son.

But her primal reaction was overwhelming distress for her husband. She felt a fiercely protective urge to find out the extent to which he had been hurt. "Do you think Tom has any idea?"

Coco was defensive. "I have never given even the slightest indication. I may be insensitive, but I've never been cruel."

"I didn't mean to imply that you would have said anything," Caroline apologized. "I was thinking more along the lines of his own . . . speculation." Her voice was dazed. "I don't know what I was thinking. He couldn't possibly know . . ." She stopped, remembering the point of the conversation. Would Tom now, after all these years, have to be subject to a disclosure that would destroy the foundation of his life? But which would be worse: the agonizing worry about passing the disease on to his son, or the agonizing discovery of a betrayal that robbed him of his own paternity? Her mind reeled. It was too much—she couldn't possibly be expected to be responsible for a decision like this. She understood why her sister-in-law had confided in her—it was a burden too heavy for one person.

Caroline shook her head numbly, wishing she hadn't had to hear any of it. Wishing it didn't exist. At the same time she was gratified that Coco had asked for her help. "I need time to think about it. I honestly don't know what to do." She put her face in her hands. Several moments passed, and then she lifted her head, looking gravely at her sister-in-law: "Thank you . . . for taking me into your confidence. I'm . . ." she wasn't quite sure what she felt, and for a moment she was tongue-tied. "I guess—what I mean is—I'm glad you came to me. I'm honored."

Coco took her leave in her usual abrupt fashion, any warmth or familiarity that might have been fostered by the conversation locked tightly away in the emotional vault where she kept all traces of vulnerability. As Caroline watched her pull away in her shiny black DeSoto, she realized that her image of her icy, unyielding sister-in-law had undergone a fundamental shift: Instead of intimidation and wariness, what she felt now was pity.

It was about three weeks into the term that Dinah turned a corner in the hallway and saw Tru walking in the distance. Walking with him, hand clutched possessively on his arm, was Lana Gervais. Dinah stopped dead. She was still standing in the middle of the hallway when Joan and Marlys came upon her.

"Hey Dinah—are you going to lunch?"

She could only nod as she moved mechanically to the cafeteria, lining up with her friends at the counter. Numbly, she pointed to the fish sticks and the applesauce as a heavy, hair-netted cafeteria matron slopped the food onto her tray. The doughy flesh on the undersides of the woman's arms jiggled back and forth as she moved, and Dinah was starting to feel slightly nauseated.

"Don't you think it's hilarious the way they list these on the menu as 'Deep Sea Dandies'?" Marlys was holding up a limp fish stick. "Who do they think they're fooling? Just call it what it is. You can't make a silk purse out of a sow's ear." She looked disgustedly at the crumbling stick.

"You mean a cod's ear," Joan grimaced. They took their usual spots at a long table near the wall and were soon joined by Betsy and their regular crowd—Susan Greer, Patsy Jenkins, and Laurie Kowalski. Nobody seemed to notice that Dinah was unusually quiet—likely because it wasn't that unusual. Within minutes the conversation turned to the latest gossip, which happened to be the earth-shaking news that Lana Gervais had broken up with Jimmy Wright.

"I heard there was a group of seniors at Melville's last night, and Lana was sitting in a booth with Tru Stuart," Joan looked quickly at Dinah, as though she'd just remembered their connection, "and Jimmy came in and tried to start a fight. Then I guess Lana went out into the parking lot with him, and when she came back she was alone, and she sat down next to Tru."

All eyes turned to Dinah, waiting for her to confirm or deny the story, based on her insider's information. She was trying to choke down a Deep Sea Dandy.

"Does anyone have an extra napkin?" She looked around innocently, hoping the sick clamminess she felt on her skin didn't betray a ruse of bland disinterest. Blocking out the rest of the conversation, she claimed an upset stomach and fled to the bathroom before lunch was over. Standing in front of the sink, she gazed at her reflection in the mirror, imploring the face before her to answer the obvious question: Why in the world did she care?

After school, she was almost surprised when Bill showed up to walk home with her. He seemed to be in an especially good mood and was whistling as they walked. He didn't even notice Dinah's silence as he chattered away about Chuck Connors leaving the Celtics to play baseball for the Brooklyn Dodgers. She didn't really hear anything he was saying, and when he finally paused for air, she blurted out, "Is Tru dating Lana?"

Bill's smile grew. "I'm not sure. I mean, it sort of looked that way at school today. She was attached to his side like a third arm. I think they've been spending some time together at night." He seemed inordinately pleased about the prospect, which confused Dinah. She had been given the impression that Bill didn't really care for Lana Gervais.

Attempting to sound casual, she asked, "Were you at Melville's last night?"

"So you heard about that, huh? Yeah, I was there. I think Tru may have seen the last of poor old Jim Wright. I guess Lana gave him a one-way ticket to Rocky Landing. Anyone could have predicted it, as soon as Tru decided to come back. That girl won't rest until she becomes Mrs. Tru Stuart."

Dinah couldn't breathe. She stopped walking, and she had to push the words out of her closing throat. "So that means Tru has been in love with her the whole time?"

Something in her voice finally penetrated Bill's euphoric mood and he became watchful. "I don't think so," he said slowly. He was looking at her carefully. "I don't think Tru has ever really been *in love* with Lana . . ."

Dinah felt her lungs expand.

"But she's a very, um, attractive girl," he continued haltingly, "and I guess if I had someone like that throwing herself at me I might be tempted to . . . ah . . . respond." His intonation rose at the end, like a question. He looked distinctly uncomfortable, but Dinah didn't notice.

"Why did they break up before?" She had forgotten to disguise her compelling interest, but in his relief to be on terra firma Bill was oblivious to it.

"Oh, you haven't heard that story?" He was smiling again, but this time it was in amusement. "Apparently Lana didn't think Tru appreciated what he had, or he wasn't giving her enough attention, or something like that. Anyway, she started messing around with Jimmy, and Tru didn't really seem to notice, so she took it a little further, and Jimmy started to think that she was his girlfriend. And so one night—it was at the bonfire—Lana was making a big scene with Tru, and then Jimmy came over and started to pick a fight, and he made the mistake of throwing a punch, which isn't really a great idea with Tru. So Tru laid him out, and before poor old Jimmy could even get up, Tru just looked down at him and said 'She's all yours,' and walked away."

Dinah walked for a while, playing the scene in her head. Finally she said, "Do you think that's why he decided to go to St. Paul's?"

He paused for a moment, and his smile faded. "I don't think so. I mean, if a girl isn't even worth keeping when you've won the fight, why skulk away?" Then quietly, almost to himself, he said, "No, I'm pretty sure that wasn't the reason." Abruptly changing the subject, he asked her what she was doing on Friday night. "There's a big home game against Centennial—they're undefeated so far, but we've only lost two games. How about we go to the game and then grab a bite afterward?"

"OK." Her response came out automatically, before she'd had time to consider the possibilities. She had been distractedly thinking about Tru and Lana, and now she suddenly realized that, with Stan and Hayes both on the basketball team, Tru was almost certain to be at the game. Probably with Lana. What if—God forbid—Bill would want to sit with them? Of course he would—Tru was his best friend. Then it occurred to her that Bill was asking her on a date. She kept forgetting that doing something with Bill would actually be considered dating. Did people consider them an item? The idea made her feel ill-at-ease. She hoped he didn't think of her as his girlfriend.

They were coming up to her house and Bill had gone back to whistling, a slightly off-key version of "Little Brown Jug." He waved goodbye, doing a little shuffle and spin as she turned up the front walk. "Plan on Friday, then! We'll go somewhere after—maybe Clark's or something."

Dinah nodded, forcing a bright smile. "Friday—got it. See you tomorrow." She turned to go inside, and the smile faded from her lips.

On Friday, Dinah woke to a raggedy scratching in the back of her throat and a dull ache in her head. When she sat up, the ache became a jarring stab, and she winced as she slumped back into her pillow. Eventually Caroline checked in to see why her daughter hadn't come down for breakfast. Testing the temperature of Dinah's forehead with her own cheek, she pronounced her confined to her bed for the day, at least. "You have a fever. I'm calling the doctor." There had been a polio epidemic in South Carolina when Dinah was five, and Caroline was still petrified whenever either of the girls came down with anything remotely resembling illness. But Dinah was diagnosed with the flu, and the doctor prescribed aspirin and rest. She couldn't believe her good luck—a ready-made, honest excuse to avoid going to the basketball game that night. She asked her mother to explain to Bill when he called, and crawled back into bed with one of the Dickens books from the collection Tom had given her—*Bleak House*. She opened to the first page, but before she could figure out who the Lord Chancellor of the Rag and Bottle Shop was, her eyelids had become lead weights, and she nodded off as the book hit the blankets.

Somehow, with the help of additional hours at the library, Dinah managed to parlay her days of infirmity into several weeks of virtual isolation. She avoided Tru around the house, keeping a detached, polite distance at meals, and timed her comings and goings to dodge even the chance passing. She was amazed at how easy it could be to live under the same roof and go to the same school and yet keep the orbital paths of two lives spinning in distinctly different galaxies. She had even started walking to school again, claiming she wasn't quite ready when Hayes pulled up, and telling Jemima to go ahead without her. The idea of Dinah being unprepared or late was so unlikely as to be preposterous, but the ride had become the highlight of her little sister's day—Jemima was far too focused on her heartthrob in the back seat to give it any thought. If Tru noticed, he wasn't letting on.

As intent as she was on avoiding Tru, she was almost as successful in her interactions with Bill. It was easy for a while to play the health card; even when she returned to school, she could claim a lingering fatigue to explain her withdrawn, distant mood. She simply didn't feel like talking. More than that, she didn't feel like hearing. When he caught up with her in the halls or after school, her attitude broadcast a message of discouragement with a crystal clear signal. There were no more invitations to basketball games, movies, or burgers at Clark's.

By March, most of her friends had given up on her. When she wasn't working at the library, she studied. She hadn't told anyone about her accelerated plan in school, but her friends noticed she was no longer in study hall with them. When they discovered she was taking an additional history class, she had to show her cards.

"You're going to graduate early? How did you do that? Can anyone do it?" The questions were mostly couched in tones of admiration, but there were a few subtle undertones of jealously as well.

"I guess anything's possible if you don't have a social life," Joan remarked at lunch one day. Dinah didn't respond—she knew Joan was right. Her pathetic mooning over something she couldn't have was taking a toll on her friendships and robbing her of whatever social life she had developed.

That afternoon she saw Bill in the hallway during sixth period passing, and decided it was time to come out of her shell. "Where've you been? I'm getting awfully bored talking to myself all the way home every day."

"I, ah, I thought . . ." He looked bewildered. "I guess I've just had some stuff to do, you know, student council and stuff . . ."

"Well, I'll be at the corner today if you happen to be going that way." She waved as she turned the corner to the science hall.

Like clockwork, he appeared at the corner, clearly happy to see the old Dinah again. As they passed the parking lot, she noticed a small group loitering under the basketball hoop. Hayes and Stan were playing with the basketball while several girls hovered around watching. Propped against Hayes's shiny black convertible was a distinctive, sun-streaked profile. A slender figure with raven-dark hair slouched across the fender, leaning against him. Straightening her shoulders, Dinah turned away, giving Bill her full attention. They chatted about the upcoming baseball season—Bill was hoping to play catcher—and she asked him about the latest student council plans. He filled her in on the Spring Bonfire, and when he asked her if she wanted to go, she accepted.

CHAPTER NINE
One Thing

THE MORNING WAS BLEAK AND COLD. A grey blanket sprawled across the sky, covering the earth, not with a flannel warmth, but with the damp chill of canvas barn tarp. Dinah knew that Bill and the rest of the student council had been hoping for a warm night for the bonfire, but fortunately the dance and the refreshments would be inside the armory, so if it rained, they could forego the bonfire and just have a canteen. The armory was a large, Quonset hut-style building that had been used to store munitions, but during the war, Latcher Industries had built a big new factory that had its own storage facilities, and the empty building was now used for social functions by most of the organizations in town. The VFW maintained it, taking in a tidy sum in rent. The Salem High School student council had moved their annual bonfire from Collins Cove Park a few years before in order to incorporate an indoor venue for a dance.

Dinah's friends had been talking about it for weeks—the bonfire had the reputation of being a free-for-all, end-of-the-year celebration that had none of the formal propriety of Prom and all of the reckless abandon of a final send-off for the seniors. The chaperones tried to maintain a semblance of vigilance, but they were inevitably thwarted by the nature of the beast: bonfires take place outdoors, away from scrutiny and policing eyes, offering dark corners and infinite opportunity for privacy.

Bill had to spend much of the afternoon setting up. He and the others on the student council erected an enormous pyre, donated by Stuart Lumber, which accommodatingly delivered a truckload of scrap each year. The threat of rain had dissipated, but the air was still cool for April. They draped the requisite crepe paper streamers inside the armory and covered the long, industrial tables with paper cloths.

Dinah spent the day at Betsy's, trying to make up for her spotty record. She was finding that there were redeeming qualities to the banality of girl talk—a relaxing, mind-numbing break from the relentless tyranny of her own thoughts. They listened to records, painted their nails, and did each other's hair. "Dinah, are you going to wear that ponytail again tonight?" Joan asked skeptically.

She hadn't given it any thought. Her hair was longer than the other girls'—she just didn't like going to the beauty parlor, and she hated the idea of sleeping on rollers. Wearing it back every day was easy—it kept it out of her face and she didn't have to worry about the style. She shrugged. "I guess I could wear it down. It's gotten kind of long . . . I don't know."

"If I looked like Dinah I wouldn't have to bother with a permanent wave or help from Revlon," Betsy said. "Think of all the money I'd save . . . "

"But she's not taking full advantage of the possibilities!" Laurie took a few steps back and regarded Dinah, tapping a finger to her lips as though she were a film director considering the *mise-en-scène*. "I know! Let me wash it, and then we can set it in big rollers and give you the 'Veronica Lake'." Laurie had all the fan magazines; she made a study of the latest hairstyles from Hollywood.

Dinah became their pet project. The girls buzzed around her like worker bees in the hive, bringing her their nectar in the form of lipstick, mascara, and perfume.

"What are you planning to wear tonight?" Betsy got into the *Pygmalion* spirit, opening her closest and pulling out a pale aqua-blue sweater. "This would look great with your skin tone and your eyes."

As they primped and groomed, Dinah was beginning to enjoy the game. She knew she wasn't as fashion-conscious as most of her friends, and she had never really worn make-up, so she was happy to let them try to reinvent her for the night, curious to see if she would feel a difference.

By the time they had all taken turns applying each other's make-up and trying on everyone else's clothes, Mike MacEvoy called up the stairs. "Do you gals still want a ride to the armory? The bus is leaving in five minutes!" They piled down the stairs, squeezing into Mike's old Mercury coupe. "Holy smokes, you ladies look like a million bucks! I thought this was a bonfire."

Betsy rolled her eyes at her father. "This is perfectly appropriate bonfire attire. Scootch over, Patsy, you're sitting on my skirt."

Mike chuckled at the obvious effort that had gone into the preparations, shaking his head. "What time should I pick you girls up?"

"Don't worry, Daddy. We can find rides home."

"I have a ride with Bill," Dinah offered. "He can take a few more, if any of you need him to."

"Why don't you just get a lift home with your brother?" Susan's voice was teasing, and the other girls jumped on the wagon.

"Yeah, Dinah, he could give us all a ride . . . I'm sure Lana wouldn't mind."

"I'd take a ride with Tru any day. What's it like living with a movie star? Does he sing in the shower?"

Dinah looked out the window, shrugging with the contrived nonchalance she had come to perfect. "I don't know—he's gone a lot. I've never heard him singing. I've heard him whistle, though." She saw him coming out of the library with the car keys, whistling the blues, on the night of the Red Barn.

Marlys laughed. "Do you come when he whistles? I know I would!" There was loud laughter.

"Marlys, I'm sure you would bark, sit, and roll over, but c'mon; it's her stepbrother for God's sake!"

Mike MacEvoy looked like he would rather be in the car with a pack of hungry wolves. "You girls mind your manners now. I'm expecting you all to comport yourselves like the ladies you are. You certainly look the part, now be sure to act it." He pulled up to the armory, and the girls slid out and into the flow of classmates streaming through the doors.

There was a large group congregating around the record player. Bill was standing behind it, shuffling through a stack of records. Some of the kids went directly out the back to wait for the lighting of the bonfire. Bill looked up as Dinah approached the table, the record in his hand hovering over the empty turntable as it spun around. He seemed to have forgotten he was holding it. "Well hello there." He gave a low whistle. "You look . . ." He was manifestly rattled. "Wow. You look nice. I like your hair."

Dinah had been pleased with Laurie's handiwork—her hair gleamed from about a thousand brush strokes. It lay sleekly over her shoulders like panels of ivory satin, and was parted on the side so the front section draped across her face like a partially closed curtain. She felt exotic and mysterious. Maybe it was worth the effort, she thought. "Thanks! What do you have there?"

Bill held up the record—Benny Goodman. "I'm on first shift here. Want to help?"

They took turns making selections, and after a while Joey Fetzer came up and asked Dinah to dance. Bill grinned. "Try not to step on her feet, Shorty." Joey only came up to Dinah's nose, but his lack of height didn't seem to bother him, and he wore his nickname proudly.

After she danced with Joey, Hayes twirled her around to Miller's swinging trombone playing "In the Mood." She was having fun, but Bill looked bereft, standing alone at the record player, and when the song ended she passed up another dance to keep him company. Eventually Pam Morton came up to relieve Bill from his shift, but before she took over he replaced the record that was playing with Billie Holiday, skipping ahead to the last track—"Night and Day." He held a hand out to Dinah. "May I?"

He pulled her onto the dance floor with an awkward little jerk, tentatively placing his right arm around her back. Dinah was nervously uncomfortable as they danced—he was holding her more closely than she wanted him to, and his hand was slightly sweaty in hers. He swayed her back and forth, humming a little in her ear as she kept her face turned to the side. As the song ended, Bill leaned his face toward hers, and with a small clutch of panic Dinah thought he might try to kiss her, but she was saved by a sudden commotion: "They're lighting the fire!" a loud voice called, and a crush of bodies moved toward the door.

Dinah looked around as they followed the crowd, wondering if somehow she could have missed seeing Tru. Since her arrival she had been covertly watching the door, but she hadn't seen him anywhere. For that matter, she hadn't seen Lana either. As they passed the refreshments table, one of Bill's fellow student council members waved at Bill, motioning him over. He held out two glasses of punch. "Get it while it's hot, comrade," he said out of the side of his mouth. Bill winked at him and took the glasses, handing one to Dinah.

"Great work, my man. How did you manage to pass the Gestapo?"

"We planted it earlier today." He looked proud as his voice took on a conspiratorial whisper: "This here community punch bowl is pure as mother's milk . . . but that," he nodded toward the reserve bowl on the back table, "is not what it may seem."

They joined the kids around the fire, cheering as the flames roared up the towering structure. The students were rowdy, and some of them starting singing loudly. Separated from Bill by the boisterous crowd, Dinah found herself standing among a group of people she didn't really know. The warmth of the bonfire was a welcome cloak against the cold night air, and she drew close. She was relieved to see a familiar face as Patsy approached her carrying two glasses of punch, giggling and tripping a little so it sloshed over the edges.

"This is the very best punch ever! You musht have some." She thrust one of the dripping glasses at Dinah, sounding like she had sampled a fair amount.

Dinah wondered how long it would be before one of the chaperones tried some of the reserve batch. She was gazing into the flames, feeling a warm, relaxed glow, when she noticed a group coming out the back door. Stan and Carol came through first, followed by Lana, who was carrying a large handbag. She was wearing Tru's letter sweater, pushed up at the sleeves. She and Carol greeted their friends loudly, relishing their grand entrance and responding to clamorous inquiries with coy allusions to a visit to the Cove.

Dinah could not take her eyes off the door. She was on the opposite side of the bonfire, but she had a clear view, and after a minute or so a familiar figure filled the frame, pausing for a moment as he looked out at the flames. As if by homing instinct, his eyes landed immediately on Dinah, and he stood still in the doorway. As she met his gaze, he ran his eyes over her hair, her face, her clothes. His lips parted unconsciously and his chin tilted back—a slow-motion flinch—as though the vision of her in the firelight caused him pain.

Dinah felt like the essence was being pulled from her body—drawn to him like a ghost through the night air. She was transfixed; she didn't even notice Bill at her side until she felt something on her shoulders and realized that he was giving her his coat. She jumped a little, startled out of the moment.

"It's pretty chilly out here—I thought you could use a jacket." He seemed innocently unaware of the exchange, and when Dinah looked back at the doorway, Tru was gone. The glass slipped in her hand; she jerked to catch it.

"Thanks . . . it's not so bad here by the fire." As if to prove her psyche conflicted, she suddenly felt a shivering chill. She slipped her arms into the jacket sleeves. Looking back into the flames, her hand systematically brought the punch to her mouth, and within a minute the glass was empty. Someone from the student council was calling to Bill to come back in and help with the music.

"Do you want to come inside? I have to play records again." He looked at her hopefully, but she couldn't bring herself to go with him. She assumed that Tru had turned around and gone back inside.

"I think I'll stay out here for a while." In a lucky stroke of timing, Betsy sidled up and handed Dinah another glass of punch.

"Here, my dear. Better take it—it's the last of the good stuff. Gustafson just made the taste-testing rounds, and it looks like we're back to Kool-Aid for the duration."

Joan and Patsy wandered over, and Bill reluctantly left them to take his shift at the turntable. The girls huddled by the fire, their giggles becoming louder with each sip. Dinah scanned the crowd, but in the hordes of kids mingling around the bonfire, she couldn't tell if Tru or his group were outside. After a while, her glass was empty again, and she was starting to feel sick. "I'll be back in a little while," she mumbled, swaying slightly as she moved away from the fire. She felt a sudden need to walk—whatever was in the punch had taken a little time to kick in, but it was now coursing through her veins with an insistent throb. Her head felt numb and her stomach was queasy. She moved along the periphery, the mob of figures blending together as in a surrealist painting. One thought became fixed in her mind—she had to get away from the loud voices and jostling bodies. Carefully, she put one foot in front of the other, picking her way across the dark lawn, moving arbitrarily in any direction that would give her some distance from the crowd. There was a grove of trees off to the side. As she neared it she could hear voices, and a small group of people came into focus.

"Oh, Laa-na?" The summons was sing-song. "How about you open up your magic satchel and share some of that giggle-juice?" It was the unmistakable voice of Sally Vecchi. Dinah could see the silhouette of a girl holding out a glass. She stumbled to a stop, gazing dumbly at the group.

"Hey Tru—isn't that your sister? It looks like she's lost." Dinah recognized Stan's friendly voice. "Come on over here, Dinah! We're having our own private party."

Horrified, she spun around and hurried in the other direction, hoping they would think she hadn't seen them. The last thing she needed was an encounter with the Sinisters, or worse, with Lana and Tru. Blindly, she rushed toward a distant line of trees, wanting to become invisible. As she ducked into the thick arboreal cover, she could hear water rushing. The sound drew her forward. After picking her way a short distance through thick underbrush, she came across a creek running through the woods. Moonlight glinted off water, illuminating a swollen turbulence that barreled past, breaking over rocks and fallen logs. The heavy snows of the past winter had provided excess run-off that was still gorging the streams and rivers in the area, weeks after the final melt.

She watched the rampaging flow, feeling completely hidden and solitary, enveloped by the curtain of trees, covered by the blanket of night, and singularly privy to the thrilling drama of nature's performance. It was a little frightening. She knew that only a small distance away there was a throng of people—she could hear their muted voices over the rush of the water—but she felt completely alone.

A fallen tree spanned almost the width of the creek, its branches hanging down to divide the furious water racing past. The white, foamy spray leaped up to slap at the old bark, punishment for getting in the way. As the water splashed, the reflecting light revealed a shiny, glinting object dangling from one of the tree limbs. Dinah peered through the darkness, trying to discern what it was. The harder she looked, the harder it was to see. She was becoming fascinated, like a hypnotist's subject, powerless to look away from the swaying watch. The object was moving a little, pushed repeatedly into a crevice in the limb with malicious smacks from the bullying water, only to fight its way back out again. In her punch-muddled state, Dinah followed a compelling urge to get closer—it was imperative that she have a better vantage.

The toppled old tree felt as solid as a wharf pier under her hand—an immovable fortress that could staunchly withstand the unrelenting onslaught of the current, obdurate and unyielding. She sat down on the thick trunk, rubbing a hand over the rough bark—she liked the feel of it under her hand. She felt at one with nature, with the night. If she moved just a little farther forward, she could lean down onto the trunk to better see the mysterious token. She was reminded of the scavenger hunts that her father used to send her on, and in a moment of intoxicated wishful thinking she wondered if his spirit had somehow put this thing here for her to find.

She leaned down to lay her cheek on the bark, feeling an urge to stretch her whole body along the length of the tree, the absurd idea that she could magically become part of nature—a petrified wooden form that used to be a girl, but was now both vegetable and immutable—filling her mind. The tree was surprisingly warm, as if it had energy flowing through its core. She put her arms around it, just able to reach around the circumference. Closing her eyes for a moment, she thought she heard a twig snap, and then footsteps in the underbrush. As she opened her eyes, there was a creaking shift beneath her. With an inconceivably instantaneous groan the mighty trunk flipped in the coursing water, bucking her off like an awakened Brahma bull.

The fury of the freezing current snatched her tumbling body from the edge of the bank, scraping a gash in her leg as she was pulled across the rocks and sticks in her path. She felt a dull thud as her head glanced off something hard. She tried to lift her face, but something grabbed her, and the rush of the water pushed over her as she was held in the underwater grip of some ancient root or gnarled, lodged branch. She couldn't move her arms—the heavy, saturated wool of Bill's letterman's jacket had the effect of shackles, even if the shock of the frigid temperature hadn't rendered her virtually paralyzed. A slow bubble escaped her mouth and she opened her eyes, but before she could register the inability to see, she felt herself being lifted up and out of the icy, inky darkness. Someone was in the water, pulling her out of the surge, struggling to hold onto the toppled aspen whose limb had snagged her.

She gasped for breath, drinking in precious air with ragged, strangled gulps. There was an arm wedged around her middle and she folded across it like a hinged doll. Reaching solid earth, both bodies fell to the ground. Dinah continued to cough and gasp.

As her lungs filled with air, she had an uncontrollable urge to throw up; she rolled over, propping herself up on her arms just in time to regurgitate a swill of creek water and gin punch. Once her stomach had emptied, a strange lethargy covered her like a cowl. She drew back, sitting on her heels for a fleeting second, and then crumpled sideways.

She was in Beaufort, lying in the swinging hammock, idly watching the clouds form animal shapes. But it was cold—much too cold for Beaufort. She was shivering, and then a warm breeze brushed her face. The breeze smelled sweet, with a hint of cherry. She breathed in deeply, inhaling the scent. The breeze had a nice, low voice. It was saying her name, over and over. It didn't sound like her father's voice, although there was a similar quality . . . something in the way he said her name, like he was holding it in the palm of his hand. She smiled. She hadn't seen her father for a long time. She was trying to remember the last time; he was wearing his uniform and he leaned down to kiss her goodbye . . . *ouch!* Her eyes flew open with the sting of a slap on her cheek.

Dark coffee eyes stared intensely into hers. She stared back, motionless and confused. The voice spoke again. "Dinah." His mouth was inches away, and the word came out like a sigh.

She only knew one thing to say. She only knew one thing. "Tru."

"Well look what we have here!" Sally Vecchi strode through the trees, Lana one step behind her. They drew up next to the wet bodies. Lana's arms were folded across her chest, while Sally struck a casual, spectator's pose, hands on her hips. "Is this what you'd call *brotherly love?*" Sally's nasal, high-pitched voice cut through the night like a buzz saw.

Tru looked up at them blankly. Lana cleared her throat, looking pointedly at the position of Tru's body, which was propped on his elbows over Dinah's sodden, disheveled form.

Sally continued her harangue: "Did your little sister try to drown herself? We didn't know she was having problems."

He pushed himself up, resting on one knee. "It was an accident. I need to take Dinah home." He stood, then leaned down and took Dinah's hand, pulling her to her feet.

"We don't mind making a stop on the way to Clark's—do we, Lana?" That adenoidal, rankling voice again. Dinah was starting to wonder if Sally did all the talking for her friend.

"I don't know." Tru's words were clipped as he looked down at his soaking clothes. "I think I've had enough."

"You'll be fine." Lana actually spoke. "The others have already left—they're expecting us to meet them. I told them you could give Sally a ride, too." She was insistent. "You can run in and change when we drop her off."

Like a bag of trash, Dinah thought.

Tru's jaw clenched and he tilted his face toward Dinah. "Are you all right?" She nodded weakly. He turned away from the other girls without a word, gently guiding her forward with a hand on her back.

He led them in a circuitous route, intentionally avoiding the crowd still at the bonfire. Lana and Sally walked a few paces behind, giggling and talking under their breaths. Dinah walked next to Tru, shivering and dripping, and she couldn't help being disappointed when he dropped his arm to his side.

When they got to the car, Lana walked quickly to the passenger door, sliding in and shutting it with a sharp slam. Tru opened the back door for Dinah, and she looked away as she got in, shaky and numb. The fact that she was in the back seat of a car with Sally Vecchi didn't even bother her—she was too cold to care. But as she sat there, watching Lana move over to the middle of the seat and press her shoulder against Tru's, she remembered the sound of her name on his lips, and she felt a surge of warmth.

Tru swung the car past the main entrance of the armory. "Sally—go in and tell Bill that I have Dinah and I'm taking her home. Tell him . . . tell him . . . " He seemed at a loss. He turned around, resting his gaze on her trembling frame. His words came out slowly as his eyes met hers: "Just tell him I have Dinah."

The lights were on in the library, and Tru quickly turned off the headlights as he pulled into the driveway. He got out, closing his door quietly and opening the back door for Dinah. A mocking voice came from the backseat: "Hurry up, Buttercup—we'll be waiting."

Tru leaned in after Dinah got out, his eyes as icy as his voice: "Sally, shut up."

Dinah was starting up the front walk, but he took her by the arm, pulling her around to the back of the house. "Let's go in this way." They went through the service entrance, quietly. Tru's hand remained clasped around her arm. As they entered the kitchen, a voice stopped them in their tracks.

"Hello there. What do we have here?" Tom was standing at the counter, making a sandwich.

Dinah froze like a criminal caught in the act, but Tru recovered quickly. "Um, there was a little accident . . . some of the guys were horsing around, and Dinah got pushed in the creek."

Tom looked skeptical. "What were you doing by the creek? And how did you come to join her?" He indicated his son's wet clothes.

"Well, I just . . . I wanted to help her out. It was stupid—a bunch of people got pushed in, you know, and I just wanted to make sure she was OK . . ." his voice trailed off.

Tom's lie detector was clearly going off, but he couldn't define where the lie lay. His face showed a combination of suspicion, disgust, and alarm, with alarm winning out. "That's really poor judgment on your friends' part . . . that water is freezing. People could get seriously hurt. Dinah, are you all right?"

Dinah's was still shivering, but she plastered on a bright smile. "Sure, I'm fine. It really was an accident—Tru was just trying to help. I just need to take off these wet clothes, and I'll be fine." She moved to the stairway, not wanting to look her stepfather in the face. His eyes followed her watchfully.

"I'm going to change, too." Tru's voice was brusque and matter-of-fact. "I have to take a couple of people over to Clark's—some of the guys are waiting for us."

"Not so fast." Having smelled a rat, Tom wasn't about to let it go. "It seems to me that this would be a good time to call it a night."

Tru looked like he agreed with his father, but he shrugged. "They're in the car. I have to give them a ride."

Annoyance flashed across Tom's face. "Drop them off and come right back here." He was unusually stern. Dinah felt a flush of guilt for putting Tru in this predicament, but she continued up the stairs, not knowing what else to do.

It wasn't until she got to her bedroom that she realized she was still wearing Bill's letterman jacket. It was soaked; little rivulets of water continued to drip from the sleeves. She didn't know what to do with all the wet things—she thought about leaving them in the bathtub, but she worried that Jemima would get up first in the morning and broadcast it. It was hard to think—her head hurt where it had been smacked, there was a cut on her leg that was bleeding, and she was still freezing. She went into the bathroom to run a hot tub, and brought a couple of towels back to her room. Stripping off all of her clinging, clammy clothes, she looked forlornly at the ruined mess that had been Betsy's aqua sweater. She would have to replace it—she wondered how much it had cost. Wrapping the evidence up in one of the towels, she shoved the bundle into the back of her closet.

With the other towel wrapped around her, she was starting back to the bathroom just as Tru came down the steps from his room. She stopped abruptly, self-conscious and shivering. His eyes narrowed a little as he looked at her, a slow smile playing on his lips. "I like your outfit," he said softly, then turned and went down the stairs.

CHAPTER TEN
Just Lucky

DINAH AWOKE WITH A THROBBING HEADACHE. She dreaded getting out of bed—not only because she had to deal with the small lump forming on the side of her head, the pile of wet clothes in the closet, and the certain inquisition from her mother, but because she wasn't sure how to act around Tru. Last night had been a disaster in so many ways, but then again . . . What would have happened if he hadn't followed her into the woods? Why had he followed her? It hadn't occurred to her to think about that last night. And then he saved her, and she could still hear the sound of his voice saying her name. What did it mean? Was he just watching out for her, like a brother? She thought of their brief encounter in the hallway. He certainly hadn't looked at her the way a brother would.

She had come down to breakfast expecting to face a barrage of concerned questions from her mother. A heavy fog of remorse had settled in her chest—she shouldn't have so blithely sampled the punch . . . and then sampled it again. Unaccustomed not only to the sick churning in her stomach but to the morose feeling of guilt, she vaguely sensed that her unusual recalcitrance had something to do with the fact that Tru was there with Lana, but she didn't excuse herself. With a subtle sense of dread she prepared to face her mother. She presumed that Tom would have filled Caroline in on the events of the night, and she would have to admit what happened. She had no doubt that Caroline would see straight to the truth, in the strange psychic way her mother had, and she also knew that she wouldn't be able to lie about it—that would just add to the burden of guilt. But when she came into the kitchen Caroline was humming over the frying pan, and Tom looked over the newspaper at her with a wink.

Tru hadn't come down yet. With every shadow cast by the shifting sunlight, Dinah's eyes darted to the kitchen door, but he didn't show. She ravenously devoured her bacon and eggs and, in a performance fit for Broadway, put on one of her best church dresses and a bright smile. Sitting through Reverend Stallworth's mind-numbing sermon, she wished it could actually numb her aching head. The day dragged on, and Tru was nowhere to be seen.

At dinner, Dinah managed to sound casual. "Aren't we missing someone?"

"Oh, didn't I mention it this morning?" Tom looked genuinely surprised. "Tru had to go into Boston for the day, to help Harley with his cutter. Harley's paying him to wax the teak and outfit a new sail before they put it in the water. He left before you got up."

Why hadn't they told her that earlier? She had been subjected needlessly to an entire day of jumpy nerves. By eight o'clock she was exhausted, both physically and mentally. It seemed like the day had lasted for weeks. Claiming a heavy load of homework, she crawled between the sheets and fell asleep with the lights on, listening for sounds of a car in the driveway.

For the first time ever, Dinah overslept. She scrambled to shower and find something to wear, and was hastily pulling her tan cardigan over a white blouse when she remembered what day it was—the start of recitations for the poetry unit of Honors English. She had chosen the Yeats poem her father had written in a letter sent just before his ship was hit. Caroline had received it just a week before they learned the news, and she had shown it to the girls with a private sort of smile.

"This is a poem Daddy first read to me when I was expecting you," she told Dinah. I was reading a novel with my puffy, swollen ankles propped up on his lap, and he was paging through a copy of Yeats, and he read this to me as he massaged my poor feet." She looked a little embarrassed, as though the moment was probably too personal to share like that. But she let Dinah read it aloud to Jemima, and although it was slightly beyond her twelve-year-old grasp, Dinah was pleased and proud that her mother considered her worthy of the honor.

She knew the poem like her own name, having read it about a hundred times since her father died, but she was nervous at the thought of reciting it in front of the class; not only was she the only sophomore, but some of the Sinisters were in the class, and the thought of having to read something so personal in front of them put a knot in her stomach. A horn honked in the driveway.

"Dinah!" Her mother called up the stairs. "Do you want a ride with Hayes?"

She hadn't realized what time it was—she hadn't even had breakfast yet. "No thanks," she called out her bedroom door. "I'm running a little late." For once it wasn't a lie. "Tell them to go ahead without me." Grabbing a piece of toast, she ran out the door and made it to school just in time for the first bell.

Her nervousness had changed key—from minor to major—as she waited for June Larkin to finish her recitation. June moved toward her seat, and Miss Arnold's gaze fell on Dinah. "Are you ready?" she asked. Dinah liked her English teacher; Miss Arnold seemed to actually enjoy her students, unlike most teachers Dinah had known. She rose from her desk and took her place at the front of the room. She didn't know where to look, so she stared slightly over the heads of her classmates and locked eyes with President Truman on the wall, a pointed and unwelcome reminder. Why had she accepted the opportunity to skip up to Honors English? She knew that Tru was sitting on the far side of the room, even though she hadn't been able to bring herself to look over at him. She hadn't been able to look around at anyone. She felt a little light-headed.

"Dinah?" Miss Arnold was looking at her questioningly.

She drew a breath, looking down at Stan Thompson's loafers. In a slightly shaky voice, she began to recite:

> *When you are old and grey and full of sleep,*
> *And nodding by the fire, take down this book,*
> *And slowly read, and dream of the soft look*
> *Your eyes had once, and of their shadows deep;*

Her throat had unexpectedly grown tight, and she had a sudden panicked feeling that she would start to cry. She closed her eyes and paused for a moment, then continued:

> *How many loved your moments of glad grace,*
> *And loved your beauty with love false or true,*
> *But one man loved the pilgrim soul in you,*
> *And loved the sorrows of your changing face;*

Her voice broke, and she couldn't continue. She hadn't realized that the memory of her father would overwhelm her like this. She stood stock still, and then turned to Miss Arnold with a look of bleak desperation. The class was silent, and seventeen pairs of eyes stared intently at this peculiar demonstration. Dinah could sense their anticipation—emotional displays such as this, if the inability to continue could be called a display, didn't happen all that often, and the students waited with undisguised eagerness to see what she would do next.

"That was lovely, Dinah," Miss Arnold came to the rescue. "What do you think Yeats meant by 'pilgrim soul'"?

With relief, Dinah found her voice again. "Well," she said quietly, "I think that a pilgrim is someone on a spiritual journey, like the pilgrims who came here from England. So I guess a pilgrim soul might mean someone who is on a journey or a quest to find the truth in life."

Miss Arnold smiled and said, "That's a beautiful interpretation. I can tell you've given the poem a lot of thought. Thank you." She made no mention of the omitted last verse, and Dinah made her way back to her seat. She couldn't bring herself to look in Tru's direction—she didn't want to know if he shared the same predatory enjoyment the others had.

Several other students were called upon to recite, but Dinah found it hard to concentrate. Her mind reeled with the mortification of her performance. She was replaying the scene once again when she was suddenly jolted back to class, as Miss Arnold called out, "Tru Stuart?"

Tru walked to the front of the room with his loose and easy stride. Turning to the class, he looked pensive, but not nervous—secure in the knowledge that they were all his friends. He had no arrogance—it had never occurred to him that he was admired. He was simply at home with himself. He was simply Tru. Miss Arnold asked which poet he had chosen, and he replied, "Robert Browning." He looked down for a few moments and then, as he began to speak, he looked directly at Dinah:

> *She should never have looked at me*
> *If she meant I should not love her!*
> *There are plenty . . . men, you call such,*
> *I suppose . . . she may discover*
> *All her soul to, if she pleases,*

And yet leave much as she found them:
But I'm not so, and she knew it
When she fixed me, glancing round them.

Dinah was motionless, moored to the unwavering, dark intensity of his eyes. She could sense that the class was transfixed by this exchange, and she lost track of what he was saying, too keenly aware of the scrutiny and curiosity of the other students. Finally, she looked down, unable to stand the acute tension of the moment, and as she focused on her folded hands, she heard him continue in a low, steady voice:

There are flashes struck from midnights,
There are fire-flames noondays kindle,
Whereby piled-up honors perish,
Whereby swollen ambitions dwindle,
While just this or that poor impulse,
Which for once had play unstifled,
Seems the sole work of a life-time,
That away the rest have trifled.

After this she heard no more. Her heart was beating a feathery, staccato double-time, which she feared was actually visible beneath her cotton blouse. He finished the poem, and if he was still looking at her, she didn't know it. She couldn't make herself look up. She was afraid she had misunderstood; she was afraid that she hadn't.

Tru's was the last recitation of the day; Miss Arnold adjourned the class when he was finished. Dinah was vaguely aware that he had answered some standard questions about meter and rhyme, but she hadn't absorbed a word of it. Browning's words reverberated in her head, and she tried to make sense of what it meant. Could it be possible that his gaze was inadvertent—that he hadn't realized he was looking at her? It was just so . . . blatant. A memory came floating back, and she saw the copy of *Twice-Told Tales* fall open to the bookmarked page. Then she heard Bill repeating Hayes Swanson's remark at the Red Barn.

She remained seated as the others filed out, becoming aware of her surroundings just in time to notice Sally Vecchi pass Tru in the doorway, giving him a look that could pierce steel.

Thanking the gods of baseball, Dinah walked alone after school. Since the season started, Bill had been at practice every day, and now she was relieved that she wouldn't have to face him to explain why she had left the bonfire. She knew the team had a home game that day, to make up for a rained-out game last week, and she carefully avoided passing the field, instead walking around an extra block on her way to the library.

She was also glad for the diversion of the library, welcoming the insularity and cloistered effect of the hushed, staid rooms. Every time she replayed the poetry scene in her head, her heart started to race. How would Tru act when she saw him next? What should she do? How could she be expected to live in the same house with someone whom she . . . whom she . . . She couldn't bring herself to finish the sentence.

The library was unusually empty—forsaken for an azure sky and a brilliant sun. Dinah was scheduled to work at the check-out desk, but Jane was there and she directed Dinah to work in the periodicals room, cataloguing new materials. There was a calming quality to the systematic work; she routinely filed and categorized, giving her mind a respite from the angst that had roosted there. Occasionally pausing to scan the odd interesting article, she moved from drawer to drawer of the old, oak cabinets, scooting along on a wheeled stool for the lower ones. She was about halfway through the stack when she came across the latest edition of the *Boston Journal of Medicine*. The words loomed on the cover: *Huntington's Disease: Why No Cure?* Sinking onto the stool, she quickly opened to the article.

Since the day he had broken the news, Tom hadn't mentioned his disease, and at times Dinah almost forgot about it. She didn't notice any obvious symptoms; he seemed to be free of the tremors that had plagued him at Christmastime. Her mother's mood had lightened noticeably as well, which Dinah attributed to the evident health of her stepfather.

She perused the article, forgetting to feel guilty about being on the clock. Struggling to absorb the detailed and arcane medical jargon, she was suddenly jarred by a passage that leapt off the page:

> *Huntington's Disease is a familial disease, passed from parent to child through a mutation in a normal gene. Each child of an HD parent has a 50-50 chance of inheriting the gene. Symptoms usually develop in middle age and include the degeneration of vital functions, such as speaking, walking, swallowing, and*

eating, as well as dementia. At this time, there is no way to stop or reverse the
course of HD.

Dinah was stupefied. A fifty percent chance of inheriting the disease?
Did Tru know this? Did Tom? She felt sick to her stomach. Dementia?
Loss of vital functions? When would this all occur? She couldn't believe
that her hale and hearty stepfather could possibly harbor this insidious
disease. What would become of her mother? Could there be a God so
callous, so vengeful, as to impose that kind of tragedy and heartache on
one person? One truly good and loving person? One person who believed
in a benevolent God, and who gave thanks to that God on a daily basis?

Dinah pored over the rest of the article, desperately searching for a glimmer
of reassuring information—something, anything, to indicate that not all
cases were hopeless. But the nearest she could find was the cold comfort of
the possibility of a slow demise; in many cases symptoms appeared over the
course of ten to thirty years. So she could pray for that, she supposed. But
pray to whom? What possible purpose could prayer have? It was plain to see
that there was no compelling evidence of any real effect. As she sat on the
low stool in the hushed privacy of the reference room, the circling doubt that
had flickered in her heart throughout a lifetime of trying to find meaning in
the obligation of Sunday services suddenly disappeared. The moth that had
been hitting futilely against the lamp flew away as the light snapped off, and
she realized with amazing clarity that she did not believe in God.

All the lights were on, and there was a delicious aroma coming from the
kitchen when Dinah got home. Caroline was in the dining room, putting
final touches on the table setting. There were candles and extra place settings.
Dinah was mystified. It was Monday—what could the occasion be? Her
mother looked up at her as she came in with a distracted and slightly harried
expression. "Run up and change, Sweetheart. Reverend and Mrs. Stallworth
will be here any minute, and the Koenings are coming too."

"Why are we having company on a Monday?"

"The pastor has a very busy schedule. I've been trying to get them here
for months, and this was a date that we could all agree on. Now scat—put
on something nice, and hurry back down here to help Gloria with the hors
d'oeuvres."

Jemima was coming down the stairs as Dinah went up. Dressed in her Sunday best, she tripped along with an exaggerated flounce in her step and a regal tilt to her chin.

"Mimer, I don't think you need to wear a hat for dinner. Or gloves." Dinah tried to keep the amusement out of her voice—Jemima took her wardrobe very seriously.

"Momma said I could wear my church clothes, because the Retheren Stallworth is coming. And this is what I wear to church." She sounded suddenly uncertain; Dinah realized that planting a seed of doubt about her little sister's wardrobe choice could prove disastrous.

"You're right. You look very nice. Everyone will notice how pretty you are."

Crisis averted, Jemima continued her dramatic descent, pausing briefly on the landing to see if she had an audience.

Dinah went to find something to wear, feeling anything but festive. She stood at her closet, dismally considering her choices, and as she reached for the ivory twin set, she noticed the wet bundle in the corner. She had forgotten to put her clothes in the laundry, and they had started to give off a wet, slightly moldy odor. Sighing, she closed the closet door, feeling a heavy weight on her shoulders. She changed her clothes mechanically, trying to put the information from the *Journal of Medicine* out of her mind. She didn't feel capable of being polite and charming to her mother's guests with such a heavy burden pressing down on her. As if summoned, the one-handed mover once again offered his gruesome consolation, and Dinah sat down heavily with the shuddering realization that her faithful old friend—the comforting device on which she had unconsciously come to rely—had finally met his match.

As she came downstairs, the doorbell rang. Her mother welcomed Martha and Walter Koening effusively, exclaiming her pleasure that they had been available on a Monday evening.

"Caroline, dear, we are simply delighted to be here. Wouldn't miss it for the world, would we, Walter?" Mrs. Koening noticed Dinah at the foot of the stairs. "Hello dear! My stars, you are lovely! Where does the time go? Caroline, this young woman gets more beautiful by the day! Such a stunning complexion! And that hair—it looks like spun gold! Isn't she lovely, Walter?

Dinah felt like a science specimen. Mr. Koening seemed to sense her embarrassment. "She is lovely, indeed. Does she have a name?"

Realizing Mrs. Koening was momentarily stumped, Dinah quickly introduced herself, hoping her smile didn't look strained. Jemima relieved her, appearing in the hall like a minnow to a morsel—as eager to welcome the guests as Dinah was reluctant. She curtseyed and introduced herself. "I'm Jemima. I'm in second grade. It's so nice to meet you—please come in." She gestured with a sweeping arm to the living room. Dinah and Caroline crossed their eyes at each other but the Koenings were charmed by their small hostess.

"How perfectly sweet you are!" Martha Koening was clearly delighted with the floor show, a convenient distraction from her gaffe in forgetting Dinah's name. As they followed Jemima into the living room the doorbell rang again, announcing the arrival of Reverend and Mrs. Stallworth.

The guests of honor were greeted with a fanfare fit for visiting dignitaries, and Dinah couldn't help a feeling of discountenance as she watched the minister accept his due.

They were sampling the canapés that Gloria was passing when Tom hurried in. "Hello there! So sorry! I hope I didn't hold up the party. We had a couple of snafus at the mill." He smiled widely at the group, stopping to lean down and kiss his wife. "A truckload of lumber destined for Maine somehow ended up in Delaware . . ." Shrugging, he proceeded to charm the room with his warmth and wit, and Dinah watched him with awe. How could he be so optimistic and congenial, knowing the grim fate that awaited him? She was almost bowled over by her admiration for his courage and selflessness, and she had to look away as he entertained their guests with characteristic grace. Her mind started to wander down the path of philosophical choices, and she was thinking about the concepts of determinism and stoicism when Tom's voice broke through her thoughts. "Dinah?"

She looked up, startled. "I'm sorry, what did you say?"

"I was wondering if you might know where Tru is. It looks like Gloria is ready to serve, and we wouldn't want to keep her extraordinary culinary effects waiting." He winked at Gloria, who was standing in the doorway.

"Um, no . . . I haven't seen him." A vision of Tru standing at the front of the class that morning flashed through her mind.

"Well, let's go to the table then. The loss is his!" He stood and gestured with one hand toward the dining room as the group moved to be seated.

Gloria was serving her exquisite beef Wellington when Tru breezed in, looking surprised to see a dinner party in progress.

"Hello son—so nice of you to join us." There was more than a hint of sarcasm in Tom's voice. "May I introduce the Reverend John Stallworth?" Tru strode forward to shake his hand. "And Mrs. Stallworth . . ." Tom made all of the introductions, with Tru obligingly greeting the guests and shaking hands. He turned to his father with a contrite smile.

"Sorry, I was at the baseball game."

"Why don't you go wash up—you're just in time."

Dinner progressed with the inevitable strain of polite conversation, with Reverend Stallworth holding forth on a variety of topics, on all of which he seemed to be an expert. Dinah was seated between Mr. Koening and Mrs. Stallworth, but she was saved from having to make small talk by their complete disregard. The adults chatted across the table, to the extent they were able given the Reverend's pontifications. Dinah focused intently on her food, trying desperately not to look at Tru.

As Gloria cleared the dishes, Tom cleared his throat in an effort to gain the floor, interrupting a rambling discourse on apostolic succession for American bishops. "Excuse me, would anyone care for a glass of port wine with the dessert?"

Both of the other men indicated they would, and Tom looked at Tru as he handed Gloria his plate. "Will you please go to the pantry and find three port glasses?"

The women preferred coffee, with Mrs. Stallworth requesting milk, not cream. Caroline turned to Dinah. "Honey, go tell Gloria that she should bring both milk and cream with the coffee service, and remind her to bring it out first, and then the dessert."

Excusing herself, Dinah made her way toward the kitchen. She didn't think about the fact that she would have to pass through the butler's pantry until she pushed open the swinging door and almost walked into a figure standing in the center of the small space, staring bewilderedly at an open cabinet of crystal. Tru turned toward her and they both froze. After a moment, he said slowly, "I don't know which ones are for port."

Dinah tore her eyes away from his and looked up at the shelves. She saw the short stems at the top. "It's these," she stepped forward and reached up, rising on her toes to grasp one from a high shelf. As she did, she tipped a little to the side, brushing into his chest. Instantly, his arms wrapped around her and his mouth covered hers. He kissed her with a deep, desperate hunger. She dissolved into him, a raindrop in a fathomless sea. His hand wrapped into her hair and he held her so tightly she felt her breath leave. He continued to kiss her, wrapping her against his body, drinking her in as though desiccated, unable to pull his mouth from the fountain.

There was no way to tell how much time passed—it could have been moments, it could have been a lifetime. It was the loud clatter of silver and the thud of a shoulder on the swinging kitchen door that penetrated their oblivion, pulling them back into earth's orbit with such a shock that Dinah released her grip on the wine glass and it crashed onto the worn tile of the floor. Gloria stood in the doorway, holding the silver coffee service on a tray, eyebrows raised. "Excuse me." She gave them a long, penetrating look. Shaking her head, she nodded at the broken glass: "You take this tray on out, I'll see about cleaning up this here mess."

Dinah and Tru stared at her blankly, and she thrust the tray at Dinah. "Go on now." She turned to Tru: "Get them glasses and skedaddle. You shouldn't be keeping your daddy waiting." She fired off one more pointed look, and the tray rattled slightly as Dinah took it and turned toward the dining room.

All eyes were on the doorway as she came out of the pantry. Caroline was smiling, but her eyes were concerned. "Did I hear something break?"

"It was one of the port glasses. It, um, fell off the shelf."

Tru came out behind her, holding three glasses. "Sorry about that—I should have been more careful."

His father gave him a peculiar look as he opened the bottle of port. "I thought maybe you'd gotten lost."

Tru shrugged apologetically. "I must have missed the lesson on wine glasses."

Dinah looked straight ahead and set the tray on the table to her mother's right, hoping that no one would notice her flushed face. Caroline looked at the tray. "It's nice of you to help Gloria, dear, but where is the milk?"

"Sorry, I forgot," Dinah mumbled, and turned to go back for it. Her mother's eyes followed her, squinting a little in puzzlement.

Returning with a small silver pitcher of milk, Dinah took her seat and a couple of deep breaths. She couldn't hear a word that was being said, but fortunately it didn't matter, because the adults were engaged in a discussion about local politics. She stared at her angel pie, unable to take a bite. She felt intolerably warm, and it was hard to catch her breath, as if she had just run a race. Finally, she raised her eyes and dared to look across the table. There it was—the source of the heat that covered her skin: Tru was staring at her with a look so feverish she was afraid the tablecloth would ignite. She almost gasped at the boldness of it, certain that everyone at the table must be aware of the crackling friction between them. But no one seemed to notice, and she was saved from her fear of impending spontaneous combustion when Walter Koening suddenly changed the subject, addressing Tru.

"I believe we have someone here who must have some college plans in the works, haven't we?

Without missing a beat, Tru casually joined the conversation. "I haven't really decided yet." His voice was even.

Tom looked at his son with affectionate exasperation. "Tru has been offered a football scholarship at William and Mary." He fairly beamed with the announcement. "I'm certain that he will come to his senses and sign on the dotted line any day now." Tom understood his son's reluctance to leave, given the Huntington's diagnosis, but he was adamant that Tru should not pass up such an opportunity, and he had taken pains to convince him to go.

"Strong work, my boy!" Mr. Koening looked impressed. "I used to play a little football myself. What position do you play?"

"I've been playing quarterback, but they may switch me to receiver. We'll have to see how it goes."

Mrs. Koening leaned forward, eager to join in the congratulations. "William and Mary is a fine school. Isn't that where Thomas Jefferson went?"

"And George Washington was a chancellor, if I'm not mistaken." Tom was incapable of masking his pride.

Everyone seemed to know someone who had gone to the college, and they took turns offering tidbits of lore while Dinah sank into a bewildered fog. William and Mary? Wasn't that in Virginia? Why hadn't she known about this? She supposed it was her own fault—she hadn't exactly invited dialogue about Tru over the past few months. But Virginia! She was shaken. He would be leaving again. It was already almost May. When would school start? There was football practice . . . that had to begin early. Would it be August? July?

She looked back at him, but he was still engaged in conversation with Walter Koening. Suddenly she felt an extraordinary fatigue. Everything that had happened over the past few days seemed to reach some sort of boiling point and she was utterly exhausted. She looked hopefully at Jemima, and to her vast relief found her little sister nodding off quietly, her head tipped toward her shoulder. Her hat was still held in place by the thin elastic band under her chin, but it had been tilted askew as her head bobbed gently against the back of the chair.

Standing abruptly, Dinah mumbled a hasty goodnight to the group, latching onto the convenient excuse. "I think I'd better help Jemima up to bed. It was nice to see you all . . . come on, Mimer." She almost stumbled in her rush to leave the table, taking her little sister by the hand and leading her up the stairs.

She was lying on her bed, still dressed and trying to study European History, when there was a soft knock on the door. Her heart thumped in her chest and she sat up, staring at the door. It opened to reveal the concerned face of her mother. "May I come in?"

"Sure. What is it?" Dinah's face felt flushed again from the momentary rush of anticipation.

"I just thought I'd come up and see how you're doing." Caroline came over and sat on the bed. "You seemed awfully quiet at dinner . . . I thought maybe you weren't feeling well." She looked closely at her daughter's face, putting a hand on her forehead. "In fact, you look like you may be running a fever."

"I feel fine. I was just tired."

Caroline studied her silently for a moment, and then said quietly, "Are you sure there's nothing wrong? I'm a pretty good listener, you know."

Was there something wrong? The question resonated in Dinah's mind, twisting its syntax to better frame the dilemma: *Was something wrong? Was the thing wrong? Was it wrong?* But she couldn't begin to speak her thoughts aloud, and she defaulted to her other pressing worry, feeling guilty about the convenience of it: "I read an article today at the library. It was about Huntington's Disease." She proceeded to fill her mother in on the details of the article, without an iota of satisfaction in her ability to quote whole passages verbatim.

When she had finished, her mother wore a sympathetic expression. "I'm sorry you ran across that, to tell you the truth. I think that, in some cases, too much information can be harmful. I don't mean in terms of research, but in terms of expectations and attitude . . . How can I say this?" She bit her lip in concentration, trying to find the right words. "Tom and I have talked about this at length, and we both firmly believe that one's physicality can be directly affected by one's mentality. You've heard the expression 'mind over matter'? Well, not to oversimplify, but we have decided that the best way—the only way—to proceed under the circumstances is to embrace life to its fullest capacity and not let this vile thing ruin any more—not a single second more—than it has to. It isn't denial, it's simply a refusal to submit to fear or worry. You could call it limiting one's losses, I suppose. We don't want the disease to rob us of life when it's good. And in doing so, I hope—we hope—that there will be a positive effect on his health." She paused and then looked at her daughter with a smile that was heartrending in its fragility. "It's the only way I can cope, I guess. Perhaps it is denial, but it's all I have. And I do believe that it could be years, even decades, before we have to . . . well . . . face reality."

Her face took on a cryptic expression. "As for the heredity part of the equation, I don't think you should worry about that. Please don't say anything to Tru about it." Her gaze went to the window, and she seemed lost in thought for a moment. Then she turned back to Dinah, her face still unreadable. "I can't explain why I believe this, but I want you to trust me when I tell you that it's extremely unlikely that Tru will inherit this disease. That's something you should put out of your mind altogether."

"But the article said . . ."

Dinah was cut off by her mother's uncharacteristic interruption: "Please—listen to me." Caroline's tone was almost urgent. "Put the article out of your mind. It is not your burden, and I don't want you to shoulder it. The best thing you can do for Tom, and for me, is to celebrate life every day and be grateful for all that we have." She leaned forward and took Dinah's face in her hands, kissing her on the forehead. "You're right, you don't have a fever. Get some sleep, Sweetheart." She noticed the textbook on the bed, adding, "You can't let your studies overwhelm you, or you'll have to cut back on the workload. Early graduation is an option, remember, not a requirement."

"It's fine—I don't have that much work. I just want to finish this unit, and then I'll go to bed." Dinah gave her mother a reassuring smile.

"All right, then." Caroline stood and moved to the door. "Goodnight, Angel. Sleep tight."

Angel. As her mother closed the door, Dinah heard the word echo in the room. It had been her father's endearment for her. Nobody had called her that since he died. It seemed to have come out of her mother's mouth lightly and naturally—a familiar sobriquet that bore no weighty implications. It sounded nice. As she picked up her history book, she heard a car pull out of the driveway. She knew that all the guests had left, and she assumed that Tom must be taking Gloria home. The clock read nine-thirty.

It wasn't until an hour later that Dinah finally finished the last review section on the Hundred Years War. She had been amused to read that the second half of the war, when France fought England, was called the Caroline War. She wondered if her mother knew that. Stretching, she got up to put her pajamas on, but decided first to grab a glass of water from the kitchen. Walking down the hallway she noticed that her parents' bedroom was dark, and she wondered when Tom had returned. She hadn't heard the car in the driveway.

There was still a light on in the kitchen. As she stood at the sink she could see her reflection in the window. She filled her glass and was about to turn away when a movement caught her eye. Someone was standing outside, watching her. Frozen, she peered through the reflection in the glass, trying to see. Then the figure moved into the square of light that fell from the window, and she had no trouble recognizing a form that had become all too familiar to her mind's eye.

Tru put a finger to his lips and then held it out and slowly crooked it twice, beckoning her to come out. Dinah turned and walked straight out the back door, still clutching the glass of water. Tru was in the shadows again, and as she approached, he took the glass from her hand and dropped it on the grass, where it landed with a soft thud. Then he took her by the hand and led her away, around the side of the house and across the lawn. Neither of them spoke. They had walked past several other houses when Dinah saw Tom's car parked on the street. Tru opened the passenger door and she got in. As he started the engine, the radio was playing softly; Nat

Cole singing "Nature Boy." Dinah leaned her head back on the seat, not knowing where she was going and as happy as she had been in a long time.

When they crossed the causeway onto Winter Island she was mystified, but content to remain silent. The only thing she knew of on the island was the Red Barn. Tru swung the car in a different direction, pulling up at a rocky stretch along Cat Cove, in the shadow of Fort Pickering. He parked the car along the edge of the gravel road and went to the trunk. When he came around to open the door for Dinah he was holding a woolen Hudson Bay blanket. Without a word, he took her hand and led her over the large, craggy rocks that lined the cove. The rocks were slippery, and Tru grasped her elbow firmly. Dinah could hear the surf gently lapping against the rocks. As they came around an outcropping she could see an enormous, flat rock illuminated in the moonlight. Tru jumped down several feet and turned to lift her gently onto the plateau. They stood for a moment, watching the play of the moon on the ripple of the water.

Finally, he spoke. "That's Jacob's Ladder," he said, indicating the pattern of light that made rungs of the waves, leading up to the sky. "My dad and I used to come here a lot." He moved to spread the blanket near a smooth, stone wall that rose up behind them, then, thinking better of it, wrapped it around Dinah. They sat down, leaning against the rock. Their hands came together again. Tru's voice was quiet. "After my mom died, my dad couldn't sleep very well. Even after we moved here. So sometimes he would get me out of bed, and we'd come out here and look at the stars. Most of the time I fell asleep, and a couple of times it was almost morning when we went back to the car. I got kind of used to sleeping out here, in fact." He looked into her eyes. "I haven't been back here for a long time."

Dinah felt like he was trying to tell her something. She wasn't sure what it was, but she felt like she understood part of it. "When my dad died," she replied softly, "we would go down to the river and wait for boats to go by. I used to hope that somehow he would be on one of them . . . that there had been a mistake and he was really on his way home. I don't really know what my mom was thinking—I guess she just liked the sound of the water flowing past." She paused a moment. "Maybe she was wishing she could just float away."

As she finished speaking, Tru very gently put his hand on the back of her head and kissed her. The kiss was tender and sweet—intended not to ravish, but to revere. But the instant she responded he was helpless. He kissed her with a yearning so intense that Dinah felt herself swept away, spinning. She returned the kiss with an urgency that shocked her. He moved over her, pressing his body against hers, and she felt as though she might burst out of her skin. As she moved beneath him, a whimpering sigh escaped her lips. Suddenly, he drew away, dropping his head onto his forearm with a groan. He took several deep breaths, and then looked back at her. "What am I going to do?" His voice was tormented.

Dinah couldn't speak. She felt like there was a furnace inside of her, and she couldn't think at all. She simply stared at him, breathing in soft gasps through her mouth.

Tru closed his eyes briefly, with a frustrated sigh. "It would help a lot," he said slowly, "if you didn't look at me like that." He rolled onto his back, staring up at the night sky. His hand reached over to clasp hers.

Finally, Dinah found her voice. "What about Lana?" She couldn't help it—she needed to know where she stood.

His eyes didn't leave the pattern of stars above them as he took a deep breath. He seemed to be choosing his words carefully, and his voice was strained. "I've never done anything harder in my life than try to stay away from you. And, obviously, I can't. It wasn't fair. I should never have let her back in my life. I just . . . I needed something else to think about. I thought I would lose my mind living in the same house with someone that I . . . that I couldn't, or shouldn't, have. It was stupid. It didn't work. I guess I never really thought it would." He turned onto his side to look at her, propping his head on his hand. "I've known it from the first time I saw you. I never even had a choice." He traced a finger along the side of her face, looking amazed at the sheer good fortune of being able to touch her.

"But you acted sometimes like you didn't even like me! I thought . . . I wasn't even sure you liked me . . ." her voice trailed off.

Tru laughed. "I didn't think I could have been more obvious. Not that I wanted to be—I just couldn't help it. There you were, just . . ." He gave a small, exasperated sigh. "Just, so . . ." He shook his head slightly, trying to find the words, but his vocabulary seemed to fail him, so he leaned in and covered her mouth with his. Then he tipped his head back and studied her face. "Just so you." He smiled softly. "I used to imagine what you would taste like. But I have to admit, I underestimated." He kissed her again, and then he became solemn: "And it looked to me like you were interested in Bill. God knows he's interested in you. And he's my best friend."

Taken aback, she looked intently into his eyes. "You're the only boy I've ever wanted."

He gazed at her like Galahad discovering the Grail. "You need to be careful with that accent of yours," he murmured. "It's a lethal weapon. I think you could tell me to walk off a cliff and I'd do it."

"I'll never tell you to walk off anywhere," she ran her finger over his mouth, thrilled by the simple act of being able to touch the slight lift at the top of his upper lip that she had always found so achingly attractive. "Where were you tonight?" she asked softly. "And why were you standing in the yard?"

"I went over to Lana's house. I had to tell her it was over. After what happened in the pantry, I knew there was no way I could keep on trying to fool myself. And it sure as hell wouldn't have been decent of me to keep on fooling her. As for why I was in the yard—" he gave her a wicked grin—"just lucky, I guess. You saved me a trip up the stairs. I was coming to get you."

They lay on the rock for a long time, unwilling to relinquish the delicious privacy of the night. Their shared experience of loss made conversation natural and easy; they talked quietly about things they hadn't shared with anyone else. Their connection was primal and innate—something they had simply been waiting for.

Driving home, Dinah couldn't remember ever feeling so happy—it was as if a piece of her that had been missing was finally fitted into place. She sat close to Tru, his arm around her shoulders, and she couldn't help thinking back on the signs and the rumors and the hope that had been whispering in her ear. Everything was true. Everything was Tru.

As they turned onto Chestnut Street, Tru pulled the car over and parked several houses away. He kissed her softly before opening the door and pulling her out the driver's side. "Are you going to leave the car here all night?" Dinah asked.

"I'll come back for it once you're inside. I figure if the engine wakes anyone up, it would be best if I was the only one in it." Dinah felt a little thrill of danger, impressed with his foresight. Her watch read 1:30. They walked silently through the yards, and when they reached their own backyard Tru picked up the water glass, now empty, from the grass. "If anyone hears you come in, just get a glass of water and say you fell asleep in your clothes."

As she took the glass, she glanced up at their parents' window. *Their parents' window.* The phrase reverberated in her mind, and she turned to him with sudden apprehension. "Is this wrong?" she whispered.

Taking her face in his hands he kissed her deeply, a slow, engulfing kiss that was both possessive and prostrated. Then he moved his lips to her ear and whispered softly: "Can't be."

CHAPTER ELEVEN
Dreams

THE FOLLOWING DAYS DRIFTED BY in a hazy dream. By unspoken agreement, they tried to behave as though nothing had changed. The subjective taboo of their situation hung over them like a sword. Dinah's imagination drew a parallel to the Salem Witch Trials; she couldn't help a shivery feeling of empathy. Tru continued to make himself scarce, spending most afternoons and evenings in Boston, working on Harley's sailboat, but maintaining the guise of indifference was an impossible challenge. Any opportunity for privacy brought them together like magnets. It would have been easier to avoid each other at school, but Tru had taken to waiting for her in a secluded alcove by the custodian's closet where he knew she would pass after fourth period.

One afternoon, as he was pulling her into his arms, a girl from Dinah's American History class happened to pass the alcove. Dinah didn't miss the look of surprise and discovery on her face. "I think people are starting to wonder," she said worriedly. "You *know* my friends saw you today in the lunchroom," she scolded. "You have to stop looking at me like that . . . in public."

"Like what?" he asked innocently. "Like this?" He narrowed his eyes and ran them down her body and then back up again. "Or like this?" He leaned in and kissed her with his eyes open, penetrating deeply into hers. It was a kiss of symphonic virtuosity, lingering with a sweet sostenuto that made her weak.

Her friends *had* been very curious that day as they waited in the lunch line. "Geez, Dinah, if I didn't know better I'd think your stepbrother over there was staring at you," Marlys remarked.

"He's clearly looking at me," Joan joked, vamping a little as she looked across the cafeteria. "Whoa! He is *definitely* looking at one of us . . . and Marlys, I don't think it's you." She paused a beat. "Or me." Her eyes narrowed as she turned to Dinah. "What is going on?"

Flustered, Dinah fought to control the color rising in her cheeks. "You're both imagining things," she stammered, but she didn't think she was very convincing, and she saw them pass a loaded look.

Now she drew away and looked at Tru seriously. "The other thing is Bill," she said. That morning, climbing into Hayes' car, she felt Tru's hand linger on her back as he pulled the front seat forward. Moving away, he slid his hand up and across her shoulders. As she looked up she saw on Bill's face an expression that left no doubt—he had noticed.

Tru swallowed, suddenly somber. "I know. I need to talk to him."

"You'd better do it soon," Dinah warned. "He already knows."

Dinah's uncertainty about what to say to her friends was put to the test that afternoon, as Betsy caught up with her after the last bell.

"Don't you think there's something we should talk about?" she asked pointedly.

Dinah didn't even try to feign ignorance. "Yeah, I guess so." She was slightly abashed, but couldn't keep a giddy note of jubilance out of her voice. "I, um, well, I suppose you're wondering about Tru," she began.

"Yeeesss," Betsy drew the word out, with a sidelong look. "I am definitely wondering about Tru . . . and you. Looks like Lana wasn't far off the mark, hmm?"

Dinah couldn't help smiling. "Lana must be a fortune teller," she said cheerily.

Betsy giggled. "Let's just hope she's not also a witch. I wouldn't be surprised if she had a Dinah doll in her bedroom with needles stuck right through the eyes." They laughed, but after a moment Betsy was serious: "What do your parents think?"

"They, uh, don't really know yet . . ." Dinah's apprehension was as plain as Nebraska. "There just hasn't really been the right time." She and Tru both knew the time would come when they would have to confront the issue with Caroline and Tom. Now, with Bill figuring it out and Betsy in on the secret, she realized that time was probably here.

"Look on the bright side," Betsy offered some consolation. "If Lana and her coven are anywhere near as wicked as they seem, you'll probably be croaking away on a lily pad before your folks ever find out."

When Dinah got home, her mother and Jemima were in the kitchen, practicing Jemima's spelling list for the week. "Well, hello Sunshine!" Her mother smiled. "And what has put that happy look on your face, may I ask?"

Dinah hadn't been aware that she was smiling. She seemed to be smiling all the time lately. She also wasn't prepared to divulge her secret quite yet. She needed to talk to Tru again; they needed to have a plan. For the moment, she dissembled, latching on to the first idea that popped into her head. "I was just thinking that I might like to have some friends over for my birthday next Saturday."

"Sweet sixteen! I was thinking the same thing. Would you like to have a dance? You could roll the rugs up and play records . . ."

"I was thinking maybe just girls. You know, a slumber party or something."

"That sounds just fine. I'll make my famous caramel popcorn, and you can invite as many friends as you like. Just have them bring a pillow—you can all pile on the floor in your bedroom."

"A slumber party!" Jemima's face radiated excited anticipation. "I love slumber parties! Well, I've never been to a slumber party, but I know I will love it. Can Fuzz come too? He's never been to a slumber party either, unless you count sleeping with me and Clang."

Dinah looked at her mother, imploring her to find a way to head her little sister off at the pass.

"You know, it will be awfully crowded in Dinah's room." Caroline thought quickly. "Maybe you should invite a special friend to come and spend the night with you in your own room. You can have your very own batch of caramel corn, and stay up late playing games."

"Can I invite Peter?"

Caroline hesitated. She realized too late that she had practically painted herself into a corner on this one, failing to foresee the obvious dilemma. "Well, honey, I think it would be best to choose one of your girlfriends. Boys and girls should sleep in different rooms."

"Why? You and Tom sleep in the same room."

The ludicrousness of social mores that trickled down to seven-year-olds struck Caroline, and she sighed. "When you're married, then you can sleep in the same room with a boy. Until then, I'm afraid you'll have to stick to inviting other girls to sleep over."

"Could I sleep in the same room with Tru?"

"Well, that's different, of course, because Tru is your brother. But we all have our own rooms here, and you have your nice, big bed to sleep in with Fuzz and Clang."

Dinah felt like the wind had been knocked out of her. She stared at the table, every private moment of the past days flashing before her eyes as her mother's words reverberated. *Tru is your brother. Tru is your brother.* She felt a wobbly flutter of guilt and uncertainty in her stomach. How could she ever explain how she felt? What they felt for each other? He wasn't her brother! How many times would she have to say it? She couldn't bring herself to look at her mother, afraid her feelings would be transparent. Turning abruptly, she lurched out of the room, mumbling an incoherent excuse about homework.

Baffled, Caroline watched her daughter hurry away, wondering what had caused her to rush off. She had started to notice that Dinah had been acting peculiarly lately, but she knew better than to try to fish it out of her. As she stared at the now-empty doorway a flickering thought hovered just outside of her consciousness; a faint, intangible breeze lifting at the curtain.

That evening Tru was home for dinner for the first time in a week. He was laughing at the table, teasing Jemima about her spelling test when Dinah came down the stairs.

"Well, I think you need to know how to spell *perspicacity* if you want to be the best speller. I mean, you are definitely in the top three of all the second-grade spellers I know, and *guardian* is impressive, but if you really want to blow the other kids out of the water we're talking *euphemism* and *pneumonia*, not to mention *vacuum*."

Jemima giggled, lifting her face toward Tru's and practically tumbling into his lap.

"Mimer, sit back in your chair. You're going to fall over if you're not careful." Caroline looked up as Dinah took her seat. "Did you finish your homework?" She was still curious about her daughter's hasty exit that afternoon.

Dinah kept her eyes on her plate, afraid to look at either her mother or Tru. "Not quite. I still have some English."

"I thought you just finished the poetry unit."

"We finished recitations and analysis. I'm studying for the unit final."

"Say, Tru, aren't you in that class?" Tom looked at his son with a glimmer of amusement, baiting him. "I haven't heard anything about a poetry unit. What poet did you study?"

"Browning." His answer was directed to his father, but his eyes were on Dinah.

"Why don't you give us a little sample of your recitation?" He grinned at his son, clearly enjoying the opportunity to put him on the spot.

Dinah's head jerked up, a look of alarm spreading across her face. Tru looked at his father evenly. "I don't remember it anymore."

"As I thought. I'm afraid the men in this family aren't particularly poetic." Tom smiled at Caroline, shrugging a little apology. "We have to make up for it in other ways." His eyes twinkled and he held his wife's gaze, so that she missed the exaggerated wink that Tru gave Dinah. She didn't miss the incarnadine blush that covered her daughter's face, however, and again the nebulous waft of intuition fluttered just outside of her grasp.

Managing to get through dinner without any more obvious visual exchanges, Dinah fled back upstairs as soon as the last dishes had been cleared. Since her mother's chance remark after school, a mass of dread had lodged in her chest, making it hard to breathe. She just wasn't able get a read on how their parents would react—she could not envision the outcome. After an hour or so of nervous pacing, she couldn't bear trying to work it out by herself any longer. She simply had to talk to Tru. Peeking into the hall, she saw a light coming from under Tom and Caroline's door. That would mean that her mother was in bed, reading. She had no illusions that Tom would have gone to bed already—he was always in the library until late at night. She didn't know where Tru was, but she hadn't heard the car leave. Closing the door behind her, she moved quietly toward the third-floor stairway. There was a light at the top. She crept up the stairs, moving to the far right on the fourth step and skipping over the seventh one entirely to avoid the squeaky floorboards. She couldn't help thinking that Tru's circumspection was wearing off on her.

There was no need to knock—the door was already open. He was sitting on his bed, leaning against the headboard, one leg bent with a calculus textbook resting on his knee, pencil in hand. When he saw her in the doorway a smile curved obliquely across his mouth. "Come on in."

He drew the words out slowly. "And close the door behind you." Then he rose from the bed, crossing the room in a few long strides. Before she could shut the door, he reached past her, pushing it closed as he pushed her against it, covering her mouth with his own before she could utter a word. "To what do I owe this honor?" he teased, when he finally drew away. He was leaning with both arms against the door; she was captive inside of them.

"I needed to talk to you." Dinah was breathless again. It was becoming a familiar sensation—he seemed to take her breath away each time they met.

"That's good to hear, because I need you to talk to me." He moved his mouth to the space just below her ear, tracing a trail of soft kisses down her neck, and the tingly, fuzzy feeling started to sweep across her body again.

"Wait—please. I really have to talk to you."

"What's wrong?" There was a tenderness in his voice that reminded Dinah of something . . . it was after she had fallen in the creek. It was the way he had said her name.

"I . . . I'm not sure about what we're doing. I mean, I'm sure about us, but . . ."

"Come here." He took and hand and led her to the bed, and her eyes widened. "We're just sitting down." He patted the spot next to him. "I'm not about to let you take advantage of me."

She had to smile. He could always make her smile—even now, when she was worried and confused. She sat down next to him, running her hand over the buffalo-check bedspread.

He picked up her hand, tracing his finger across the palm. "I thought something was wrong at dinner tonight. What happened?"

Her voice was halting. "I was thinking today that we'd have to tell our parents pretty soon. Our friends know, and pretty soon everyone else will too. But then after school I was talking to my mom and Jemima . . ."

Tru straightened up, looking at her intently.

"No—I don't mean I was talking about us. We were talking about other stuff, and Mom happened to say something to Mimer about the fact that you are her brother. It's just that I hear it *all the time.* Everyone seems to see it that way. You are my putative brother."

He laughed. "Well, I'm not your brother, and I sure as hell hope I'm not putative. What does that even mean?"

"Supposedly, you are my brother."

He placed his hand under her chin and turned her face to his. "Look. Two years ago we didn't even know each other. Just because my dad happened to marry your mom, it doesn't mean there's something wrong with . . . us. There's nothing wrong with us, and there's nothing wrong with this." He brushed his lips softly over hers. "Everyone else can choke on their putative opinions."

And just like that, it was all gone. The nagging doubt and worry disappeared magically, as she accepted his statement as the truest thing she had ever known. The gospel according to Tru. She felt like there was a light shining in her heart, and she wondered if maybe, just possibly, that could be God.

There was a woodpecker tapping on the enormous old chestnut tree in the backyard; the one that rose to the top of the house, occasionally scraping against a third-floor window in a storm. A third-floor window. Tru's window! Dinah's eyes flew open as she realized the woodpecker was audible through the window of Tru's bedroom. The sun was just beginning to stain the sky a salmon pink, and she sat bolt upright from under the weight of an arm draped across her chest.

They had fallen asleep in the same position where they lay talking quietly into the night. Nothing drastic had happened—Tru made it clear that he wouldn't allow himself to take advantage of the situation, literally wincing with the effort. Once, when their kisses had become urgent, he pulled away, looking deep into her eyes. His voice was barely audible: "Don't move. Please don't move." At times his restraint was called upon to serve them both, and at one point he laughed softly at her febrile hunger: "You are something. You're going to get us both kicked out of the house. Be a good girl and lie still." He shifted his weight, and they lay face to face on their sides. Dinah could feel the tension of Olympic restraint in the slight tremor of his body. They remained motionless, lost in the infinite space of the other's eyes. A lifetime of communication passed between them, and then a tear slipped down Dinah's cheek.

"You can't go." Her voice was tremulous. "You just got here."

"I just got here," he repeated softly. He gently wiped the tear away with his thumb. "Don't worry, I'll be back. As long as you're here, I'll be back.

But I can't stay here like this. It's too . . . dangerous." He ran his hand down the side of her body, ruefully following it with his eyes. "It will be easier for both of us. Believe me, I won't be able to stay away for very long. Just don't go anywhere." Then his eyes narrowed and a small smile tugged at the corners of his mouth. "Hell, go anywhere—it won't matter. I'll find you."

Now she jumped off the bed as Tru rolled over and clutched the pillow. She was tip-toeing out the door when she heard his voice, groggy and amused: "Nice of you to drop in. Do come again."

She was smiling as she crept down the stairs; when she poked her head into the hallway it mercifully empty. She slipped into her own room without a sound, heaving a sigh of relief and climbing into her own bed, still fully dressed.

When the alarm rang an hour later she could have sworn she had just closed her eyes. She stuffed her wrinkled clothes into the hamper, which reminded her that she hadn't returned Bill's letter jacket yet. Gloria had done a great job restoring Betsy's sweater—somehow the drenching it took hadn't ruined it after all. Thanks to the Sinisters, everyone had heard about her dip into the creek. She'd had to dispel the rumor that she tried to drown herself, but no one really seemed to believe it anyway. She had simply said she fell off a log, and given the pack of the punch that had been served, her friends accepted it as a plausible and not surprising outcome.

Showered and dressed, she was finishing her peanut-butter toast when Hayes honked the horn. She hadn't seen Bill since yesterday morning, and there was a nervous lump in her stomach at the thought of facing him. As much as she hadn't wanted to admit it, she knew how he felt about her and she was sorry that she might have hurt him.

Tru was coming down the stairs as she and Jemima came into the foyer. Ignoring Dinah, he swept Jemima up, spinning her in the air. "You must be lost—the Miss America pageant is in Atlantic City. That's down in New Jersey. Would you like me to give your chauffeur directions?"

Jemima squealed with delight, gazing at him like he must certainly have hung the moon. "My chauffeur is Hayes," she giggled. "You can tell him!"

As they got into the car, Dinah saw that she needn't have worried about facing Bill—he wasn't there. Tru turned to Hayes, a shadow crossing his face. "Where's Bill?"

"He said he needed to go in early. Something to do with student council."

Tru looked pensive, and he was quiet for the rest of the ride.

If the whispering, focused attention they received as they walked into school was any indication, their secret was definitely out. As it turned out, the girl from her history class happened to be the cousin of one of the Sinisters, and the news had spread like wildfire. But aside from the curious looks and low-level buzz, it wasn't too bad. Dinah figured they were probably somewhat protected by the enormous respect Tru commanded. She did have to weather some poisonous looks from some of the Sinisters, but Lana was nowhere to be found. In fact, it occurred to Dinah that she hadn't seen any sign of her for several days. She wondered whether she had been out sick. When she had asked Tru how Lana had taken the break-up, he was vague, only saying that it hadn't gone well.

At lunch, she invited everyone to sleep over for her birthday. "We can go for burgers first at Melville's or Clark's—my mom offered to treat."

"Let's go to Melville's, better malts, fewer seniors."

"Well, there may be at least one senior there. Will Tru be joining us for the slumber party?" Marlys looked coyly at Dinah, but the resulting giggles had a slightly nervous twitter. No one seemed to know quite how to act; there was an inherent awkwardness to the situation, and the reality of it made them squeamish.

Dinah tried to bluster through it, breezily dismissing the idea as absurd. "I don't recall attending any slumber parties where boys were invited." Remembering where she had slept the night before, her cheeks turned red. "I'm sure he has better things to do than look at fan magazines and paint his toenails." The image made everyone laugh and the moment was diffused, but Dinah was becoming aware of the delicate balance that would be required to walk the thin line that she and Tru had painted.

After school she went home with Betsy to help her with her math homework, and Laurie tagged along. "I will never understand polynomials, no matter how hard I try," Laurie moaned.

"Just remember the rule," Betsy instructed. "Add, subtract, or multiply, but don't divide, and don't ask why."

When they entered the kitchen, they found Mike MacEvoy pulling some cold cuts from the refrigerator. "Hello, ladies. Would anyone care for a sandwich?"

They sat around the kitchen table, eating and studying, while Mike looked on, offering whatever help he could. They teased him that he couldn't remember any algebra, and he pretended to be wounded, claiming old age and too much dust in the attic.

When he excused himself to get back to his own work correcting papers, Betsy turned to Dinah: "So, did you have any trouble with the Sinisters today? I heard a rumor that Lana refuses to come to school. Apparently she's pretty broken up."

"It wasn't too bad. Sally's as nasty as ever, but I'm getting used to her." Dinah felt a flash of pity for Lana. As hostile as she and her friends had been, Dinah felt sorry for her. She tried to imagine what it would be like to lose Tru. Her stomach flipped over. It had been hard enough just wanting him; now that she had him, she didn't think she could survive letting him go.

As she walked home, she saw a distinctive black DeSoto parked in the driveway. Dinah hadn't seen Coco or Harley since Thanksgiving, and she wondered what the occasion could be.

The adults were all seated in the living room when she came in. "Hello, Sweetheart," her mother called. "We'll be having dinner soon—Coco and Harley are joining us."

Dinah went into the living room to greet everyone. "It's nice to see you again." She stood there awkwardly. Coco and Harley had the strange ability to rob her of articulation.

Coco graced her with a weak, obligatory smile, but Harley looked as though he hadn't even noticed her. He was holding a small sheaf of papers, and he didn't raise his eyes from whatever it was he was examining. Dinah excused herself and went upstairs with her books.

When she had washed up and come back downstairs, they were moving to the dining room. The front door opened as they passed through the foyer. Making his customary last-minute entrance, Tru gave Coco a kiss on the cheek, and Dinah was amazed to see the woman's standard expression of bored superiority soften into a countenance that was almost tender. "The hometown hero has arrived! I've been told the news about William and Mary—an excellent school. You'll have to give my regards to

Chancellor Bryan. He's a personal friend. By the way, Senator Guilford's daughter will be a freshman there as well." She turned to Tom as they took their seats at the table. "You remember Frank and Mary Guilford don't you? I was at Radcliffe with Mary. Frank is in his third term now— representing Virginia. I believe he's on the Committee of Foreign Affairs . . . and another one . . . what is it now? Anyway, they have an exquisite daughter, Nancy, who is utterly charming." She looked pointedly at Tru. "You'll have to be sure to look her up."

Dinah suddenly envisioned a parade of beautiful college girls sashaying in a conga line to form a circle around Tru. Her expression was so forlorn that Tru laughed. "I'm sure she'll have plenty of other guys to charm. I'll be pretty busy trying to keep up with the studies on top of football and everything."

"Well, there will certainly be social functions that require an escort. Are you familiar with the King's Ball? The school has a charter from the King of England, you know. Every spring they have a magnificent ball . . . it's the event of the year. You'll have to keep her in mind."

Tru just smiled, and he was rescued by the distraction of Jemima precariously setting his plate in front of him. Caroline had prepared lamb chops, and, as was generally the case when Gloria was off-duty, the girls were enlisted to help serve. Jemima delivered the plates from the kitchen while Dinah poured water. She moved around the table, taking extra care to hold the linen towel against the sweating silver pitcher as she filled Coco's glass. She could have sworn she felt a distinct drop in the temperature of the room in the area surrounding Coco's chair. Subconsciously, she left Tru's glass for last, and as she leaned in to pour she felt the subtle pressure of his finger tracing a line up the back of her knee. It sent a shiver up her spine, which caused her to overfill his glass, sloshing icy water onto the tablecloth.

"How very clumsy of you," he teased, pinching her lightly on the inside of her leg.

Jemima was asked to say grace, and after she recited a simple prayer Tom lifted his glass in a toast. "We are happy to have Coco and Harley sharing our table tonight, as we give thanks for the gift of family. We are not a very large clan, but we have each other, and it is my greatest hope that our children will know how lucky they are to be blessed with the rich reward of a loving family." He gazed around the table as they all drank to the toast. "Remember," he added meaningfully, "the most important thing is to love each other."

Suddenly Tru's napkin flew to his mouth as he choked on a mouthful of water. "Sorry," he coughed. "I, ah, swallowed wrong."

Dinah struggled to stifle a giggle, looking down at her own napkin. They had just started to eat when Jemima piped up with her latest fixation: "Momma? Can I have a sleepover with Tru tonight?"

Caroline sighed. She should have known that yesterday's passing remark was by no means past—she was well accustomed to the single-minded determination of her youngest daughter. "Honey, I'm sure Tru has other plans for the evening. And he only has one bed. You don't want to sleep on the floor when you have a nice, soft bed of your own."

"I can sleep in his bed with him, like Dinah."

There was complete silence. It was as though the volume had been turned off in the room. Then, a quiet, nervous cough from Tru and a loud, honking burst of laughter from Harley: "Tru, old man, do you have something you'd like to share?" Harley looked positively tickled by the inconceivable horror of the moment.

Caroline's face was frozen. She seemed unable to comprehend what she had just heard. "I'm sorry, Jemima. What did you say?"

"I want to sleep with Tru. Dinah gets to."

Tom's eyes were riveted on his son, but Caroline looked slowly, almost painfully, at her older daughter. "Dinah, do you have any idea what she's talking about?"

Tru attempted to intercede on her behalf. "It's not what you think. I mean, I wouldn't . . . we didn't . . ."

He was interrupted by his father, who stood abruptly, eyes still locked on his son. "If you'll excuse us, I'd like to have a word with Tru. Caroline, perhaps you and Dinah would join us?" His voice was steely, and his gaze didn't waver as he said, "Jemima, I'm sure you won't mind keeping Coco and Harley entertained, will you? Please continue with the meal." With that he turned and walked stiffly toward the library without a backward glance.

Feeling like she was moving under water, Dinah stood slowly, placing her napkin carefully on the table. As she turned to follow Tru from the room, Jemima sang out, "I'd be delighted!" and Dinah couldn't help thinking that her sister had seen way too many Shirley Temple movies.

Tom stood by the library doors as they filed in, closing them soundly behind them. Tru and Dinah were standing helplessly in the middle of the room, unsure of what to do next. "Why don't we all sit down?" Tom's voice was calm, but it was impossible to miss the taut strain of tension lacing his words.

Dinah sat on the edge of a tufted leather sofa under the south window, and to her surprise, Tru sat down right next to her.

"It was my fault." Dinah's voice came out a little hoarse, and she had to clear her throat. Her mother was still standing by the door, with the stunned look of someone who had suddenly found herself in a strange, new land. "I went up to Tru's room last night to talk to him. I just . . . I just wanted to talk about something, and then . . . we talked for a long time, and I fell asleep. I guess we both fell asleep. It wasn't his fault. Mimer must have come upstairs during the night—we didn't even turn the light off."

Tom cleared his throat quietly. "I'm going to ask you both a question, and I'd like to think that you have enough respect for your mother and me to give us an honest answer." He paused, trying to form the language. "Do you have feelings for each other that are not . . . ah . . . that would not be considered . . . sibling-like?" He winced at his inept articulation.

Dinah turned to Tru, who simply picked up her hand. Neither of them spoke—the answer was in the deep, brown depths of his steady gaze.

With a sigh, Tom dropped his head, staring blankly at the Persian carpet on the floor. Then, remembering Caroline still standing silently by the door, he went over and put his arm around her shoulders, drawing her over to a chair. No one spoke for what seemed like a very long time.

Caroline's voice finally broke the silence, uncommonly tense as she fought to control her emotions. "I should have seen this coming. This is my fault." The pitch of her voice was escalating as her emotions took over. "But this is simply not permissible. We cannot allow any kind of . . . romantic relationship between you. It's . . . it's just not right." She struggled to find the right words, stammering a little. "There are too many reasons to even comprehend. Not the least being the utter inappropriateness of two young people living under the same roof in a situation like that. I can't even begin to list the complications." Her voice had grown more and more agitated. "You are step-siblings. You'll be thrown together for the rest of your lives." She took a deep breath, continuing in a more subdued tone:

"Think of the implications. What if, for instance, this would somehow turn into a serious relationship? What would happen if or when it didn't work out?" Bewildered, she looked back and forth between Dinah and Tru. "How will you bear being around each other? Think of the hurt, the repercussions! Think how it could affect our family!" She shook her head sharply. "It's beyond inappropriate—it's treacherous."

Tom picked up his wife's hand and gave it a small pat, signaling his comfort and support. "Your mother is right." He looked up at the ceiling briefly, as if he might find an answer, then sighed in exasperation. "You see, right there. That's the problem. *Your mother.* I was addressing both of you. We are a family." Tom looked toward the doors, remembering their dinner guests—waiting hungrily, no doubt, to witness the outcome of the extemporaneous tribunal. His words became clipped: "This is not the ideal time to have this discussion. Tomorrow your mother and I will have had some time to digest this . . . development, and I hope we will all have given some thought to the situation. We will deal with this in the morning. For now," he glanced again at the doorway, his voice sardonic, "let us resume where we left off."

They returned to the dining room to find Jemima charming Coco and Harley with an enthusiastic rendition of the Chiquita Banana jingle. There was a moment of acute awkwardness as the quartet took their seats, with Tom elaborately shaking out his napkin and Caroline brightly applauding Jemima's performance. The revelation hung in the air like the aftermath of an explosion, and it was clear that everyone was struggling a little to breathe normally through the dust. Dinah tried not to look at their guests, but she couldn't miss the look that Coco shot her way as she sat down.

Mercifully, in her role as entertainer, Jemima seemed to have forgotten her sleepover request. She segued into a description of her much-beloved teacher, and Dinah noted that her little sister had picked up Tru's penchant for amusing observations: "Mrs. Lifson has really neat hair. It's huge. And it used to be brown, but then she killed it. She killed it red, and now it looks like a giant raspberry sitting on her head."

Everyone at the table looked confused, except for Caroline, who had a mother's ability to decipher her child's meaning. "You mean dyed, Sweetie. She dyed her hair." Jemima just shrugged, not interested in drawing too fine a point about what seemed to her like semantic subtleties.

With the saving grace of Jemima's chatter they all managed to get through the rest of the meal, but Coco stood up as Caroline collected her dinner plate, declining dessert without ceremony. "We must be going. Thank you for dinner. It was both delicious and . . . edifying." She turned to Harley, who obediently rose, offering a similarly perfunctory thank-you. As they left, Coco paused for a brief moment as she passed Tru's chair, leveling a reproachful look at her nephew. Tom escorted them to the door, while Caroline stood silently by the table, staring at the empty plate in her hands.

Working as a team, Tom and Caroline did the dinner dishes. In light of the terrible strain of the evening, Caroline had excused Dinah, asking her to take Jemima to bed. Tru, pleading a heavy study load, had escaped to the third floor. At the sink, Caroline stared into the window, unaware of her reflection. Her thoughts circled around the magnitude of evening's revelation. It had been so obvious she could have slapped herself for not seeing it. She should have listened to her instincts—she knew there something going on with Dinah, but she hadn't been able to put her finger on it. How could she have missed it?

As she absently rubbed the back of her neck, Tom stepped behind her, resting his hands on her shoulders. "It seems that the handwriting on the wall was too close to read." He looked at her in the reflection of the glass. "I could never figure out why Tru seemed to continually avoid Dinah. I was worried that they didn't like each other!"

"I feel so foolish," Caroline said. "How is it possible that it never even occurred to me?"

"It's not your fault. I didn't see it either. I should have paid more attention. When Tru suddenly decided to go to St. Paul's, I thought it was because he was uncomfortable with the new . . . family situation." With an ironic smirk, he gave a short, bemused huff. "I guess that's exactly what it was. He was trying to save himself from . . . well, from himself." He shook his head wonderingly. "Looking back, I think they really must have tried to keep this thing at bay—that's probably why we couldn't see it."

"Well, it's out there now." Caroline's voice was bewildered. "What are we going to do? I honestly don't know how we can control this. I mean, certainly there have to be rules, but we can't mandate feelings. This is a disaster."

Tom chuckled, and then apologized. "I'm sorry, my love, but I can't quite qualify it as a disaster. If it is indeed the most disastrous thing we ever encounter, I will count us as among the luckiest of all people." He kissed her cheek. "Don't get me wrong—I agree that we can't allow this to go on. But you're right about the fact that we also can't regulate their emotions. Even if they try to follow every rule we lay down, one can't always rely on one's best intentions. Especially at that age."

He was momentarily lost in thought, and he tilted his head to the side, his voice speculative: "I hate to say it, but I think this may really be something. Did you notice the way he looked at her tonight? Tru used to have a girlfriend. Her name was Lana Gervais. They dated for quite a while. He didn't bring her around very often, but when he did, well, I can tell you that he never looked at her like that."

"I noticed. That's what scares me." She pulled the plug from the drain as she rinsed the final plate. "Let's call it a night. Things may seem clearer in the morning, when we've had a chance to sleep on it." Handing Tom the last piece of china, she thanked God for the strong steadiness of his hands. There had been barely a quiver for months; it was tempting to believe the diagnosis had been wrong. Tom had not yet spoken to her of any fears he had for passing it on—she had been holding her breath for the moment that he did, agonizing over her choice. She had vacillated, one day deciding that she would have to tell him—that sparing him the torment of worrying about his son would be the right thing to do—the next day burying her knowledge with the hope that Tom would cling to the idea that Tru had been lucky enough to escape the odds. The thought of wielding the knife that would carve such a hole in her husband's world was unbearable. No wonder Coco had unloaded on her—it was an overwhelming burden, and her sister-in-law seemed much lighter in spirit since depositing it on Caroline's shoulders. The vague notion in the back of her mind was that she would make the decision spontaneously, responding to her instincts when and if Tom broached the subject. And so she waited for the penny to drop.

At least Tru felt confident enough in his father's health to take the opportunity offered at William and Mary. She couldn't imagine what would happen if he wanted to stay in Salem—it was as though fate had thoughtfully intervened to provide a safe distance to protect Dinah and Tru from themselves. The Lord works in strange ways, she thought.

This led her to consider the change in Coco since hearing of Tom's diagnosis. She had become much more sisterly to Tom, and even civil to

Caroline. Of course, the fact that she and Harley needed Tom's power of attorney to adjust the terms of the trust may have had something to do with that. Their visit that evening had not been purely social—the loan Tom had given them hadn't quite made the stretch to the next disbursement, and Coco had persuaded Tom to speed up the process.

Accordingly, Tom seemed to have softened toward his sister since he learned of his disease. He had been patiently cooperative, telling Caroline that he would just as soon let Coco have the entire bulk of her inheritance at once, but their father, in a moment of prescience, had identified a trait in his daughter that had compelled him to schedule the distribution to his own satisfaction. There were parts of the trust that Tom simply couldn't revise—they were iron-clad. At any rate, Coco and Harley continued to enjoy a pattern of living that exceeded their means, and Tom had called them to come to the house so he could again give counsel on practical finances. It was a mystery to Caroline how a successful lawyer like Harley could be so completely irresponsible when it came to managing his own finances, and she couldn't help wondering whether he had, indeed, overcome his gambling problem. The meeting seemed to have gone well. Although Harley was his usual taciturn self, Coco was in rare good spirits, and Caroline was surprised when her invitation to stay for dinner was accepted.

Now she wished she had never extended it. Jemima's inadvertent disclosure couldn't have happened in worse company. She could not stand to have Coco's censure aimed at her daughter. Whatever contempt she had endured from her sister-in-law had been harmless—she simply didn't care what Coco thought of her. But the idea of this woman judging her child was unbearable.

Caroline turned and put her arms around Tom. "I feel sorry for them. I mean, it isn't as though they're physically related in any way. It's just the impropriety of the situation . . . It just can't be. Thank goodness for Harley's old cutter. That will provide some diversion, at least. June can't come soon enough."

"Tru's catboat is ready to go in the water, too, so that should keep him busy."

Turning out the lights, Tom stopped as they headed toward the stairway, pulling his wife into his arms. He started to sing softly into her ear—"Time After Time," their wedding dance. Moving slowly across the old marble floor, they danced in the quiet darkness of the kitchen. As he reached the final verse, the words took on a new meaning, and Caroline had to close her eyes to hold back her tears:

> *I only know what I know,*
> *The passing years will show—*
> *You've kept my love so young, so new;*
> *And time after time,*
> *I tell myself that I'm*
> *So lucky to be loving you."*

It was exactly 2:22 when Dinah looked at the clock. Her Westclox alarm had a glow-in-the-dark face, so she only had to open one eye to see the time. After lying awake until after midnight (the last time she checked it had been 12:12), she slept fitfully and found herself once again conscious and replaying the scene in the library. She didn't know what she had expected, but she hadn't been prepared for the shock and agitation in her mother's reaction. She dreaded the sunrise, wanting to postpone the family meeting for as long as possible. The clock ticked on, and the next time she opened her eye it read 5:55. She wondered if there was some sort of supernatural meaning in the weird synchronicity of the numbers, but when she looked again it was 7:15.

The smell of coffee announced the fact that Tom and Caroline were already up and in the kitchen. Dinah went down the back stairs, subdued and reluctant. Her mother's smile was gentle and disarming as Dinah poured a glass of juice, and Tom gave her arm a little pat as he brushed past her to pour another cup.

After a sprinkling of rather stilted small talk over their coffee and juice, Tru appeared, looking as if he hadn't slept very well either. His hair was disheveled and his T-shirt, although clean and pressed, was inside out. But despite the bleary look in his eyes, he crossed the room purposefully and sat down next to Dinah. Saying nothing to Tom or Caroline, he picked up her hand very deliberately and held it in his, resting them both on his leg. Then he simply sat back and looked at their parents.

"Well," Tom cleared his throat, "it looks like we're all here. It seems like this might be a good time to take up where we left off last night, while Jemima is still upstairs. We've had a little time to think about and discuss the situation, but the answers are not easy." He sighed and made a small, overwhelmed little whistle. "The circumstances are such that it would be extremely difficult to maintain the proper boundaries. We need to try to come to some kind of agreement . . ."

Caroline took over, placing both of her hands on the table. "It isn't a bad thing . . . I want you to know that. Feelings like that for another person can be wonderful. It's just that we didn't anticipate the possibility. We shouldn't have been so blind. Of course it could happen. I don't know why it didn't occur to us. It isn't your fault. But you must realize that we cannot allow this . . . situation . . . to continue while you live here together as, well, as siblings. It just isn't appropriate."

Tru finally spoke. "I've thought about it. I'll be leaving soon—it's only a month until graduation, and then I'll be teaching at Genoa for the summer. Then I'll only be back for a few days before I have to leave for football camp."

Dinah's face was pale. This did not sound like good news to her. Sensing her dismay, Tru squeezed her hand and continued. "I know—we know— that it probably isn't a great idea for us to be living under the same roof. But I promise," he looked straight at Caroline, "I would never do anything to . . . compromise Dinah."

Again there was silence, as Tom and Caroline seemed to be pondering the options.

"Thank you, Tru—I would like nothing more than to take you at your word." Caroline smiled at Tru for his obvious sincerity. "Unfortunately, your honest intentions may not be enough to protect you both from . . . well, from yourselves."

Tom's voice was firm as he outlined a plan for compliance. After enumerating several specifics, he wound up with a more general, all-encompassing safety net: "We will have to operate under the presumption of honor and obedience, and we expect you both to respect the rules."

Caroline continued the disquisition: "And Dinah, I'd like to think that we can also count on you to behave in a manner that is appropriate and careful. You are not allowed to visit the third floor, at least while Tru is here.

And there is another thing." She looked grave as a thought occurred to her. "This . . . situation . . . would be very confusing to Jemima. That needs no explanation—I'm sure you both can see how damaging it could be if she were to . . . catch on. I have to insist that you maintain an impeccable standard of behavior in this house. There can be no sign of anything . . . well, anything unseemly."

Tru and Dinah both nodded silently; he was still holding her hand. Dinah realized that Tru had been right, and she was struck by the irony: Not until they lived apart would they have the freedom to be together.

The weekend passed quietly. Tru spent most of it in Boston, making an uncharacteristic point to inform Tom and Caroline of exactly where he was going and what his plans were. Dinah spent most of Saturday working—the library was having a used-book sale beginning Monday, and it took the help of every single employee to get ready for it. Late in the afternoon on Sunday she was getting ready to return; anyone who agreed to work on Sunday was offered overtime pay, and she had drawn the evening shift. She didn't mind— Jane had offered to bring in coffee, lemonade, and her raspberry crumble bars. Without the restrictive presence of the public, the mood would be casual and relaxed. She put down her homework and slipped on her loafers. As she walked past the third-floor stairway, an arm reached out, pulling her up and around the corner to a small landing.

"I can't be up here! When did you get home?"

"Shhh." Tru put his finger over her lips. "You're not actually 'up here'— this isn't even half-way." He kissed her, moving her subtly against the wall as she glanced nervously toward the hallway. "No one else is upstairs," he murmured. "I checked. Just give me a minute. I just want to . . . touch you. The teak on Harley's old boat has never been so waxed . . ." Within moments his kisses became urgent with the force of pent-up need. He seemed to teeter on the brink of actually devouring her. Dinah couldn't constrain her response, helpless against the sway of his ardor.

As she felt herself sliding to the floor, she managed to pull away. "This can't be what my mom meant by 'impeccable standard of behavior.'" Her voice was thick and quavering.

Tru smiled as he moved over her. "I can't imagine a higher standard." He had both of her hands locked in his, and he raised her arms over her head, pushing against her on the soft carpet of the stairs. He was kissing her hard, and she found herself involuntarily moving beneath him, rhythmically, incoherently, losing all sense of time and place. She heard a muffled, throaty moan that seemed as though it was coming from a long distance away, until Tru whispered "Shhhh" in her ear and covered her mouth with his own, smothering her cry as she felt a seizing, shuddering cataclysm. Her body was exploding, shattered and scattering across the universe while a million stars danced behind her eyelids. She opened her eyes, dazed and wondrous, and for a brief moment, she thought Tru's eyes had actually turned black as they bored into hers. Then he closed them, burying his face in her hair, and his voice was strangled as he repeated her name over and again: "Dinah . . . Dinah . . . Dinah . . ."

They lay still, listening for any sign of discovery. Tru lifted his head, a mischievous grin spreading across his face: "Oops."

She was still stunned. She gazed at him with awe. He studied her tenderly, kissing her fingers, still laced in his hand. "That wasn't supposed to happen. Normally people take their clothes off first."

Dinah wasn't able to find her voice. She simply looked at him with complete and utter reverence. He was about to speak when a voice came from the hallway.

"Momma? I can't find her. My turn was yesterday—she has to do it today."

They waited tensely as Jemima passed by the door to the stairway, going back down to the kitchen where Caroline was evidently waiting for Dinah to set the table before she left. "I think that's your cue." Tru got up, pulling Dinah with him. "Just say you fell asleep in your clothes and you needed a glass of water," he teased, alluding to his previous advice as a mea culpa in her on-going orientation to the finer points of prevarication.

Her legs felt wobbly as she went down the few stairs from the landing, and she had to take a moment to collect herself, pausing in the hallway. She thought Tru had gone up to his room, and she jumped when she felt a finger trace lightly down her spine. As she turned around he placed both of his hands on her shoulders, looking at her solemnly. "There's one more thing." He leaned in and put his lips to her ear, sending a tingling thrill across her skin as he breathed the words: "I love you."

Coming home after her shift at the library, Dinah was still tingling. She had been floating on air all evening—barely able to focus on the carts of books she was supposed to catalogue and deaf to most of the conversation around her. Jane had been concerned; she asked if Dinah was feeling all right. Smiling vacantly, she assured Jane that she was just fine, but she didn't hear what Jane said after that, because all she could hear was Tru's voice whispering "I love you."

Closing the front door softly, she could smell the pleasant, slightly sweet aroma of pipe tobacco. She heard the customary strains of Verdi, or was it Puccini? Tom would be working at his desk in the library—his vast collection of opera playing as usual. Tonight, however, the strains were faint. As she passed by, she started to look in to say goodnight, but stopped short of the door when she realized Tom wasn't alone. Tru sat on the long, leather sofa under the window with his forehead resting on the palms of his hands, elbows propped up on his knees. His sun-streaked hair fell over his fingers in feathery disarray, and it struck Dinah as the image of a bird's wing. She then noticed another figure standing by the fireplace. It was a middle-aged man in work-a-day clothes. His arms were crossed and he, too, was looking down silently. He looked vaguely familiar, but Dinah couldn't place him. Tom noticed her in the doorway and said, "Dinah? Can I help you with something?"

At that, Tru raised his head and looked at her. It was the most unfathomable look she had ever seen. His eyes seemed both empty and stunned, but there was something more. It was a look that contained a plea, a question, and an apology all at once. After an agonizing moment, he turned away. Dinah felt rooted to the spot. She didn't know what had transpired, but she knew it wasn't good. Tom repeated, "Dinah?" and she snapped out of it, embarrassed to have imposed on their meeting.

"No, nothing, I just wanted to say good-night," she mumbled and started to move away.

"Wait," Tom called. "Would you mind closing the doors, please?"

That request underscored the seriousness of the situation. Tom never worked with the doors closed—he enjoyed seeing Caroline and the kids coming and going. Dinah gently pulled the heavy, mahogany pocket doors closed and headed upstairs to her room.

Her homework left a lot to be desired that night, as she found herself reading several pages without having absorbed a word. What could Tru have done to precipitate the meeting in the library, and who was the other man? She thought she had seen him somewhere before. Where was it? She finally put down her books and climbed into bed. She had a sick feeling in the pit of her stomach.

That night, she dreamed of a football game. It seemed at first to be against Centennial, their arch-rivals. But then it segued into a game against the Marines—the actual Marines, not a high-school team. They wore uniforms, but they were military, not football, uniforms. Tru was quarterback, and Dinah's father was on the other team, leaning into three-point position with his dog tags dangling down. Then her dream-vantage moved to the sidelines, where she noticed a man in a windbreaker holding a clipboard. The man looked at her and she recognized him as the same person who stood by the fireplace that night. It was Larry Gervais, football coach, boys' gym teacher, and father of Lana Gervais.

PART TWO

DAMAGE

CHAPTER TWELVE
Maybe

IN THE MORNING, Tru was nowhere to be seen, but Tom was notably present. He always left for work well before anyone else was awake; seeing him sitting at the kitchen table reading the paper confirmed the feeling that Dinah had from the night before—something was terribly wrong. Caroline was bustling around the kitchen, her bright "Good morning!" a little too forced. Jemima was oblivious to the tension in the air, happily eating a bowl of cereal, wondering aloud if grapes really had nuts and chattering about the upcoming May Day party at school.

"We get to bring May baskets to the hospital. There are some kids who have to stay there for a long time. Even longer than me. I'm going to show my friends my room there, and my bed. Maybe I'll get to see Nurse Wagner!"

Tom was nodding, but his eyes were fixed on the paper, and Dinah could tell he hadn't heard a word Jemima said. Caroline refilled the juice glasses, only contributing a distant "longer than *I*." When Hayes pulled up, she quickly ushered the girls to the door, explaining that Tru wasn't feeling well, and he wouldn't be going to school that day.

The morning crawled by. In Honors English Dinah noticed Sally Vecchi and Ginger Novak whispering together, giving her peculiar looks. It wasn't their usual menacing stare; it was more speculative, and almost . . . gloating. At lunch Laurie noticed the same thing. "Dinah, I don't mean to scare you, but that whole table of Sinisters is looking over here. I'd watch out if I were you."

"There's something weird going on," Betsy remarked. "Did something happen that you're not telling us about?"

Dinah was pale. She had no idea what was going on, but her friends weren't making it any better. "I don't know . . . Maybe . . . maybe they're just worried about Lana. I haven't seen her around lately."

"She hasn't been around. Maybe she's suicidal! That's it! Lana probably tried to kill herself, and her friends are all broken up about it!" Joan was triumphant, proud of her powers of deduction. They all looked at her, aghast.

"Don't sound so excited about it. That's horrible." Patsy was clearly worried that Joan was right. She looked at Dinah. "I hope, for your sake, that's not the case. I, for one, wouldn't want to be responsible for something like that."

Could it be? Dinah was jittery for the rest of the day. Grotesque visions of Lana Gervais hanging from a rope in her garage or slumped in the bathtub with rivulets of blood draining from her wrists appeared like a horror movie in her head, over and over. Walking home, she was playing out different scenarios of asphyxiation when she heard her name in the distance. As she turned around she saw Betsy running across the school lawn.

"Dinah, Dinah wait up!" Panting, her friend caught up, trying to catch her breath. "Listen, you should probably sit down." Her voice came out in huffs. "Over there—there's a bench. Come here." She grabbed Dinah's arm, pulling her toward a park bench at the edge of the school property. Dinah stared at her friend, waiting for the other shoe to fall.

Betsy sat close, facing her with their knees touching. She picked up one of Dinah's hands in both of hers. "I just heard . . . I just heard something. It's why the Sinisters were looking at you like that." She let out a final panting breath, and then looked Dinah in the eye, pausing for a moment before dropping the bomb. "Lana's pregnant."

Standing at the window in the second-floor guest room, Dinah watched as two figures worked in the grove of cedars at the far edge of the back lawn. Of about equal height, one of them was broader, with graying hair and a plaid workman's shirt over dark grey cotton work pants. The other was dark blond, with loose-fitting chinos slung low on his waist. He was shirtless, and even from a distance Dinah could see the delineation of muscle under smooth skin, already tanned from the hours of working on Harley's boat. They worked in tandem, pruning the branches, taking turns with the saw as the other held the limbs. There was a large pile of trimmings on the grass.

She hadn't thought anyone was home. Tom's car must have been in the garage, and Caroline's little Nash was gone. But moving numbly through the halls, she noticed a movement through the guest room window as she passed. Now she was incapable of drawing away, her forehead propped heavily against the glass—a crutch to support the weight of knowledge. She simply watched, drinking in his movements, unconsciously suspending time, hording the moment. She couldn't deny reality, but she could temporarily sustain the illusion, postponing the instant that it would be acknowledged—the instant he looked her in the eye.

The late April sun beat a warm, mellow light; Tom stooped down, taking off his gloves to lay them on the ground, and then he stepped back, hands on hips, surveying the project. He said a few words to Tru, then turned and walked toward the garage. Dinah continued to watch. She watched Tru raking the limbs into a neat pile; she watched as he picked up the hedge-clipper to even out a patch; she watched as he dropped the tool to stand motionless in the sun, head down, eyes fixed on the ground. Seeing him like that—solitary, defenseless—she felt something crack in her chest.

He had not moved when she approached him—a garden sculpture devoid of life, a granite rendering of what used to be a boy. "Hello." Her voice was shaky. He raised his head slowly, and when he looked at her the expression in his eyes was so utterly lost that she had to look away. "I heard . . ." She swallowed hard—anything else she had intended to say was stifled by the swelling of her throat. He said nothing—his head dropped again, as though he might find an answer somewhere in the Kentucky bluegrass of the lawn. Dinah didn't know what to do. Her chest was swelling along with her throat; she was helpless against the tears that slipped down her face. A tear fell to the ground—a single tear, glistening on a blade of grass, which broke through the seawall.

"I'm sorry . . . I'm sorry . . . I'm sorry." He wrapped his arms around her, his voice ragged. Her face was pressed against his chest; she could hear his heart beating through the skin and muscle and bone, and the inexpressible loveliness of being held against his bare torso almost shattered her. They stood that way for a long time; her memory absorbing the sweet smell of his skin, his heart absorbing her tears. Finally, they moved across the lawn and sat on the grass in the shade of the big old chestnut tree, leaning against its broad trunk.

"What are you going to do?" She struggled to get the words out.

"I don't know. I don't know." He shook his head slowly, pausing for a long time. "I don't even know if I'm the . . ." He couldn't bring himself to say it. "If I'm the right guy."

Her head spun toward him. "You mean, it could be Jimmy?"

He nodded. "I think so."

"But . . . it could be you?"

He hesitated, and then, with a dazed and empty look in his eyes, he simply nodded.

"Isn't there some way to tell?"

"I don't know. Maybe. I guess after it's . . . after it's . . ." He let out a tortured sigh, leaning forward to press his forehead against his arms, which were crossed over his drawn-up knees. "I should have known." His voice was muffled. "I should have known."

"What do you mean?"

He took a deep breath, letting it out slowly as he stared at a spot on the grass. "Lana is used to getting what she wants."

"Do you mean she did this on purpose?" Dinah was shocked.

He didn't answer for a moment; he seemed to be turning the possibility over in his mind. Then a look of defeated acceptance spread over his face, and a word pushed out of the grim set of his mouth: "Maybe."

Tru was gone. He left for Camp Genoa and his position as a sailing instructor the day after graduation. Tom had insisted; in fact, he would have sent his son off sooner if not for the formality of finishing the school year. The past weeks had been wretched. Tru had withdrawn to the point of complete detachment, living as much with Coco and Harley in Boston as he did at home, and often staying at Hayes's or Stan's house during the week. Dinah barely saw him. He didn't have to say it; being near each other was torture. At school there was a hushed carefulness around Tru; everyone knew, but no one said a word. Dinah felt like she was in a fugue state; she didn't even try to pretend around her friends. They heard the requiem, low and mournful, and for once they silenced their ever-clanging cymbals.

Lana had come back to school after a week or so, looking wan and fragile and beautiful. Her friends flocked around her, clucking like mother hens over a wounded chick. It was as though her star had risen with her new condition—a martyr Madonna, bearing the cross of spurned love, of fertile abandonment. For several days, Dinah scarcely saw her—she made it a point to avoid the hallways where the senior classrooms were, and her friends had thoughtfully moved with her to a remote table in the cafeteria, far from the hub where the Sinisters reigned.

She didn't know if Tru had spoken to Lana. It was something that she blocked out of her mind—she just couldn't bring herself to think about it. But as it turned out, her mental discipline was wasted; she turned a corner one day and there they were—close and intent. They were in a corner of a quiet hallway in the math wing—Dinah wouldn't even have been there except for the signature required by the trigonometry teacher to register for summer school.

Tru had one elbow propped on a row of low lockers; he was supporting his forehead with his hand. Even at a distance, Dinah could tell his expression was strained. It looked like he had a crushing headache. Lana had her arms crossed over her books, and Dinah realized she was crying. Tru reached his arm out, laying a hand gently on her shoulder, saying something that Dinah couldn't make out. Lana leaned into him and he draped his arm around her. As she buried her face against his shirt, Dinah felt a roiling wave crest in her stomach and she had to run to the bathroom, locking herself in a stall and leaning her head against the cool metal of the door as she fought to overcome the feeling of sick despair.

She was still standing in the stall, sweating and shaky, when the door flew open and there was a violent retching sound at the sink. Moments later the door opened again and she heard his voice.

"Are you all right?"

"No." The voice at the sink was bitter.

"Is there . . . anything I can do?"

"Yes."

"I mean . . . right now?"

"Don't worry about it, Tru; I'm used to it. It happens all the time. You should be around in the mornings. That's really fun." The words dripped with sarcasm.

Dinah was stunned. Tru had come into the girls' bathroom. It was Lana at the sink. She unconsciously drew back, squeezing into the narrow space next to the toilet, praying they wouldn't notice the occupied stall. She heard the water running as Lana rinsed out the sink. "I'll be fine—you can go."

"Look . . .Lana . . . you have to think about what I said. Please. Please. You know it makes sense. Don't do this. It's not fair—to you, or to the baby, or to . . ." His voice trailed off.

"Stop it!" Lana practically screamed at him. "Stop thinking that. I told you, I'm sure. It's you. It's you, it's you, it's you . . ." her voice was becoming hysterical, and she was crying again. Dinah heard footsteps cross the floor. Lana's sobs became muffled; it didn't take much imagination to know that Tru's arms were around her.

"Shhh. All right. It's all right. I believe you. It will be OK. Please don't cry. We can talk about this later. Shhh."

"I don't want to talk about it later." Her voice came out in gasps. "I'm not giving it away. I'm keeping it. I don't care what you say, this is what I want."

Tru was silent, and the sobs waned to soft, stuttering sniffles. After a while he spoke; quietly, patiently, as though addressing a child: "Lana, you know I'm leaving. I'm going to school. I won't be here. You can't just . . . You just can't do this. We're not old enough and . . ." his voice was cracked ". . . and I don't love you. I'm sorry. I'm sorry—I can't help it."

Dinah flinched as a loud, stinging slap resounded off the tile walls.

"You can't help it?" Lana's voice was enraged. "Well guess what? I can't help it either. I can't help that I'm having your baby . . . and you can't help—" she drew a sharp breath. "You can't help that you want to fuck your sister." Her footsteps echoed, heavy and furious, as she stormed out the door.

The room was silent. Dinah huddled against the wall, praying that Tru would leave. After several moments, she couldn't restrain herself from leaning forward to peer through the crack on the side of the door. She could just make out the back of his form, leaning forward, balancing his weight on his arms as they gripped the edges of the sink. She couldn't see his head, because it was it was slung low, hanging from his shoulders. Then he raised it and she could see a sliver of his reflection in the mirror as he stared into his own eyes. He was riveted there when the door opened again. For several beats he didn't move, but then, as a girl stood confused in the doorway, he turned around. "It's all yours." He moved around her and was gone. Dinah sat down on the toilet, still shaking.

That evening, as she was going toward the bathroom to brush her teeth, she heard her mother's voice behind the bedroom door, uncharacteristically raised in affronted anger: "Do the right thing? He's only eighteen years old, for God's sake! He's not even an adult! How can you possibly expect him to . . ." Her words became muffled, and Dinah couldn't make them out, but the meaning was clear; she felt her legs buckle.

CHAPTER THIRTEEN
Dust of Its Hooves

THE CLASSROOM WAS HOT. Dinah had never realized how warm the school could get during the summer. Her legs were sticking to the varnish on the wooden chair. There were only five other kids in the trigonometry class—all rising seniors who hadn't passed the class last year. As miserable as the climate was inside the building, she was thankful for the class. It was something to do to pass the time. In the four weeks since the school year ended she hadn't been able to bring herself to do much of anything but go to her class and work at the library, where she had taken on extra hours. Betsy, Joan, and Laurie had all left for camp—they were counselors-in-training at Camp Winnawog in Vermont. Joan and Laurie had been going as campers for years, and they recruited Betsy to go with them. They had tried to convince Dinah to sign up—it was a great summer job, and there was a boys' camp down the road that held a weekly dance. This was considered compelling motivation, but it didn't succeed. Now more than ever, Dinah sought solitude—the long, quiet days of June and July a much-needed reprieve from the tumult of April and May.

She hadn't heard from Tru, but she on some level she understood; his future was balanced on a fulcrum—it could tip either way. They were both caught in a kind of limbo. Proceeding with any kind of normalcy was impossible. At the graduation ceremony, Dinah had sat in the rear of the auditorium with the family—they had been a little late getting there, and the room was packed. She couldn't see where Tru was sitting, and she watched as most of the alphabet was called to the stage. When Lana crossed the stage, Dinah noticed her mother sitting forward to get a better look.

Her heart skipped a little when Tru's name was called. Just hearing his name in a public forum still incited a thrilling little rush, and she wondered sadly if it would ever go away. Watching him walk across the stage, somber and remote, she was struck again by how extraordinarily handsome he was; she thought every girl in the room must be secretly in love with him.

After the ceremony, when all of his friends were going out to celebrate, Tru returned to the house to pack his bag. He went straight up to his bedroom, and Dinah drifted to hers, with the surreal feeling that time had somehow regressed—that it was January again, or February, and she didn't really know him at all. She wondered how they would say goodbye. He was leaving early in the morning, but he hadn't said a word about it. The idea of going to him pushed at her persistently, but deep in her heart she was waiting for him to come to her. She drifted off to sleep with a book on her chest, open to the same page where it had stayed for the better part of an hour, the lines blurred, the words unread.

In the morning she was aware of only one thing when she awoke; he was gone. Even from her bed, she could feel his absence. There was a hole in the house, and through it drained happiness.

After her trigonometry class she walked home slowly in the heat. Kicking off her sandals in the foyer, she felt like stripping out of her clammy shorts and blouse as well. She didn't remember the summer being this hot last year. She could hear Jemima chattering to Gloria in the kitchen, and it occurred to her that she could take her sister to the pool. As she started toward the kitchen she noticed a pile of mail on the mahogany Pembroke table against the foyer wall. An envelope on top stopped her in her tracks. It was Tru's handwriting, and it was addressed to Tom. She picked it up, staring at it for several minutes, wishing she had a way to see through the envelope to the letter inside. Reluctantly, she started to put it back when she saw the next letter on the pile. It was the same handwriting, addressed to her. In slow motion, she picked it up, gazing at it with a mixture of exhilaration and trepidation. Without realizing it she had started to walk slowly in a circle around the foyer, tapping the envelope lightly against her palm, her subconscious accomplishing a dual purpose—prolonging a sweet anticipation while postponing a fearful possibility. Silently, she slipped her sandals back on and went outside—she couldn't bear to have anyone intrude on her privacy when she opened it.

She wandered to the backyard, with no real destination in mind. But the chestnut tree provided a lovely shade, and she sat down beneath it, leaning against the trunk. She looked at the handwriting on the envelope for a long time, drawing out the moment, memorizing the exact shape of each letter.

Finally, she tore it open.

There was a single sheet inside—it slipped out easily. She closed her eyes, afraid. When she opened them she saw that there was only one line. Only one line and only six words:

I kiss you in my dreams.

One line—six words. But what words! They rose up from the page and enveloped her. They lifted her into the leafy branches of the chestnut tree. They twirled her around like a ballerina on a music box. It took her an hour to finish reading it—she read it a thousand times. She knew that the future was uncertain, but now she also knew this: He held her in his heart. Whatever happened, she knew. He loved her, and she knew it. She would always know it. A light breeze ruffled her hair, and suddenly the day didn't feel so oppressive, the air wasn't so heavy. It was, after all, a pretty nice day.

At dinner that night, she waited to see if Tom would mention his letter from Tru. When he didn't, she decided to broach the subject, hoping she sounded casual.

"I thought I saw that you had a letter from Tru today . . ."

Tom's head came up sharply. Exchanging a glance with Caroline, he cleared his throat: "Yes, I did get a few lines. He isn't much for details . . . I believe everything is going well as far as the sailing goes. It was, ah, mostly of a personal nature." He looked pointedly at Jemima, who had perked up at the mention of Tru's name.

"I miss Tru. When is he coming home? He said he would take me sailing again—I'm going to be his crew." Jemima's voice was almost petulant—the fact that Tru was gone made her cross. Dinah could sympathize.

Caroline stepped in: "I'm afraid you're going to have to wait a few more weeks, Sugar. He'll be here for a few days at the end of July, and then he'll be off again for football training camp at school." She gave the last part of the sentence a weighty emphasis, looking meaningfully at Tom.

"That would certainly be the ideal." Tom's voice was wistful. He suddenly looked tired and sad. He addressed Caroline: "We should clear up, I guess."

"Yes, they're coming at around eight o'clock." Caroline turned to Jemima, changing the subject. "Why don't you go up and start getting ready for bed? Dinah can read with you tonight." She looked back at Tom, sighing. "I'll make coffee."

Dinah didn't need to ask who the guests were—she could read between the lines. She was curled up on Jemima's bed reading a chapter of *Betsy and Tacy* when she heard the doorbell ring. Jemima was getting sleepy, and Dinah hurried to the end of the chapter. "'Night, Mimer." She kissed her little sister on the forehead. "Sleep tight." She quietly closed the door behind her, but instead of going to her own room, she crept to the top of the stairs and sat down. She could hear voices, but she couldn't make out the words. If they had been seated in the living room, she wouldn't have had any problem eavesdropping; they must have gone into the library. She should have known—it was turning out to be the room where all serious discussion took place—the heavy paneling containing the heavy problems, quarantined from the rest of the house.

On a rogue impulse she decided to go downstairs. She didn't even know what her intention was—her feet just started down the steps. She had the idea that she could always use the glass of water excuse, which sent a sharp pang through her chest. But instead of going to the kitchen, her legs took her directly to the library, where the doors were partially open. Inside she saw her mother serving coffee on a silver tray; she was bending down to the couple seated on the sofa. Dinah recognized Mr. Gervais. The woman seated next to him would have needed no introduction—she looked like an older version of Lana. Her hair had a few silver streaks, and it was drawn up in a neat bun, but the eyes were the same—a deep violet that Dinah could see even from the doorway. She stood there for a moment, unnoticed, until Mr. Gervais finally saw her and everyone else followed his eyes.

"Yes, Dinah?" Her mother looked at her expectantly.

"Ah, I just thought I would say hello." She looked nervously at Mr. and Mrs. Gervais. "Hello."

She felt completely foolish, realizing her curiosity was transparent, but Tom covered for her with aplomb: "Hello, dear. Come in. May I introduce Mr. and Mrs. Gervais? You may know Mr. Gervais from school. This is our daughter Dinah."

She crossed the room to shake their hands, wondering why in the world she had come down here. "It's nice to meet you." They nodded and smiled, without the faintest glimmer of recognition. Suddenly Dinah understood her impulse: She hadn't known until that moment that she was curious to see if Lana had told them about her. She wanted her relationship with Tru to be acknowledged. She wanted to assert her presence—to be recognized. But clearly, Lana hadn't mentioned her name. She felt an odd disappointment. "Well, I was just, um, going to the kitchen. It was nice to meet you." She hurried out of the room, intentionally leaving the doors slightly open behind her.

Hovering in the kitchen, she hoped to catch at least part of the conversation in the library. It was no good—after a few minutes of polite small talk she heard the doors sliding shut. She went back to her room, walking very slowly as she passed the library, but she could only hear the murmur of low voices. As she went to bed, a sequence of the different plausible purposes and outcomes of the meeting ran through her mind, all jockeying for position as the frontrunner. But there was one dark and terrible mount that raced harder and faster than the others, one beast that jumped the gun and charged ahead, pushing all challengers into the rail. It buried her dreams in the dust of its hooves; it tore up the track of their lives; it carried Tru's future on its runaway back.

As Dinah fell asleep, she thought she heard a baby cry.

CHAPTER FOURTEEN
There's No You

TOM WAS EXCITED about the fireworks. He and Caroline had been on their honeymoon last year over the Fourth of July so he hadn't been able to take the girls to the annual extravaganza at The Willows, and he had been talking about it for days. From experience, he knew that the limited parking would be a nightmare, so they took the trolley, which ran from downtown Salem straight into the park. Tom carried the Hudson Bay blanket from the trunk of his car—the sight of it made Dinah's chest contract—and a picnic basket containing ham sandwiches, peaches, and iced tea. They arrived while the sun was still lolling above the horizon and disembarked at the seaside pavilion to a buzzing throng of spectators milling about in shorts and sandals, holding hot dogs and ice cream cones.

Jemima was enchanted by the beautiful pavilion—there was a Sousa band playing on the orchestra stage, accompanying the skaters on the roller rink with rousing renditions of patriotic tunes. She made Caroline promise that she could come back and learn how to roller skate. She also wanted to try the "Best Batter-Fried Shrimp" advertised on a placard at the base of the stairway leading to the large, upstairs restaurant overlooking the cove. When Caroline explained to her that her father had helped design the building, Jemima seemed confused.

Looking on, Dinah realized that her little sister didn't have many memories of their father—Jemima had been very young when Gideon was shipped out. She looked around at the details of the building, wishing she had seen more examples of his work. He had taken her once to a library that he designed, and she could remember being dazzled by the graceful arched domes of the soaring ceiling, supported by slender iron columns. But for the most part, she had taken his vocation for granted. Now, with the perspective of maturity, she was beginning to realize that her father had possessed a real talent. She gazed around, bracing for the constricting squeeze of sadness. Suddenly she realized that something was missing: It was her grief. She was thinking about her father without an ache in her heart.

They wandered through the park, settling on a grassy slope to have their picnic and wait for the fireworks show. "It's not Boston, but they do a pretty bang-up job," Tom joked, earning groans from Caroline and Dinah. The hillside was getting crowded with families laying out blankets, opening picnic hampers, and swatting at mosquitoes.

As they ate, Dinah looked around to see if any of her classmates were there. She saw a couple of kids from the class ahead of her, and June Larkin was sitting with her family on a blanket nearby, but she didn't see any of her friends, or any of the Sinisters. They finished their sandwiches and sat back to wait for the show. Although it was past eight-thirty, there was still enough daylight left to foretell a dragging interim. Jemima was antsy, repeatedly pestering them with the same question: "When is it going to start?" From her impatience grew a cranky frustration; she slapped a mosquito on her leg. "I'm thirsty. I don't like iced tea." Her voice had taken on an aggrieved whine.

"Come on, Mimer. Let's go get something to drink." Dinah took her sister by the hand, heading toward a lemonade stand near Restaurant Row. They passed a small pagoda where Al's Barbershop Quartet was singing "Sweet Adeline." There was a line at the lemonade stand, and they fell in behind a little old lady who was talking to a Pekinese sporting ribbons of red, white, and blue:

"Now remember, Twinky, the fireworks won't hurt you. Mommy brought your earplugs—we don't want you to have another accident on the blanket like last year."

Dinah pictured Bel cowering under the bed when there was even a dim crack of thunder, and thought the dog would certainly have a heart attack if they had brought her along. She couldn't believe anyone would subject an animal to the uncomprehending terror of fireworks, but she forgot her indignation when she noticed two figures standing beneath a willow tree off to her left, engaged in what appeared to be a heated discussion. There was something familiar about them, but in the gloaming, it took several moments to make out the faces. It wasn't until the girl turned her head sharply that it registered. It was Lana, talking to Jimmy Wright. Even from a distance, Dinah could tell that they were arguing.

She jumped when someone tapped her shoulder, and couldn't have been more surprised to find Bill at her elbow. Since the bonfire she had hardly seen him. It was clear that he had been avoiding her, and she didn't blame him. She missed him, but it seemed selfish to expect him to be her friend when it was obvious that she couldn't return his feelings for her. Sadly, she had resigned herself to sacrificing his friendship, hoping that Tru wouldn't have to make the same sacrifice. In poignant proof to the strength of their bond, Tru had survived the threat. Bill counted Tru's happiness in equal measure to his own, and with loyal generosity he seemed to have had accepted the situation.

She smiled at him warmly. "How've you been?"

He returned her smile. "I've been all right. Keeping busy. I'm a working stiff, you know. The days fly by when you're checking dipsticks and scraping bugs off windshields."

Dinah laughed. "That's right—I heard you were working at the Skelly station. I never guessed you for the grease-monkey type."

"You underestimate my skills—I can change a tire in two minutes flat. On the other hand, there isn't a lot of call for any of the stuff we learned in calculus or European history. In fact, I can sum up the extent of my verbal requirements in three words: Fill 'er up?"

The topic of the conversation attracted Jemima's scattered attention; she piped up excitedly: "Do you know how to do the gas guns?" Jemima had long been intrigued by the pistol-like shape of the nozzles—from her small vantage the looming pumps held a strange menace.

"I can sling 'em like a cowboy. Who is it that you named your club after—Tex Granger?"

"Tex Granger the Midnight Rider." She rattled it off as one name. "If I come to the filling station, can you show me how you do it?" Her eyes were wide with anticipation.

"You bet. Next time your mom or dad needs to fill up the car, you tell 'em to come see old Billy the Kid." He made a quick-draw gesture from an imaginary holster.

Jemima was dancing a little at the thought of it, hanging onto Dinah's hand and bouncing on her toes. Dinah was laughing at Bill's hackneyed cowboy impression. "Speaking of verbal requirements, I heard about your scholarship at Bowdoin. Congratulations!"

"Thanks. It's not Harvard, but I'll take it."

"It's a very good school. Nathaniel Hawthorne went there. So did Longfellow."

"I guess I'm in good company. Who knows, maybe I'll be a writer someday."

"Or a poet . . ." Dinah couldn't keep her eyes from wandering back to see if Lana and Jimmy were still there, under the willow tree. Bill followed her gaze silently.

After a few moments, when Jemima was distracted, he quietly stunned Dinah with a flat statement: "Jimmy thinks it might be his."

Dinah stared at him. She didn't dare hope she had understood. "What did you say?"

"Jimmy thinks it might be his baby. He's been pressuring Lana to wait and see. To give him some proof that it isn't." He paused, watching them. Lana was turning away, and Jimmy was clutching her arm.

"It's kind of weird. It's like he thinks it's another contest with Tru." Bill's face became pained. "I can tell you this; that's one contest Tru doesn't want to win."

Dinah stared at the couple, moving away in the distance. What if it wasn't Tru's baby after all? She could hear Lana's voice in the bathroom, insisting through her sobs that Tru was the father, but what if she was wrong? What if she was lying?

She suddenly had the feeling that her heart actually leaped, and couldn't help a clinical observation of the sensation. She was always a little wondrous when metaphors actually rang true. With new buoyancy she ordered three lemonades at the window, and then tapped her glass against Bill's. "It's on me. Happy Fourth of July." Taking his arm, she insisted that he join the family for the show. As they led Jemima back to the blanket on the hillside, the first of the fireworks exploded in the night sky—a shimmering, cascading harbinger of hope.

Caroline was peeling rhubarb for a pie when Dinah wandered into the kitchen, idly picking up a piece of cleaned rhubarb and munching on it. Caroline was almost surprised to see her—Dinah had been hard to reach lately. In fact, Caroline hadn't felt the close, familiar connection for quite some time. Over the course of the past year she had attributed her daughter's increasing emotional distance to the natural cycles of maturity, but now she knew there had been other forces at work; forces that had recently stripped Caroline of her maternal prerogative. She was powerless to kiss the scraped knee and take the hurt away. It wasn't hard to imagine the pain that Dinah must be feeling, given the situation. In fact, she didn't even have to try—Caroline could feel it like it was her own. But as strong as her instinct was to take her daughter in her arms and comfort her, she could sense that such overt sympathy would be not only unwelcome, but rejected. Dinah had erected a wall to hold herself together, and it was so clearly friable that Caroline was afraid to touch it.

Smiling, she picked up another knife, holding it out by the blade. "Would you care to give your mom a hand with the chopping? I'm going to can the extra rhubarb in sauce." Rhubarb sauce on vanilla ice cream was one of Dinah's favorites. She took the knife and grabbed another piece of the sour plant, peeling off the some of the outer skin.

Reaching across the sink to the wide windowsill, Caroline turned on the old Philco radio, adjusting the knob to find a station. Gloria listened to gospel; there was only one station in Salem that it came through on, and the dial was practically on a permanent setting. She turned it until the warbling voice of Jo Stafford floated out from the tinny speaker: "There's No You." For a lovely, serene interlude they worked together, as a light breeze drifted through the open window, softly ruffling the curtains on a lazy July afternoon.

After a while, Dinah revealed her purpose: "I was wondering . . . Um, I was just wondering if you could tell me what's going on. I mean, you know, with Tru . . . and Lana." She kept her eyes on the chopping board. "I mean, I think I have a right to know. What's going to happen? Is Tru . . ." she hesitated, trying to find a palatable way to phrase it. "Is Tru still going away to school?"

Caroline's heart almost broke for her daughter. She knew exactly what Dinah was trying to ask, and she hated the answer she would have to give. But she had to be honest with her—Dinah deserved that much. She cleared her voice, trying to choose the right words. "It seems that Lana and her parents feel, and we can't disagree with them, that Tru has a responsibility here. They aren't happy about it, but they make a valid case that Lana shouldn't have to shoulder this alone."

The knife Dinah was holding fell to the floor. Caroline just looked at it, leaving it where it lay. "The baby is due in November. There haven't been any final decisions made yet, but it is possible—no—probable that Tru will need to notify William and Mary that he won't be attending this year." She felt like crying at the preposterous unfairness of life. She could barely stand to think of that poor boy having to scrap everything—his entire future—to pay for his mistake. And the fact that her daughter, too, would suffer the consequences of this sad circumstance doubled the loss.

Dinah hadn't moved. She was still staring at the tiny pieces of rhubarb scattered across the soapstone slab. She was holding her bottom lip in her teeth, and Caroline was afraid to say anything else. But then, slowly, Dinah spoke. "Jimmy Wright thinks it's his."

CHAPTER FIFTEEN

Your Son, Tru

THE SALEM MUNICIPAL POOL had been crowded all summer, a popular alternative to the tide-bound peril of the beaches. The unusually warm days turned out crowds of bathers seeking relief, and Dinah and Jemima were among the regulars who staked out a spot by the shallow end on the hot afternoons. Jemima had a new swimsuit. Caroline bought it for her before their first foray to the pool. Unable to see her own back, Jemima had been blessedly unaware of the scarring that covered her skin, still angry and red after eight months. But when Jemima had put on her favorite blue gingham bathing suit, Caroline felt a piteous pang in her chest, and she knew that she would have to find a way to protect her little girl from both the sun's damaging rays and the innocent cruelty of other children. As she gently explained to Jemima that she would need to protect the delicate skin on her back, her daughter craned her head back and forth over her shoulders, with a perplexed furrow on her brow. Finally, Caroline picked up a silver hand-mirror from her vanity, and positioned Jemima with her back to the wall-mirror, adjusting the hand-mirror before her to provide a vantage to view the scarring. Silently, Jemima studied the reflection. Caroline watched as small lips pursed and struggled to suppress a trembling quiver: "I don't feel like going swimming, anyway. I hate the pool." Jemima's voice was taut—an over-wound fiddle string about to snap.

Wondering if she had done the right thing by showing her daughter the mirror, Caroline tried to explain that the scars would get better over time, but Jemima simply shook her head, finding a sudden urgent need to inspect Bel's ears.

That afternoon, Caroline drove to Boston with single-minded purpose, combing every shop and department store until she found a perfectly-designed swimsuit that would cover Jemima's back. It was red with white polka-dots, and it had a wide ruffle around the neck and shoulders. Jemima loved it. She asked her mother to hold the hand-mirror once again. After careful scrutiny, a wide smile spread across her face. "I guess I do like the pool, anyway. I changed my idea." Clearly taken with the movement of the ruffle across her shoulders, she gave a little shimmy.

Since then, Jemima seemed to have put the troublesome scarring out of her mind—a capability that Dinah couldn't help noting with envy. Dinah had become her sister's regular chaperone, offering to take her swimming as a way to pass the days, lounging in the sun with whatever library books she had taken out that week. Her fair skin, after an initial pink sunburn, had taken on a golden tan; she couldn't deny that being outdoors gave her a feeling of physical well being that the library just couldn't provide. Some days she ran into Marlys and Susan, but they preferred to sit near the diving board, where the high-school boys showed off their cannonballs and swan dives. Dinah needed to keep an eye on Jemima, an excuse that played perfectly into her preference for reading quietly, isolated in a bookish bubble within the sea of people.

She was midway through *Howards End*, looking over the pages at regular intervals for Jemima's bobbing head, when Marlys and Susan hurried over. Their bare legs were moving in a quick stutter-step and their arms were locked down straight, trying to disguise their eagerness. "Sandra Vecchi is here—you know, Sally's sister." Susan's whisper carried an excited urgency. "She's over at the snack shack—don't look! We don't want her to know we were listening. Anyway, we were standing over there, waiting in line, and she was talking to some of her friends about Lana and Tru. Is it true? Are they really getting married?" Their eyes gleamed with nervous anticipation—the titillation of melodrama combining with a worried concern for their friend. Dinah put down her book, trying to appear calm and collected despite the shudder that ran through her body.

"No. It isn't true." The answer echoed in her mind—how she wished the phrase would apply in another form: *It isn't Tru.* She regretted that she had no god to whom she could pray: *Let it not be Tru. Please, whatever mystifying, obscure mind that might be out there, please, let it not be Tru.* She realized that Marlys and Susan were looking at her expectantly, waiting for more. "He's going to William and Mary. What happens after Lana has her baby, well, I'm not sure." She didn't want to even think about it, much less speak the possibility.

After she had told her mother about Jimmy, Caroline had grabbed both of Dinah's arms, unintentionally squeezing them a little. She couldn't keep a note of stern injunction out of her voice when she commanded Dinah to tell her everything she knew. Although Dinah explained that she didn't know anything more, there had been a flicker in her mother's eyes—a glimmer of light from the window that had just been cracked open. Caroline forgot about the pies and the sauce, rushing to the phone to call Tom at the mill. They treated the news as if Tru had been given a reprieve from the executioner's block. Even though it was only a possibility, there was at least a chance that he would escape this life sentence.

After an awkward phone call, another meeting with Lana's parents was arranged. Tom and Caroline had requested Lana's presence, but Mr. and Mrs. Gervais had shown up without her, explaining that their daughter wasn't feeling well. Once again, the library doors were firmly closed, denying Dinah any access to the processes of the inner sanctum. But when the doors finally opened again, she was strategically seated on a sofa in the living room, with a clear vantage of the foyer. Ostensibly engrossed in her book, she watched as Mr. and Mrs. Gervais took their leave, studying them for any evidence of the spoils. Lana's mother was holding her chin at a jutting, upward angle, keeping her eyes straight ahead at the door, while Mr. Gervais smashed his hat firmly onto his head, nodding a curt goodbye with a notable lack of handshake. Dinah wanted to stand up and cheer— Tom and her mother must have stood their ground. She unconsciously let out a long breath after the front door closed.

Caroline came into the living room and sat down on the sofa next to her, dutifully offering a summary of the meeting. It had been decided that it would be terribly unfair to Tru to make any drastic decisions until there was absolute proof that he was, indeed, the responsible party. He would go to school, accepting the football scholarship as planned. There would be a blood test after the baby was born, at which point further decisions would be made. She didn't volunteer anything more about just what those decisions would entail, and Dinah couldn't bring herself to ask. It was too painful to contemplate.

Now, hearing the rumor made the possible consequence all too real, and she quickly picked up her book again, dismissing Susan and Marlys with a not-so-subtle turn of the page. They looked disappointed. "Well, it sounds like Lana has other plans," Marlys warned. "Sandra was saying that Sally has been spending all sorts of time helping Lana make plans for a wedding, and baby stuff, and they've even been talking about where Tru and Lana could live. Lana wants to get a little apartment . . ."

Dinah couldn't hear her anymore—the image of Tru and Lana living together in an apartment, with a baby, caused a deafening roar in her ears. The page in front of her was starting to swim when she was yanked back into the sunlight by Jemima's wet body dripping cold water all over her.

"I want to get an ice-cream cone. Do we have any money?"

Dinah had a dollar in her beach tote. "No—sorry, Mimer, we're all out. It's time to go, anyway." She stood up quickly, turning her back on Marlys and Susan. They looked at each other and shrugged.

"We'll let you know if we hear anything else." Susan's tone was conspiratorial. They were clearly thrilled by the idea of a reconnaissance mission, assuming the role of spies on Dinah's behalf. Dinah wasn't so thrilled. The thought of hearing anything more from her friends about Tru and Lana made her dizzy.

"Sure. Let me know. I'll see you later." She shoved the towels into the tote and grabbed Jemima by the hand, practically dragging her to the exit turnstile.

The pencil in Dinah's hand had become dull; she finished the last problem of the trigonometry final using a worn nub of lead. Flexing her fingers, she shook off a cramp in her hand and picked up her test. It had been difficult, but she thought she had gotten most of the questions right. Because it met for three hours each morning, the six-week summer session had covered the full course and Dinah was glad it was over. She wasn't a natural math student, but given her sedulous nature she had managed a high average. The long mornings had been tiresome, but she hadn't minded as much as the other kids in the class; it had given her something to do. Now a feeling of relief rolled off of her shoulders, and she headed toward the teacher's desk with a light step, the first to turn in her test.

As she moved to the doorway, a boy with dark, curly hair waved a little goodbye. Kenny Mitchell had become a friend over the summer—he struggled with math, and on a few occasions he had asked her to help him study. She had invited him to come home with her for lunch after class, going over their assignments at the kitchen table. He played trombone in the band and wrote for the newspaper, and he was funny and self-deprecating. He had been encouraging Dinah to join the newspaper staff, where he was the incoming editor. She waved back, mouthing "Good luck" as she went out the door.

Walking home she felt a small raindrop on her face; the sky had darkened as swollen clouds rolled in. By the time she neared the house the clouds had opened, drenching her with fat, bursting drops. Her camp shirt and Bermuda shorts were soaked. Rushing through the door, she was still in the foyer when she heard a car in the driveway. She waited, dripping water on a small Persian rug, for her mother and Jemima to come in. A loud crash of thunder shook the house as a sudden torrent broke from the sky. The front door flew open and a body rushed in, head down, hauling a large canvas duffle over his shoulder. He slammed the door behind him without looking up, and proceeded to run straight into Dinah. Drawing back, he dropped the bag, rivulets streaming down his face. Dinah could hear the car backing out of the driveway, and she turned toward the sound, confused.

"I hitchhiked." Tru answered her unasked question, keeping his eyes locked on her face. They looked at each other for a long moment, and then he gently put his hand on her hair and kissed her. It was so light, so tender, that she could hardly feel it; just a soft, lingering brush on her lips. Inhaling deeply, he closed his eyes and pressed his forehead against hers. "I remember you," he murmured. They stood like this for a long time, breathing in the sweetness, soaking in the nearness. After a time, they both opened their eyes. Their faces were still pressed together; they were literally eye to eye.

Without moving, without taking her eyes off of his, tears began to roll down Dinah's face. She couldn't help it—seeing him made her feel like an infant who doesn't cry until its mother returns, then suddenly realizes an inchoate terror and fury at having been abandoned. Her voice quavered like the string of a cello. "You didn't say goodbye. You just . . . left."

His response was barely a whisper: "I just came back." He rubbed his cheek against hers, wiping off the tears.

"What's going to happen?" She had to choke out the words.

He was silent for a moment. Dinah could hear him swallow. "Nothing that keeps me away from you." His words resonated with unconditional resolve. He drew back a little, smoothing his hands over her wet cheeks, and she leaned her head onto his chest. He wrapped his arms around her, pulling her close against him. She heard the phrase echo in the room: *Nothing that keeps me away from you.* In that moment, she loved him more than she had ever thought possible. She felt like the past months had all been a terrible dream, and she had finally woken up.

"I thought you were coming home next week," she murmured.

"I didn't stay for counselor's week. The campers left yesterday." He took a step back, gently grasping her shoulders, his eyes traveling up and down. "You look nice wet." Tru's voice was still subdued, but a familiar grin was playing on his lips, and Dinah could see the ghost of a gleam in his eyes. "All tan, and soft, and . . . damp . . ." He swallowed hard, taking in the soaked, clinging blouse. "Maybe I'm still at Genoa, dreaming . . ." The sound of another car pulling into the driveway finally separated them.

"I should go upstairs . . . my mom and Jemima are home." Dinah hurried toward the stairs to get out of her wet clothes and let Tru explain his unexpected appearance.

"Wait." Tru looked up at her on the stairway. "I need to talk to you— alone. Do you have to work at the library tonight?"

"No, I work tomorrow night."

"Can you say you do?"

Dinah just nodded, thinking it was the best idea she'd ever heard.

"I'll pick you up there at eight o'clock." He smiled his oblique smile, a trace of the old Tru surfacing through the worn strife. "If I'm lucky, it will still be raining."

Jane was surprised when Dinah showed up at five o'clock. She was just leaving and Joanne O'Connor had arrived to take the evening shift. "Honey, I have you on the schedule for tomorrow night."

"I know—I'm just here to check out some books."

"It couldn't wait one more day? You are the most inveterate bookworm I've ever come across." Chuckling and shaking her head, she patted Dinah's shoulder on her way out.

Dinah let out a breath of relief; lying was still a challenge. She had already struggled to sound casual and convincing when she told her mother that Joanne was sick and she had been called to fill in. Now she had three hours to kill, and she moved into the stacks to find something to read, choosing another E.M. Forrester title: *A Room with a View*. She sat at a long table in the reading room, pulling the chain on one of the low lamps that were spaced at intervals along the center of the table. Although she had liked *Howards End*, she was having trouble concentrating on this one; her eyes kept wandering to the clock on the wall, which for some reason had slowed its pace. The minute hand was dragging around in mocking hesitancy. At 7:30 she couldn't sit still any more. She said good night to Joanne and went outside to sit on the wide stone steps and wait. The thunderstorm had passed in the afternoon, leaving a calm heaviness in the air; it was warm and it smelled of rain and grass and flowers. It was Dinah's favorite time of day, the last, lingering light—mellow and soft—before dusk. She could hear the evening call of the larks, and a lone cricket, warming up for the show.

She was glad when she saw the Buick turn the corner at 7:50, ten minutes early. The library closed at nine o'clock, so they wouldn't have much time before Dinah had to be home, playing out the ruse. Tru pulled up in front of the steps, windows rolled down, and leaned toward the passenger window. "Excuse me—can you give me directions?"

Dinah walked to the car, leaning in. "Are you lost?"

He held her eyes for moment. "Not anymore." He leaned over and opened the door, and she slid in.

They drove across town to the causeway, and Dinah knew where he was headed. It didn't take long to get onto the island, and when he pulled the car over on the gravel road she hurried out; time was playing a twisted joke, the hands now rushing around the face of her watch like a mad, over-wound mechanical toy.

He took her hand as they climbed over the boulders, once again lifting her down from the last promontory to the smooth, dry surface of the flat rock. He didn't have the blanket—they didn't need it. They settled against the wall, the warmth that had been stored from the late afternoon sun emanating onto their backs and legs. Tru leaned his head back and closed his eyes; Dinah leaned against him, their intertwined hands resting on his leg. It was so peaceful that Dinah wished they could stop time and stay there forever, watching the last traces of light on water as the sun set behind them, reflecting muted shimmery light onto their faces, warming the frozen winter of their souls. They were reluctant to speak, to shatter the illusion of a tranquil, untroubled existence. Finally, Tru gave a long sigh.

"I guess you know that there have been some plans in the works that involve . . . my future."

Dinah swallowed and nodded, painfully aware of what those plans were.

"It's been . . . hard," he continued. "Confusing. I mean, it's impossible to really confront the issue until it's certain . . . So that's why, I think, it took me so long to see it. To see the obvious thing. People tell you one thing, and, especially when it's someone like your dad, you feel like you have to listen. And you won't believe it, and you hope it will go away, and it's just . . . overwhelming. You don't know what to do. But then it came to me. I guess I had to get away to think clearly, but finally it came to me. I can't do something that would be so wrong, so fundamentally wrong, that it would ruin the lives of several people. No matter what everyone says is the right thing, the honorable thing. They're wrong. I can't . . . I can't marry someone I don't love. No matter what. Even if I am . . . the one, it wouldn't be fair—to anyone. I can take responsibility, I can work until my back breaks to support whatever needs supporting. I can be . . . a father." He turned away from the reflecting water to look into her eyes. "But I'm not letting you go. I can't."

Dinah was dumbstruck—she gazed at him in wonder, blessing every defiant bone in his body, utterly overwhelmed with loving him. Tru looked back at the warm, pink light of the setting sun on the calm water of the cove. "I think I have it figured out. If it turns out to be, um, necessary, I'll ask my dad for help. Until I graduate. I know I'm lucky—it wouldn't be a big problem for him, financially, and I'll pay him back someday. So I guess . . . I guess what I'm asking is, is that OK with you? I mean, can you live with that?" He looked at her, and his face was so vulnerable, so hopeful, that she had to smile. She put her arms around him and leaned in to give him her answer.

By the time they returned to the car, Dinah was looking at her watch. "You'd better drive fast. It only takes me a few minutes to walk home from the library."

Tru didn't seem to be in a hurry, reaching over and popping open the glove compartment. He pulled out a small package, wrapped in plain white paper with a slender blue ribbon. "Happy birthday."

Dinah's birthday had come and gone in the horrendous week following Lana's announcement. She had cancelled the slumber party, and she hadn't had the appetite or inclination to accept Tom and Caroline's invitation to go out to dinner at Donovan's—the nicest restaurant in town. Her mother had made her favorite birthday cake, German chocolate, but she didn't have the heart to tell her that she couldn't taste it as she forced down a small piece. There had been several lovely gifts from her family: a book of Auden's poetry from Tom, who had inscribed the inside cover with the notation that although he was no poet, he could recognize the gift in others; a small patent-leather coin purse with a silhouette of a horse's head on it from Jemima; and from her mother, a beautiful silver vanity set with her first initial engraved on the hairbrush and the hand mirror. Her friends had pitched in together and given her a black cashmere sweater, elegant and sophisticated. But it all seemed wasted—she felt sadly incapable of appreciating the beauty of the gifts and the thoughtfulness behind them.

She stared at the gift in her hand, amazed that he had remembered.

"Go ahead, open it."

The narrow ribbon was satin—it slid off easily. Her fingers fumbled a little as she gently tore open the paper. Lifting the lid of a small black box, she took out a delicate silver necklace, twinkling in the light of the dashboard. Suspended from a fine chain was a little sailboat that seemed to tack in an imaginary breeze.

"This is beautiful. I love it. It's . . . it's you." She opened the clasp, holding it out for him to put it around her neck.

"I found it at a silversmith's shop near camp—the Penobscot tribe still makes jewelry there." He reached around her neck to secure it. It fell to a point just below the hollow of her throat, and he touched it gently. "Listen," he spoke softly. "I want you to know that I'm sorry. Not just about everything that's happened, but about missing your birthday and, you know, deserting you like that. I just thought . . . well, I thought it would be easier for you, and being anywhere near you would have been a hell of a lot harder for me—"

She interrupted him with a soft, slow kiss. "I know. You don't have to explain. It's all right—everything's all right." And then, looking into deep pools of dark coffee, she told him what she felt like she had known for her entire life: "I love you."

He dropped her off a block from the house. She was late, but not alarmingly so. "I'll see you later." He picked up her hand and kissed the back of it.

"Where are you going?"

"I need to go over and talk to Bill."

He didn't elaborate, but Dinah understood—Bill was his best friend; he would want to know what was going on.

When she got home, she found Jemima in bed but still awake, percolating like a coffee pot. "Dinah—you missed dinner! Tru gave me a present!" She was holding out a small birch-bark canoe; in it were two miniature braves in headdresses, holding tiny oars. They were carved from wood, with amazingly intricate detail. "These are Penobscots. Tru said they used to live all over in Maine, but there are only a few left. And I have two of them!" She laughed at the joke, her eyes dancing with the excitement of having Tru home again, and then she studied the little figures intently. "I think the real ones are bigger, though."

Dinah laughed. How could her sister be so sincerely naive? She was touched that Tru had remembered how much Jemima loved tiny things—he had a way of noticing things without seeming to. She sat down on Jemima's bed. "Look, Mimer—I got a present too." She pulled the sailboat pendant away from her neck, leaning toward her sister.

Jemima looked at it carefully, reaching out to run her finger over the smooth silver of the little boat. "Did you say *woliwoni*?"

Dinah didn't have the slightest idea what she was talking about. "What?"

"*Woliwoni*. That's how the Penobscots say thank you. Tru told me."

"I didn't know that. I had to thank him in my own language."

She kissed her little sister goodnight, and Jemima placed the canoe on her nightstand, adjusting it carefully, so that she could see it from her pillow.

Nervously, Dinah poked her head in to say goodnight to her mother. Caroline was propped up against the headboard on a pillow, a book resting on her lap.

"Hi—I'm home."

"Hello. How was work tonight?"

"Fine. Nothing special—it was quiet."

Her mother nodded, looking at her evenly. "I hope Joanne doesn't have anything contagious."

"No, I don't think so. I mean, nothing serious. It's probably just a cold or something."

"Well that's good. I'd hate to think she had anything serious."

She knew. Dinah realized with certainty that her mother knew she hadn't had to work that night. Swallowing hard, she backed out of the doorway. "Well, I'm pretty tired—I guess I'll go to bed. Goodnight!"

"Goodnight, Dinah." Caroline hesitated. "One more thing . . ."

Dinah looked back in, her heart pounding. "Yes?"

"I like your necklace."

Lying in bed, Dinah wondered how her mother had known. Was it just from spotting the necklace? Dinah had the sudden panicked feeling that maybe her mother knew everything about her, all the time. Maybe there was some weird power that mothers had to read their children's minds or to sense their behavior. She felt a horrible flash of embarrassment at the idea, replaying scenes from her private encounters with Tru. The way her body responded to him was completely out of her control—she was constantly astonished at her lack of restraint. If it hadn't been for Tru's iron discipline, she didn't think she would have been able to draw any lines. It was as if all standards and expectations flew out the window in the face of her overwhelming love for him. Being with Tru felt completely right, and she couldn't make her body believe that there was any reason to say no. She heard her mother's voice, insisting that their good intentions may not be enough to protect them from themselves, and she saw the truth in it.

As she drifted off to sleep, her fingers went to the pendant still around her neck. She hadn't taken it off for bed, and she didn't think she ever would. Twisting the little boat between her fingers, she fell asleep with a smile on her face, and dreamed of sailing.

Her dream came true the next day, when Tru came down for breakfast and asked her if she'd like to go out on the catboat. Tilting his head, he made a show of sizing her up, then came over and put his hands on her waist. "You look like perfect ballast. How'd you like to come out on the water with me today?"

Dinah looked around quickly, glad her mother and Jemima were out in the backyard tending the flower beds. "I guess so. I've never been sailing before."

Raising one eyebrow, Tru looked surprised. "Is that a fact? Hmmm." His voice was low as he leaned down and kissed her just below the ear. "Well, I'd say it's about time somebody showed you how it's done." She felt the tip of his tongue trace lightly across her skin. "And I'm just the guy to do it."

In what was becoming a regular occurrence, the capillaries beneath her skin swelled to a flush, just as Jemima ran through the back door. Tru stepped away, laughing when he saw that Dinah was blushing. Addressing Jemima, he kept his eyes on her sister. "I was just saying that it's about time someone took Dinah sailing. That *was* what we were talking about, wasn't it?"

Dinah was flustered. She picked up the box of corn flakes and turned to Jemima. "Do you want anything else for breakfast?" Her hand was a little shaky.

"No, thank you," she said politely, but then turned to Tru. "I want to go sailing! You said you'd take me as soon as you got back." She looked at him accusingly.

"Listen, Skipper, I need you for tomorrow." He gave Jemima his full attention. "Tomorrow is important. I should take Dinah today, because there isn't much wind and I don't need a good sailor. But tomorrow is going to be windy, and I need someone who knows what they're doing." He tousled her hair and it was almost possible to see her ego inflating.

"OK, I guess. Dinah doesn't know how to do anything. She doesn't even know how to come about. You'll have to show her everything."

Tru flashed a wide smile. "That I will." Grabbing an apple from a bowl on the table he made toward the doorway. As he past Dinah, he leaned down furtively and whispered into her ear.

Several minutes later her cheeks were still burning with the echo of his teasing words: "You have a dirty mind."

Both of his boats were moored in Marblehead. Tru wanted to take out the twenty-foot catboat he had spent the winter refurbishing with Tom. Dinah was tentative as she moved from the little dinghy to the sailboat—she felt like an awkward landlubber, unsure of what to do. She scrambled aboard, quickly sitting down as the boat lurched on a small swell. Grabbing the halyard, Tru grinned at her obvious inexperience, dryly suggesting that she'd better move over as he raised the gaff rig. She scooted out of the way as the boom swung around, shooting him an accusatory glare. He patted a wooden bench in the stern, and she gingerly crab-crawled to the back of the boat, sitting primly next to him as he adjusted the keel and trimmed the sail to a lovely, beam-reach tack.

There wasn't a lot of wind, but Tru expertly worked the rudder, moving the boat smoothly out of the cove into the open, sun-kissed bay. Dinah felt herself relaxing with the rhythm of the water, leaning back to let the sun warm her face and the breeze blow through her hair. She kicked off her sandals and put her feet up on the step, stretching out her bare legs. They sailed for the better part of an hour, Dinah watching as Tru easily maneuvered the sail to catch the wind. He didn't need a crew—that much was clear. She embraced her role as passenger, closing her eyes for long moments to relish the serenity of it all. It was during one of those moments that she felt the boat start to slow. She opened her eyes to see Tru spinning the winch. A minute later, the sail was down and they were drifting idly.

Peeling off his shirt, Tru stood and stretched. "Come here." He held out his hand, pulling her up as she took it, and led her to the front of the boat, stretching out on the smooth wood of the bow. They sprawled in the sun, bobbing on the gentle swells that rocked the boat. "How do you like sailing?" Tru's voice was relaxed to the point of drowsiness; he absently traced his finger up and down her arm.

"It's nice. It's different than I expected. When we watched you race last year, it was so wild and fast—it looked dangerous. But this is peaceful."

"Mmmm." He rolled onto his side, facing her. "Well, I'm not really wild and fast, as you can see. It's a common misperception." His head was resting flat on his arm, and he smiled his teasing smile, lazily wrapping a tress of her hair around his finger. "Aren't you hot?" He looked at her blouse, which was clinging to a light film of perspiration that covered her chest. Dinah had worn cotton shorts and a sleeveless blouse, confident that she would be comfortable enough, but now she regretted it.

"It is a little warm without much breeze. I should have worn a swimsuit."

"Hold your breath." Before the words left his mouth, he had pulled her on top of him, wrapping his arms around her as he rolled them both off the boat and into the cool depths of the bay.

She barely had time to register the words before they hit the water. He didn't release her, clutching her tightly against him as they sank, and she had the odd sensation that she was part of his body. In the seconds they were underwater she felt no panic—only a sense of complete security, of absolute faith that he would provide the air for her to breathe when she needed it. She opened her eyes as they surfaced, and once again she was met with the mooring of his steady gaze. She drew a deep breath, and he kissed her, then he swiveled her shoulders so that he was holding her from behind.

"Lie back." As she leaned back, he dove under the water, surfacing to float on his back beneath her legs. She was perfectly, effortlessly buoyant—his body supporting the part of her that would otherwise sink. Puffy, cirrus clouds danced across an azure sky and the world disappeared as they floated, listening only to the sonic echo of the sea.

Lulled to the point of sleepiness, Dinah started when Tru took her hand to pull her toward the boat. There was a small ladder off the transom, and they swam to it.

"We should head back. We're losing what little wind there was. If it hits dead calm, we'll have to stay here all night. Then again . . ." Tru raised his eyebrows as she pulled herself up on the ladder. Perched on the second rung, she looked down to discover that everything she had on had become semi-transparent. She dropped back into the water, looking at him helplessly.

"You're going to have to get on the boat sometime." His grin was diabolic.

"You did this on purpose, didn't you?"

He looked affronted. "Absolutely not. Some days," he smiled and shrugged helplessly, "things just seem to go my way." Pulling himself up, he stood dripping in the stern with his hands on his hips. "Can I give you a hand?"

"I think I can manage." Dinah climbed the rungs, but her hand slipped a little on the edge of the boat and Tru grabbed her arm, pulling her in. The breeze, seemingly nonexistent before, brushed her wet skin with goosebumps and she shivered.

Dinah could tell immediately that they could be in trouble. She saw her mother's face as she asked if she could go sailing with Tru, and the long look Caroline had given her—a mix of worry, warning, and weary resignation. She couldn't very well deny Dinah the opportunity when Jemima would be going the very next day.

Pulling away from him, she crossed her arms across her chest. "Are there any towels on the boat?" Her voice was small, apologetic.

He followed her drift. "Trying to keep me honest, huh?" Moving away, he grabbed a towel from a small cupboard under the bow, looking back with a wistful expression. "I need all the help I can get." He wrapped the towel around her snugly. "Just don't make it a habit."

They were almost dry by the time they tied up. Tru carried the towel over his shoulder, laying it on the upholstery of the Nash before Dinah got in. It had been a perfect day—the magic of the sun and the sea bestowing tranquil contentment on both of them. They drove home in relaxed silence for several minutes, until a thought occurred to Dinah. "Have you talked to your dad about . . . your plans?" The question came out unbidden—she hadn't intended to ruin the day by inviting the problem into the car, but her subconscious had a stronger agenda.

"He knows. I wrote him a letter a while ago."

Dinah pictured the envelope on the Pembroke table. "What did it say?" She couldn't help herself.

He didn't answer for a moment, and then he gave her a knowing look, his voice taunting. "You want me to say it, don't you?"

She was mortified—he had seen through her before she had seen through herself. She couldn't even respond, turning her head to look out the window.

He waited, and she kept her eyes glued to the passing trees. Finally he took pity on her, laughing softly at her embarrassment. "I'll say it—I don't mind. Look at me." He kept one eye on the road as he reached over to turn her face toward his. "It said: Dear Dad—I'm going to marry Dinah. Your son, Tru."

CHAPTER SIXTEEN

Something You Know
How to Do

THE DAYS DISAPPEARED LIKE FOG in the sun. Tru spent most of them on the water, taking Jemima out a couple of times on the catboat and sailing with Bill as his crew on the catamaran. On his last day home they competed in a big regatta in Boston—this time in the adult class. Despite shifting winds, they took both races. Tom and Jemima were there to cheer them on, but both Dinah and Caroline had to miss it. Dinah was scheduled to work at the library, and Caroline had a Ladies' Auxiliary meeting.

What had been planned as a farewell dinner at Donovan's that evening now became a victory celebration as well. Dinah was home from the library, getting dressed for dinner, when she heard them all come in, jubilant with the win. She was happy to hear that Tru had won, but it couldn't mitigate her despondence that he was leaving for Williamsburg in the morning. She pulled on her dress—an ice-blue polished cotton with narrow shoulder straps and a low back. It was perfect for summer, showing off her tan and her figure. She had loved the dress when she picked it out with her mother several weeks before, but now she couldn't summon any appreciation for the light, silky fabric or the beguiling cut. He had only been home for nine days. Nine days, and now he would be gone for months.

They had tried to spend as much time together as they could, grabbing any opportunity for privacy, but Tom and Caroline were particularly watchful, making it difficult to be alone. Whenever she voiced her despair at his leaving, Tru would lighten the moment by making her laugh with outrageous promises. He promised he wouldn't smile even once until he saw her again; he promised he would write long poems about her for the school newspaper; he promised that he would have her name tattooed on his arm; he promised that he wouldn't go out on Saturday nights, or have any fun ever, for that matter. He promised that he would dream only about her. He promised he would go to church every Sunday to pray that she still loved him. But most outrageous of all was the promise that the time would go by quickly. That one, she knew, was a lie.

When she came downstairs, Tru and Tom had gone up to shower and dress. Caroline was ready and waiting. Dinah couldn't help noticing how beautiful her mother looked in a simple black sheath with the double strand of pearls that Tom had given her for her birthday. They were to replace the strand that Caroline had passed on to Dinah, and they were a beautiful, lustrous ivory.

Caroline smiled at her daughter. "You look very nice." It was an understatement, as custom. In truth Caroline had been overawed of late whenever she looked at her older daughter. The luminescent beauty that Dinah had possessed all of her life had burgeoned into something almost startling. It was more than just the happy accident of extraordinarily fine features and silken hair. There was a nearly palpable allure that seemed to resonate around her, and Caroline had to conscientiously avoid thinking about the source of this phenomenon. "Where is that pony-tailed little bookworm that I used to know?"

Dinah just shrugged, feeling self-conscious. "Where's Mimer?"

"She went up to change—no help allowed. She is old enough to decide what to wear by herself, didn't you know?"

The words were no sooner out of her mouth than Jemima descended the stairs, wearing the pink peony dress from the wedding. It had become a little short on her, but it was still her favorite. She was rummaging through a small white patent-leather purse. "Has anyone seen my lipstick?"

Dinah looked at her mother with an expression of disbelief, trying not to smile.

"I don't believe I have. What color is it?" Caroline played it straight.

"Um, I think it's red. It has a name. It's on the bottom. It's called Copa Banana, or something like that."

Now it was Caroline's turn for disbelief. "Do you mean Copacabana?"

"Maybe. That might be it. I know it was in here before . . ."

"Jemima, just where did you get this lipstick?" Her mother looked suspicious, and Dinah was now wearing an amused grin.

There was a pause, and they could see Jemima thinking quickly as her eyes darted back and forth. "I found it somewhere. I found it outside. At school."

"I see. Well, that's quite a coincidence. Coco wears the very same shade.

Won't she be pleased to know that you two share the same taste in lipstick? I'll have to be sure to tell her the next time she's here."

Jemima's olive complexion turned a different shade—something more akin to the flowers on her dress. "Oh, well, it might not be the same. In fact, I'm pretty sure it was called something else. Like . . . Denver Omelet."

Dinah burst out laughing. That was exactly what Tom had ordered the last time they had gone to Melville's.

Caroline was trying, without much success, to look stern. Her mouth quivered as she spoke: "Well, I certainly hope that whoever . . . lost . . . her lipstick will be able to replace it. Some poor woman is probably looking high and low for her signature shade, thinking about just exactly where she had it last."

They could both read Jemima's thought process; a fleeting nervousness turned to bold confidence as she plastered a smile on her face. "I'm sure that whoever it was hasn't seen her lipstick for a long time. She won't remember where she was when . . . it got lost. I'm going to wait in the car." With that, she snapped her purse closed and sashayed outside.

Tom came down the stairs as Caroline and Dinah were staring at the door, open-mouthed. He gave a low whistle. "What do we have here?" He surveyed the scene. "I am surrounded by beauty." He kissed his wife on the cheek, and turned to Dinah. "You are as captivating as your mother. We are lucky men in this house." There was an awkward moment as the implication settled in. Tom looked surprised by his own words; it was an acknowledgement he hadn't intended. They were spared by more footsteps, as Tru tripped lightly down the stairs, whistling as he buttoned a cuff.

His hair was still damp. He was wearing a tie and blazer, the crisp white of his shirt collar complementing his deep tan. Looking up at him, Dinah felt a little flutter in her heart. The feeling must have been mutual—Tru stopped mid-step when he saw her. He stood motionless, hand frozen on his cuff, one foot on the stair behind him, staring. His eyes narrowed as his mouth slowly curved up at one corner, and he moved his head very subtly, very slowly, back and forth, as if in warning, as if no one else were in the room. He held her in his gaze like that for an indecently long moment, and Dinah felt the same heat that had covered her at the dinner table on the night they had met in the pantry.

"OK then!" Tom's voice was brusque as he gave a sharp clap. "It looks like we're all here. We have reservations at seven." With a bewildered shake of his head he grabbed his hat and waved an arm to usher them all to the door.

The doorman at Donovan's greeted them effusively. They were taken by a tuxedoed maitre d' to one of the large, semi-circular leather banquettes that lined the walls. The ambience was supper-club snazzy—low candles on the tables, velvet curtains lining the walls, and the Bobby Sweet orchestra playing from the bandstand in the corner. Tom extended an arm, indicating that the women should be seated first. Caroline slid in, followed by Jemima and Dinah. The men took a position at each end, with Tom sitting down next to Dinah, leaving Tru to sit by Caroline. To Dinah, it didn't seem arbitrary. The waiter brought a relish tray and the adults ordered cocktails.

There was a lightness in the air that had been notably absent for the past few months. It was like they had all decided to paint the looming possibility out of the picture for the moment, savoring the festive moment. Tom toasted his son with a short but poignant speech, crediting his focus and determination, and his prowess on the water. He wished him luck for the football season, threatening to drive to Williamsburg for every home game. When the waiter took their orders for dinner, he asked for a bottle of champagne, magnanimously pouring glasses for everyone at the table, with just a splash in Jemima's water glass.

They were finishing the salad course when the orchestra struck up. Tom held his hand out to Caroline. They danced a foxtrot, navigating among several other couples who had taken to the floor. When the song ended, Caroline raised one foot delicately as Tom leaned her backward in a deep dip, and Jemima clapped. They returned to their seats, flushed and laughing, as the main course was delivered.

Dinah and Jemima had both ordered lobster; when the waiter offered bibs Jemima took personal offense, scolding him sternly: "Do you think I'm a baby?" Tom and Caroline shared a Chateaubriand, and Tru had a T-bone steak. Tom was particularly ebullient during the meal, entertaining the table with an enthusiastic accounting of the regatta, while Tru looked on with a slightly pained expression.

The bottle of champagne was perplexingly empty; Tom ordered another. On the wings of amnesiac determination, the little party was almost boisterous, laughing and joking throughout the meal. Of the group, only Jemima was unaware of the ghost in the attic, but they were all intent on holding tight the ceiling door, willing the specter to recede into the darkness, unwelcome in their evanescent, shining circle.

Like many of the better restaurants in Boston and New York, Donovan's employed a house photographer. He went by the name of Sal, introducing himself as he looked down into the camera, enjoining them to lean in and smile. "Would you look at this table? Such a bounty of beauty has not graced this humble room in the centuries I've been here. What's your name, Sweetheart?"

"Jemima." Her reply burbled through a giggle.

"Jemima! What a fabulous name. It sounds like an exclamation. I bet you have all the boys following you around, don't you?" He snapped the picture as she beamed into the camera, his shameless fawning eliciting smiles of amusement all around.

The orchestra had taken a small break during dinner, but they returned as the plates were cleared, and Tom ceremoniously asked Jemima to dance. He lifted the little girl into his arms, doing a modified soft-shoe shuffle onto the dance floor. It was easy to hear Jemima's laughter as he dipped and spun her around the floor, and Dinah was touched by the sweet happiness on her mother's face, softly smiling at her husband's antics.

As the song ended Tom shimmied Jemima back to the table, and in the spirit of conviviality he challenged his son to best his performance. "Am I the only Stuart who dances here?" The dare was unexpected, to say the least. Recently, there had been a marked effort to discourage this type of interaction between Tru and Dinah.

The champagne had clearly gotten the better of his father's discretion, but Tru wasn't about to pass on the opportunity. "I dance. Dinah, do you dance?" His voice was mockingly formal.

Panic hit Dinah in the chest. She couldn't dance like he could. A vision of Tru and Lana at the Red Barn flashed before her eyes. "I, ah, haven't danced all that much . . ."

The words weren't out of her mouth before Tru was standing next to her, holding out his hand. "It's easy. If he can do it"—he nodded at his father with a contained smirk—"anyone can."

She stood nervously, taking his hand as he led her onto the floor. As they moved away from the table, Tru spoke out of the side of his mouth: "I like your dress."

"Thank you."

"Do you enjoy torturing me?"

"What do you mean?" Dinah was smiling.

He turned to put his arm around her back, his voice low. "I believe it's what you would call a paradox." His lips brushed her ear. "It looks so good on you that I want to take it off you."

In a stroke of profound confluence, the band struck up a sultry, groaning version of Woody Herman's "Blues in the Night." This was Tru's music—it was what he loved. He pulled her close, with the secret, Cheshire-cat smile of someone who has just learned that the game has been rigged to his advantage.

Dinah stuttered: "I don't really know how to—."

"Shhh. Don't talk. Just listen. Here," he placed his hand on her lower back, pulling her even closer. "Can you feel this?" His thigh pressed against hers. "Just keep your legs close to mine. That's all you have to do. And relax." The music swelled with a guttural trombone slide, and he started to move her. She was looking down, trying to watch his feet, but he cupped her chin in his hand, tilting her face up.

"Look here. Look at me."

She looked into his eyes, and magically her body started to follow his. He kept his right hand pressed on the small of her back, holding her against him; his other hand clasped hers lightly, almost imperceptibly informing her direction. It wasn't difficult after all—following Tru was easy. Dinah felt like she had turned into air. He moved her slowly, sensuously around the floor. While the band's phrasing had started out swaying and deliberate, the tempo gradually heated up to an undulant, pulsing rumba. Tru matched the rhythm smoothly, finessing an intricate series of quick steps and subtle twists that Dinah miraculously followed.

It wasn't until the horns sighed their last fading wail that Dinah became aware of the other dancers. She and Tru had been caught in a vortex of physical communion, oblivious to anyone else, but now she realized that most of the couples on the floor were watching them. She knew it was Tru they were really watching—she could see the envy on the faces of the women and the self-conscious impotence on the faces of the men. It seemed that even the orchestra had noticed them; when she looked up, the trombone player winked at her. As they started to leave the floor, a voice called, "Hold for a shot, please," and they turned to find Sal aiming his lens at them. Dinah smiled and was momentarily blinded as the flash bulb sparked, but the reassuring grasp of Tru's hand on her arm led her safely to the table.

As they took their seats, her eyes readjusted just in time to notice the ambivalent looks on their parents' faces. Tom seemed torn between disapproval and admiration. He addressed his son: "That was quite . . . something. When did you learn how to dance?"

Tru shrugged. "It's not really something you learn—it's just something you know how to do." Dinah had heard that before somewhere; it was exactly what Bill had said about painting.

"It's not the old box step we learned in school, I'll say that much." Tom cleared his throat, and both he and Caroline looked down at their plates. "Well, I took the liberty of ordering your dessert—it's the house specialty." As they picked up their forks to try the New York Cheesecake, Tom raised his glass and gave another toast: "Here's to dancing."

Caroline came out of the bathroom in her nightgown, rubbing Caswell's Gardenia Lotion onto her bare arms, to find her husband sitting on the edge of the bed, staring at the floor.

As he raised his head she was greeted with a bewildered expression: "What *was* that?"

She shook her head. "I don't know. Was it my imagination or did the room actually get warmer while they were dancing?"

"It wasn't your imagination. I was afraid some of those women on the dance floor were going to leave their partners and form a line."

Absently massaging her right temple, she sat down next to him. "This is a runaway train. I don't think there's a single thing we can do about it. Just cross our fingers and pray, I guess."

Tom looked at her tenderly: "You know, if Tru is anywhere near as in love with Dinah as his father is with her mother, I don't think we have anything to worry about. He won't ever hurt her."

"That's not all I'm worried about. What's going to happen to those poor kids when the blood test is done? How can they manage to survive the responsibilities . . . the complications . . . the unforgiving strain of it all? I just don't see how they'll ever be able to overcome the hurdles. Dinah is only in high school! How will they manage to wait for each other?" She paused for a moment. "Look at what happened to us," she said softly. "The timing just wasn't right. And we were older than they are."

Tom brushed his hand across her cheek, his voice tender: "It wasn't a coincidence that I moved to Salem, you know."

Perplexed, Caroline turned as he picked up her hand.

"After I went to Pennsylvania, I knew I had made a mistake; whatever my ambitions were, they hadn't been worth letting you go. By the time I realized it, it was too late." He absently regarded his thumb, moving in slow circles around hers: "I came back. I don't know what could have made me believe that you would still be available—any idiot would have known that some other guy, someone with more intelligence and foresight, would be waiting in line. But I never got the chance to plead my case. I stopped in Boston on my way back, and Coco was kind enough to give me the newspaper clipping of your engagement."

Caroline was stunned. He had come back for her? What would have happened if she had known? She couldn't bring herself to think about it; her love for Gideon had been overwhelming, but no more so than her love for Tom now. The knowledge was jarring, and better left in the past. She didn't want to even ponder the choice she would have had to make.

"I think Margaret always knew there had been someone else—someone that . . . haunted me," Tom continued. "It wasn't really fair to her—it was like I had lost a part of my heart and it didn't grow back." He smiled sadly. "After she died, something just . . . drew me here. I think I wanted to be in the place where you used to live." He hesitated for a moment, and then with a sheepish look he said, "I used to stop by and see your mother once in a while. I made her promise not to tell you. I knew you were happy—she filled me in on the basic details. I also wondered how it would feel if I ever ran into you. I was afraid, actually, that it would happen, and I'd have to see you with your husband . . . Anyway, I hadn't seen Cecelia for quite a while when I heard she had died. I felt terrible for missing her funeral. But I guess I would have blown my cover if I had shown up and seen you there."

Caroline digested all this with astonishment. He had visited her mother? It seemed surreal—he had never mentioned it until now. "So that night at Melville's—did you know . . . ?"

"I didn't realize it was you. I wasn't paying attention—and I had long given up the fantasy of bumping into you. I figured you wouldn't have much reason to come back, with both of your parents gone. It took me a minute to process the reality of . . . you. I was completely blindsided. In fact, I can't even remember what I said." He smiled sheepishly. "Probably something inane. I remember wondering where your husband was . . ." His voice grew solemn. "I didn't know he was gone. And that, of course, is why I didn't phone, or stop by. But when I saw you in the parking lot at the mill, there was something . . . I don't know what it was, but something told me that you were alone. You just looked so . . . lost." He kissed her hand. "So now you know my secret—I loved you all along. I should have never let you go."

The dawning of an understanding spread across his face, and he looked almost surprised. "I guess I have to respect Tru for knowing what he wants, and for holding on to it. As complicated and difficult as the situation is, I think he has his priorities straight—you just don't let a love like that go."

As he reached for her, Caroline knew that what he said was true. She closed her eyes and felt the strength of his steady arms around her, and she offered up a prayer, a plea to a higher power: *Please, please, dear God—let us know that love until we are very, very old.*

The night air was warm and languid. Although the windows were open wide, the still blanket of August covered Dinah's skin and she kicked off the bed sheets. The thin lawn nightgown she wore clung slightly, due as much to nervous anticipation as to the sultry heat. The house had been dark for hours, but it seemed like eons. She had turned off her lamp early hoping to speed up time. In a stroke of luck, Tom had gone to bed when Caroline did, instead of staying up late in the library. Dinah saw it as a sign—it was meant to be.

They had been leaving Donovan's, walking through the parking lot, when Tru pulled her aside, speaking in a covert whisper. "I'll see you later."

"Where?"

He smiled: "Just be sure to leave your door unlocked."

"You're coming to my room?" Dinah's voice rose in alarm.

"Unless you'd like to announce it a little louder . . ." His voice was teasing, but he stopped walking and turned serious as he looked her in the eye. "I made the mistake once of leaving without saying goodbye. I won't do it again."

Now the moon hung outside her window, not quite full. *What was it called again? A gibbous moon.* The doorknob turned silently, but she could see it. She had been watching for it.

Within seconds he was next to her in bed, kissing her throat.

"What if they hear us?" she whispered.

"They won't hear us if you don't talk." He breathed it into her ear.

"But I won't be able to talk to you for a long time. I have things to tell you." She maintained a hushed whisper.

"You can tell me things without talking, you know . . ." He moved over her.

She smiled up at him. "Tonight was fun. I liked dancing with you."

"I told you it was easy. You just have to feel the rhythm."

"That's not the only thing I felt." She was appalled at herself before the words even left her mouth.

"Dinah Hunt!" His whisper held exaggerated shock, but his dark eyes glinted in the moonlight. "Shame on you—that's obscene." As her face grew hot, he kissed her deeply, murmuring, "Obscenity becomes you . . . What do you feel now?"

Imminent separation created a new paradigm—a confluence of urgency, desperation, and recklessness—the last of which threatened to make Tru a liar. "Am I compromising you?" he whispered. "Because I promised I wouldn't, so you're going to have to tell me if this is a compromise . . ." Dinah gasped and shook her head. "How about this . . . ?" He gave her his crooked, wicked smile, ". . . or this?"

Slowly, reverently, they explored the mystical destinations of a dream, stopping short of the one fundamental compromise that Tru refused to risk. Even when she had surrendered all restraint, he held back; he loved her too much to take her there. Quaking with desire, he moved to find a compromise to avoid compromising her. As he held her tightly against him, she buried her face in his chest to contain her shuddering response, and she almost didn't hear him when he whispered in her ear: "Someday, I promise, I will show you how to sail."

CHAPTER SEVENTEEN
Obscure and Illuminate

THE HALLS OF SALEM HIGH seemed foreign—Dinah felt like she was in a different school. It was an odd sensation to be an upperclassman; the absence of last year's senior class still echoed off the tiled walls. The current class of seniors was benign, their new-found superiority targeting only the incoming sophomores. Dinah was in a strange limbo, not a member of the junior class, but not really part of the senior class, either. She still ate lunch with her friends, but all of her classes were with the seniors.

Kenny Mitchell was in her calculus class—he had managed to pass the trigonometry final at last. Sitting down at the desk next to her on the first day, he smiled as he handed her a flyer advertising positions on the newspaper staff. "Be the first to submit your application—I'll put in a good word for you!"

Dinah laughed; as editor-in-chief, he would be talking to himself. She also knew the paper was having trouble filling posts—Kenny had told her that summer that they were looking for anyone who could hold a crayon. "I'll think about it. When is the application deadline?"

"It's Friday—but there's no need to wait. In fact, I can fill it out for you—what would you like—editorials, photography . . . how about the gossip column? No, you'd be wasted there—I can give that to someone else."

"I know just the girl—have you met Joan Marconi?" She was promising to think about joining the staff when the teacher came in, and Dinah spent the rest of the class trying to ignore Kenny as he stealthily placed flyers, one after another, in a pile on her desk.

After school she stopped by Bentley Elementary to wait for Jemima. It had been almost a year since she had walked home with her little sister—the elementary school ended later than the high school, and Jemima had insisted that she could walk home with Peter, who lived just a few blocks away. But it was such a beautiful autumn afternoon that Dinah wanted to prolong the walk, and she waited on the steps for her sister.

When the bell rang, a horde of small bodies scrambled through the doors. Dinah stood to look into a sea of brightly colored shirts and blouses for a white sailor's shirt. It was Jemima's favorite thing—Tru had given it to her before he left, telling her that a real sailor should look the part. She had insisted on wearing it for the first day of school. Caroline bought her a navy plaid skirt to go with it.

When the trail of children had tapered to the last couple laggards, Dinah started to be concerned. Could she have missed her? She looked across the schoolyard toward the street, but there was no sign of Jemima. She went into the school, wandering down the hallways full of welcoming, construction-paper cutouts, looking for Mrs. Hazlet's room. After a minute or two she found it.

The door to room 107 was open. When Dinah peeked in she could see the teacher at her desk, grading a pile of wide-lined papers. Across the room, standing on a footstool, was a girl cleaning the blackboard: a girl in a sailor shirt, with curly brown pigtails. "Hello?" Dinah looked inquiringly at Mrs. Hazlet.

"May I help you?"

Jemima had turned around at the sound of Dinah's voice. When she saw her sister in the doorway, tears began to trickle down her face.

"I'm Dinah Hunt—I was just looking for my sister . . ." Her voice trailed off, confused.

"Oh . . . I'm sorry if you were concerned—Jemima didn't say that someone would be waiting outside. As you can see, she has had to stay after school today to clean the blackboard."

In her attempt to be amiable, Mrs. Hazlet fell short. Dinah could detect a note of something else. Antipathy? Contempt? Maybe it was just weary aggravation. Whatever the case, Dinah saw behind the teacher's smile.

"Why?" Seeing her little sister, perched on the footstool, crying silently as she tried to wipe the upper reaches of the blackboard, Dinah could feel a protective indignation start to simmer. Whatever Jemima had done, she couldn't imagine that it could merit making an example of her on the very first day of school.

"Perhaps you would like to ask Jemima about it?"

Dinah crossed the room to her sister. "What happened, Mimer?" The little girl's shoulders began to heave, and she turned silently to the board, blindly swiping her arm back and forth across the slate.

Dinah couldn't take it. She grabbed the long eraser and whisked the rest of the chalk away, then took her sister's hand, pulling her off of the footstool. "Come on—we'll talk about it on the way home. She turned to the woman at the desk. "Is Jemima free to go now?"

Mrs. Hazlet stood, a tight, condescending smile on her lips. "That will be sufficient. Please be sure that Jemima informs you fully of the incident. If there are any questions, I will be happy to speak to your parents." With that, she sat down and turned back to the papers on her desk.

Outside the building, Dinah knelt down and put her arms around her little sister. "Tell me what happened."

"I don't know . . ." Jemima started to sob again.

"Shhh. It couldn't be that bad. Don't worry, everything will be okay. Calm down and tell me about it."

Through spasmodic hiccups, Jemima tried to explain. "I was saving a place for Peter at lunch. He always sat by me every day last year. And Mary tried to sit there, but I told her it was for Peter. And then I was waiting for a long time, but I couldn't find him. But then Raymond said that Peter was sitting by Greta Wilson, and then he said Peter probably wanted to sit there because Greta is pretty and Peter likes her better than me. And I said he did not, and then Raymond said it looks like it to me, and then . . . um . . . then I spit in his milk."

"You spit in his milk? Oh Jemima! That's disgusting"

"I know." Jemima's voice was breaking again.

"Well, what happened after that?"

There was a long pause—long enough to alert Dinah that there was something more. "Then I went over to Peter, and I told him that I hated him and he could never sit by me again, and then I told Greta that she looked like . . . something . . . and she cried and told the teacher."

"What did you say she looked like?"

They walked twenty yards before Dinah had to ask again. "Mimer, what did you say?"

"A wart on a witch's bottom."

Dinah had to choke back a laugh. A wart on a witch's bottom? Where did her little sister come up with these things? She had no idea what to say. Not only because she was a little revolted by Jemima's behavior, but because on some level she could empathize. Not with the spitting, or the invective, but with the feeling of abandonment. She knew what it was like to see the boy you loved sitting next to another girl at lunch. She really couldn't blame her.

"I hate Mrs. Hazlet. She's mean. I'm not going to school anymore."

All of Jemima's humiliation and heartbreak was handily transferred to a burning grudge against her teacher. Dinah could see the cogs in motion, the mechanics of self-protection that moved the pain away from her heart and into her gut, settling there in a focused animosity toward the convenient target. This was shaping up to be a very long year for Jemima.

"Mimer, it isn't Mrs. Hazlet's fault. You spit in someone's milk! And you can't go around calling people names like that. Did you apologize?"

"Mrs. Hazlet made me. I had to give Raymond my milk, too, but he said he didn't want it. He said it was probably poison."

Beyond the obvious inappropriateness of Jemima's behavior, Dinah was struck by the honesty in it. It was so immediate—so visceral. She thought it must be something someone is born with—wearing one's feelings right out in the open—not bothering to look before leaping. Certainly that had never been her problem. Dinah couldn't count the times she had practically drowned in hesitation and introspection.

"Are you going to tell Momma?"

She had to think about it for a minute. "If I don't tell her, Mrs. Hazlet probably will. You have to tell her yourself, Mimer. Just explain it to her like you did to me. I can't promise you won't get into trouble, but it will be a lot easier than if she has to hear it from the teacher." She was relieved that she could so easily pass the buck. For the first time, she realized how hard it must be to be a parent. She was glad that Jemima's behavior wasn't her responsibility.

The mail was piled in its usual place on the Pembroke table. Under a small stack of letters was a large manila envelope. Jemima grabbed it up, enthralled by the mystery and surprise of mail delivery. Dinah couldn't deny that she felt the same way. She could see the printed name on the top left corner—Donovan's. Jemima had already torn open the envelope by the time Dinah could deduce the contents. Two large, black and white photographs slid out.

"Look, Dinah! It's from the restaurant!"

They were all there, smiling at the camera, with Jemima laughing in the middle. It was a picture of the quintessential happy family—celebratory, light-hearted, leaning together toward the center. It occurred to Dinah that photographs could be oddly misleading. She studied their faces, marveling at the inability to sense the many sorrows that had been laid at their doorsteps. There appeared to be no shadows behind the smiles, no dark clouds hanging overhead—nothing more than a handsome, fortunate, carefree family. She hadn't realized, until now, how very little a photograph could reveal.

When Jemima picked it up to study it more closely, the second photo was exposed. This was the one taken as Tru and Dinah were leaving the dance floor. Dinah could remember the blinding light of the flash. Looking at the picture, she realized why Tru had been able to lead her so easily back to the table: Instead of looking into the camera, he was looking at her. She was smiling directly into the lens, flushed and bright-eyed from dancing, but Tru was in profile, gazing down at her with an expression of such naked adoration that it made her heart lurch. If she hadn't known he loved her before, she would have known it now. The contradiction was striking: Not only could a photograph obscure, it could also illuminate.

She took it to her room, hesitating as she stood before the bulletin board. For some reason, she didn't want it there, crowded among the snapshots and memorabilia. She didn't want it anywhere that others could see it—invading their privacy, leeching the magic from the glossy paper. She tucked it into her desk drawer, carefully laying it between two sheets of velum.

The light in the hallway was still on, but Caroline knew it was after midnight. She didn't need to look at the clock to know that something was off—that it was long past time for Tom to come to bed. She lay still, allowing the sense to settle; there was something wrong. The knowledge was there before she was even fully awake, fatalistic and certain. Cognition began to arrange itself into neat rows in her mind, and she walked each one, examining the crop, looking for signs of pestilence or decay. What was it? There was Jemima, who had come to her while she was preparing dinner, tears of remorse streaming a channel for her confession. Caroline had been disturbed by her daughter's ungoverned behavior, but no . . . that wasn't it. The next row contained the obvious difficulties with Tru and Dinah, never far from center, but that problem, too, was less immediate; it couldn't explain the sense of lurking ambush. There was something else—something more ephemeral. She snapped on the lamp—three o'clock. The obvious thing stared her in the face: the empty pillow. It had to be Tom. The symptoms must have returned. But how bad were they? What fresh hell could render him unable to come to bed? She sat up unsteadily—dizzy with the rush of sleep departing, dizzy with the rush of fear descending.

He was tilted back in his desk chair, feet resting on the desk, ankles crossed. Absently he puffed on his pipe, a sheet of paper in his hand and a vacant look in his eyes. The quiet was foreboding—the turntable on the phonograph was still spinning slowly, but the needle had reached the end of the record, a hushed, scratchy static repeating over and over as it moved in place. He didn't even seem to notice Caroline as she lifted the arm and turned off the machine. She approached him, putting a hand on his shoulder. Neither of them spoke for several moments. Finally, he held up the paper.

"The results of Tru's blood test arrived today."

Caroline felt the air leave her lungs; she hadn't realized she'd been holding her breath. *It wasn't the Huntington's.* Inhaling deeply, her shoulders fell in relief and she took the report. "This won't really tell us anything until after the baby arrives, though . . ." Tru had taken a blood test before he left for school. When the time came, they would have all possible information. It wouldn't necessarily be conclusive, but it could be exclusive. Caroline took the paper, trying to decipher the medical jargon.

Tom was silent for a moment. "It doesn't tell us if he is a father . . . yet. But it does tell us something else." His voice was remote, distracted, as if he were trying to see something through a dense fog.

Caroline froze. Her eyes fastened on the blood type: A positive. Suddenly she knew that this information was of vital importance. She couldn't speak—she didn't know what to say.

Woodenly, he continued: "Margaret and I had the same blood type: O positive. We counted it as a good omen when we were getting married, one more sign of compatibility. I remember Margaret joking that she wanted to add a line to our wedding vows: I promise to love, cherish, and give blood if necessary."

With a pressing need to sit down, Caroline moved to the leather wingback chair, slumping heavily into the cushion. She looked at her hands, still holding the paper. "Tom . . . I need to tell you something. I don't know how to . . . I haven't been able to decide how to do it."

He looked at her oddly, baffled by her timing.

"Coco came to me some time ago . . . I don't remember exactly when it was . . . well, it doesn't really matter. At any rate, Coco came to me with . . . with . . . some information. She wanted me to help her . . . with the burden of it. Because . . . it was Whit." She hesitated for a moment. "And Margaret."

Tom continued to stare at her blankly.

"I don't know what to say." Caroline's stammering hesitancy proved the words. "I could say that I'm sorry I didn't tell you before, but that wouldn't really be true. I honestly didn't know what to do. If it hadn't been for the Huntington's, Coco would have never . . . shared this." She shook her head at the memory of her sister-in-law's anguish. "I'm so sorry." She looked at her husband with wrenched compassion. "Coco knew about Margaret and Whit . . . she knew about Tru. She just couldn't admit it to anyone. It's not surprising, really—you know how proud she is." She paused, trying to gauge her husband's reaction. She was afraid to continue the . . . assault . . . of the disclosure, but she knew she had to tell him everything. In a thin voice, she went on: "It was astonishing—her concern for you was . . . so loving, so real. She didn't want you to know. She kept it to herself all these years." She closed her eyes, cringing at the cruelty of life. "I don't know anything more. That's all she told me. You'll need to talk to Coco."

That was it, then. She really had nothing else to tell him. Tom was staring at the tips of his shoes on the desk, trance-like, unresponsive. Caroline had no idea what to do next. What could be done in such a catastrophic, earth-shattering moment? How could he be expected to absorb something like this? It occurred to her that she needed to remind him of Coco's motivation in the first place. "I know this may not help, but you have to consider why she came to me with this: Tru will never, ever, inherit the disease. It's something she thought . . . well, we both thought you would want to know. Need to know." She stood and went to him, laying the lab report on his desk and picking up his hand. "Nothing, not one thing, has actually changed about who Tru's father is. It's you. It always has been. No one could have been a better father, and no son could have loved his father more. And now you know that he will be safe from this . . . affliction. And I think I'm glad you know."

He turned to her then, stunning her with his next words: "I knew."

Caroline never went back to bed. They stayed awake for the remainder of the night, while Tom admitted what he had never told anyone. His explanation was so eloquent, yet so simple, that it brought tears to her eyes: "The answer was there, if I had chosen to ask the question. But I didn't. He deserved better than that." As the morning light dawned, she began to understand; when Tom looked into those dark eyes, he saw only Tru. It was pure, selfless love—conscientious, yet unexamined, able to overcome the most threatening knowledge ever to confront a man. A love so unconditional that it made her weep.

She also discovered the reason for his stunned reaction: He hadn't realized that Coco knew. The likeness was strong—light hair and dark eyes were an unusual combination—but Tom had made the decision the instant he discovered that his wife was pregnant: This would be his child. The awareness had always been there, hiding in the reeds of a misty midnight fen, but he had never cared to flush it out, to hunt down a conclusion. Allowing consensual opinion was not even a consideration. And so he had never admitted the possibility that his sister, too, had made a decision based on love. He saw now how very little he really knew Coco.

Ultimately, he revealed what had been tormenting him: He had been suffering, not from worry about Tru's physical well being, but from the same wracking indecision that had plagued both Caroline and Coco: Which course would be the wiser?

"I have been guilty of ignoring the obvious. I have the reassurance— the essential relief—that Tru deserves, yet I've denied him that. It hit me when this arrived." He indicated the blood test. "It's right there, in black and white: He needs to know. He can't go through his life wondering if and when the axe will fall."

"Isn't there some way to . . . pretend? To tell him that he doesn't have the disease—that the doctors can tell?"

"I can't lie to him—he can easily do the research. I can't let him believe that he could end up like that." Then, looking at his hands, he sadly, confoundedly corrected himself: "Like this."

CHAPTER EIGHTEEN
Ego Etiam Sapor Vos

LIFE WITHOUT THE SINISTERS had a rosy hue. Dinah was surprised at the difference in her days. She hadn't realized how the ever-present threat of hostility had colored the last year. Without the minatory presence of the older girls, she was relaxed and confident. But just when she thought it was safe to go back into the water, a single predatory shark started to circle.

Lucy Hancock was the newspaper's answer to Sally Vecchi. Bossy and overbearing, she preyed on any hapless soul who happened to drift anywhere near her feeding ground. She was threatened by anyone who displayed potential competition, and mounted a defense based on offense, preempting any challengers by chewing them to ribbons before they could recognize their advantage. She hated Dinah from the moment Kenny introduced them.

"This is Lucy. She's the assistant editor. She'll show you how to do layout, and you'll be submitting most of your articles to her. Lucy, this is Dinah Hunt—the answer to our prayers. She's here to make your job easy. You'll be obsolete in no time!" He winked at Dinah behind Lucy's back. If Kenny had only known the effect of his teasing, he might have thought better of it. After four weeks of unnecessary rewrites and overt hostility, Dinah had just about had enough. She was finishing yet another revision on an article about the history of Homecoming at Salem High when a fin crested the surface.

"I hope you didn't have any plans this afternoon—we need you to stay after and finish the layout for the ads this week." Sliding into the cramped copywriter's room, Lucy leaned imposingly over the desk where Dinah was working.

"I'm not on the advertising staff—they do their own layout. And I have to work after school." Dinah was intentionally curt—she knew that polite deference would be futile.

"Well, call the plant foreman and tell him you won't be punching the clock today—Warren is out sick and Tammy has cheerleading practice, so you're it. I would have expected you to realize that a certain *esprit de corps* is taken for granted from our staff. It's poor form to limit one's effort only to one's own concern. It lacks . . . initiative and sportsmanship. You have a responsibility to make sure that you are contributing on all levels, which includes advertising."

Dinah knew this was baloney. None of the staffers ever crossed over departmental lines. If she had been asked to help another writer, that was one thing. But someone from the writing staff did not, ever, get involved with the advertising or photography staff, and vice-versa. It just wasn't done. Lucy's motivation was clear—as assistant editor she was responsible for taking up the slack when needed; it was one of the reasons the position existed. She was obviously trying to pass what was widely considered the most tedious of all assignments on to Dinah. But Dinah wasn't having it.

"Maybe you should ask Kenny to do it—he probably doesn't have anything else to do." They both knew that Kenny was stretched beyond the limit covering several unfilled positions, wearing hats from all three staffs. "I'm sure he'll understand that you don't have time for something like this."

Lucy's face reddened and seemed to swell, like it was containing steam. "I'm sure one of the other staffers will be happy to help." She turned and marched away, stopping at the door. "It's lucky we have an editorial meeting with Mr. Dean tomorrow; he always likes to be informed about the performance and effort of the staff. I've been working on evaluations—I'm sure he'll agree that it may be necessary to do some housecleaning. After all, we need to ensure that we have everyone's full commitment." With that, she marched off, slamming the door behind her.

Dinah just shook her head. Mr. Dean was the faculty advisor, but he didn't know a thing about publishing a newspaper. He was an aging, befuddled biology teacher who had to take his turn in the rotation of faculty assignments. He attended advisory meetings with the bewildered expression of a messenger mistaken for a messiah—he would no sooner get involved with personnel problems than deliver the Sermon on the Mount. She finished the article and put it in the layout bin, turning out the lights as she left. Generally, she tried to get her assignments done during sixth hour, which was study hall; that way she didn't have to stay after school when she needed to get to the library.

As she approached her locker, she was met by Joan, Marlys, Susan, and Betsy. By the look on their faces, she knew something was up.

"Where have you been? We've been waiting for you—why weren't you in senior study hall?" Betsy's voice was urgent.

"I was in the copywriter's room. What's going on?"

They all looked at each other, waiting to see who would claim the honor of news-bearer. Grabbing the opportunity, Joan fairly burst with import: "Lana had her baby!"

Dinah actually fell back against her locker—the words had the effect of pushing her down. *Lana had her baby? Lana had her baby. Oh, no. No. It couldn't really happen.* She hadn't expected it to ever become real. It was something that was supposed to stay in the future, a dangling threat that would never actually impose itself. She had not assimilated the fact that there would be an actual, flesh-and-blood human being in existence, a baby that most likely belonged to Tru. And Lana. Together. She slumped to the floor, legs splayed, books tumbling between them. In an automatic gesture of solidarity the other girls sat down around her, with Betsy and Marlys close on either side.

Betsy put her arm around Dinah's shoulders. "Honey, listen to me. Lana had her baby . . . this morning. Today. October 7. What does that say to you?"

Bewildered, Dinah just looked at her. She swallowed. "I don't know what you mean."

"Supposedly, the baby was due in November. Now, we know that babies can arrive early, but this is suspiciously early, if you ask me."

The other girls were nodding. "Way too early," Joan concurred. "There's something fishy going on here, and I'm willing to bet that Jimmy Wright will be going down to that hospital before the day is over."

It was still hard to believe, even after learning that Tru was conclusively ruled out as the father. Dinah didn't know all the details, but she had overheard her mother and Tom in hushed voices, discussing something about type B, and impossibilities, and strokes of luck. It was about time luck gave them a fair shake, she thought. Tom put a call in to the residence advisor at William and Mary, saying only that he needed to speak to his son at his earliest convenience. It was almost midnight by the time Tru called back, and Dinah happened to be nearest the phone in the hallway when it rang. She grabbed it up, a thousand butterflies lifting off in unison as the operator's voice said, "Will you accept reverse charges from Williamsburg?" It wasn't until the nasal voice repeated the question that Dinah realized she had simply nodded. By the time Tru said hello, Tom was at her elbow.

"Dinah?" Tru's voice sounded worried. "Is everything all right?"

"Yes, um, yes . . . it is. I think . . . I'd better let your dad talk to you . . ." She couldn't think of how to tell him, how to give him such an enormous gift. She wasn't sure it was her place, and she thought that maybe Tom should be the one to release his son from the chains around his ankles.

When Tom took the phone, Dinah moved away, granting him some privacy. A minute later he held out the phone to Dinah. "He wants to speak to you." Tom was smiling as he moved away, thoughtfully retreating up the stairs and out of earshot.

"Hello?"

"Hi."

She could hear the smile in his voice. "Hi."

"Do you miss me?"

"Yes."

"Why don't you come down here?"

"To Williamsburg?"

"Yeah."

"If I start walking now, I should be there in about, oh, a couple of months at most."

He laughed. "When I get home I'm teaching you how to drive. I need to see you."

"How much?"

"What?"

"How much do you need to see me?" The elation of the moment made her uncharacteristically flirtatious.

"Much."

"Are you having fun at school?"

"Of course not—I promised I wouldn't."

Dinah was smiling. "Well, I suppose it's OK if you smile once in a while . . . just don't make it a habit." The phrase echoed back to the day on the boat, and suddenly she missed him with a sharp, breathless longing.

"I'm serious. I want you to come down here. My dad's coming to a game in early November. See if you can come with him.

"Won't that be close to Thanksgiving?"

"I don't think I'll be home for Thanksgiving."

"What?" Now it was her turn to sound confused.

"It's playoffs. It looks like we have a good shot at winning the conference, and that's a big game weekend."

Her heart fell. She had been counting the weeks until Thanksgiving, and now it would be Christmas before he came home. She tried to disguise her crushed dismay, but her voice was small, betraying her as it wavered a little. "So you're having a good season?"

"I love you."

Suddenly there was a lump in her throat. He had caught her distress like a perfect pass, responding with his ever-impeccable timing. He always knew what to say, but that didn't make it any easier. Her lip actually quivered as she spoke: "I miss you."

"Then come and see me. You'll only miss one day of school. I need to . . . look at you."

"Aren't there lots of girls at William and Mary for you to look at?" She cringed at her poutiness, and her conspicuous fishing expedition.

"Are there girls here? I hadn't noticed. In fact, I can't see much of anything anymore. Even when I look up at the stars at night, all I see is your face."

Dinah laughed at his obvious coddling. "Right. And the sun, and the moon, and the flowers in June . . ."

"I mean it. I knew I was in trouble when the old geezer who teaches economics started to look like you."

"OK, that's pathetic. And sort of grotesque. I'll see what I can do." Wild horses couldn't have kept her away.

"I already know what you can do. That's why I want you to get down here."

She was smiling broadly. "You are nothing but trouble. My mother told me about boys like you."

He laughed, but his voice grew soft: "Did she tell you that boys like me wouldn't know what to do without girls like you? Did she tell you that this particular boy will make it his mission in life to prove that you will never be sorry you stuck with him?"

The earnestness in his voice almost melted her: He had done it again. Was there no end to the ways he could turn her into jelly? "No, she didn't, but that's all right. I'd rather hear it from you."

There was a momentary silence, and then he spoke again, serious and halting: "Dinah . . ." A slight break in his voice was just discernible. "Thank you . . . for, you know, hanging in there. I'm sorry I put you through this. I want you to know that I'm going to make it up to you . . . " He broke off, and she could tell that the impact of learning that he was exonerated, that his life was his to live as he chose, was settling in.

She swallowed hard, moved by his emotion. "It's all right . . . I knew it was worth it. You don't have to make anything up to me." Lightening the mood, she teased him with a warning: "I'll come down and watch you play, but you'd better be good. I expect at least three touchdowns if I'm going to come all that way."

"That's a pretty tall order. Would you settle for a fumbled pass and a ten-yard penalty?"

She could hear that the smile was back on his face.

"Oh, by the way . . ." A private familiarity crept into his voice. "There's a dance that night. Bring the blue dress."

Tru had warned her that he wasn't much of a letter-writer, but he had obligingly replied to each one she had sent, in his own fashion. Foregoing salutations and signatures, each was different from the next. Dinah saved them all, carefully tucking them in the desk drawer next to the photo from Donovan's. For the umpteenth time, she took them out, curling into the worn, floral chintz armchair by the window in her bedroom. The first one was the closest to a standard letter, offering at least a sentence or two of referential observations:

> *You'd like it here—the beach isn't too far, and it stays warm for a long time.*
> *The guys on the team are great—I'm playing receiver.*
> *A squirrel fell right out of a tree and onto Charlie Mulligan's head today—it*
> *was pretty funny…he had to change his pants.*
> *A lot of the people here are from the South—they all sound like you. It's distracting.*
> *Coach thinks there's nothing in the world but football.*

Professor Snedeker thinks there's nothing in the world but chemistry.
I think there's nothing in the world but Dinah.

The next one didn't bother at all with mundane reporting:

Probably should have cracked the book, but I got stuck on the cover.

D I S C R E T E M A T H E M A T I C S

i	u	l	e	a	h	v	o	l	a	e	x	o	n	o	n	r	k
n	f	o	a	c	o	e	m	w	s	r	q	u	d	u	c	e	i
a	f	u	s	h	u	r	e	a	t		u	t		c	e	a	n
h	e	d	o		g	y	n	y	i		i	h		h	n	m	
	r	e	n		h	t	s	n			s			i	d	y	
	d		t			g					i			n	i		
											t			g	a		
											e			r			
														y			

There are a couple of other versions, but it wouldn't be polite to show them to you. And I might go to jail.

The last one wasn't even in English. Tru knew that Dinah had never taken Latin, so she could imagine the smile on his face when he envisioned her trying to translate:

Numquam aliud natura, aliud spaientia dicit;
Difficile est subito deponere amorem,
Nec leve fit, quod bene fertur, onus.
Non est ad astra mollis e terra via.

Ego etiam sapor vos...

She had taken that one to school with her, hoping to find someone from advanced Latin to help her with it. As it turned out, she didn't have to look far. Sitting on Kenny's desk in the newspaper office was a Latin textbook, Level 5. He took the letter, grabbed a pencil, and quickly made the translation for her. When he had finished, he looked up with a peculiar expression on his face. "May I ask who this is from?"

Caught off-guard, Dinah wasn't sure what to call Tru. "It's, um, from a friend . . ." Her voice rose at the end like a question.

"Uh-huh. Must be a pretty good friend." He slid the letter back to her, with the translated words at the bottom, and Dinah thought she felt a chill in the air. She picked up the letter, turning away to read it:

> *Never does nature say one thing and wisdom say another;*
> *It is difficult to suddenly give up love,*
> *But the burden is made light which is borne well.*
> *There is no easy way from the earth to the stars.*
>
> *I still taste you . . .*

No wonder Kenny had given her a strange look! She felt the blood rising in her cheeks. She should have known better than to let someone else read anything that Tru had written to her—incorrigible boldness was one of his most distinctive traits. Then she realized that he had done this on purpose. He set her up!

She threw a hurried goodbye over her shoulder, quickly leaving Kenny at his editor's desk. She couldn't bring herself to look back at him, afraid that he would see the smile on her face.

Now she put the letters back in their envelopes and looked at the one that had arrived earlier that day:

> *There's a big Halloween party this weekend. I'll be the one dressed as a beggar, with no relief for my hunger, staggering with starvation and thirst. Or maybe I'll decide to wear a costume.*
> *Have Jemima ready at 7:00—Hayes will pick her up.*

Dinah realized her little sister hadn't even spoken about a costume that year—the image of riding around in Hayes's convertible seemingly faded from her memory. It occurred to her that Jemima might be afraid to go trick-or-treating again. This would be the perfect solution to put the trauma of last year behind her for good, and she was touched that Tru had remembered. She hadn't even known Hayes would be back, but it made sense; Halloween happened to coincide with Homecoming weekend this year, and the drive from New Haven wasn't that far. She decided that she would take Jemima to the Homecoming game on Friday night, so she could see the queen and her court. Jemima was predictably dazzled by all forms of glamour and celebrity. There was a good possibility she would be inspired to dress up after all.

Crisp fallen leaves drifted in piles on the sidewalk, emitting little bursts of autumn aroma as Jemima kicked them into the air. Dinah wished there were a way to bottle it—it was one of her favorite scents. It was already dusk as they made their way toward the stadium, and she could hear the low rumble of the fans in the bleachers, riled up for the big game. As they reached the brick archway with its gothic, wrought-iron gates, she could see that the stands were already packed. Looking around for her friends, she hoped it wouldn't be impossible to find them in the crowd.

Jemima wanted popcorn. They tagged onto the snaking line to the concession stand. The stadium lights were bright against the night sky, and the air was crisp and chill. Students and alumni of all ages crowded the small stadium, toting thermoses, car blankets, children, and the odd pair of field glasses. Dinah purchased two popcorns and Nehi sodas: root beer for herself, grape for Jemima. She scanned the tiers, searching for familiar faces as they moved along the outer edge of the football field. Finally she spotted Betsy's bright green jacket—an anomaly in a sea of maroon. They wended their way up the rickety stairs, the old wooden bleachers groaning with bloated capacity.

Joan spotted her and started to wave, but it wasn't until she and Jemima had shuffled past a long row of knees that Dinah saw another group of familiar faces. Sitting directly behind them, just two rows up, were the Sinisters. Carol Grisham served as the bellwether; Dinah turned away the instant she saw her, using Jemima as a diversion. She squeezed in beside Laurie, but after they were settled she couldn't resist the impulse to glance casually backward, up the rows, ostensibly searching the distance for a phantom friend, peripherally searching the foreground for one particular face. The hair on the back of her neck stood up as she stumbled into a pair of deep violet eyes. For several moments they were engaged in a visual stand-off, gazes locked like crossed swords, but Dinah conceded the battle with the *noblesse oblige* of one who knows she has won the war.

The prickly sensation of a dozen eyes on her back crawled over her as the pep band struck up the national anthem and the crowd rose. Staying on her feet for the school fight song, she fought the urge to turn around again, to take another look. She knew that Lana had decided, after all, to give the baby up for adoption. It had been the talk of the school for several days running. Jimmy had offered to take responsibility—she heard that he had shown up at the hospital with a ring, but Lana refused to see him. It gave Dinah a sick feeling of pity—of sadness for everyone involved. She couldn't even resent Lana for what she had put Tru through; Dinah truly felt sorry for her. But she felt even worse for Jimmy. In her opinion, he was the biggest victim of all. She didn't see him anywhere in the crowd, and she wondered if he was there, somewhere in the stands, mourning his loss.

She managed to pretend an interest in the game, cheering along with the others as the Spartans scored, leading by two touchdowns at the half. The energy of the crowd accelerated as the Homecoming floats took the field—convertibles festooned with banners and balloons, driven by faculty on the asphalt track surrounding the perimeter. The queen led the way, seated atop the back seat, graciously waving a white-gloved arm in a sweeping motion toward the stands. She was a pretty brunette, whom Dinah recognized as a member of the school band. It was common knowledge that someone from the band usually won—the numbers provided a large voting bloc, and they always supported their own. Jemima was captivated; Dinah caught her stealthily emulating the wave, her wrist rotating slowly back and forth as she tried to get it right while keeping her arm hidden by her side.

The parade circled away and through the far gates, and there was an exodus from the stands as people made for the concessions and the bathrooms. Dinah stood up to allow passage to a young couple carrying a toddler. As she turned she noticed the Sinisters descending the stairs in single file. She craned her neck when Lana passed, still curious and slightly awed by the fact that she had actually had a baby. It was impossible to tell that she had given birth only three weeks before. Although she was wearing a boxy woolen jacket, she appeared almost frail. Her face was pale against her dark hair, and again Dinah felt a pang of empathy—she knew exactly what it felt like to love Tru. As she watched Lana disappear in the crowd, she felt a tug on her sleeve. "I need to go to the bathroom." Jemima was subtly hopping from one foot to the other.

Dinah sighed. Her little sister inevitably chose the worst possible times to use public facilities—always when the lines were longest. Taking her hand, she led Jemima down the row to make their plodding way to the restrooms. At the bottom of the stairs they were funneled into a stream of people, and suddenly she felt a yank on her ponytail. She turned to find herself face to face with Stan and Joey, both back from the University for the weekend. She smiled as Stan scooped Jemima up out of the dense forest of legs, hoisting her onto his shoulders.

"What's a princess like you doing way down there? Royalty deserves a loftier position!" He tugged on her legs as she laughed and clapped her hands over his eyes. "Hey! I can't see anything . . ." Stan made a show of weaving and swaying, while Jemima tipped precariously back and forth, giggling and shrieking.

He had started to bounce on his toes, jostling her up and down like a wild horse, when the obvious occurred to Dinah. She grabbed Stan's arm, a warning on her lips, but she was too late. Jemima went pale at the exact moment that Stan froze, trying to mask the revulsion that was spreading over his features. Dinah could see the wet trail snaking its way down the back of his jacket; nobody moved except Joey, obliviously walking ahead of them. Stan's eyes met Dinah's as they both registered the calamity. Jemima was stricken, silent tears running down her cheeks. The crowd pushed against them, and Dinah quickly stepped behind Stan to block the view. She was mortified for her sister—the last thing the little girl needed was for some wise guy to point out the spreading stain below her perch. Dinah put her hands on Stan's shoulders and propelled him forward.

"Do you think you could walk with us to the gate? We need to go home—it's getting late for Mimer." She was praying he wouldn't say anything—she could feel her sister's humiliation, heavy and cleaving.

Luckily, Stan managed to maintain his composure. He quickened his pace, moving assertively through the crowd. "I'm leaving too . . . we've got the game in the bag, anyway. I need to get home—I'm sweating like a racehorse in this jacket." Dinah was impressed by his gallantry. He called to Joey that he'd see him later, keeping a tight grip on Jemima's ankles as he led them through the exit and into the parking lot. Outside the glare of the lights, he lifted her over his head, setting her gently on the grass. She kept her head down, tears drizzling down her face. Getting down on one knee, he put a hand on her shoulder. "I'm sorry I can't carry you all the way home, princess. You're just getting too big—I'm sweating right through my shirt! I hope I didn't get you wet. I guess I'm just out of shape. I'm gonna have to work out a little more—then I'll give you a ride all the way to Brickman's for an ice cream cone, OK?" Jemima nodded and sniffled, still looking at the inky grass. Stan stood up. "All righty then—you girls be careful going home, now."

Dinah gave him a grateful smile, relieved that he had been able to think so quickly. "We'll be fine. It was nice to see you, Stan."

"You, too. Say hello to Tru for me. Tell him I have money on Virginia Tech in the playoffs." He gave her a wink, waving as he walked off into the darkness, but before he disappeared, Dinah could see him rolling his shoulders, contorting to pull the soaking jacket away from his back.

She took Jemima's hand, leading her across the parking lot toward home. Concentrating on what she could possibly say to make Jemima feel better, Dinah was so lost in thought that she didn't notice the group standing at a nearby car until it was too late. She and Jemima walked right past the Sinisters. They were gathered in a loose circle, several of them leaning against a dark blue Chrysler, the smoke from their cigarettes curling into the cool night air. Dinah felt like she was walking over land mines. They watched her silently. One particularly abrasive, needling voice was noticeably absent—Sally Vecchi was missing from the group. Dinah thought she and Jemima had made it past without incident when a thin voice caught up with her: "Wait."

She turned to see Lana walking toward her, distancing herself from her friends. Dinah was rooted to the spot, still holding Jemima's hand as she watched the dark-haired figure approach. When Lana reached them, she stood silently for a moment, hands in the pockets of her coat. She was looking nervously into the distance over Dinah's shoulder, absently scuffing her right foot back and forth on the pavement.

"I thought maybe you could tell Tru . . ." Her voice was thin and hollow, and she swallowed. "I thought you could tell him that I'm sorry . . . and that I didn't . . . it wasn't . . ." She looked around, as if the words were floating somewhere in the air and she might find them. Dinah waited quietly, while Jemima continued to stare at the ground, submersed in the miasma of her own embarrassment. When Lana finally found her voice again, it echoed the empty sorrow on her pale, drawn face:

"I really thought it was his."

She was turning away before the words had left her mouth, but this time it was Dinah's turn to call out: "Wait."

Lana turned back cautiously.

"I . . ." Dinah throat was dry. "I'm sorry, too. I know . . . I can imagine how you must feel, and . . . I'm sorry."

Lana's color rose and her eyes narrowed as she lifted her chin. When she spoke, her words were bitter: "You don't know how I feel." She gave Dinah a long, stony look, but in the darkness a glistening betrayed her, and she quickly turned away. Dinah watched as she walked back to her friends, head down and shoulders hunched up, as if she were very, very cold.

Halloween came and went without incident. There were no costumes this year for Tom and Caroline, and Dinah stayed in, watching *The Original Amateur Hour* in the library. Hayes had pulled up for Jemima at seven o'clock on the dot, and she was ready for him, decked out in a cut-down dress that her mother had worn to a debutante ball. Caroline found it in a trunk in the attic, along with several other flouncy gowns from dances past—she had no idea that her mother had saved them for all these years. Jemima had her tiara at the ready—the wise man's crown from the Christmas pageant. Her white church gloves completed the outfit. Caroline had even helped her apply a bright layer of Copacabana to her lips, hesitating only briefly before shrugging her shoulders and deciding to overlook its provenance.

Hayes pulled away, with Jemima sitting on top of the back seat, waving to an imaginary crowd. Caroline and Tom settled in with Dinah to watch Ted Mack and the latest talent. The spinning wheel filled the television screen, as a sonorous voice intoned: "Round and round she goes, and where she stops, nobody knows . . ."

The first act was a seven-year-old girl singing gospel—a soulful rendition of "Show Me the Way." She was remarkable, performing with astounding maturity and poise. "It's absolutely amazing the talent these people find," Caroline remarked.

"What was that rumor going around about the first guy, the one who used to host . . . what was his name . . . Bowes? Something about the Nazis . . . ?" Tom looked up, squinting with the effort of remembering.

"I remember," Caroline said. "People thought there was a conspiracy, that after each of the radio shows, an American ship sunk, so there must have been some sort of coded information being passed by the broadcast."

"That's ridiculous. I thought he was a personal friend of Roosevelt's."

"He was. It was just one of those crazy witch hunts." Caroline shook her head at the ludicrous notion.

"Well, there's no system of national security that can defend against the hysteria of paranoia—it's a dangerous thing." Tom stretched, his feet resting on a round ottoman. "Speaking of danger, did you read that the Soviets are testing an atom bomb?" His eyebrows were raised as he looked at his wife.

"What will become of us?" Caroline looked sad, contemplating a new society, where the push of a button meant the end of the world.

"I read something today," Dinah offered, changing the subject. "RCA is coming out with a television that's in color!"

"You don't say! I'll have to check into it." Tom smiled at her, glad to move on to a brighter topic.

"You can order one in the Sears & Roebuck catalogue."

He chuckled at her optimistic suggestion. "I'll see if Mort knows anything about them, down at the place on Dearborn. Let me do some investigating before you get your hopes up."

They were watching a tap dancer who juggled flaming torches when Jemima pranced in, with Hayes behind her carrying her little bag of treats. "I'm home!" She was fairly floating from the thrill of the evening, spinning around in her gown. "We went all over the place, even around the square, and I waved at everyone who was at the bombfire, and guess what? I saw Peter and Clarence, and then I saw Veronica and Greta Wilson. I waved at them, but Greta stuck out her tongue. But I don't care, because I know she just wanted to ride in the comvertible. And Hayes took me to lots of houses for candy, too. We didn't go by any jack-o'-lanterns, though, because this dress could get on fire." She nodded sagely at her own wisdom, and Dinah could see that both the humiliation of last night and the devastation of last year were behind her.

Tom told Hayes to pull up a chair, and they chatted for a while about life at Yale. Hayes was the fourth-generation Swanson to attend the Ivy institution; he would undoubtedly follow the footsteps of his ancestors right into the family law firm. He asked about Tru. Tom told him that they would all be going to the game next weekend. "He's having a pretty good season, so far. They have him at receiver—the kid who plays quarterback is a senior. It looks like they have a good shot at the conference."

"Tell him we'll miss him at the Turkey Bowl. We'll have to get Butchie Briggs to heave the old pigskin again."

"Are you kids still keeping up that old tradition?" There had been an annual pick-up game of touch football on the Saturday following Thanksgiving for generations. "I don't remember Tru saying anything about it last year."

"He was supposed to be there, but he didn't show up. I think he went back to St. Paul's early."

Dinah remembered—he had taken a swing at Carson the night before. She was amazed now that she could have been so obtuse—she hadn't been able to see what was right in front of her. She was smiling as Hayes said goodbye—the only one in the room who knew the real reason Tru hadn't been at the game.

CHAPTER NINETEEN
Deep Blue Sea

THE BUICK WAS WAITING OUTSIDE the main door when Dinah came down the front steps of school on Thursday afternoon. Tom and Caroline had already picked up Jemima, and she was waving out the window. The trunk was packed with their overnight bags—with Dinah's blue dress spread carefully on top—and the car was packed with a picnic hamper, thermoses, a pile of children's books, and two pillows in the backseat. They would drive until Tom was tired, intent on getting a good jump on the next day's stretch. Williamsburg was over six hundred miles away—they had a long drive in front of them, and they wanted to get there by dinnertime Friday.

Dinah bundled in next to Jemima, slipping off her shoes and settling in for the duration. Tom and Caroline were already sipping coffee from their thermos cups, and a sententious voice reported world events on the radio. They had only been in the car an hour when Jemima had to use the bathroom. Tom pulled over at a Texaco station and walked her to the restroom.

"Maybe we should have brought a bedpan for Mimer," Dinah grumbled, irritated at the prospect of hourly delays.

Caroline shrugged helplessly. "We'll just have to watch what she drinks . . . and hope she falls asleep."

They had a picnic on the road: Gloria's fried chicken for everyone but Dinah, who still couldn't stomach it. Caroline had packed her a peanut butter and jelly sandwich. By seven o'clock, they had all tired of listening to Jemima sound out laborious paragraphs from *The Children's Book of Wonders* and *Buddy and Nan*. Caroline turned the dial on the radio until she found a clear signal. Jemima drifted off to Rosemary Clooney singing "You Started Something." Somehow time went faster without her non-stop prattle and repeated demands to know how much longer it would be until they stopped for the night. Dinah leaned back against her own pillow, resting against the edge of the window. She dreamily watched passing headlights, and made her own game out of counting the cars with one light out—what her father had referred to as "Popeyes." She could hear her mother and Tom chatting quietly in the front seat, but their words were unintelligible. The sound of their voices was soothing . . . she was startled to suddenly find that they were parked next to a flashing neon sign that read:

Seaview Motel
VA ANCY

"The C is missing," Dinah pointed out groggily.

"Truer words were never spoken." Caroline made a show of looking around the cracked parking lot.

Tom laughed. "I'd say the sea is about twenty miles east. The only view from here is a long stretch of highway and the moon on a clear night."

Through the lobby window, Dinah could see a middle-aged man rise from the center of the room. A few long strands of hair were pulled across a shiny scalp, and his shirt was unbuttoned to reveal the dingy white T-shirt beneath. He adjusted his glasses and stretched as Tom entered. Dinah surmised he must have been sleeping on a sofa. She watched as the rumpled, skinny figure ceremoniously checked the ledger, scanning down the page with his index finger. There were no other cars in the parking lot. When Tom got back into the car, the man disappeared below the window. Dinah guessed he was going back to sleep.

They drove to the end of the single-story row of units, parking in front of number 3. There was a ramshackle portico fronting the weathered, white clapboard façade. Tom opened the trunk and deposited their bags under the portico. He pulled out two keys, unlocking the doors to rooms 3 and 4. A slight musty odor greeted them. Spare but clean, both rooms featured linoleum floors and worn, white, chenille bedspreads covering twin beds. The rooms were adjoining, and Jemima was taken with a door in the wall that opened to another door, which opened to their parents' room.

"A secret passage!" She closed and opened the door a few times, squeezing her eyes shut and popping them open each time, as if she would see something new there instead of the mirror image of green linoleum and twin iron beds. "If I had this door in my room I would wish it to go into any room I wanted. I would go in the kitchen if I was hungry, and I would go to Momma's room if Fuzz had a bad dream. Sometimes I would like it to be for the bathroom, and for sure I would go in Tru's room if he would only be there."

The last part caught Dinah's attention, and her mother's words echoed as she crawled between the scratchy sheets: *Truer words were never spoken.*

They were back on the road by eight o'clock the next morning, after breakfast at the Round-the-Clock Truck Stop. They had been seated in a booth next to a large window overlooking a gas pump, where for a good part of the meal a semi-trailer had been idling with a noxious rumble. Sitting in the booth next to them was an obese man in a taut blue shirt. To everyone's mortification Jemima loudly pointed out the absence of most of his teeth.

In the car, they amused themselves with impromptu games. Caroline challenged them to make up a poem about something in the landscape—a contest Tom won when he managed to rhyme *mutton fleeced* with *skunk deceased*. Since he had driven until almost midnight the night before, even with all-too-frequent restroom breaks and a short stop at a roadside café for lunch, they were in Williamsburg by six o'clock. Dinah thought if she had to play one more game of Twenty Questions she would throw herself out the car window.

They drove down Henry Street to Francis Street, marveling at the quaint, historic buildings, their ancient brick tidy with neat, white trim. Turning onto South England Street, they pulled up at the Williamsburg Lodge, while Tom gave a running commentary on the local history: "John D. Rockefeller is the man to thank for the preservation of this town. Junior, that is. He funded it all. Planned it along with a man named Goodwin. Eighty-five percent of the buildings of colonial Williamsburg have been preserved." He turned to Caroline. "I think you'd enjoy a little tour—and the girls, too. Maybe we can fit it in tomorrow."

They entered the elegant, red-brick inn, feeling scruffy and sluggish from the day's drive. The porter showed them to two large rooms furnished with colonial period antiques. The walls were covered with Virginia cypress paneling, and the polished wood floors were covered with bright, handmade rugs.

"We'll have to hustle and clean up," Tom called over his shoulder as he tipped the porter. "Our dinner reservations are at seven."

Showered and refreshed, they set out on foot, past the restored blacksmith's forge and the post office of the charming village, turning onto Gloucester Street to The King's Arms tavern.

"Most of these taverns have been here since revolutionary times. Just think," Tom turned to Jemima, "George Washington used to eat here!"

Eyes wide, Jemima gazed around at the rustic beams and wide-plank floors. A matronly woman in period costume led them to a scarred oak table in the corner. Jemima watched her with wonder. As the hostess placed the menus in front of them, the little girl couldn't contain her curiosity: "Did you ever wait on George Washington?"

"Darlin', I'm old, but not that old." The woman gave her a wink. "I did wait on President Truman, though. He was here last year—the college gave him an honorary degree. Doctor of Laws, I believe. He's was right friendly. Ordered the Oysters and Corn Pye. You might want to give it a try." She moved away, snood bobbing on the back of her head.

Dinah pretended to study the menu, but her eyes kept going to the door, a nervous anticipation growing by the moment. Several times it opened, and several times her heart fluttered, only to be squelched by the arrival of more tourists. Then it opened once again and Tru was there, with all the dazzling brilliance of the Perseides. He stood in the doorway, eyes fastened on Dinah, his expression a portrait of deliverance and redemption. It was a moment wholly theirs—a private exchange in a crowded room, an entire opus passing between them in the sliver of time granted before the rest of the family turned and saw him.

Tom stood up and waved him over, clutching his son in a warm embrace. There were hugs and kisses all around. When Tru got to Dinah he chastely kissed her cheek, but his hand squeezed hers with a secret, intimate possession.

He sat down next to her, shining his incandescent light, restoring the warmth that had been missing from their lives for the past three months. "Sorry I'm late—Coach called an extra-long practice." His hair was still slightly damp, and Dinah had to force herself not to stare at the way it brushed across his forehead . . . and at the slight hollow under his cheekbones . . . and the way his smile always started on the left side . . . and his flawless profile . . .

She was saved from herself by the waitress, who came to take their order: "Hey there, Darlin'! I didn't know these nice folks were with you! Is this your family?" She was smiling broadly at Tru.

"This is my family," he nodded, smiling back. "Family, this is Dotty. The prettiest waitress in Virginia."

Dotty beamed and ruffled his hair. "He's such a flirt. He's gonna give some poor girl a run for her money." She turned to Tom and Caroline. "But don't you worry—we're keepin' an eye on him for you. Only comes in with his pals from the team. And all the girls followin' him around like stray kittens after the milk wagon! He's a mystery, all right." She looked at Jemima and Dinah. "These must be your sisters. I'll bet you're right proud to come down and see your big brother play football. What a handsome family y'all are!"

Dinah felt Tru's hand on her knee—he gave it a tight squeeze, making her jump, but he didn't offer comment. Tom kindly changed the subject, ordering for the table. They had lobster and scallops. To Jemima's rich hilarity, they all wore the bibs. Tru kept them entertained with stories about his teammates, his classmates, and his roommate, who liked to practice his tackles on unsuspecting friends as they came out of the shower. "He never actually hurts anyone, but plenty of guys have had the spit scared out of them. I like to think of him as my bodyguard. He plays offensive tackle. Tough as nails. You'll see him tomorrow—number 54. Just watch—he has no regulator. He's just a machine out there. And here's the funny thing: He likes opera. He keeps a little record player in the room, and he blasts the tenors at night. I can't believe our walls are still standing after the hammering they've taken from the guys on the hall. I told him I thought I'd finally escaped from Puccini prison—he couldn't believe I knew some of that stuff." He turned to Tom. "Get this: I came in the other day to full volume "Nessun Dorma" and the guy was sitting on the bed with tears in his eyes! This mammoth country boy from Georgia, who would go up against a freight train on the field, just sitting back with tears running down his face, listening to some fat guy sing!"

By the time they finished dinner, Tru was looking at his watch. "There's a ten o'clock curfew on game nights—can you believe that? Coach comes around doing spot checks; if you're not in your bed, you won't play."

"We should get Mimer back to the Lodge at any rate—it's been a long day." Caroline looked meaningfully at Tom. "Maybe Tru could just show Dinah around for a few minutes . . . it's such a lovely little town."

Dinah was surprised by Caroline's suggestion—she hadn't expected her to advocate for their privacy. Sympathetic understanding was one more quality she was beginning to appreciate about her mother. Tom went along. "We'll see you at the game, son. Don't let those Maryland guys try that left counter-trap on you . . . and tell 'em to watch out for Johannson—he's a rocket."

The early November night was almost balmy—unseasonably warm weather covered the southeastern seaboard. Tom and Caroline took Jemima and started back toward the Lodge. Tru and Dinah watched them go, and then he took her hand and started walking in the other direction.

"Why don't you tell me exactly which sights you'd like to see . . . I'll give you a private tour." He turned into a narrow lane as he spoke, pulling her into his arms in the shadows of a Colonial courthouse, complete with stock and pillory. "This is a very historic spot." Tru's voice was muffled as he kissed her. "It's the exact place where a Yankee from Massachusetts told some little Southern chippy that he couldn't have made it one more day without her." He continued to kiss her, murmuring, "You got here in the nick of time; I was flat out of oxygen."

Suddenly Dinah screamed, practically jumping into his arms. A small meow wafted up from the ground as a scruffy stray cat snaked its mangy body around Tru's ankles. Tru laughed. "If you wanted to jump on me, all you had to do was ask. No need to use some old alley cat for an excuse."

She was breathless with the shock of the furry brush against her legs, but she managed to stand up straight, swatting him lightly on the arm. "Very funny. That's so creepy. Where did it come from?"

"There are strays all over the place down here. I guess the warmer climate suits them." He looked reluctantly at his watch. "Speaking of strays, I'd better get back to the pound before the dogcatcher makes his rounds. I wouldn't want you to come all the way down here just to see me sit on the bench."

He led her down the lane and around the next corner, the quiet streets dark but for the gas lamps on the buildings. South England Street was only a couple of blocks away. He kissed her goodnight on the wide steps of the Lodge, under the watch of the costumed doorman. "I'll see you after the game—wait by the locker room. If we're lucky, we won't have to listen to an endless tirade about why we lost."

She blew him a kiss for luck as she went inside, giving a small wave with one hand, while the other reached up to her neck, unconsciously grasping the tiny silver sailboat that hung over her heart.

The day dawned bright and beautiful—a perfect game day, with a clear blue sky and the crisp, sunny dryness of autumn. Spending the morning touring the town, the foursome watched while costumed colonists demonstrated butter churning and wool dying, and they saw a reenactment of Revolutionary soldiers on the march. Jemima wanted a souvenir; Tom bought her a little tin soldier, complete with tiny musket. Caroline found a delicate milk pitcher made of English creamware in the Dry Goods Shoppe. Dinah looked through the wrought-iron doorstops, willow baskets, and tinwork bric-a-brac, but she didn't see anything that caught her eye.

At noon, they made their way to Cary Field, where the unmistakable aroma of hot dogs wafted in the air. The subliminal enticement to a captive market provided plenty of custom for the vendor who operated from a kiosk under the bleachers. They loaded up, carrying dogs and drinks into the stands. The stadium was crowded—students waving green and gold pennants filed in and filled the rows. A rowdy section of boys with megaphones led the stands in cheers, while Tom led the way to their seats on the forty-yard line. When the team loped onto the field, Dinah studied the uniforms, looking for Tru's number. She discovered that he was distinguishable from the other players by the lean, graceful lines of his physique. Only the quarterback and another receiver shared the same build—the other players looked thick and hulking in comparison.

The score was tied at the half. Dinah found herself biting her thumbnail whenever Tru took a hit, which happened on a fairly regular basis—he seemed to carry the ball the majority of the time. Tom's enthusiastic cheering rivaled that of the student section; at one point Caroline had to pull on his sleeve, sarcastically reminding him that the people behind them were not gifted with x-ray vision. He picked up Jemima and spun her around each time Tru made a play, tossing her right into the air when his son scored. The final score was 24 to 7, with Tru chalking up two touchdowns.

They waited along the ivy-covered brick of the stadium wall, next to the door to the locker room, chatting idly with other families who were there for the game. When Tru came out, he was walking next to a giant with a freckled, snub-nosed face and a crew-cut. "This is Percy Talton,"

Tru made the introduction, "roommate and savage beast. Percy, this is my family." The leviathan shook hands with everyone; Dinah thought hers had never felt so small. Jemima was looking at him with a hint of fear in her eyes—clearly envisioning child-eating giants who lurked in the woods.

"Tru tells us that you're an opera fan," Tom offered.

"Yes sir." Percy was respectfully formal, and a note of reverence crept into his voice: "I hear you have a copy of Titto Russo and Caruso singing *Otello.* They say it's the greatest vocal recording ever made."

"That's a rare one, all right—I may have to agree with them. I found it in Venice last year."

"Venice! Did you happen to get to the Fenice?"

"You bet. It was the highlight of the trip . . ." Tom and Percy had started to drift off, walking away from the stadium toward center campus, engrossed in their mutual passion.

The little group toured the campus—the ancient, pale bricks mellow in the late afternoon sun. In the large, oblong, sunken courtyard students relaxed on benches and in the grass, reading or talking in small groups. At one end a croquet match was in progress. Tru showed them to his dorm, but only as far as the lobby; women weren't allowed in the living quarters.

Percy was shaking Tom's hand. "Next time you come down, I would love a chance to give the *Otello* a listen." He sounded piteously hopeful.

"I'd be happy to bring it along. In fact, I'll keep my eyes open for another copy. If I ever find one, you'll be the first to know." It was clear that Tom was delighted with his son's roommate assignment.

Percy turned to Caroline and the girls. "It was sure nice to meet y'all." His Southern manners made him seem almost bashful. It was disconcerting in someone so physically intimidating. "I'll keep an eye on your son," he smiled at Caroline. "Make sure he doesn't get into any trouble."

He was whistling "Si, Pel Ciel" as he walked away, and Tru shook his head. "What did I tell you? When he's not on the field, old Percy is nothing but a big pussycat."

"He's charming," Caroline replied. "I think we should ask him to join us for dinner tonight."

"That's a good idea." Tom turned to Tru: "Why don't you meet us in the dining room of the Lodge at, say, 6:30? That should give us plenty of time before you have to move on . . ." He looked quickly at Jemima, who continued to pose a quandary. In the tricky equation of the family dynamic, she was unquantifiable. They had all avoided mentioning the dance to her, and Dinah hoped that Caroline and Tom could distract her before she caught on. She wondered how long they could go on without explaining the situation to her.

They were seated in the rustically elegant dining room when Tru and Percy came in. Dinah wore the blue dress; the boys had on rep ties and blazers. "You football players clean up right nice," Caroline greeted them.

Percy look distinctly uncomfortable in his jacket—it pulled across the shoulders and the sleeves were a little too short. "I don't get much chance to spiff up. I probably wouldn't be goin' to the dance tonight if Tru hadn't talked me into it."

Jemima perked up like a crocus through April snow. "Dance? What dance? Are we going to a dance?" She looked expectantly at her mother.

"No, sweetheart, we are not going anywhere. We have an early morning, and a long day on the road tomorrow." Caroline looked at Dinah and winced. "Your sister may be going along with Tru and Percy to meet some of their friends," she continued, "but that's because she's older and she can stay up a little later."

Jemima's chin fell, and her lip began to quiver.

"Hey Smidgen," Tru leaned across the table. "Just wait until I come home for Christmas—I'll teach you how to dance. You'd better start practicing right away. We're going to burn a hole in the rug."

Literal as always, Jemima's eyes widened.

Percy stepped up to the opportunity: "I didn't know your sister was coming with us! That's great. Maybe she'll take pity on your poor old roommate and give him a dance." He looked so hopeful that Dinah felt a surge of guilt. Tom actually sighed and closed his eyes, the onerous complexity of the situation clearly testing his limits. But when Dinah looked at her mother, she was amazed to see her simply shrug, giving a little wink and a smile. It was as though Caroline had decided that there was nothing to be done but have a sense of humor about it.

Dinah smiled at Percy. "I'd be happy to dance with you."

"Just don't let him step on your feet. We wouldn't want any broken bones." Tru raised his eyebrows dubiously as he glanced down at Percy's size-fourteen shoes.

When they had finished eating dinner, Tom got up and held his hand out to Jemima. "Come on, Sassy—I think there's an ice cream cone with your name on it just down the street. If we hurry, we can get there before the parlor closes."

Jemima jumped up, forgetting about the dance as Caroline and Tom led her toward the lobby, her voice incredulous as it floated across the room: "How does it know my name?"

Dinah excused herself to go to the restroom, and Tru nodded: "I need a minute to explain something to Percy. We'll meet you out front."

When she found them on the broad steps, Percy gave her an exaggeratedly disappointed look. "Does this mean you won't dance with me?"

Dinah smiled as Tru took her hand. "Of course not. Tru doesn't know how to dance, anyway. Maybe you can show him how it's done."

The Autumn Cotillion was held in the second-floor reception hall of the Wren Building, a magnificent room with high, coffered ceilings, ornate plaster mouldings, and tall, Palladian windows. The orchestra was already in full swing when the trio came in—a full assemblage in white tie and tails on a raised platform. Quite a few couples were on the dance floor. Percy split off from Dinah and Tru, calling back to Dinah as he wandered away: "I'll find you for that dance. You can run, but you can't hide."

Tru took Dinah by the hand, leading her to the bar. "Would you like a glass of milk?" His expression was serious, and she laughed.

"I guess so. If I remember, you made it perfectly clear at the Red Barn that I wasn't allowed to drink beer."

He looked at her with a guilty smirk. "So I did." He turned to the bartender: "Two ginger ales, please."

As they moved through a sea of chiffon and organdy, Dinah couldn't help noticing that quite a few of the girls seemed to watch her as she passed. She had the uncomfortable feeling of being judged, like an entry at the county fair. She wondered if her dress was too casual, or if she should have worn her hair up. Several of them turned away from their dates, calling out, "Hey, Tru."

He returned their greetings with a polite smile and a perfunctory "Hi, Connie," or "Hi, Fran." Dinah was starting to wonder if he knew all of the girls on campus. It seemed like most of them knew him.

They wandered over to a group of football players congregating by a wall of windows, clean and shiny in coat and tie, boisterous with their win. Several of them had dates by their sides. Tru put his arm around Dinah, pulling her into the group.

"Well, look who's here!" A short, compact boy with dark, Mediterranean features clapped Tru on the back. "If it isn't our very own Red Grange. And who do we have here?" He leaned inquiringly toward Dinah.

"This is Dinah Hunt. And this disreputable lot," Tru turned to Dinah, "are my teammates. This is Marty Santoris, would-be place kicker."

"Would-be, my ass—whoops, I mean fanny. I'll place a kick where you can feel it—."

He was cut off by a tall, lanky player, who lurched a little, sloshing the drink in his hand: "So this is what's been keeping Tru honest." He gave Dinah an exaggerated leer. "Now I see why he's been so blind to the temptations of the flesh." His words were slurry, giving the impression of a lateral lisp. He grabbed the arm of another player who happened to be within reaching distance. "Hey Charlie, get over here and meet Mrs. Stuart."

Dinah blushed at the reference, as Charlie turned with a drink in each hand. "Hey pal," he elbowed Tru, "you owe me one. I didn't see a play all day long." He looked at Dinah, nodding at the drinks to excuse a handshake: "You must be the reason old Tru here convinced Frankie to throw every pass his way. Wanted to impress the missus." His eyes roved over her dress. "Can't say I blame him."

"Dinah, meet Charlie Mulligan—squirrel tamer." Tru smirked as Charlie shot him an indignant glare. "And this charmer," Tru inclined his head toward the tall, slurring one, "is our esteemed quarterback, Frank Simmons."

"Don't let this guy fool you," Marty broke in, nodding at Tru. "He doesn't normally see so much action. Yessirree, it was the Tru Stuart show today. He had old Percy covering him like a shroud . . . ain't nobody gonna get through that."

Grinning, Tru shook his head: "Betrayed by my own teammates. Where is the loyalty?"

There was a round of self-congratulatory banter as they basked in the afterglow of the afternoon's success, while Tru introduced Dinah to more of the players and their dates. The girls seemed polite, but timid, and Dinah was secretly relieved that Tru didn't know most of their names. None of them offered anything in the way of conversation, standing mutely next to their dates, as the boys took turns good-naturedly skewering each other and recounting big plays. After a couple of minutes, Tru turned to Dinah, intentionally overt: "I hate to disappoint you, but I've had enough of these clowns." He looked back at his friends: "If you'll excuse us, I heard there was a dance here somewhere." He led Dinah away, depositing their empty glasses on a linen-draped table.

Dinah couldn't shake the feeling of scrutiny as they moved into the crowd of couples on the dance floor, but as soon as Tru pulled her close she forgot anything else but the feeling of floating in his arms and the rhythm of his movements. They danced song after song. He taught her several new steps, including the Lindy, which reminded Dinah of the first time she had seen him dance—it was with her mother at the wedding. It was fun, and Tru was impressively good at it, showing her how to do an aerial step and swinging her with a smooth, facile control. At one point Dinah looked up to find Percy watching them. He shook his head sadly, and when the dance ended he came over. "I thought you said he couldn't dance. I don't know if I can follow that act."

"Sure you can," Tru graciously stepped away. "Just don't get too close," he warned with mock severity. "I've got my eye on you." As he moved off, Percy led Dinah into a standard foxtrot. His agility surprised her—he had a grace unexpected in someone so big.

He read the surprise on her face. "Miss Palmer's School of Dance. Required by law in the state of Georgia."

Dinah laughed, looking up at the childlike face looming over her. He looked down at her thoughtfully: "I figured Tru must have a girlfriend somewhere," he said as he spun her around the floor. "He doesn't say much about his personal life, but I've never met a guy so immune to . . . well, you know, other girls. This explains a lot." He chuckled. "He is one whipped hound, all right. And y'all actually live together? How does that work out?" He suddenly looked appalled at his own impertinence, his pale, freckled skin turning pink.

Not sure how to respond, Dinah looked absently past his elbow, thinking about her answer. How did it work out? There wasn't any way around it—it was a very unorthodox situation. When she didn't reply, Percy cleared his throat. "Sorry, I didn't mean to pry. It's just . . . unusual, you know? And I can imagine that things get a little tricky . . ." He sounded as if he were trying to dig himself out of a hole, trailing off uncertainly.

Dinah felt sorry for him—she hadn't been offended, just stumped. "No, it's all right, really. I was just thinking about it. You're right, it does get tricky. And it hasn't been easy, but Tru isn't home very much . . ."

"Well, by this time next year y'all could be living in married students housing, and that's not so long from now. Seems like a pretty easy solution."

Dinah practically tripped over her own two feet. Married students housing? The idea of it was absurd. She had always planned to go to her mother's alma mater—Smith College. Suddenly she realized that would mean four more years away from Tru. How would she manage? How would they manage? Maybe she should be thinking about applying to William and Mary. Would that be what Tru wanted? Percy's offhand remark set off a minor avalanche, and it wasn't until he made a small bow that she realized the dance had ended.

"You're an easy partner—thanks for the dance. I'm glad I didn't do any damage." He made a show of inspecting her feet. When she looked up, Dinah noticed that Tru was talking to the bandleader. The orchestra had been playing mostly popular standards and swing, but when they struck up again, the strains of a smoky saxophone began to wail and the sultry notes floated out over the room. Tru came back for her, wearing the same satisfied smile he had at Donovan's.

"I believe the next dance is mine." He took her away from Percy, cinching her tightly against him as the horns heated up. They moved together, lost in an intimacy that belied the crowded floor, and Dinah forgot all about the questions that had blanketed her only moments before.

When the song ended, the band took a break. Dinah and Tru started back toward the bar. On the edge of the dance floor, a tall, striking brunette approached them, a wide smile on her elegant, patrician face. "Hey there, Tru! I haven't had the honor of being introduced to this lovely creature." She reached out, lightly clasping Dinah's arm, her eyes travelling from tip to toe. "You must be the lucky girl who holds the key to this one's heart," she inclined her head toward Tru. "We've all been wondering who could possibly keep him so true . . ."

She laughed at her pun—a tinkling, musical sound.

"Nancy Guilford, Dinah Hunt." Tru made the introduction as Nancy took one of Dinah's hands in both of hers.

"I probably shouldn't tell you this," her tone was confidential, "but there are about a hundred broken hearts here tonight. And who knew that he could dance like that?" She turned to Tru, lightly swatting his arm: "You've been holding out on us. That's not fair!" Looking back at Dinah, her voice was as smooth as syrup: "Aren't you just sweet? Such a pretty little thing!"

Dinah felt like a child sitting at the adults' table. Suddenly she was tongue-tied and insecure. The girl's name fluttered around in her memory. In an instant she captured it: This was the daughter of Coco's friends—the senator and his wife. This was the "exquisite and utterly charming" girl that Coco had wanted Tru to meet. Dinah felt like she was shrinking—becoming smaller and smaller, as the sophisticated beauty patted her on the shoulder like a pet. Nancy's smile was gracious, but Dinah could read something else in her eyes.

"You must be his high-school sweetheart. Where do you go to school now?"

Dinah's voice sounded thin and tentative to her own ears: "I'm still in high school—I'm a senior." At least she could claim that much—she sent a mental thank-you to Principal Dawes.

"Really? My! I imagine that must be difficult—having your boyfriend off at college, with all the changes and new experiences, and there you are, still in high school, doing the same old thing. You must be very . . . tenacious!" The word came out sounding like a euphemism.

Unable to muster a response, Dinah looked helplessly at Tru, who had a sly smile on his face: "I can think of a lot of words to describe her, but that wouldn't be one that comes to mind." He draped his arm across her back. "It was nice talking to you, Nancy, but if I don't get Dinah alone in the next five minutes I may get us both arrested." With that, he turned and led her away. Even Dinah was shocked; she wondered if she would ever get used to his audacity. As they reached the doorway, she couldn't help glancing back, a little thrill of vindication coursing through her as she saw Nancy standing alone, staring at the floor in complete stupefaction.

In between kisses in the languid night air, she tried to scold him: "You have the propriety of a pirate."

"She deserved it. Besides, it was true." He started walking again, leading her away from the lights of campus.

"Where are we going?"

"There's a little lake through the woods—Lake Matoaka. It's part of my tour . . . but you have to pay extra to see it."

He loosened his tie and took off his jacket, slipping it over her shoulders as they lay down on the soft grass of the bank, now covered with fallen leaves. The glassy water reflected a crescent moon in the quiet darkness.

"So what would a pirate do now?" His eyes held a familiar gleam as he began to work his own brand of thievery.

Only one word came to mind, and it escaped before she could swallow it. "Plunder?"

He threw back his head and laughed, looking at her with undisguised adoration. "I knew there was something I liked about you."

A lone, croaking bullfrog performed its rhythmic serenade as Tru traced a trail of kisses down her neck, charting a course for the deep blue sea.

CHAPTER TWENTY
Innocence

THANKSGIVING WAS QUIET THAT YEAR. Coco and Harley had somehow managed to find their wings again, and they had decamped for Palm Beach, along with most of their social set. Tom convinced Caroline to forego inviting May and Roger—he said he didn't think it would be wise to establish a pattern. "At most, let it be biannual," he pleaded.

With just the four of them, it didn't seem practical to roast an entire turkey, so they decided to join the other scaled-down families for dinner at the country club. The waiters were dressed as pilgrims, and there was a turkey coloring contest, which Jemima labored over for the entire meal, sneaking crayoned strokes in her lap between every bite. In a production unfit for even the most rudimentary summer stock, Miles Standish (normally Seamus the bartender) made the selection, announcing the winner with hackneyed schmaltz, taking every opportunity to insert a 'thou' or a 'thee' in an attempt to lend verisimilitude to his character.

Jemima didn't win. A boy with a suspicious shadow on his upper lip who claimed to qualify for the under-twelve category produced a museum-quality piece, walking away with the pumpkin pie. All was not lost, however. Peter Campbell was there with his family, and he made his courageous way over, shyly admiring Jemima's efforts. They examined the other entries, Peter insisting that the judge must have made a mistake—that Jemima's turkey was a hundred-million times better than any of the others. He was hard at it, pitching third-grade woo with fierce determination, while Jemima maintained a haughty distance worthy of her step-aunt. Dinah had to smile when she heard her little sister tell Peter that he could sit by her at lunch on Monday only if he promised to write on the chalkboard that she was his best friend and also the only girl that he liked.

As they gathered their coats in the cloakroom, Jemima handed hers to Peter and turned her back expectantly. Looking over her shoulder, she raised one eyebrow and waited. Peter looked at the coat in his hands, momentarily confused, but his expression cleared as he figured it out. Gallantly he put it on, struggling to squeeze his arms through the too-tight sleeves, and then he obligingly took his own coat from the hook and presented it to Jemima.

The Plaza Hotel cast its regal French Renaissance shadow over Central Park South, festively trimmed with evergreen boughs and sparkling lights. A red carpet descending the steps produced a doorman in a cap and long woolen coat who opened the door of the cab. They had taken the train to Grand Central Station, arriving in the early dusk of December to cool blue shadows on yesterday's snowfall, already dirty with the grime of traffic.

The opportunity had come up suddenly for Dinah; there was an American Library Association symposium being held at the New York Public Library to which Jane was invited, and which also happened to coincide with Betsy's birthday. The MacEvoys had spontaneously decided to make a family trip of it, and wisely reckoned that Betsy's experience would be improved upon considerably if she could share it with a friend. The timing was perfect—Dinah had been staring at the calendar for the past weeks, willing the pages to turn, and the final, plodding days until Tru's return had a Himalayan pitch.

Betsy and Dinah were dazzled—they gazed at the Beaux Arts splendor of the Plaza, overwhelmed with the elegance of the marble floors, the crystal chandeliers, and the rich, polished mahogany. Jane was equally wide-eyed, pulling them into the Palm Court to marvel at the beautiful stained-glass ceiling. Raised in the Midwest, she was as green as the girls—this was also her first trip to the big city. "If we hurry, we can take a carriage ride before dinner." She ran her hand along the ornate scrollwork of the elevator plaque.

On the sixth floor, they wandered down the hushed hallway, the paneled walls reassuring each guest of his or her supreme privilege and secure station in life. Betsy and Dinah were just down from Jane and Mike; they felt incredibly adult with their own hotel room, putting on exaggerated airs of sophistication as they changed their clothes. They were in for a rare treat that evening: In an unprecedented gesture of extravagance, Mike MacEvoy had presented his only child with a dream birthday gift—tickets to the smash Broadway hit *Finian's Rainbow*. The tickets had only become available at the last instant. Mike knew someone in the drama department at Salem State who had a cousin in show business—somehow he had managed to procure seats to the perpetually sold-out show. Dinah and Betsy had spent the past few days trying to hide their excitement from the other girls and planning what they would wear.

Jane was waiting in the lobby when the girls stepped off the elevator. Mike was already waving down a carriage. Riding behind a dappled grey Belgian, they drank in the city, shimmering with holiday spirit. The statue of Pomona cast her lovely *Abundance* over one end of Grand Army Plaza. At the other end, General Sherman sat beneficently on his gilded bronze steed, reminding the republic of his estimable contribution. The aroma of roasted chestnuts wafted from corner carts, accompanying them past the brightly adorned store windows, brimming with the desideratum of the holidays. The carriage driver circled around the block and turned up Fifth Avenue, heading into Central Park for a quick jaunt across the south end, down through Columbus Circle and back to the Plaza, where they disembarked. Their dinner reservations were at Merriman's. Although it was within walking distance, they hailed a taxi to save their shoes from the slushy pavement.

In Dinah's limited experience, Donovan's represented the height of culinary sophistication, but when she saw the army of tuxedoed waiters at Merriman's—there for the sole purpose of catering to their table—she knew she had been woefully underexposed. They ordered extravagantly, caught up in the spirit of the city. Dinah couldn't imagine how Mike and Jane were paying for the luxury of it all. Surely the salary of a professor and his librarian wife didn't cover this. It wasn't until the waiter had cleared the last plate, inquiring as to their satisfaction, that Dinah realized her stepfather had arranged to be billed for the tab: "I'm sure Mr. Stuart will be pleased to hear you enjoyed the meal," he said, whisking the crumbs from the tablecloth with a sterling utensil.

Jane leaned over to Dinah. "You be sure to tell Tom that he didn't have to do this, but we certainly appreciate it!"

They hailed another cab to 46th Street. Inside the theatre, the buzz of the crowd sent a shiver of anticipation across Dinah's skin. The orchestra struck up the overture and she could hear Mike quietly singing along with "How Are Things in Glocca Morra?"

"Jemima would love this musical," Dinah remarked. "Leprechauns are right up her alley."

The evening swept by in an enchanted minute. As they left, Mike spied a placard advertising recordings of the show. Through a window in the wall of the lobby a young woman in a white blouse and thin black bowtie was selling copies. Mike bought one, delighted by the prospect of being able to listen to the production at will. They rode back to the Plaza on a cloud of contentment, the score repeating in dreamy catches as they all found themselves humming the odd stanza.

As they entered the hotel, however, they encountered something different. A strange, unearthly-sounding voice floated across the lobby. Jane gravitated toward the Persian Room, beckoning the others with a furtive gesture of her hand. Poking their heads through the door, they saw an exotic-looking woman warbling into a microphone next to a shining grand piano. "That's Eartha Kitt!" Jane couldn't contain her star-struck excitement.

"Who's Eartha Kitt?" Betsy was as clueless as Dinah.

"I heard her singing on the radio just the other day. She has the most unusual voice. Isn't she something?" The proximity of celebrity clearly had an intoxicating effect on Jane, and it was contagious, spreading to the girls, and even to Mike.

"Maybe we can get a table," he said, optimistically scanning the room.

"Let's see if we can get her autograph," Betsy whispered nervously.

As if on cue, the maitre d' approached, carrying a leather-bound diary. "Do you have a reservation?" He somehow managed to sound both unctuous and officious.

"No, I'm sorry to say we don't, but the girls here were wondering if they might just get an autograph from Miss Kitt." Mike used his most sincere, friendly tone—hoping his rustic approach would buy entry. The self-important little man gave them the once-over, looking over the narrow eyeglasses perched on his nose, and snapped shut his diary. He was clearly ready to turn them away when an exotic, purring voice came over microphone.

"What's going on over there, Harry?" Miss Kitt's unmistakable voice undulated through the room. "Do we have more guests? Let's invite them in—there's room for everyone." The crowd was smiling at her personal, attentive banter.

Jane's eyes were wide, and Mike was smiling broadly. The girls fell in line behind them as Harry led them past the great length of the bar to a small table in the front corner, off to the left and almost behind the singer. He turned and went back to his stand, gliding across the floor like a debutante flaunting her finishing-school comportment.

"So nice to have you here with us tonight." Miss Kitt turned around to engage them. "Where are you lovely people from?"

Mike spoke up, proud in his moment in the sun. "We're from Salem."

"All the way across the country from Oregon?" The chanteuse was taking the opportunity to connect with the crowd.

"No," Mike chuckled a little. "Not quite so far away. Massachusetts."

"Ah, the other Salem—the infamous one." She gave the crowd a wink. "I think I've got a little something for you." With that, she launched into a sultry, inveigling performance of "I'd Rather Be Burned as a Witch."

Dinah looked around at the warm, elegant décor. The rich reds of the room reflected a rosy glow on the patrons; everyone was bathed in the luster of the low, intimate lighting and the sensual, feline voice.

It wasn't until she heard the distant, dreamlike sound of laughter that Dinah realized she had drifted off to sleep, resting her chin on her hand. She sat up quickly.

"Ah, the princess has awakened." Eartha Kitt's voice was teasing, and Dinah sensed she had missed something. Mike, Jane, and Betsy were grinning at her, amused and tickled to find themselves once again in the spotlight. Dinah was mortified—she realized she must have been the center of attention for at least a few unconscious moments.

"As I said, I never considered that one a lullaby." The singer was smiling at her. "Let's try this—a tribute to the sleepy young lady from Salem." She smoothly slid into "Wake Me When It's Over."

At the end of the set the songstress moved away to the dressing room, and the maitre d' reappeared, pointedly inquiring as to whether they would be occupying the table for the remainder of the evening. They sheepishly took the hint. Walking to the elevator, Dinah took some good-natured ribbing about drifting off on Eartha, and she had to laugh at her own country-cousin transparency.

Snuggling into the luxurious, silky sheets, Dinah could hear Betsy, still giggling. She fell asleep with a smile on her face.

The next day was a blur of museums, monuments, and a fair amount of window shopping. Mike and the girls had arranged to meet Jane after the symposium, and late in the day they found her on the wide steps of the Library, where Patience and Fortitude, the iconic marble lions, looked on. In the echoing elegance of Astor Hall an enormous Christmas tree twinkled with hundreds of lights, and when Dinah gazed up at the frescoed ceilings in the Rose Main Reading Room, she thought this must be what Catholic pilgrims felt in the Sistine Chapel. It made her almost giddy to think she was in the presence of Jefferson's own manuscript of the Declaration of Independence, not to mention the actual Gutenberg Bible. Wandering through the exquisite rooms, each one more magnificent than the last, she had no idea that two hours had passed when Betsy finally grabbed her by the wrist: "My parents gave up—they're waiting for us at the hotel. I'm starting to worry about you," she teased as she pulled her friend toward the towering doors. "You're like one of those saints who had ecstatic trances—St. Bernadette at Lourdes. I'm afraid you might suddenly fall to the floor in a fit, seeing visions of Shakespeare and Noah Webster." She tugged more forcefully as Dinah slowed down to gaze into the Map Division, and was still pulling her along as they emerged into the noisy rush of the Manhattan night.

Mike had parked the car at the train station, and they dropped Dinah off late on Sunday afternoon. She called out a final "Thank you!" as the car backed away, with Mike waving the bright cover of the *Finian's Rainbow* recording out the window, a goofy salute to the success of the whirlwind trip.

Opening the door, she was greeted by inordinately loud music coming from the library. This time it wasn't Tom's opera, however. Dinah recognized the piece: "Tango Por Una Cabeza." It had been popular on the radio a couple of years earlier. She wondered why Tom was playing it so loudly, and then she heard something over the music—it was the sound of wild laughter. Curious, she started toward the library. Passing the living room, she discovered the source: Jemima was swaying dramatically, feet barely touching the ground as Tru swept her across the room in an exaggerated tango. Dinah watched them for an appreciative minute before they pivoted sharply and noticed her in the doorway.

"Dinah! I'm learning how to dance." Jemima giggled crazily as Tru dipped her backward with a flourish. "But we're not really burning a hole in the rug," she assured her sister, looking a little worriedly at the Aubusson carpet.

"You said you wouldn't be home until Tuesday." Dinah wasn't really complaining.

"Our Latin prof decided to make the final optional." Tru had to raise his voice to be heard over the music, calling over his shoulder as he whipped Jemima around and moved away. "I changed my ticket at the last minute." As the song came to its snaking end, they slid back again, Jemima matching Tru step for step.

"Maybe you two should try out for the Ted Mack show," Dinah teased.

"Can we?" Jemima's eyes shone with the light of fervent aspiration as she looked up at Tru.

He gave Dinah a pained look. "I don't know, Smidge. You could probably pull it off, but I'd have to practice a lot. Maybe when you get a little older you'll find a partner who can keep up with you."

Jemima continued to hang on Tru's arm, determined to keep his attention. He turned his face away from her, silently mouthing something to Dinah.

Dinah shrugged and shook her head, unable to read his lips. "Jemima, go find Mom and ask her if she needs help with dinner," she instructed.

"Why don't you go ask her?" Jemima was justifiably indignant.

"Because I want to tell Tru what I got you for Christmas."

Tru raised an eyebrow, impressed.

With a wide, anticipatory smile, Jemima skipped off to the kitchen. Dinah watched her sister go, casting her glance quickly around the hall to see if anyone else in the household happened to be lurking about. She looked questioningly at Tru. "What did you say?"

His eyes narrowed slyly. "If I told you, you'd have every right to slap me. Get over here."

She moved into the living room, away from the exposure of the doorway. He reached out and pulled her close as she approached, wrapping his arms around her waist. "I turn my back for a second, and you run off to New York." He was kissing her when they heard footsteps in the hallway.

Tom cleared his voice loudly, calling out ahead of himself. "Dinner's almost ready. Did I hear Dinah's home?" He poked his head around the archway, blustering through the awkward moment as the two moved apart. "Well hello there! How was the show?"

"It was great." She moved toward the doorway. "Mr. MacEvoy even bought the recording. They both said to thank you for dinner, too."

"You'll have to tell us all about it." He was in high spirits, motioning them along. "Come on then, we'll be graced with a full menu tonight; not only a delicious meal, but sparkling conversation as well!"

Relishing the cheerful harmony that surrounded the table, Caroline allowed herself a moment of unfettered happiness. There was a lightness that had been missing the last time they sat there together; the improvement in Tru's circumstances had cleared the air significantly. But there was a shadow behind her husband's easy smile of which she alone was aware. She knew that he was making an extra effort—that his light-heartedness was, at least partially, contrived: He had decided that it was time to explain everything to Tru. Although Tom's symptoms remained sporadic, they were still evident, and he could no longer bear the thought of his son living with the gnawing fear of a similar fate. Before Tru left for school, Tom hadn't been able to bring himself to add to the burdens already weighing on his son's shoulders. Now that Tru was no longer vulnerable, now that he stood firmly on solid ground, Tom thought it was time to give him the gift of truth. He had decided to wait until just after Christmas, allowing the holiday an untarnished festivity. So it was with selfless determination that he joined in the banter, obscuring the dread that pressed on his heart, preserving the innocence of the moment.

CHAPTER TWENTY-ONE

Lost Purchase

THE BENTLEY ELEMENTARY NATIVITY PAGEANT had been a popular topic for several weeks. Jemima had pulled off a major coup—snagging the coveted donkey role. It was a perennial favorite, due to the fact that it was a dual part, requiring two actors to fill the costume. Predictably, Jemima had enlisted Peter to be her co-star.

"Let me see if I have it straight," Tru said. "You are the head of the ass, and Peter is the—"

"All right, I think we all understand which part of the donkey Peter will play." Tom cut his son off with a reproachful glance.

In a rare dereliction of parental duty, Tom and Caroline had asked Tru and Dinah to take their places in the audience, bowing to the demands of profession—the production happened to take place on the same evening as the annual Stuart Lumber Christmas party. Tom was ruefully apologetic, but Caroline had taken it in stride. "I think Jemima would rather have Tru there than all the rest of us, anyway. Don't worry," she kissed her husband's cheek as he helped her into her coat, "there will be plenty of Nativity pageants to come. We'll be there when she manages to convince them that she should play both Mary and Joseph."

Dinah asked if she could drive. Over the past few days Tru had been taking her out in Caroline's Nash, and she had become quite confident. After a fitful start, when she couldn't seem to get the hang of the temperamental clutch, she had taken to driving like a bird to flight. She attributed it to natural prowess, but Tru insisted it was his superior instruction.

Their parents, however, thought better of giving her the keys that evening. It had been snowing lightly all day, and they didn't feel that Dinah had the experience to maneuver the slippery roads. "You need to have a driver's license before you can take your sister anywhere. It's fine to practice, but not with children in the car," Caroline insisted.

"I don't want Dinah to drive, anyway," Jemima stated emphatically.

"She goes too slow. I'll miss the whole show."

They arrived in plenty of time. Jemima headed backstage to find Peter, while Tru and Dinah nabbed good seats, front and center. Tru was making jokes as they waited, describing possible scenarios in which Jemima would manage to upstage Baby Jesus, somehow promoting the character of Donkey into a pivotal role. They both burst out laughing when they heard her voice from backstage, hollering through the donkey costume: "Quit touching my bottom!"

"God, I hope she's talking to Peter, not the janitor," Tru wisecracked, wincing as Dinah slugged his arm.

The pageant progressed with predictable grammar-school hitches: Joseph's beard slipped on one side, hanging off his face like a dangling possum, and one of the Wise Men forgot his line, announcing to the holy family that he came bearing the gift of Frankenstein. Jemima and Peter didn't exactly steal the show, but they did manage to distract the audience with antsy shuffling that made it look as if the donkey were rooting for truffles, and several times it appeared that the poor animal was sprouting spontaneous tumors in the general vicinity of its ribcage. During the final scene, as the cast serenaded the audience with a sweetly moving rendition of "Silent Night," the donkey did a slow soft shoe, throwing in the odd little hop for good measure.

Waiting in the hallway outside the school gym, Tru and Dinah examined the art projects displayed on the walls. Dinah led the way to room 107, and they searched among the paper snowflakes and red felt Santas with cotton-ball beards to find something with Jemima's name on it. Finally they found it: a construction paper Christmas tree adorned with sequin ornaments, with two brightly wrapped gifts beneath it. She had cut out real wrapping paper, and there were miniature ribbons tied in tiny bows and glued on top. Most prominent, however, were the real gift tags, enormously outsized for the dimensions of the gifts, that dangled by strings from the tops of the bows. There, painstakingly printed in capital letters, were two names. The first tag read, "*TO TRU, FROM JEMIMA*". The second one, accordingly, "*TO JEMIMA, FROM TRU.*"

"Wow." Tru looked a little intimidated by the implied message. "I guess I'd better get going on my Christmas shopping."

Dinah felt a disturbing twinge of guilt. She looked up at Tru with worried seriousness. "How do you think she'll take it when she finds out about . . . you know . . . us?"

She didn't get to hear his answer—they heard Jemima's voice before they saw her running down the hall, demanding to know what they thought of her performance. "Could you hear me singing? I was the one who sang really high. Peter kept on saying the wrong words—he messed me up a little, but I sang quiet on those parts."

"Everyone in the audience has been saying that the Donkey had the best voice of all," Tru said, sweeping her up and giving her a little spin. "I like your picture," he said, indicating the tree.

"Oh . . ." Her face turned red. "Oh, that. Well, um, it's not really finished. I ran out of time, so I couldn't get any more presents on it." She squirmed to get down, quickly changing the subject. "Can we go out for ice cream? Peter gets to go to Brickman's."

They piled into the Nash. A light dusting of snow covered the windows. Tru wiped them clear with the sleeve of his coat and turned up the defrost dial. They followed the parade of cars leaving the lot, several of them leading all the way to Brickman's. "It seems a little strange to be going for ice cream in December." Dinah mused. "Shouldn't we be getting hot chocolate or something?"

"It's always a good time for ice cream," Jemima countered. "Even when it's cold. Why do you think there are Eskimo Pies, anyway? It's because Eskimos love ice cream. Even their pies are made out of ice cream. And you know it's cold whenever Eskimos are eating anything." She sat back with authoritative satisfaction, tracing her finger on the fogged window to draw a little igloo.

They got the last booth at the crowded ice-cream parlor. Jemima invited Peter to join them, while Mr. and Mrs. Campbell took seats at the counter. Tru and Dinah both had milkshakes, but Jemima wanted a chocolate sundae, and Peter ordered a towering structure called a Shebang. "I get a free lollipop if I can eat the whole Shebang," he informed them.

He industriously made his way toward the bottom of the dish as they chatted about the production. Peter and Jemima had been unable to see most of it—Jemima led from a small slit in the mouth of the costume, while Peter blindly followed. Dinah found nothing at all surprising about that. Tru and Dinah did their best to describe the performance of the rest of the cast, assuring them that none of the other characters had the stage presence of the donkey.

Abruptly, Peter put his spoon down, looking a little queasy. Tru eyed him warily. "Take it easy, Champ. You don't want to put it all back on the table—I don't think it counts unless you keep it down."

Peter looked at the rest of the ice cream mournfully. "I don't feel very good. I'm not sure I want the rest."

"That's all right—at least you gave it the old college try. That's the most important thing."

"Tru's in college—he knows," Jemima bragged. He goes to William in Mary."

A spray of milkshake spewed from Dinah's mouth, landing on the table, with a dribble on the front of her sweater. Tru shook his head, trying to suppress a grin. "It seems that someone at this table is given to lewd interpretation," he said, picking up a napkin and dabbing at the stain. Jemima and Peter looked uncomprehending, while Dinah swatted his hand away. "Just trying to help," he said with wounded innocence.

"Are you going to William in Mary, too?" Peter asked Dinah.

Tru looked at her pointedly. "That's a good question, Peter. Where will Dinah go to college next year?"

It was a loaded question—one of the first things Tru had done when he came home was to put the application for admission on Dinah's desk. She found it there after dinner the first night, a rush of adrenaline jangling through her nervous system. He wanted her to come to school with him! It opened an enormous vista, and she felt almost dizzy with the view. "I don't know yet," she managed to reply, her heart beating a little faster. "I haven't sent in all of my applications . . ."

Peter's parents were making their way over, looking skeptically at the melting pool in front of their son. "Did you try to finish that monstrosity again?" Mr. Campbell sounded a little disgusted, shaking his head. He looked at Tru and Dinah resignedly: "He insists on going for the prize every time. Come on, Petey, what say we throw in the towel and I buy you a lollipop tomorrow at the Five and Dime?" He held out his hand, leading Peter away as Mrs. Campbell thanked them and slid fifty cents onto the table.

The snow had stopped falling by the time they started home—the leafless trees covered in a silvery icing that glittered in the night. As they pulled away from the parking lot, an urgent voice came from the backseat. "I have to go to the bathroom."

Dinah looked at Tru, aware of the weight of those words, given their source. "Maybe we should go back in. This could be a disaster."

"I'll take a shortcut," Tru said over his shoulder. "Can you hold it?"

Jemima was squirming a little on the seat. "I guess so. But hurry up."

They turned onto Grove Street, out of the thoroughfare of cars and stop signs. There was a slight incline to the railroad crossing. As they approached it, the warning lights started to flash. "Hang on," Tru said as he stepped on the gas. It was clear that they had enough time to sneak past—the train was blocks away. As they raced up the rise, Dinah could feel the car lose ground, slipping on the slick road. The tires lost purchase entirely as they hit the track, spinning around in a buzzing, whining futility.

"Damn." Tru threw the gears into reverse, punching the accelerator. The car lurched, but the tricky, fickle clutch betrayed him and jammed as he stamped furiously on the pedal. He slammed the stick shift into forward again, and in a moment of hopeful optimism the car jerked ahead, but the back wheels stalled on the slick patch at the crest of the rise, spinning futilely on the black ice of the asphalt.

"Come on . . . COME ON!" He was shouting now, pleading with the tires to grab traction, to move the car, while a single yellow light appeared to the west. "GODDAMMIT!" Tru was rocking the transmission back and forth, struggling with the treacherous clutch, desperately trying to find an inch of dry pavement, and there was something else—a whimpering from the backseat—but to Dinah it all sounded very far away. There was a distant blare of the train's whistle, and a crunching thud as the crossing arm landed on the back of the car. The whistle had become insistent—a loud, honking blast. Dinah was frozen, staring out of the passenger window at the approaching light, growing larger and brighter by the second.

"GET OUT OF THE CAR!" She heard the imperative, but she was strangely incapable of reacting. There was a lunging movement—Tru was throwing himself over the seat, grabbing for Jemima—but Dinah was transfixed, unable to look away from the light. She felt herself drawing away, floating into the distance as the light became as big and as bright as the sun. There was an acrid smell of burnt rubber, and the long, continual blast of the whistle as the engineer hung on the cord in frantic warning. And then there was the tearing screech of steel wheels on steel tracks, and another shrieking sound . . .

CHAPTER TWENTY-TWO
Cruel Proof

VOICES AGAIN, drifting like clouds. Dinah felt like she was floating. "It's hard to predict; every case is different. She will most likely have no memory of the accident . . ." Someone was talking. She didn't recognize the voice. "Dinah? Can you hear me?" The words were becoming clearer now.

"Sweetheart, can you hear me?" That was her mother; Dinah knew she should respond. Her head felt fuzzy. As the room came into focus, several faces looked back at her. She thought her mother was sitting on a chair by the bed, but for a moment she wasn't sure—Caroline looked different. Something was wrong—her expression was hollow and lifeless, without the familiar sparkle in her eyes, and her hair was lank and messy. Tru was standing on the other side of the bed, but Dinah felt like she was looking at him through fog. There was something odd about the way he stood— his shirt looked swollen and lumpy, while the right sleeve dangled uselessly at his side. There was a trail of what looked like tiny spiders across his cheekbone. With his left hand, he picked up hers. "Dinah?" Mustering up as much energy as she could, she gave a little squeeze. She wanted him to know that she heard.

"Hnnm." It didn't sound the way she meant it to sound, but her voice had the effect of ringing a gong. Her mother stood quickly, leaning down to stroke her hand across Dinah's brow.

"Hey there, Sunshine." Dinah thought her mother's voice sounded strange—there was a trembling tightness to her words. "You've been sleeping for quite a while. How do you feel?"

"You'll have to explain things to her, once she regains full consciousness." The unfamiliar voice again. It was a doctor—Dinah gazed at his white coat. "For now, you can expect her to drift in and out." His voice faded as Dinah struggled to stay awake. The doctor was talking to her mother. Everything had been murky, but the haze was beginning to lift. She knew she was in a hospital—that much she could comprehend. She looked up at Tru. His shirttail had ridden up slightly—Dinah could see the edge of a cast on his right arm, protruding from a sling. There was a line of black stitches running from his right temple to just below his cheekbone. Not spiders, stitches. Her eyelids were heavy; it was an effort to keep them open, but she thought there was something else about him—something more than the stitches and the cast. His face was gaunt and pale, but it was his eyes that caused a distant flicker of alarm to echo through the fog—they were empty and dull, as if he wasn't really there.

"What happened?" Dinah managed to say the words, but they came out in a faint croak. A sharp pain stabbed at her lungs.

"Honey, there was an accident. You were hurt, but they've been taking good care of you here at the hospital. You're going to be fine. You just have to keep resting for a while." Dinah gazed at her mother like a somnambulist. Her eyes found focus on Caroline's neck—she could see her mother's throat move as she swallowed. It looked like the words were painful as they came through. An accident . . . She looked around the room. Tom had appeared beyond her mother's shoulder, smiling down at Dinah, but there was something missing in his smile. He didn't seem happy. She knew she should wonder why . . . an accident . . . she was in an accident . . . she was so tired . . .

The doctor was holding a small light: "Hello there, Dinah. I'm Dr. Greer. I'm just going to take a little look into your eyes. This will be bright, but will only take a second." He leaned over, pulling up on her right eyelid as he shined the light into her eye. Following his instructions to move her eyes side to side, up and down, she heard Tom's voice.

"Hello again, Bright Eyes. Nice to see you back." He picked up her hand as the doctor made some notes on a clipboard. Dinah gazed around. No one else was in the room. She felt confused, with the disturbing, slightly panicked sensation of having slept through an important exam. Tom must have read the distress on her face. He sat gently on the edge of the bed, while the doctor moved to the door. "Can you remember waking up over the last couple of days?" Dinah started to shake her head, but then a vision of Tru with stitches on his face appeared, and she remembered that she had been in an accident. Evidently he had been in the accident, too.

"I remember a little. I thought it was a dream. Where is everyone?" Her throat felt rusty.

"Your Mother and Tru needed to get a little rest and clean up—they'll be back soon, along with Batty and Bee."

"Batty and Bee are here?" She was just lucid enough to understand that her aunts' presence was unusual. An alarm was going off in a remote region of her brain. Once again, she asked the question—but this time she was determined stay awake to hear the answer: "What happened?"

Tom looked down at her hand, still clasped in his. Then he looked into her eyes. "Honey, it was a car accident. You and Tru and Jemima were coming home . . . there was ice on the train tracks . . . do you remember anything at all?" Dinah just shook her head, trying to make her memory work.

"It had been snowing—the streets were icy, and Tru . . ." Tom's expression took on a look of infinite sadness. "Tru tried to beat the train. He was trying to get Jemima home—she needed to use the bathroom. The car stalled on the tracks."

"A train . . ." Dinah repeated the word absently, struggling to process the information. "And it hit the car."

Tom nodded, almost imperceptibly. "Yes—you and Tru and Jemima were coming home from Brickman's. It was after the Christmas pageant. Do you remember that?" His words were quiet—almost reluctant.

Bits of memory began to flicker in the distance, but they were elusive. She managed to grasp one—it was something about the Christmas pageant: Jemima was the donkey. Jemima. Dinah looked around the room slowly. "Where's Mimer?" Her voice was lethargic, the question reflexive. But Tom didn't answer. Dinah's eyes travelled back to her stepfather, and a pain stabbed at her chest as she drew a deep breath. Cautiously, Dinah repeated the question: "Where's Jemima? Everyone's OK, right?"

Tom cleared his throat, closing his eyes briefly. After a moment, he swallowed, and his voice was thick. "You're going to be just fine. You've been unconscious for a few days, but we've got you back now. Your leg is broken—you can feel the cast." He moved Dinah's hand to the top of her right leg—she felt the hard shell reaching nearly to her hip. "Both the tibia and the femur were fractured—that's your upper and lower leg—it's quite a cast. You also have some broken ribs. Be sure to tell the doctor or the nurses if you need more pain medication—taking a deep breath will be painful for a while." He blinked a few times, and then continued: "Tru's arm is shattered— they had to operate and put in a few pins . . . it may require more surgery . . .

He took a pretty good gash to the face, as well, but he'll be all right. You both have some cuts and bruises . . . contusions, I believe they call them." His words tapered off, and he looked down at his lap.

"What about Jemima? Is she all right?" Tom's patient explanation had lulled Dinah into an optimistic complacency, but now his shoulders slumped.

With a deep sigh he turned to look into her eyes: "Dinah . . ." The color had drained from his face; he squeezed her hand tightly. "Jemima was in the back seat. She . . ." He drew a deep breath. "Honey—the back of the car was directly in the path of the train." He closed his eyes; his chin fell to his chest. "Jemima . . ." His voice cracked at her name, and Dinah felt a sense of urgency press through the enervation. Suddenly she was painfully, acutely awake, as the tears Tom had been fighting rolled down his face.

"What? Jemima what? Is she hurt? Is she here—at the hospital? Where is she?" Although still weak, Dinah's voice was imploring. Tom couldn't answer. He simply shook his head, back and forth, and his shoulders heaved as the tears continued to stream, falling onto Dinah's hand where it was cradled in his.

And then she knew. This was what she had read in Tru's eyes. This was why she hadn't recognized her own mother. The room began to tilt and she was slipping back—into to the salvation of oblivion. Her last conscious thought came unbidden, as the image of the one-handed furniture mover appeared in all of his living, breathing glory—taunting her with cruel proof of the torturous truth: There is some damage that cannot be measured; there are some sorrows that can't be conceived.

PART THREE

LOOK AHEAD

CHAPTER TWENTY-THREE
Echoes

THE REFERENCE BOOK LAY OPEN on the table, but Dinah had stopped reading a long time ago. She was tired. It had been a long struggle to catch up with all of her schoolwork. Back in November she had decided to use Elizabeth Peabody's letters as the basis for her thesis for a history honors project, and she wasn't getting anywhere in her search for more information about the relationship between Peabody and Nathaniel Hawthorne. Leaning back in the hard chair, she straightened out her right leg, still aching in a walking cast. She tried to take a deep breath—the constricting tightness around her chest remained. The doctor told her the ribs were healed, but she could feel a painful stab each time she filled her lungs. She couldn't think. The cloudy, dense aura that cocooned her—that kept the raw, excruciating grief at bay—also suffocated her curiosity and acumen. She felt like a zombie. She didn't care.

Resting her head in her hand, she closed her eyes, allowing her mind to wander toward the edge of the precipice. She drifted to the days in the hospital: the stunned, empty days, when she was incapable of anything but sleep and numb denial. When she was finally released, Tom took her home to a strange house. It looked the same from the outside, but inside it echoed with an emptiness that bore no resemblance to the house she knew. The Christmas tree was gone; there was no evidence of the gaily wrapped gifts that had waited beneath it. Her mother was in bed—something that Dinah would come to expect. The door to Jemima's room was closed. Aunt Batty was quietly crocheting in the sunroom—she and Bee had swooped in after the accident like Sisters of Mercy, tenderly taking over the funeral arrangements and ministering to Caroline's grief. They were regular visitors at the hospital, sitting by Dinah's bed for hours, their soft, worn hands stroking her forehead, gently combing her hair, bestowing the strength of their implacable love.

After a couple of weeks, Bee had gone back to Beaufort, leaving Batty to tend to the detritus of their lives. In the months since the accident, neither

Dinah nor Caroline had been able to surface from the inconceivable grief—it wasn't possible. It wasn't even something they could conceptualize. Tom struggled to bear them up, to keep them from sinking to the bottom of the well, but it was an effort that he could ill afford. Dinah had seen him one night at his desk in the library, head bowed, chest heaving with pent-up sorrow.

But Dinah's bereavement had another aspect—an extra layer of anguish that doubled the loss: In addition to losing her sister, she had lost Tru. He was gone. She couldn't feel him anymore. She had always been able to feel his presence, even when he wasn't there. She had come to accept it as a truth that was as constant as gravity. But the truth was gone; it had disappeared like a forgotten dream.

She had seen him last the day after she regained awareness, the day after she finally woke to the nightmare. She had opened her eyes to find him there, alone with her in the room. His body leaned forward from the chair onto the edge of her bed, his forehead resting on his left arm. She stirred and he raised his head, and that's when she knew: Even through the fog that lingered, she could see it. He looked at her and she knew; she was losing him. The person behind the dark eyes was being buried alive, entombed by guilt and pain and sorrow.

He tried to speak, but no words came out—just a strangled gasp. He closed his eyes and tried again: "I'm sorry . . ." choking on the words, he hung his head. "I can't . . . I'll never be able to . . .fix it." His voice was shattered, and his shoulders shook. She wanted to hold him, to beg him not to let it swallow him whole, but all she could do was watch as he drifted away. He couldn't help himself, and she couldn't help him. Hopeless tears filled her eyes. She knew—he was already gone.

He left the next day. Dinah learned later that Tom insisted Tru return to school for the spring term—he felt it was essential that his son at least go through the motions of living. She learned that Tru's shoulder had been crushed, along with his humerus. He wouldn't play football again, but Dinah knew that whatever pain he had endured would never be enough to punish himself as he wished.

She closed the book, snapping off the library lamp and picking up her papers. Limping on the rubber stump of her cast, she moved through the empty rooms to the lobby, smiling sadly at Jane as she left. "I'll see you tomorrow."

"Honey, you know you don't have to come in if you don't feel up to it. I know you have a lot of work to catch up on at school . . ."

"It's fine—I like having a place to go . . ." She didn't elaborate, but Jane knew what she meant. She couldn't imagine what it would be like to live in a house with so much sadness.

The house was still; Aunt Batty had left earlier in the week to go back to Beaufort. On the day before she left, she had taken Dinah on the trolley to St. Mary's Cemetery. Dinah had been terrified. Batty held her hand as they sat on the wooden bench. The trolley ran along North Street, and as they passed Brickman's, Dinah closed her eyes. At the cemetery, they walked across the thick lawn, wending their way through the ancient headstones, and Dinah drifted away—transported from the present as she became immersed in the history of the dead. She escaped to centuries past, losing herself in the names and the dates and the imagined life stories. Batty had to tug gently on her arm to pull her back, to face their real purpose. She led Dinah over a knoll to the far side of the cemetery and a small, alabaster headstone with the likeness of a dove—wings outstretched— carved at the top. As Dinah stared at it, a thousand images of Jemima overwhelmed her—so real, so visceral, so intensely present that she knew it must certainly be a mistake. Her sister could not lie there, in the cold, dark ground. She could not be gone. It simply wasn't possible. She felt Batty squeeze her hand; there were tears running down the soft lines of the worn face. Then she heard Jemima's voice, and the utterance that had echoed in the hospital after the fire—a single sentence that floated back from two summers past. It struck her like lightning and she sank to the ground, face down on the soft grass, prostrate with heaving sobs. Her arms pressed into the earth with the unsparing need to hold the small body that lay below, and the words repeated in her ears: "It's not nice to leave people alone."

CHAPTER TWENTY-FOUR

Vestiges

THE PHILLIPS LIBRARY WAS LOCATED in Plummer Hall, a Southern Colonial-style building that had once housed the Salem Athenaeum. The library was part of the Peabody Essex Museum, and Dinah had started using the research facilities there for her history project on Elizabeth Peabody. Over the course of the past weeks she had found a crucial escape—a story that transported her from the devastation of her own life to that of a real heroine. The rich, productive life of this fascinating woman had taken root in Dinah's mind and seemed to grow of its own accord.

Crossing the room, she noticed a heavy, walnut-framed portrait hanging in a prominent position on the inset mahogany paneling. It was the original Charles Osgood painting of Nathaniel Hawthorne. The author was widely acknowledged as an extremely handsome man, even in Victorian times, and this portrait proved it. But in all of the various images that Dinah had come across, none had captured as Osgood had the quality of Hawthorne's gaze. There was something familiar about it. She couldn't define it at first, but then she stepped back and realized what it was. His eyes were the deepest shade of sable—almost ebony—and there was something else . . . a compelling, magnetic pull from which it was nearly impossible to look away.

Dinah backed away a few more steps, until she bumped into a library table. She dropped her books on the table as she sat down, taking a deep breath. Her grief for Jemima—the overwhelming anguish that left her empty and numb—had buffered her from her grief for Tru, and it shook her to the core when it snuck up on her like this. She felt weak against the power of it—the loss and longing washing over her like a wave. After a moment she squeezed her eyes shut and shook her head, forcing her attention to the books scattered on the table.

She scanned the titles, giving them one last look to be sure she had gone over everything. While Peabody's life had grown ever more fascinating, Dinah still hadn't found any corroborating evidence of the private relationship between Elizabeth and Nathaniel Hawthorne. She had exhausted all available documentation in the archives, and now she stood and started putting the books back on the shelves. It was as she slid the last one into meticulous Dewey Decimal order that she noticed a tattered cardboard file, pushed behind a collection of Transcendentalist publications. It was wedged in tightly, the top edge of the file hooked behind the upper shelf, and she had to pry it out carefully, so as not to tear the folder. She sat down and began to leaf through the file. One look inside confirmed what she had expected: It contained the usual documents detailing the "conversations" held at Peabody's West Street Bookstore, dissertations on Transcendentalism by Ralph Waldo Emerson and Henry Thoreau, fledgling women's rights discourses by Margaret Fuller, copies of lectures on Unitarianism by William Ellery Channing, and documentation of the seminal Temple School that Peabody had started with Bronson Alcott.

Dinah was already familiar with the basics of these records; she had been challenged to pare down the incredible depth and breadth of accomplishment in Peabody's life in order to conform to the maximum permitted length for her paper. She was tempted to return the file to the shelf, but her natural diligence drove her to empty the sections, stacking the contents in neat order on the large oak library table.

It was near the back of the file that her perseverance paid off. Hidden in the leaves of a Margaret Fuller critique on traditional social and religious authorities were six postmarked envelopes. But they were not letters from Fuller. There, in the upper left-hand corner, on each and every one of them, were the initials N.H.

And they were all addressed to Elizabeth Peabody.

Here it was, then. His own hand, his own words. Finally, the other side of the story. Dinah hardly dared hope that she might find something that would shed light on the mystery of Elizabeth's enigmatic notes, but as she opened a nearly-translucent envelope, she hoped anyway.

At the top of the page was a date. A date! It was too good to be true. Right there, in faded India ink: *19 August, 1842*. With utmost restraint, she put the page down and systematically withdrew all of the other letters. She didn't allow herself to read a single line until they were arranged chronologically. Then, picking up the earliest one, she began to read:

Dearest Lib,

Let me begin by saying straight away that I cannot agree with you and Mr. Emerson on all points. Man is not delivered from evil. I will never be persuaded that evil is simply the absence of good. But I do agree on several. Most important, that what I know about us—about the forces that drive this madness—is not born from reason. You speak of Divine Intellect, and this is the only answer I can find—I cannot defend what we are in any other way. Defend! What a meager term. If God, Humanity, and Nature are one, then what we do must be of God. If I am to answer to anyone, it must be to myself. But I suffer! Your Mr. Emerson says "No law can be sacred to me but that of my own nature." The law of my own nature. How can I deny it? Am I fed by a fire whose foundation is Divine? I am—

Your wretched disciple
NH

Resting the letter on her lap, Dinah sat back thoughtfully. What did he mean by *"defend what we are"*? Was he referring to greater society, or did he mean it personally: *we*, as in you and I? And what about *"the forces that drive this madness"*? These sounded like the desperate words of a man who had lost his bearings. She studied the letter again. There was something about the Emerson quote . . . it reminded her of something. She couldn't think of what it was. Something about nature. Nature. *The law of my own nature.* And then she envisioned the translation that Kenny had scratched at the bottom of her own letter. The letter that was written in Latin. The letter from Tru. *"Never does nature say one thing and wisdom say another."* She stared at the onionskin paper. It seemed as if Hawthorne were using the intuition concept—the *Divine Intellect* doctrine of Transcendentalism—to justify his relationship with his sister-in-law. Suddenly the pale script was replaced with voices. She heard her own whispered fear as she stood in the midnight darkness under their parents' window: *"Is this wrong?"* And Tru's voice—resolute and certain—breathing softly into her ear: *"Can't be."*

There was no need to define the doctrine. She knew about intuition.

Shakily, she picked up the next letter. It was dated 24 January, 1844, and the salutation alone made her sit up straight:

My Lib, My Libation, My Libretto, My Liberty—

What an immense joy you must feel for your proud accomplishment! Tell Bronson I send my best—your new school will set the standard, it is certain. What an odd tale about Abba Alcott—why would she open your mail? The entire clan is quite eccentric, but Bronson has some fine ideas. The German education model is the way of the future, I think.

I have been working on the story of the Ingersoll place. Pondering calling it something else—something to feature the actual structure of the house. There is something in it—the walls hold a fearful power, and such melancholy! Perhaps about the gables, there are quite many. Poor Susanna, to have grown up in such a place! If ever spirits did walk this earth, they would abide there. As a child I would quake with nerves during the night, certain the specters of my frightful ancestors were hovering near. Do you think I bear the weight of their sins? Old William with the Quakers in that horrendum aestate of 1692, and his son John with the Witches not 40 years late—is this grievous life I have come to live penance for their ghastly abominations?

The indisputable intimacy of the pet names seemed evidence enough. What was it that Tru used to say? *Res ipsa loquitur. The thing speaks for itself.* Dinah stared at the endearments for several moments, and then back at the date. Hawthorne had married his wife in 1842, two years earlier—the same year that the first letter was written.

The rest of the message could easily have been interpreted as a friendly exchange, congratulating Elizabeth on her new educational enterprise with Alcott in forming the Temple School, and discussing his work on *The House of Seven Gables.* While Dinah found it interesting to learn more of Hawthorne's own personal experience in the house, she had already seen transcripts of notes Hawthorne had made on this topic. She also knew that his ancestors had been involved in the persecution of the Quakers and the travesty of the Witch Hysteria, and that their culpability haunted him.

But the last line brought home the familiarity of the first. Was the *"grievous life"* to which he referred a product of his guilty conscience?

The next letter was dated 16 June, 1846:

My Libbet,

Yesterday brought the dubious fortune of a meeting with your friend, Jones Very. He was violently excitable. A strange man, Very. Very strange, indeed! He was ranting about being a savior, and insisted that he had taken it upon

*himself to perform your baptism! Is this what comes of being born into a
Godless household? Or could it be the result of the union of first cousins? He
bears a tinge of lunacy. I read some of his poems—somewhat too syncopated
in style, I think. He mentioned a reading at your store—you'd do better to
keep Margaret Fuller on the bill.*

*Julian is crying in his cradle. One last line—stolen from you friend Jones,
but decidedly apt: "'Tis a holier thought than that in which my spirit lived
before . . . earth wears a lovelier robe than it wore."*
Only but for you, my dearest love
—N.

There could be no doubt; it was as she suspected. Elizabeth was his
dearest love. But Hawthorne didn't seem as plagued by guilt as he had been
before, and the reference to his baby son was confusing. The comment
about Jones Very had also struck Dinah. *First cousins.* Was she imagining
it, or did this reference to a union complicated by family ties draw a faint
parallel to her own life? A shiver rushed over her skin, and she had to
shrug it off, turning abruptly to the next letter.

11 November, 1848
Libby my Love—

*I was with Margaret at Brook Farm. She had some extraordinary ideas.
In many we share a like mind. Her treatise on men and women is intriguing.
Do you agree with her? What of marriage? Meg says you have been fortunate
to channel your own talents and intellect to their fuller development without the
burdensome role of wife and mother. But what of the union of souls? Is there
no holiness in that bond?*

*I walked in the garden at Brook Farm last night;
the ebon sky glittered with shimmering light.
Every object in shadow bore visions of thee,
and from each star I felt thy gaze rest upon on me.*

A simple rhyme, a bedeviled truth.
Your Nate

The next letter, as those before it, was written after a two-year span.
Dinah wondered if there had been others, or if the correspondence could

have possibly been so sporadic:

> *8 July, 1850:*
> *My Own Sweet Lib,*
>
> *I heard the anguishing news about Margaret and her new husband, the Marquis. To think they sailed across the vast expanse, only to founder on the rocks at journey's end. I'm told Emerson sent Thoreau and Channing to search for poor Meg—the wreck was off Fire Island—so close. There is no doubt she is debating ferociously with Poseidon. He stands scant chance!*
>
> *I will be in Concord a fortnight hence. Until then I must conjure your presence. My fantasies fall woefully shy.*
> *Your Most Grateful Author*

This was the terrible shipwreck that had taken the life of Margaret Fuller. Dinah had read about it. It had been a tragic loss to the progressive ideological movement of greater Boston and to women everywhere. She knew Peabody had been stricken with grief for her friend.

Hawthorne's closing line reminded Dinah that Elizabeth Peabody was not only his sister-in-law—and apparently his lover—but also his publisher. Dinah had been impressed from the outset that he had entrusted this woman, the first female book publisher in the country, with the immensity of managing his literary career. His respect for her must have been tremendous.

She moved on to the penultimate letter. It was brief—only a few lines. The first few were achingly poignant in their simple brevity, but it was the last one that jumped from the page:

> *Elsabetta—*
> *Do I ever think of you? Can you possibly wonder? It is all that I do.*
> *I kiss you in my dreams*
> *—NH*

How could it be possible? The uncommon syntax, the very same words. Dinah sat perfectly still, staring at the line. She felt lightheaded, but at the same time it felt as though her head must weigh a hundred pounds, and she dropped her forehead to her arms, folded on the table. She was unaware of anything but her own rapid, shallow breathing.

Finally, she lifted her head and sat back. She realized her cheeks were wet. Absently, she wiped at them with the sleeve of her sweater. *I kiss you in my dreams.* It was too coincidental, too uncanny. She was starting to believe her entire project had been predestined. Was this a sign? Was this God, laughing, proving her wrong about His existence? She had never believed in fate, but now she was beginning to wonder.

There was only one more letter. Dinah was almost afraid to pick it up. Steeling herself, she looked at the date: *4 October, 1850.* Only a few months later. The pattern was broken. She closed her eyes for a moment, and then she forced herself to read:

> *Dear Heart,*
>
> *Could I ever conceive a greater torment? I can scarcely force pen to paper. Sophia has returned—she is not well. My moral aspect has been revealed to my mind's eye, and I am tortured with frightful dreams and desperate thoughts. Though I would cling to the dictums of wiser men—"Let me not to the marriage of true minds admit impediments"—I cannot allow my heart its wont. I cannot, Libbet! I cannot! There is no escape from the demons which haunt me. I pray for sanctity. I pray for sanity. The only recourse is to repent.*
>
> *I can offer you naught but the knowledge of my eternal sorrow, and that my heart is forever yours*
> *—N.*

That was it, then. Dinah put the letter down, swallowing a lump in her throat. He had told Elizabeth goodbye. He had left her. This was the final letter—there were no more.

Walking home from the library, Dinah could hardly feel the sidewalk under her feet. She was rocked by her discovery—proof of an adulterous affair between one of the most renowned moral paragons of his time and a woman that Dinah had come to revere—but she was even more unnerved by the eerie parallels to her own life. The coincidence of the identical phrase had rattled her nearly senseless.

The familiar black DeSoto was in the driveway—an increasingly common sight. In a perverse twist of fate, Tom seemed to have gained a sister since Dinah had lost hers. Coco had come through the tragedy with flying colors, arriving each week with bags of groceries, new recordings for Tom, the latest cologne from Paris for Caroline, a bestseller or one of the classics for Dinah, and other astonishingly thoughtful gifts. Even more surprising, she seemed to have established a real rapport with Aunt Batty, paging through the latest issue of *Vogue* or *Harper's* in the sunroom while Bat worked her crewel, companionably biding their time. It was bewildering. Coco had an innate sense of sympathy of which no one had been aware. She didn't say much, but her determined presence, by its very unexpectedness, provided a touching support.

Harley didn't come with her. Coco never revealed much, but she had made several references over the weeks to a new, unspecified venture. Dinah didn't really pay attention, but she knew that Tom had taken Coco into the closed sanctuary of the library to discuss the subject on several occasions.

She was unpacking groceries in the kitchen when Dinah came in. "Oh, hello. I'm just getting these things put away." Coco moved busily around the kitchen. "I haven't seen your mother; she may be upstairs. I believe Tom is still at the mill. I thought maybe I could whip up a little dinner . . . I have a divine recipe for chicken cordon bleu. I managed to get it out of an old chef at a darling little trattoria in San Remo. It was in his family for years—I don't think he had ever given it out before."

Impossible! Coco was going to cook for them? Dinah looked around for flying pigs. Batty had been doing most of the cooking since she had arrived, with Gloria pitching in every now and then. Evidently Coco was willing to fill Batty's apron now that she had left.

Dinah wandered upstairs to see if her mother was aware they had entered an alternate universe. It was quiet—she thought Caroline must be asleep. The possibility was more likely than not; her mother hadn't really been able to wake herself since the accident. Dinah was envious. She wished she could turn herself into Rip Van Winkle and sleep for a hundred years—it would be a welcome relief from the horrible, heavy grief that made a fresh assault each morning when she opened her eyes.

She went to her room and sat down at the desk. Her history project was almost finished—she simply needed to write the conclusion. She wasn't going to use the letters. After she had finished reading them, she sat motionless on the heavy oak library chair for almost an hour. She was torn about her discovery. Although she originally intended to use the letters as the crux of her thesis, she now felt an odd protectiveness toward them.

The mystery was solved, and she realized she didn't really have the stomach to share it. Her own familiarity with the subject of taboo relationships had produced a unique sympathy; she just couldn't bring herself to disclose the secrets to which, by all standards of common decency, she had no right. In the end, Dinah had decided not to betray the woman whom she had come to think of as a friend. She had put the folder back on the shelf, hiding it deep behind a collection of aged issues of *The Dial*.

Now, as she finished the last paragraph, she was glad about her decision. She had written a thorough, reflective study: a portrait of a woman whose blazing passion was the dissemination and discussion of literature; a woman who spent a lifetime finding ways to promote and publish works; a woman who had found, in the thrilling and sweet concourse of books, what she had lost in love. In this, Dinah felt a painful empathy.

Gathering the pages, she inserted them neatly into a three-ring binder and snapped it shut. She laid it on the desk and absently ran her hand over the cover. It felt like she was saying goodbye to a good friend.

Still shaken by the unearthly parallels in the letters, she was exhausted. She was also hungry, and she stood to go and see if Coco had risen to the challenge of finding her way around a stove. Especially that stove.

Quietly, she moved down the hallway, wondering if her mother was awake. Caroline's bedroom door was ajar, and Dinah peeked in. The bed was unmade, but no one was there. Quietly, she padded across the carpet, looking toward the bathroom. She noticed a lump in the bed—just a small little hump under the blankets. Vague curiosity compelled her to pull back the sheet. There, sprawled beneath the covers, looking dazed and a little lost, was Fuzz Monkey. Dinah closed her eyes. Her mother had been sleeping with Jemima's beloved Fuzz. To her knowledge, no one had gone into Mimer's bedroom in the past months; the door remained closed at all times. But clearly someone had. Caroline had taken a vestige of her baby girl into her bed with her—a heart-wrenching surrogate whose very presence howled Jemima's absence. Dinah sank onto the bed, holding Fuzz in her arms, and hung her head in sorrow.

CHAPTER TWENTY-FIVE
Truer Words...

PULLING THE LAST OF THE GERANIUMS from the flower box, Caroline wiped the back of her gardening glove across her forehead. In late September the air still carried the heavy warmth of summer, and she wondered if it was too soon to put the mums in. She could probably get another month out of the red geraniums, but she was in the mood for autumn colors—the pale golds and burnt oranges that signaled a slowing down, a quiet, restorative withdrawal from the hectic brightness of summer. She sat back on her heels, gazing around her. It had been almost May when she had slowly begun to emerge from the somnolent stupor of her grief and pour herself into the gardens. They provided an earthy anodyne that soothed her soul; each tiny shoot, pushing through the ground with earnest need, gave her a purpose—a life to nurture. The effects of her single-minded industry had been dazzling—the gardens burst forth with spectacular, lush blooms—every one of them a tribute to Jemima. It was the only form of therapy Caroline knew, and somehow it had helped.

She thought back to the dark days of winter and early spring, when she had been unable to function at all. She didn't really remember much of those weeks and months, but she did know that she had been incapable of helping herself, let alone anyone else. The sad fact that she had emotionally abandoned her oldest daughter still aroused a queasy regret; she hadn't been there when Dinah needed her most. It had been a complete transposition, in fact. Dinah had been the one to care for her, worriedly checking on her day after day. Sometimes Caroline would wake to find her daughter sitting on the edge of the bed, softly stroking her forehead. It always seemed like a dream, and she would drift back to sleep with the feel of the smooth hand on her face.

Caroline was also aware that Dinah had suffered more than the loss of her sister. Her worries about Dinah and Tru had played out in the worst possible way. She knew that Dinah's heart was broken, and, again, she had no ability to fix it. Tru hadn't come home for the summer; Coco had arranged an internship in Washington with Senator Guilford. Tom had been to visit him a few times over the course of the year—each time returning with a sad helplessness. He worried that his son was irremediably broken. Tru went through the motions, applying himself to his studies and his work, but his spirit seemed to have flown away that night on the tracks, leaving a hollow impersonator.

One evening, after Tom had returned from his second visit, Caroline noticed his soup sloshing over a quivering spoon during dinner. She stared at her husband's hand, aware that he was struggling to camouflage the tremor—unsure of whether to try to bring the spoon to his mouth or simply give up and put it down. He saw her watching him: "It isn't as bad as it looks—just the odd spasm. I don't really think it's getting any worse." He smiled reassuringly, but the effort showed.

Caroline couldn't help wondering if the cruel strain of all that had happened could have an effect on the progress of the disease, but she couldn't bring herself to say it aloud. She still couldn't speak of the accident. Instead, she asked the difficult question: "Have you told Tru . . .?" Her voice trailed off; she didn't need to finish the sentence.

Tom stared at his soup for a long moment. "No . . . no, I haven't. I just can't make myself do it. I don't know . . . maybe there isn't any right time, but I have to believe that it would be better to wait a while."

Would it help? Caroline wondered. Would that be all it took—simply waiting a while? If only she could believe it—if only time truly did heal all wounds. It was a miraculous hope, and she couldn't make herself hold onto it.

Now she stood, pulling off the gardening gloves and stretching. She was alone; Tom had to see about something at the Vermont mill, and he wouldn't be back until tomorrow. Dinah was in Northampton—she had left to start school at Smith several weeks earlier. The house was silent but for the clicking of Bel's paws when she walked across the kitchen floor and the scuffing sound of her stomach brushing against the carpets. The dog had taken to following Caroline around like a shadow, confused and unsettled by the empty house. It was sadly apparent that the poor thing was all too aware of the loss. Now, with Dinah gone, she attached herself to Caroline in bewildered desperation—her worried eyes communicating the fear that soon she would be left entirely alone. Caroline was growing inordinately attached to the trundling, pathetic basset hound; she pictured herself old and gray, surrounded by slobbering, flea-bitten mutts, shuffling around in her slippers and bathrobe with her pockets full of doggie biscuits. It was a parody that reflected her wry awareness of her reliance on Bel's company. The dog followed her back to the house as she brushed the traces of soil off her knees, stopping to put her tools away in the potting shed.

As the bathwater ran, she realized she had no reason to get dressed for dinner. She could just as well wear her nightgown—not even Gloria would be there to know, and Coco's visits had come to an abrupt end as she flew off to Argentina. Harley had a new venture, undertaken with Tom's wary approval: He had invested in a horse farm and was now in the business of breeding racehorses. Although the details were murky, Caroline understood that the other partners in his law firm had . . . encouraged . . . him to consider a new career. She was under the impression that he hadn't, perhaps, contributed to the collective success of the practice as they would have preferred. Tom admitted that it might be a good idea to place him in the environs to which he seemed ungovernably drawn, and off Harley had gone to find his pot of gold. Once he had settled on a farm near Buenos Aires, Coco followed, with trunks of strapless evening gowns to secure her status in the steamy social swirl of the southern hemisphere.

It was surprising to realize that she missed Coco. Her sister-in-law's weekly presence, however imperious, had become somehow comforting. Caroline supposed it was simply the poignancy of discovering that this hard, untouchable woman really cared; it was uplifting to see the workings of the human heart in times of need.

More than anything, however, she missed Dinah. It had been a challenge to settle the college arrangements; although Dinah had started the application process in November, the forms were incomplete. Everything had slipped away during the first months of the year, but Principal Dawes had been a godsend, helping to fill out applications, forwarding transcripts, and arranging letters of recommendation. With the shepherding assistance of the school, she had been accepted at Wellesley, Radcliffe, and Smith. The hard part came when it was time to make a commitment. Dinah was suddenly reluctant to leave, and Caroline knew that it was because she felt that her mother needed her at home. It took some convincing, with an earnest, reassuring effort from Tom, to get her to go.

On a rainy day in early September they dropped her off at Cushing House, the same house on the quad in which Caroline had lived as a freshman. It couldn't have been called a happy day, or even an exciting day, but it was, perhaps, a hopeful day. A bittersweet and brave day. A new day. It wasn't until they got home and Caroline wandered absently into Dinah's room, gazing around at the nearly empty closet and the gaping bookshelves, that she saw the blank form still on the desk—the sad reminder of all that was lost: the application to William and Mary.

The study lounge of Cushing House held an assortment of mostly Federal-style chairs, along with three Queen Anne sofas and various side tables. Most of the furniture was comfortable enough—Dinah had staked out a large wingback chair, with a round ottoman pulled up for her feet. There were always plenty of girls in the lounge, inevitably barefoot in blouses and slips—skirts and hose having been peeled off after classes. Someone had put a record on the turntable in the corner, and Artie Shaw played softly as Dinah nibbled the end of her pencil, trying to concentrate on Shakespeare over the constant, low chatter of the lounge. It was quieter in the library, but the lounge had a communal, slumber-party aspect that was cheerful. A short, buxom girl named Dory Bremer curled up in the chair next to her, lighting a Pall Mall and opening a math textbook. She was grumbling about the mid-term when Dinah noticed the title: *Discrete Mathematics*. She stared at the words, wanting to reach out and run her hand over them. She felt oddly proprietary toward the book, as if it should belong to her alone. She could see Tru's provocative words dropping down from the letters. She leaned her head against the side of the chair, closing her eyes. She missed him every minute of every day. She didn't know what he was doing, or thinking, or feeling. Several times she had started to write him a letter, but they all ended up in the trash can, crumpled into dry, sharp-edged snowballs. Anything she wrote sounded puny and inadequate. There were no words that could fill the void; nothing could begin to address what had happened. And there was another factor inhibiting her efforts: beyond the paltry destitution of language was the terrifying possibility that her letters would go unanswered—that she would have to live with the anxious uncertainty of wondering whether he had read them, and why he didn't respond. Worse still was the prospect of a response that she couldn't bear to read. She knew he needed time—Tom tried to explain that Tru was punishing himself and there wasn't anything anyone could do—but that didn't ease the pain in her heart.

She tried to turn back to her assignment: *Romeo and Juliet*. It wasn't the first time Dinah had read the play, but this time it seemed achingly pertinent. As she fixed her eyes on the page, the words reached out and choked her: *"Romeo is banished—There is no end, no limit, measure, bound, In that words death; no words can that woe sound."* Truer words were never spoken. She closed her book and slipped on her loafers. Suddenly the camaraderie of the lounge wasn't welcome; she needed to be alone.

"Don't let me drive you away," Dory said, stamping out her cigarette. "I won't smoke if it bothers you."

"No, it's all right. I'm just tired. I'm going to turn in early." Walking past her housemates, she repeated the explanation as they all asked where she was going. College life had surprised Dinah—she hadn't expected the ease of social acceptance, the sisterhood that came with communal living. She couldn't get over how easy it had been to make friends—a far different experience from being the new girl in junior high. The past months had been a relief; the diversions of college life and the change of scenery were a balm that she hadn't anticipated. She had formed a particularly close friendship with her roommate, Ann Donahue. Ann was possibly more bookish than Dinah, and she also possessed the ability to sense hidden sadness. It hadn't been more than two nights before she sat down on Dinah's bed and asked her, in her straightforward but gentle way, what had happened. She just seemed to know. Staring at the ceiling, Dinah told her the barest details, and Ann didn't ask for more. She became Dinah's protector, ensuring that the other girls knew enough to be careful with her, and everyone seemed to go out of the way to take her under wing. Dinah felt like she had found another family, a much-needed substitute for all she had lost.

She had been admittedly remiss about keeping in touch with her friends from high school. Their well intended concern and barely concealed pity felt suffocating, and the inevitable associations pulled at her balance. It was just such a relief to have a fresh start that she felt a near-aversion to old friendships and the bridges they erected. Her life in Salem seemed far away; the day-to-day of her courses and her surroundings had removed her not only physically, but mentally and emotionally as well.

As she walked to her room, the single connection to her past presented itself, in the baleful form of Lucy Hancock. She was moving past Dinah, coming from her own room down the hall. When Dinah had returned had to Salem High after the accident, her study load had forced her to quit the newspaper staff. Kenny and Lucy had become accustomed to distributing her assignments to the other writers anyway, and everyone seemed to understand. But it was a complete surprise when Lucy approached her in the lunchroom one day, her normally superior expression contorted into something resembling sympathy. She even put her hand on Dinah's arm. "I just want you to know that I'm very sorry for what happened to you." She sounded unnatural and stiff, but she pressed on, determined to do the right thing. "I think you're a very good writer, and I hope you do something with it in the future." Her words were rushed; she seemed slightly panicked—a novice swimmer who had ventured into the drop-off area of concerned thoughtfulness. She was clearly out of her depth. Dinah thanked her, a little nonplussed as she watched Lucy walk away, her ramrod posture and stiff gait giving the impression of a mechanical soldier.

It hadn't taken long for Lucy's sympathetic generosity to evaporate in the light of their shared classes at Smith, however. Dinah was dismayed to find her old nemesis enrolled in both her Shakespeare class and her British literature class. Whenever there was a paper due, Lucy made a point of quizzing Dinah on her thesis, even going so far as to ask if she could read her drafts. But Dinah could smell the fishy odor of her competitive maneuvering a mile away, and she didn't take the bait. She nodded at Lucy as they passed one another, and Lucy simply nodded back, churlish as always.

Back in her room, Ann sat at the desk, bent over her biology assignment. Dinah quietly slipped into bed, exhausted by the weight of missing Tru. She closed her eyes, the cover of the *Discrete Mathematics* textbook burning an image on the back of her lids.

CHAPTER TWENTY-SIX

Velum

THE BOSTON-ATLANTA LINE hadn't changed much since Caroline first climbed aboard as a new bride. For some reason this took her by surprise—the constancy of the railroad cars juxtaposing a stark contrast to the changes in her life. It gave her a bittersweet feeling to see everything exactly the same as it had been so many years before. She pictured herself in the deep-claret horsehair seat of the Pullman car, so full of blithe optimism, so ignorant of sorrow. She could barely remember that girl. Looking at Dinah, asleep against the window, she felt an affronted outrage at fate—at the cruel, capricious winds that had ripped through her daughter's young life, tearing away any possibility of that kind of blissful naivety. Dinah would never get to be that young bride, certain that life held nothing but the promise of a happy future.

Tom was snoring lightly, with his feet propped up on the empty seat next to Dinah; there hadn't been any sleeping berths available when they made the decision to go to Beaufort for Christmas. Batty had written with the invitation weeks earlier, but Caroline had been paralyzed by an inability to think about the holiday. She knew she was being irresponsible and weak, but the associations were so painful that she had denied the calendar, ignoring the looming date altogether. Finally Tom took action, making the arrangements and sending a letter of grateful acceptance to Batty and Bee. He knew it would be best for all of them to have a change of scenery for the holidays.

They had been traveling since the previous morning, arriving in Boston just in time to park the car and board the ten o'clock to Baltimore. There, they had to switch lines to Charleston, where they would be met by Batty and Bee for the drive to Beaufort. Caroline had noticed Dinah gazing out the window into the dark of the night as they passed Washington D.C. Her forehead was resting against the glass, and the expression on her face was so forlorn that Caroline didn't have to guess what was on her daughter's mind. Tom had tried to persuade Tru to meet them in Beaufort, but he refused the offer. He said that Senator Guilford had offered to put him up for the holidays in his Washington townhouse, because he needed to work on summer job prospects. It was a flimsy excuse, and Caroline knew that Tom was despondent about it. It was clear that Tru hadn't even begun to recover from the accident; he still couldn't bring himself to face his own family. She worried that the longer he stayed away the harder it would be for him to come back. And while she knew that Tom's disappointment was profound, it couldn't be deeper than Dinah's. Her daughter hadn't needed to voice it—the look on her face when she learned that he wasn't coming spoke volumes.

There was a tinge of pink on the horizon—the landscape outside the window was beginning to assume form. Her thoughts were interrupted by a slow-down of the train. Tom shifted and opened his eyes as they rolled into the station, but they had to shake Dinah awake. The sun was just rising as they stepped onto the platform, stiff and groggy.

"Yoo-hoo! Halloo!" Two gloved hands were waving over a crowd of heads—they could have been a matched set, if not for the fact that they were both right hands. Below them *was* a matched set: two sweet, smiling faces beneath matching white pin-set clouds of hair.

"Lordy! I thought we'd have to take you home by lantern," Batty called out, throwing her hands in the air and bringing them down to frame Dinah's face as she leaned in to kiss her cheek. "We've been waiting here on this old platform in the pitch dark for y'all to show up. Bee nearly tipped right off the side a couple of times." The sisters clucked over the track-weary travelers like hens, enveloping them in clouds of jasmine and talc.

"Y'all are lucky the sun's comin' up—otherwise you'd have to experience the terror of Batty drivin' at night." The teasing words were no sooner out of her mouth than Bee realized her gaffe, clamping a hand to her mouth. Batty jumped in to cover for her sister's faux pas, keeping up a prattling commentary as they loaded their suitcases into the trunk of her ancient Model A. "I'm sorry we can't offer y'all any snow for Christmas, but I make a mean fig puddin' and we've got plenty of holiday spirit. Bee decked out the halls like nobody's business—you'd think we were hostin' the Baby Jesus himself!"

"And just wait until you hear our choir at First Baptist," Bee chimed in. "I declare, you'll think you're at the Mormon Tabernacle."

Dinah leaned back and let the rich molasses warmth of southern hospitality wash over her. Batty started the car, popping the clutch a couple of times in the process, while insisting that the beastly thing had an obstinate will of its own. They rattled down the highway, watching the palm trees and dogwood sway in the December breeze. Dinah thought the drive seemed longer than it had before, but when they pulled into the crushed-shell drive of the familiar old house, she was relieved to see that it was exactly the same—a tidy white bungalow with dormer windows on a gambrel roof. There was the long, low front porch, fronted with flower boxes, but instead of the usual hibiscus they were spruced up with evergreen boughs and stalks of holly.

Climbing the stairs to the bedrooms, Dinah ran her hand over the old pictures and photos that lined the wall—all just as they were before. She had loved coming to Aunt Batty's house as a little girl. Her own house was only blocks away, and she often had sleepovers with Bat. She could remember her mother washing her hair and pulling it into a ponytail, then dressing her in her pajamas before her father took her hand to walk down the quiet evening sidewalks, her special pillow tucked snugly under her arm. When they arrived, he would stay and chat a while with his aunt, until Dinah made it clear that it was her own private sleepover, and he would kiss her goodnight. Batty always made root beer floats. They would eat popcorn and play pinochle until Dinah's eyes were closing. Then Batty would lead her up the stairs and tuck her into bed.

She was delighted to find that the bedroom was just the same: There was the wedding-ring quilt—the one that Batty had sewn for her trousseau, but which had never seen a wedding bed. Batty had never married. She had lived in this house since she was a child. In fact, she still occupied her girlhood bedroom, refusing to disturb the pattern of her life by moving into her parents' larger one after they were gone. Her mother died when Batty was only eighteen, and Bee had just married and moved to Houston. With no one else to look after their father, Batty had assumed the role of caretaker and housekeeper. He died just a few years later, but she didn't see any reason to move, and she had happily stayed put for all these years. There were rumors of a tragic broken engagement; Dinah overheard her father once saying that more than one of the young men of Beaufort had asked for Batty's hand, but she had never recovered from a broken heart.

The story had alarmed her as a child, trying to figure out how someone's heart could break. Remembering it now she felt a stabbing empathy for her dear old aunt and she understood how apt the description was.

When she came back downstairs the aunts were in the kitchen, busily frying eggs and whipping up the specialty of the house—corn cakes with fresh maple syrup. Dinah pulled up a chipped painted chair and leaned her arms on the old oak table, tracing her finger along the scars of many happy meals. Before she knew it, Bee was gently shaking her shoulder, holding a breakfast plate. "This old table doesn't make such a soft pillow—let's get a little somethin' inside of you, and then you can climb into a real bed."

The week drifted by in a flurry of meal preparation, cookie baking, and a stream of visiting friends and neighbors who stopped by bearing tokens of holiday cheer. Inevitably they would hunker down on one of the porch swings to while away an hour or two with a cup of eggnog or cider. It was a lulling palliative to help them all clear the hurdle of the dreadful anniversary.

On Christmas night, Dinah wandered out to the porch after helping put away the last of the dinner dishes. Wrapped in a large shawl that one of the aunts had certainly crocheted, she leaned back in the swing, her left foot softly scuffing the wooden floor boards, and looked up through the tall southern pines to the clear night sky. The stars twinkled with a dazzling clarity—nature's Christmas pageant. The day had held a mixture of joy and sadness. Opening their gifts, it was impossible to ignore a gaping, abysmal absence. Dinah kept seeing the construction-paper tree with the enormous gift tags bearing two names, both missing that morning from their little circle around the Christmas tree. But there were moments—slivers of light illuminating the love and support that surrounded them—that revealed a poignant appreciation for one another, shared by survivors of a shipwreck thrown onto a rocky shore to learn, together, how to live.

Dinah was marking the constellations, trying to find Andromeda, when the door opened and Batty came out. Her great-aunt settled in on the swing, picking up Dinah's right foot and resting it on her lap. "It's a pretty night for late December," she said, rubbing her hand softly over Dinah's ankle. "Do you remember the year we had snow for Christmas?"

"No—I don't remember ever seeing snow here. I must have been a baby."

"Well, it started to fall on Christmas Eve, and wouldn't you know it just kept on comin'—right through Christmas Day. It was a veritable winter wonderland around here. Of course it was gone by the next day, but the timing was just so perfect. We all thought it was a gift from heaven."

Dinah had been thinking about gifts—and not just the ones they had opened that morning next to the Scotch pine in the parlor. She had never asked what had happened to the Christmas gifts that had been under the tree last year. There hadn't been many—Tom and Caroline waited to put anything out until Jemima was fast asleep on Christmas Eve, dreaming of Santa coming down the chimney. But there had been a few bright packages, and one of them had been for Tru. It was from Dinah. She had managed to track down Sal, the photographer from Donovan's. As luck would have it, he made a practice of keeping all of his negatives. She ordered a copy of the photo of Tru and herself as they had come off the dance floor—the same one that was in her desk drawer at home. When it arrived, she put it in a plain silver frame and wrapped it. Over the past year she found herself wondering where the gifts had gone, but she never asked. She wondered if Batty knew.

"Were you there last year to take down the Christmas tree?"

The old woman looked at her sadly, patting her leg. "You poor thing. It must be a strange feeling to have missed an entire chunk of time. It was probably a good thing, though. I think oblivion is the preferable state in some circumstances. Yes, Bee and I took the tree down."

"I was just wondering . . . there was a gift that didn't have a tag on it. It was blue with white snowflakes. Do you know what happened to it?"

"I know the one. I also know what was in it. Bee and I tried to figure out what to do with everything, and it wasn't a time for gifts, so we just put them up on a shelf in the front hall closet for later. But when that one didn't have a tag, our curiosity got the better of us and we opened it. Very carefully, of course—we intended to put it back the way it was once we figured out who it was meant for. Well, I guess I don't have to tell you—that photo was a heart-stopper. When we saw the love on that boy's face, it about knocked us over. I don't believe I've ever seen it captured like that before. But, you know, we weren't sure if he was the giver or the receiver of the gift, so we had no choice but to show it to him. It didn't take a diviner to tell he hadn't seen it before; I was certain he had stopped breathing. And then the most heartbreaking expression came over his face—I simply don't have the words to describe it. He didn't say anything. He just took it and walked away. The last I saw of it, he had it in his hands as he went up the stairs. So I have to presume he took it with him when he went back to school. And that's where your gift is."

Tears were rolling down Dinah's face—all the months of missing Tru spilling out like someone had pulled a plug. Gently removing Dinah's leg from her lap, Batty slid over and took her in her arms. "Oh, Honey—I'm so sorry. You've had one hard row to hoe." She was stroking Dinah's hair, while Dinah buried her face in the soft cotton of her aunt's house coat.

Through choking sobs, her grief poured out. She told her aunt everything she had been holding inside—the abandonment, the worry, the waiting—all the sorrow of the days and nights since he had vanished from her world. Finally the sobs subsided, and she laid her head on Batty's shoulder as they rocked gently together in the night.

"Darlin', there's somethin' you're not seein' too clearly here, and it's as plain as the nose on your face."

Dinah couldn't imagine what her aunt was talking about. "What is it?" Her voice was tired and small.

"Well, you know that poor boy will never be able to get through this until he can forgive himself, but how can you possibly expect him to forgive himself when he doesn't think you can forgive him?"

"What?" The idea of forgiving Tru had never even occurred to Dinah. She had never blamed him—it was an accident that had happened to all of them.

"You say you haven't spoken to him at all, not even once, since the hospital?"

Dinah nodded, beginning to see the angle of her aunt's point.

"How do you think he sees that?"

She was flabbergasted. Had it been up to her, this whole time, to reach out to him? The possibility that she had misunderstood—that she could have somehow spared him pain—made her weak with remorse. She could hardly consider it, sickened by the prospect of the missed chance.

Switching lines at the Baltimore station, Dinah looked up at the board. The short-line to Washington D.C. left from a platform across the great hall. The idea of simply getting on that train fleetingly crossed her mind, but it wasn't a real possibility. She was certain Tru had gone back to Williamsburg by then, and she had to go back to Smith for the start of classes. For the duration of the return trip she thought of nothing but Tru. Batty's words had jarred her. She now felt a pressing urgency to talk to him. She knew it wouldn't be in a phone call. The hall phones in the dorm were subject to a continuous running commentary from a long line of waiting callers—any attempt at privacy was a joke. It would be best to see him, but she knew she couldn't get to Williamsburg until at least March, when there was a break in classes, and even then she wouldn't know what his plans were.

By the time she had arrived back at Cushing House, she had come to the conclusion that the only choice would be to try writing another letter. How many times had she started, only to second-guess herself into silence? Her previous attempts had been hobbled by insecurity and confusion, but now she knew what to say.

Pulling out a sheet of pale blue velum stationary that Bee had given her for Christmas, she sat at her desk and began to write. She held nothing back. She told him how she had worried and wondered and waited, and how she had never, ever considered him anything but another victim in a terrible tragedy. She told him she saw him in every sunrise and every falling leaf and every page of every book. As a cold winter rain fell against the window, she poured every ounce of her love onto the page. It was terrifying; over and again she had to stifle the small, trembling voice that tried to whisper in her ear: *What if he doesn't want this?* But she did it. She did it not only for herself, but for Tru, for the chance that he had been waiting to hear it.

Folding the letter into a matching blue velum envelope, she sealed it without giving herself the crippling chance to read it over. Then she sat at her desk for a long time, staring at the envelope and listening to the rain. She was still there when Ann came into the room, rushing to find her book bag and get to class. She was clutching several envelopes of her own.

"Do you have any stamps? If I don't get these in the mail today, there'll be hell to pay with Mildred and Jim." Ann came from a large, tight-knit Irish clan in St. Paul, Minnesota. Her parents and older siblings had been more than reluctant to let her leave the sheltering wing of family, and they had strict expectations of weekly letters.

"I need to mail something, too. Would you like me to take your letters?" Dinah handed her the stamps.

"I'm going right by the box—I'll do it." She took the blue envelope and dropped it into her old leather book satchel, along with her own stack.

Dinah leaned against the window, looking out on the quad as her friend scurried away in her hooded anorak, head down against the rain. Her eyes fixed on the battered satchel, bobbing at Ann's side, until it disappeared, holding the contents of her heart.

CHAPTER TWENTY-SEVEN

The Thing with Feathers

THERE WAS A SMALL HOLE in the lace of the canopy on Jemima's bed—Caroline hadn't noticed it before. She gazed up at the pattern in the ivory fabric, picking out the imagined shape of a camel that she used to see as a child lying in the same bed. She had been working in the bedroom all morning, sifting through the books and toys, carefully stacking things into boxes. She held the peony-covered dress in her hands, softly smoothing the fabric that she had just folded. It was hard to make good progress; each book and toy held a memory that clamored for her attention—each tiny glove, or patent-leather shoe, or sailor's shirt painted a portrait of sherry-brown eyes and an impish smile and the guileless wonder that was Jemima.

She had finally found the strength to come into the room when they returned from Beaufort. Rather, it had found her. On Christmas Eve, as they left the midnight service at First Baptist Church, Caroline had been amazed by a feeling that she hadn't thought she would ever feel again: It was as though the flutter of wings brushed past her heart. What was it that Emily Dickinson had said? *Hope is the thing with feathers* . . . She knew, with all the clarity of a ringing bell, what it was: the hopeful, healing presence of Jemima's spirit.

She stood and placed the dress on top of a pile on the bed. It was enough for now. She had all the time in the world to finish the task. Her auxiliary club didn't take up much of her time, despite the fact that they were working on several projects to help veterans of the war. She was in charge of a quilting bee that provided hand-made quilts to patients at the Veteran's Hospital, but instead of finding joy in the prospect of providing some measure of comfort to the poor souls who had missing limbs and other afflictions, Caroline found herself increasingly angry and upset by the thought of all the wasted and shattered lives—by the cruel devastation of war. And now there was a new conflict in Korea—when would it ever end? What was wrong with mankind that it must continually endeavor to destroy God's creation? She had run out of patience—her experience with loss had given her a uniquely qualified position to view the callous disregard for human life that war imposed. She had recently read an article about the Registry of Conscientious Objectors created by the Unitarian Universalists, and she was seriously considering attending one of their prayer services.

Her dissident thoughts were interrupted by the doorbell. As she hurried down the stairs, she caught a glimpse of steel-blue wool through one of the leaded windows flanking the front door. Instantly, she recognized a uniform, and she opened the door with her heart in her throat. The Western Union delivery boy gave her a bright smile as he proffered the trademark envelope, chirping a staccato "Telegram!"

Caroline did not entirely trust the smile on the young messenger's face. It had been some time since she'd received a telegram. The last one had been years ago in Beaufort, confirming her father's death. It hadn't been unexpected, but the words were a blow, and the association was embedded: Bad news arrives cloaked in yellow and black. Caroline looked at the envelope warily as she closed the door. Moving instinctively toward the study, she opened it. She read as she walked, a curious smile replacing a nervous frown as she recognized the abrupt tone of her sister-in-law:

Require summer accommodations stop. Chairing Gala stop. Please confirm stop.

It took Caroline a moment to realize that Coco was asking for a place to stay while she organized the Centennial Gala for the Friends of the Library foundation. When Harley bought the horse farm in Buenos Aires, Coco had sold the brownstone in Boston. Now, with her presence required in Salem, she had nowhere else to go. Drifting to the wingback chair, Caroline curled up and looked at the brief communiqué, musing idly over the strange workings of a fate that would have her looking forward to the ongoing company of Coco Stuart Wells O'Grady.

Dinah looked at the itinerary in front of her. Her classmates were buzzing with excitement. The field trip to Washington D.C. wasn't mandatory, but every student in the American Politics class had signed up for it.

Dinah was fairly certain she was the only one who wished she hadn't. The registration had been during the first week of the semester's classes, when the thought of going to the Capitol held the dreamlike possibility of seeing Tru. She had envisioned arranging to meet him there—a misty, magical reunion after the long, painful months of separation. Now the screen of her imagination was dark. The only scenario in her mind was the stark reality of her failed attempt to bring him back to her. Her letter had gone unanswered. Daily she had waited for the campus mail delivery. Desperately she had listened for her name to be called to the phone in the hallway—but there was nothing. She had even pictured him showing up at her door. For several weeks she had taken extra care with her dress—brushing her hair each morning until it shone—on the slim chance that this would be the day she returned from class to find him waiting. But the only person waiting for her was Ann, commenting on the attractiveness of her carefully chosen wardrobe. She felt like a fool.

It wasn't the agenda of the trip that caused the heaviness in her chest; normally she would have been eager to see the White House and the Capitol and the Senate in session. It was the association—the futile proximity to Tru—that had robbed her of any inclination to go. It was the city where he had only recently been, where he would likely spend his summer again this year. She didn't know if she could stand it. But her mother had generously written a check for the cost of the trip, non-refundable; and so she waited, reluctant and forlorn, to board the bus.

As the driver squeezed through the crowded streets of the nation's capitol, Dinah was intrigued to find that they were staying at the Willard Hotel on Pennsylvania Avenue. She recalled a quote from Nathanial Hawthorne: *"The Willard Hotel more justly could be called the center of Washington than either the Capitol or the White House or the State Department."* Despite her reservations, Dinah couldn't deny a thrill of excitement at being surrounded by the import of the most powerful government in the world. She was awed by the vast sense of history that hung in the air.

The week passed in a hectic rush to see everything. The city had recently added new features: The Jefferson Memorial was lovely—Dinah was drawn to the symmetry of the Neo-Classical architecture; and they were all amazed by the new building called the Pentagon—it was said to be the largest government building in the world. Someone made a joke about having to polish the floors of over seventeen miles of hallways. They went to the National Gallery, the Museum of Natural History, and Arlington Cemetery. True to form, Dinah's favorite tour was of the Library of Congress. She could hardly believe she stood in the largest library in the world—it was what she imagined heaven would be. She felt the same overwhelming awe that she had in New York, and she couldn't help remembering Betsy's teasing remarks about her library fixation…and wondering if maybe her friend had a point.

On the final night of their stay, the chaperones agreed to allow the girls to stay out until eleven o'clock—an hour past the usual curfew. They were going to Martin's Tavern, an illustrious old restaurant that had seen its share of presidential customers. Afterward, some of the girls planned to go to The Backroom, a juke joint in Georgetown recommended by a tall, officious girl named Donna, who had it on the high authority of her cousin that it was "the berries for killer jazz."

After dinner, with the exception of a few quiet types who wanted nothing to do with a nightclub, the girls piled into cabs for the short trip to Georgetown. They spilled out in front of a narrow brick building wedged into a recess between two larger storefronts, one a ramshackle-looking law office, the other an army recruiting center. There was a bare bulb over a heavy wooden door. Strains of a horn section, audible from the street, swelled as they opened the door. Inside, through a haze of smoke, crowded tables lined a narrow room. A long bar ran the length of the far wall.

The girls, authoritatively led by Donna, made their way toward the back of the room where a small stage held the musicians. There were no available seats; they hovered awkwardly by a table of men in business suits who loudly proffered their laps for the girls' convenience, if only they would sit down and stop blocking the view. They sidled over to the wall, squeezing past disgruntled patrons, trying to blend in. The music was loud—a strange, new type of jazz, and Dinah couldn't identify even a modicum of melodic structure. She was beginning to regret that she had come—her soft bed at the Willard was beckoning. Donna was engaged in a conversation with a table of young men in sailors' uniforms who were eyeing the girls with the aspect of farmers at a livestock auction. The unrelieved, atonal dissonance of the music, the smoke, and the warmth of the room were starting to make Dinah feel nauseous. She looked around, wondering if she could convince any of the others to leave with her and find a cab back to the hotel. Glancing toward the door, she noticed a group of young people moving away from the bar. She had registered a crowd standing by the bar when she came in, but in the quest to find a table she hadn't paid much attention. Now, from the opposite side of the room, she saw a tall, brunette girl turn and laugh. She couldn't hear the laughter over the music, but she didn't need to. She knew that the sound coming from the wide smile on the elegant, patrician face was tinkling and musical. And there, walking next to her, was a profile so familiar to Dinah that she would have recognized it from the moon. She couldn't move. The group was making its way to the door; she saw him turn and glance back, looking toward the bar, not her. The students went out the door, and she was left staring at the space where Tru had been. And then the room caved in on her and she crumpled.

The school term had come to a grinding end. Dinah buried herself in term papers and exams, grabbing onto whatever diversion she could find to blot out the image of Tru and Nancy Guilford. There had been several end-of-the-year parties and socials. Most of the girls invited boys from Amherst to the mixers, but Dinah preferred to cloister herself in the security of her carrel at the library. She was now sitting on the floor of her room, routinely weeding through her books and papers, trying to decide what, if anything, needed saving for next year. She and Ann had been packing up their room since the day before, hauling suitcases out of the storage closet down the hall, stuffing towels and sheets into laundry bags, and generally making an enormous mess. Ann was hunting through the debris on the floor for her biology textbook—she wanted to sell it back to the student bookstore at a discount. Her parents were stretched to afford her tuition, and every little bit helped.

"It was right on the desk, I'm sure of it." She kicked a pile of papers and looked around futilely. Frustrated, she grabbed her old leather satchel—the one that had been her father's when he was a student at the University of Minnesota—and dumped the contents onto the floor. There was nothing in it but an array of old class notes and a few graded papers, marked up in red pencil. Irately, she gave the bag a sharp shake, more for effect than any real purpose. As she did, something blue fluttered to the floor. Both girls looked at it curiously. A pale blue velum envelope landed on top of a pile of old biology notes. Dinah stared at it, afraid to turn it over; afraid to touch it. Ann looked puzzled. She leaned over and picked it up. As she read the address on the front side, her expression turned to dismay. "Oh, my gosh! Is this that letter you gave me to mail? How could it still in my bag? She peered into the satchel, examining the empty pouch. Scowling, she pulled at the lining. "There's a tear right here—right on the top edge. It must have been stuck in there." She looked at Dinah apologetically. "When I mailed my packet of letters, I thought I had them all. How could I have missed it?"

Dinah closed her eyes, picturing Ann's head tilting down as she hurried through the rain. She could see how it happened. "It was raining," was all she could manage to say. Numbly, Dinah took the envelope that Ann held out to her. Tru had never even received her letter. He didn't know how she felt. He might still believe that she blamed him. There was a sick knot of regret forming in her stomach. What if she had lost him because of it? What if he had fallen in love with someone else—someone like Nancy Guilford—because she hadn't been able to reach him? What if it was too late? She stared at the envelope, dazed by the possible implications. When she had seen him at The Backroom, she assumed he had read her letter. She thought he had chosen not to answer—that he didn't want to see her. It had been agonizing; she had borne the crushing weight of it for weeks. Now a new possibility arose from the ashes of her incinerated hopes: What if he still loved her?

Her mind raced . . . she could send the letter now . . . or maybe she should just get on a train and go to him . . . Then she remembered—her mother had hesitantly informed her last month: Tru was studying abroad for the summer, in an exchange program that William and Mary had with Exeter College. When she heard it, Dinah felt a jolt of fresh misery—it was painfully clear that he was trying to distance himself even further. He would be well on his way to Oxford by now.

She continued to stare at the blue velum. She had no idea how long it would take to send a letter overseas—it could be weeks.

Ann sat down on the floor next to her. "I can't tell you how sorry I am." She was looking at Dinah with concern, clearly disturbed by the shock on her friend's face. She put an arm around Dinah's shoulders, nervously asking the obvious question: "Is it too late to send it now?"

Dinah closed her eyes again, wishing she knew the answer. Swallowing a dry lump in her throat, she responded the only way she could: "I don't know."

CHAPTER TWENTY-EIGHT
Posterity

IT HAD BEEN A PLEASANT SURPRISE when Dinah showed up for her first summer shift at the library to find a dark head of curls bent over the returned-book cart. She peered at it curiously, thinking there was something familiar about the intensely focused set of the shoulders, and then she saw why: When the new employee raised his head, Kenny Mitchell was looking up at her. "Kenny!" Dinah was delighted to see her friend. "I didn't know you were working here this summer!"

"Thought you'd gotten rid of me, didn't you? Well, don't worry, I can't boss you around anymore—you have seniority here." His sardonic smile was still the same.

"I didn't even know they were looking for extra help. Is Joanne still here?"

"Yep, she's here, but Mrs. MacEvoy is moving, so Miss O'Connor is taking her place."

"Jane is moving? The MacEvoys are moving?" Dinah was shocked. How could she have been so removed from her friends in Salem that she hadn't known about this? "When are they moving? Where are they going?" She looked around for any sign of Jane in the reading room.

"I guess at the end of the summer—they've been getting their house ready for sale, and taking trips to Wisconsin to look for another one."

"Wisconsin? Why Wisconsin?"

"I heard that Mr. MacEvoy took a position at some college there . . . Ripon, or something like that. My dad said there was some big blow-up at the college—I'm not sure what it was." Kenny's father was also a professor at Salem State—ironically, in the math department. When Dinah had learned this she had laughed. Evidently, the only thing Kenny had inherited from his dad was his thick head of curly hair. "Maybe he didn't get tenure or something," he added.

Until that moment, Dinah hadn't realized how much Jane and Mike had meant to her. All the time she had spent at the MacEvoy house, laughing with Betsy and her parents; the generous, exciting trip to New York; the inestimable gift of her job at the library—she was moved by a sudden sentimental onslaught of love and appreciation. And Betsy! She had been Dinah's best friend since Dinah had come to Salem. How could she have so callously distanced herself from her closest friend? She was ashamed. Whatever connections her subconscious had been avoiding, she couldn't justify the loss of friendships she had been only too willing to sacrifice. She took the returns cart from Kenny and started toward the stacks, feeling guilty and remorseful.

After her shift, she hurried home to call Betsy. Rushing along, she kept her eyes to the ground, careful to avoid turning an ankle on the old cobblestones still extant on many of the streets. As she turned onto Essex Street she was vaguely aware of a body moving toward her, but it wasn't until they were face-to-face that Dinah looked up. She would have recognized the deep violet eyes in a coal mine. They both stopped short, and for a long, strange moment their gazes held.

Finally Lana spoke: "I'm sorry," she said quietly.

Dinah was confused. Was Lana apologizing to her? Their history seemed like a lifetime ago, yet seeing Lana still provoked an uneasy wariness. She was struggling to form a reply, but in the next moment she realized that she had misinterpreted.

"I'm sorry," Lana repeated in a halting voice, "about your sister."

The ground shifted slightly under Dinah's feet. "Oh." She couldn't summon any other response. "Oh." She was completely blindsided by the unexpected sympathy, and to her embarrassment she felt her throat swell. Closing her eyes, she tipped her head down and tried to maintain her composure.

"Is Tru . . . all right?" Lana's words were hesitant.

There was no question—it was right there, in the way she said his name. She still loved him. She probably always would. If Lana only knew how much they had in common. Dinah felt a strangling squeeze around her chest. Any modicum of control she may have had crumbled, and she was helpless against the treacherous tears that streamed down her face. She took a small step backward and her foot slipped on a stone. Lana surprised her even further by gently grasping her arm, steadying her.

"Are you okay?"

Dinah couldn't answer. She turned her face to the side, nodding through her tears.

"Could you tell Tru . . . that I'm sorry about what happened? To all of you."

This was the second time that Lana had asked her to relay a message to Tru, but this time Dinah couldn't oblige, even if she wanted to. She couldn't tell Tru that Lana was sorry, because she didn't know how to reach him. Silently she turned away, unable to tell her yes, and unable to tell her why.

It was strange to have Coco staying at the house on an extended basis. Dinah imagined it must have been like this for Tru while he was growing up, after his mother died. Her step-aunt was less frosty than she once was, but there was still a formality in the atmosphere that hadn't existed before. Regular weeknight dinners felt like special occasions. But Dinah was glad to have another person at the table—it was so obtrusively pitiful with just the three of them. Coco contributed a stream of self-centered dialogue, keeping them all occupied with the eminent aggravations of planning the Gala: the incompetency of the catering staff; the impossibility of getting a decent fois gras in the United States; the problem of finding a large enough canopy to cover the dance floor; the plebian sensibilities of the other board members who had approved an appallingly insufficient budget . . . the list went on. On the evenings Coco was engaged in one of her myriad social obligations, the table seemed empty.

Dinah was curious about life in Buenos Aires, but whenever the subject was broached, Coco was vague, giving only a sketchy account of her home life with Harley. The horse business was "fine," the house was "livable," the farm was "not too far from the city." She did volunteer detailed descriptions of the fabulous cocktail parties thrown by the Jefe De Gobierno and his wife, with whom Coco had become a close personal friend. Dinah surmised that "the Jefe" must be something like the mayor. But although the names of South American politicians, American celebrities, and European nobility cropped up with regularity, Harley's name was rarely mentioned. It seemed almost like Coco had been living there independently, taking the elite of Argentina by storm as an amusing diversion to the provincial offerings of greater Boston. Dinah overheard

Tom remark to her mother that, while Harley's business acumen had finally found its mark, his success threatened to violate the accepted premise of his relationship with Coco.

"In other words," Caroline confirmed, "she needs him to need her."

Dinah's summer schedule at the library was light—she worked only a few days each week, and the occasional evening. Coming home from an afternoon stint, she found Gloria in the kitchen, humming along to the gospel station on the radio, stirring an aromatic pot of soup. Although it was dinnertime, no one else was home. "Hi Gloria—what's cooking?" She peered over an apron-clad shoulder into the steaming vat.

"Cream of celery. Just somethin' light tonight, Chickadee—ain't anybody here but us."

"Where is everyone?"

"Well, I can't speak for the Empress, but your Momma called a little bit ago to say she and Mr. Stuart wouldn't be here—somethin' about a doctor."

That was odd. Doctors didn't normally keep evening hours. Dinah had noticed that Tom's tremors seemed to have worsened lately; he had taken to laying the newspaper flat on the table instead of holding it up, and he was notably last to finish a meal, cutting his food and drinking his wine with slow and deliberate determination.

She wandered up to her room, trying not to worry. As she set her latest library acquisition—Fitzgerald's *This Side of Paradise*—on the desk, her eyes fell on the blue velum of her letter to Tru. It had been sitting there since she got home, a derelict casualty of her uncertainty. She had agonized over what to do with it. The risk of sending it overseas, only to have it lost or delayed, made her skittish—she had first-hand experience with the potential for postal mishap. But the thought of waiting another couple of months to deliver it to him was tormenting. She picked up the envelope, tapping it against her palm as she once again deliberated its fate. She looked at the address, now obsolete. Impulsively, she tore it open, sitting down at the desk to read the words she had written months ago. She needn't have bothered—they were etched on her heart. Clutching the pale sheet, she moved instinctively out of the bedroom and down the hall to the stairway. She hadn't been up to the third floor since she had been home; Coco had chosen to stay in Tru's room instead of the second-floor guest room, as it afforded an extra level of privacy. There were two other bedrooms on the third floor, but they had long since been appropriated for the excess furniture and household items from both Caroline's house in Beaufort and Tom's house in Salem. Stuffed to the rafters, there wasn't any question of trying to carve out another guest room.

Dinah gravitated to Tru's bedroom like a pet finding its way to a former home, bereft and bewildered to discover its owners no longer there. Standing in the doorway, she felt the same unsettling sense of lonely desperation that she had as a child when she would imagine being the last person on earth. The room was familiar, but just ever-so-slightly off, like a song played out of key. Gone were the messy stacks of *Sailing Digest*, gone were the inevitable clothes draped over the desk chair, gone was the football from the deep sill of the window. Now, there was a lingering trace of *Joy* perfume in the air, and several valises were lined up in the corner— their buttery leather inviting a caress even from across the room. On the tallboy was a silver brush set, and a slender black umbrella with a bronze swan handle leaned against the doorframe. The buffalo-check bedspread and the sailing pictures on the wall were still there, but Tru was gone.

She sat down on the bed, gazing absently around her. She wondered if Coco thought about her nephew as she slept in his bed at night . . . if she missed him, too. Laying her head on the pillow, Dinah curled up on one side, remembering the night that she had fallen asleep next to him with his arm draped protectively across her body. It seemed like a lifetime ago. Closing her eyes, she let herself pretend that he was there with her now; she could feel the weight of his cheek pressed against her hair and smell the clean, soapy scent of his skin. Like a child caressing the satiny, comforting edge of a favorite blanket, her mind replayed the stolen moments in the house, and the meetings in the alcove at school, and the alley in Williamsburg, and the rock at Cat Cove . . . The last image she saw was the way he had looked into her eyes on that very bed, promising her that, wherever she was, he would find her.

A hushed, scolding voice pulled her from a dreamless slumber, accompanied by a hand on her shoulder, shaking her like a skillet on the stove. "I don't get paid extra to come up all those steps, lookin' every which way for Sleepin' Beauty. And where do I find her but cat-nappin' in Her Royal

Highness's chambers! If I were you, I'd high-tail it out of here before Her Majesty catches you sullyin' her bed, or you're gonna need all nine lives. She don't seem like the type to take kindly to strays."

Utterly disoriented, Dinah bolted up. She hadn't intended to fall asleep, and she certainly didn't want to explain herself to Coco. She voiced her alarm: "Is she here?"

"She just came in. You come on down with me—soup's on in the kitchen."

Dinah followed Gloria to the second floor, where they veered off to the back stairs.

Helping herself to a bowl of soup and a slice of bread, she ate at the kitchen table by herself while Gloria finished polishing some old copper pans. The last thing Dinah was expecting was a gleaming head of dark hair to swing through the pantry door—she had assumed the socialite had been out to dinner and wouldn't be joining her.

"I was wondering if you had spoken to your mother or Tom." Coco came straight to the point, as always. Dinah looked at Gloria, deferring the question.

"I spoke to Miz Stuart 'round five o'clock. She said she and Mr. Stuart wouldn't be in for supper tonight." Gloria had looked up as she answered, but immediately went back to working on the pans. Dinah was curious— why hadn't she mentioned the visit to the doctor? Evidently Gloria did not feel it was her responsibility to give Coco any more than the most basic facts. It was no secret that Gloria didn't like Coco—she made it clear in every reference. But Dinah thought there was something more—a protective loyalty to her mother that guarded the gate with inviolable discretion.

Coco gave Gloria a penetrating look. "Did she say why?"

"I'm not 'zackly sure." Dinah could see Gloria stalling, trying to find the middle ground between an outright lie and full disclosure.

"What do you mean by 'not 'zackly'?" Coco's tone was withering.

Gloria continued to rub at an offending spot of tarnish. "I *expect* they'll be along shortly—you can ask Mrs. Stuart yourself."

Dinah was trying not to smile—Gloria's pronunciation was suddenly the very model of Philadelphia Main Line.

Exasperated, Coco turned back to Dinah. "I have reason to believe that my brother may have had an incident at the mill today. I would like to be informed of any updates you receive. If anyone calls, please let me know."

If Coco had intended to mask her concern on Dinah's behalf, she failed. Dinah peered at her, unconsciously mimicking Coco's question, if not her tone: "What do you mean by 'incident'?"

"I'm sure Caroline would have been in contact if it were something urgent." Reassurance was not Coco's forte—her words sounded stiff and scripted. "I ran into Meredith Burns, and she mentioned that John had seen Caroline and Tom going into the hospital."

Of course it hadn't been a standard office appointment—not at dinnertime. Dinah should have known better. She felt a rising alarm—something serious must have happened. She was starting to lose her appetite when she heard the front door open.

"Anybody home?" Tom's voice was hearty. He made his way to the kitchen, followed by Caroline. There was a bandage on the right side of his forehead. "Something smells delicious. I hope we're not too late to sing for our supper!"

Setting her handbag on the counter, Caroline kissed Dinah on the forehead, and then busied herself with ladling out the bowls of soup. "Hello Coco—would you care to join us for a late supper?"

"May I ask what happened?" Coco looked pointedly at Tom's forehead, ignoring the invitation.

"Just a little spill. Took a few stitches—nothing serious. Dr. Ramsey is a veritable Betsy Ross with the sewing needle—I'll be as good as new in no time."

Everyone in the room could read the print that jumped from between the lines: Tom was starting to lose his balance.

"There's good news, too," Caroline interjected. "We met with Dr. Phelps afterward; he wanted to tell us about an experimental drug that's being developed to relieve symptoms . . ." She didn't need to specify. "It can reduce tremors and improve balance, and perhaps even promote remission." Her words were bright and hopeful, but to Dinah, they sounded forced.

They ate their soup without further discussion about the "incident," speaking only of matters trivial and light. Coco did not join them, claiming a splitting headache from the stress of her earlier Gala meeting. Dinah noticed that her mother sliced the bread for Tom, and spread the butter as well. She couldn't help watching as her stepfather picked up his soup spoon, a bitter truth revealed in the fact that he had suddenly become left-handed.

After dinner, both Tom and Caroline decided to turn in—another indication of the stress of the day. Dinah tried to watch television for a while, but the reception was off. After wiggling the rabbit ears one too many times, she turned off the fuzzy picture and headed upstairs to start in on the Fitzgerald. She was passing the front hall closet when she suddenly heard Batty's voice, explaining what she and Bee had done with the Christmas presents. Dinah stopped short, staring at the closet door. She didn't know how many gifts there had been, or if any of them had been for her, and she had no idea if they were still there. Suddenly, the door seemed ominous. She was drawn to it, curious and pragmatic, but she was also repelled—afraid that finding packages from two Christmases ago would be like tearing at a freshly-healed wound. She remained motionless, eyes fixed on the door. Finally, scolding herself for her cowardice, she opened the door and pulled the chain for the overhead bulb. The upper shelf was deep—from where she stood nothing was visible but a couple of hat boxes from Filene's and Tom's old fedora. Rising onto her toes, she tried to see beyond them, but it was no use. She went into the living room, picking up a small Regency side chair that she carried back to the closet. Slipping off her shoes, she carefully stepped up onto the seat, ducking her head under the doorframe. They were there: just a few bright packages stacked against the wall. Pushing the hat boxes out of the way, she reached to pull them forward, stirring up a fine swirl of dust. There were two larger boxes; tags bearing her mother's handwriting were attached to the ribbons—one for Dinah and one for Jemima. Dinah swallowed hard, feeling a little dizzy. She took a deep breath and pushed them back against the wall, unwilling to bring them any further into the light. A medium-sized box bore Tru's name—it was Jemima's careful printing. Dinah was starting to realize that this hadn't been a good idea—she was beginning to feel a queasy panic. Quickly, she put it aside and picked up another—a tiny box wrapped in a pattern of holly with a red ribbon—but her curiosity had evaporated as her anxiety deepened. She tossed it back with the others, pulling on the light chain as she hopped off the chair. She closed her eyes and took a deep breath, shaking slightly. Her instincts had been right—she wasn't ready to stir up those kinds of memories. She put the chair back and closed the closet door, a little shiver of relief running down her spine as she hurried up the stairs, away from the ghosts of Christmas past.

It wasn't until she was getting ready for bed that Dinah realized she had forgotten something: As she crossed the room to retrieve the Fitzgerald, she saw the torn and empty envelope lying on the desk. Somewhere in Tru's room—now Coco's unwelcoming domain—was the letter that she had been holding as she fell asleep.

CHAPTER TWENTY-NINE
He Just Does

MARLYS JAMES HAD A NEW CAR. She honked the horn merrily as she pulled into the driveway in the shiny blue Chevrolet, with Laurie and Betsy waving out the windows. Dinah recognized it as the same model as her mother's—a Styleline DeLuxe—but Caroline's was pale green. She liked driving her mother's new car; she'd been practicing for her driver's exam. It had taken Tom a long time to convince her to get behind the wheel again, but everything that Tru had taught her came back in an instant, and she was surprised to find that she wasn't afraid—she still loved driving.

She slid into the backseat with Betsy. They had reunited in fine fashion, taking up where they had left off, as good friends do. Betsy graciously overlooked Dinah's year of neglect, and the past weeks had seemed like old times. Her friend also seemed to accept the fact that her family was moving. By way of explanation, she vaguely cited politics at Salem State. She would be spending most of the year away at college anyway, which mitigated the impact. They made plans with the other girls, and if Dinah wasn't working at the library she met her friends at the pool, or went to the beach, or out for burgers and shakes at Melville's or Clark's. The group no longer felt obligated to fuss over her; the time for condolences was past, and they had moved on to the easy chatter and gossip that came naturally. They all refrained from asking about Tru—mindfully pulling Dinah along like a kite on the carefree breeze of summer

That evening they were going to Clark's to celebrate Marlys's birthday. The car had been a gift from her father, an investment banker who commuted to Boston every day. Susan and Joan were already there when the girls arrived, and they all squeezed into the same booth, three on a side. The mood was boisterous. True to form, Joan kept them all entertained with gossip about old classmates as they scanned the menus. Dinah was oddly disappointed when she heard that Lana Gervais and Jimmy Wright were together again. She felt sorry for Jimmy—he would always play second fiddle in Lana's orchestra, and everyone knew it. But she had an especially pitying empathy for Lana—she knew the measure of her loss.

They hadn't ordered yet when another group came through the door. Dinah looked up to see Bill Lange, followed by Stan, Joey, and Hayes. As the boys approached their table, she realized it was likely pre-arranged—Stan and Marlys had been seeing a lot of each other over the summer. The boys slid into the next booth, but within minutes there was a re-shuffling, as Marlys angled to sit with Stan. In the end, Dinah, Betsy, and Laurie sat with Bill and Hayes. Bill and Dinah shared one side of the booth and a plate of French fries. Their rapport was relaxed and teasing—it reminded Dinah of the first months she had known him. He was showing her a trick he had learned—an illusion of bending a spoon—when another familiar face came in.

Kenny Mitchell was with his father—a replica of Kenny, but taller and wearing round, black-framed glasses that gave him the aspect of an owl. As they passed the booth, Kenny stopped short, while his father moved along to find a table. He looked intently at Dinah, and then at Bill, and then back to Dinah.

"Hello." There was a question in his tone.

"Hi, Kenny. Meet my friends—you know Betsy, and this is Laurie, and Stan, and this is Bill."

With customary directness, Kenny turned to Bill, his voice flat: "Are you the friend who sends letters in Latin?" It took a second for Dinah to register the reference; she felt her cheeks grow hot.

Bill looked confused, but then a flash of amusement crossed his features. "No, I can't say that I am." He looked levelly at Kenny. "That's someone else. Our loss."

Dinah thought Kenny must have been the only person in the entire high school who wasn't aware of her situation with Tru. His intense focus blinded him to anything that didn't have direct bearing on his world. Since they had started working together their friendship had grown. It was a fun challenge to keep up with his intellectual wit, and she appreciated the literary bent of their conversations. He invented games to keep them occupied when things were slow, which, during the summer months, was fairly often. One of them was called "Predict the Genre." It was easier than it sounded—Kenny had a system that proved the stereotype: Cardigan sweaters gave away mystery lovers; floral dresses meant Romance; teenage boys were only there for summer school, so that meant one of the Classics, and so forth. Young children didn't count—they inevitably choose whatever book they could find with the most pictures. So far Kenny was ahead, but it was close. He hit it out of the park one day with the bold assertion that a portly, bespectacled man with a grey goatee would walk out the door carrying Proust under his arm. Dinah still suspected a set-up, but she hadn't been able to prove it. The same day, Dinah misread a little old lady in a straw hat with plastic fruit on it. She saw something in the way of horticultural instruction, like *The Spirit of the Garden*. Kenny, who predicted Romance, won by association when the prim biddy checked out Kinsey's *Sexual Behavior in the Human Male*.

Now she wondered whether he had construed their friendship as something more. She hadn't missed his expression at seeing her there with Bill. And then Bill had implied that she was still receiving letters in Latin. If only that were the case. She didn't even know what had become of her own letter to Tru. She had scoured the room after Coco left the next day, but there was no sign of it. At first she waited for Coco to say something—her embarrassment at having been exposed as an intruder surpassed exponentially by her mortification at Coco being privy to her most private thoughts. She had nervously waited for a caustic comment about trespassing or, worse, the nature of the letter, but Coco seemed oblivious, and Dinah hadn't been able to bring herself to broach the subject. A cigar box labeled *Panama Gold* and a certain tattered cardboard file had come to mind. She remembered her vow to never leave anything so personal to posterity, and had to admit a glaring poetic justice.

Finally, she concluded that it would be easier to simply write another letter. She didn't know if she would ever discover what had become of the first one, but by that time she had decided it would be best to wait until Tru returned from Exeter at the end of the summer—what good could a letter do from thousands of miles away? It had been over six months since she had first written—she was starting to wonder if it would make any difference at all. And so, as desperately as she wished otherwise, there were no letters. Kenny had nothing to worry about.

However, he now looked about as uncomfortable as it was possible for Kenny to look—his normally unflappable self-possession just slightly disturbed, as revealed by the flare of his nostrils and a sharp swallow. "I'll see you at work." He gave her a pointed look, nodding curtly to the others as he moved away.

A merciless August sun fell on the shoulders of the volunteers as they worked to set up for the big event. Weather had been the topic among the group for days: A predicted nor'easter had dissipated somewhere off the coast of Newfoundland, the clear blue sky answering the prayers of the committee as they nervously anticipated a sell-out crowd. The Centennial Gala for the Friends of the Library was the biggest thing to hit Salem since the Witch Trials. Coco had succeeded in drawing not only the most prominent contributors in town, but some very well-heeled acquaintances from Boston, who had donated generously in anticipation of a superlatively glittering evening.

Dinah and Kenny were among the laborers arranging chairs around linen-draped tables and stringing lights across the soaring canopies. Every employee of the library was enlisted to help, and there were countless others from the committee who were scurrying to and fro with armloads of flowers and engraved place-cards. The Willows was the chosen venue, with sheets of wooden flooring hauled in to cover the grassy expanse overlooking the harbor near the bandstand. Three enormous canopies had been erected, providing shelter for the guests in the event of rain, but Dinah suspected that the rain knew better than to darken Coco's doorstep—the sky was accommodatingly clear. Tiny lights were strung throughout the willow trees on the periphery, and everything in sight was festooned with silky white organza and calla lilies—Coco's favorite flower.

To her surprise, Dinah had learned that Tom was being honored for his significant contributions to the foundation. She had been completely unaware of his charity to the Salem Public Library. Once again, her stepfather had amazed her. His quiet generosity needed no tumult or shouting—he preferred to keep his philanthropy private. In fact, he had been reluctant to accept the recognition, bowing only under the weight of Coco's insistence: He knew that she had been counting on the reflected glory to cap off her tenure as board member and chairwoman of the Gala.

The other factor in Tom's reluctance, Dinah knew, was his increasing difficulty with balance. He now walked with the assistance of a cane.

She imagined that he would prefer to avoid directing a spotlight on his trembling hands and tipsy gait. There had been no more signs of injury, but Dinah suspected that he may have fallen again on more than one occasion—his unsteadiness was treacherous. The experimental drug that Dr. Phelps had so optimistically prescribed had done nothing; in fact, the symptoms had worsened. She feared that soon her stepfather would require a wheelchair—the image stirring up an aching pathos. Pushing back a stray tendril of damp hair, she took the paper cup of water that Kenny was handing her and emptied it in one long drink.

"They're unloading more boxes of linens—looks like we'll be here all day." Kenny didn't mind the work; unlike the volunteers, library employees were actually on the clock.

"Jane wants us here early to man the registration table, so we can get going pretty soon. Did you try on your dad's suit?" Dinah was teasing—she had struggled to convince Kenny to take the opportunity offered them: As employees of the library they could attend the Gala free of charge. Kenny had promptly rejected the invitation, citing a lack of proper wardrobe as the easy excuse, until Dinah pressured him into borrowing his father's best worsted blue suit.

"Would you believe me if I said it didn't fit?" He turned to follow her gaze, which was fixed on a moving truck in the parking lot, where several men in dark green coveralls were hauling the final pieces of planking for the stage. She seemed strangely transfixed by the process. Kenny couldn't imagine what she found so fascinating. As two of the men passed with a wide plywood panel, he noticed that the taller one balanced most of the weight on his left shoulder, while his right arm swung at his side. Then he noticed the absence of his right hand. "Would you look at that? That's quite a trick. I wonder how he manages the really heavy stuff."

Dinah had a thoughtful, faraway look on her face, and she was silent for a long moment. When she spoke, her words were soft and sad, and she bowed her head as she said them: "He just does."

Pulling her dress from the closet, Dinah paused to admire the cut and the fabric. She had been hesitant to let her mother buy it for her—the price tag was shocking. But Caroline had insisted, telling her that there were times when it was folly to count the cost, and this was one of them. Dinah had to admit it was a dreamy creation—all floating chiffon and silky shantung, a delicate shell-pink that glowed like candlelight against her skin. She had never owned a strapless gown before—it made her feel as glamorous as . . . well . . . as Coco. She had just come from her mother's dressing table, where Caroline had pulled Dinah's hair up into an elegant French twist, leaning in to apply a swish of mascara and a layer of pale pink lipstick—a perfect match for the dress. Then Caroline had kissed her daughter lightly on the forehead, saying that she was the prettiest thing to come along since the magnolia. Dinah carefully slipped the dress over her head, zipping it up the side and twirling around for effect. The skirt floated around her like a cloud. She slid her feet into a pair of satin pumps, dyed to match the dress, and picked up her small silver clutch.

As she went into the hallway she passed Tom, collar and cuffs unbuttoned, tie in hand. His smiled at her tenderly, but his words held a trace of regret: "You look lovely, my dear—a vision deserving of a worthier audience." His words covered his emotion with charm and grace, but Dinah understood; the eminence of the occasion served to magnify Tru's absence—she knew Tom missed his son terribly.

She followed him to the bedroom, twirling again for her mother's approval. Caroline was still in her dressing gown, but her hair was skillfully arranged in a sleek chignon and her make-up was perfect. Dinah kissed her goodbye and headed for the door. Turning back, she unintentionally witnessed a tender, private moment, as her mother rose up on her toes to kiss Tom's cheek, while gently taking the tie from his spasmodically jerking hand.

Kenny was already in the driveway when she came down the stairs. He was nothing if not prompt. Getting out of the car to open her door, he walked with such an exaggeratedly stiff gait that Dinah had to laugh. He gave her a mournful look. "Go ahead, enjoy my misery. I'll be all dressed and ready for my funeral when I broil to death. Let's see who's laughing then." There was already a fine sheen of sweat beading on his forehead.

"You can take your coat off until we get there, Einstein. You'll be fine. It's always hottest in the car." She slid onto the warm seat, smoothing the skirt under her.

Kenny threw his jacket into the back seat. As he got back in the car he turned to Dinah, almost mumbling: "You look nice. I like your dress." His compliment sounded perfunctory, and it made Dinah smile—charm was not Kenny's strong suit. They drove with the windows down. Dinah was certain she would arrive looking like she'd been electrocuted, but Caroline's handiwork held, and the French twist was still in place when they pulled up to the park.

Their duty at the registration table lasted well into the cocktail hour. Kenny handed a table number to a last group of stragglers as a waiter in white tie and tails circled in a slow promenade, daintily striking his three-tone chimes to inform the guests that it was time to be seated for dinner. There was only one card left on the registration table: *Mr. and Mrs. Thomas Stuart: Table One.* Dinah was becoming increasingly worried—she could imagine all too easily what may have caused the delay. Kenny looked at her questioningly, and she shrugged as she picked up the card, trying to stifle her anxiety. "I guess we should sit down. Hopefully they'll get here before the program starts."

Dinah and Kenny took their seats. The library employees were grouped together on the outer edge of the covered space, farthest from the bandstand, where the presentation stage was set. The tables seated ten. The only empty seats remaining at their table were flanked by Joanne O'Connor and an octogenarian named Wilfred Woolsey, who worked only on Tuesday afternoons, as he had for thirty-five years. Mike was there with Jane, but extended conversation was difficult at the large table. Joanne contributed some interesting local lore about Captain Bertram and the history of the library, while Kenny made an impressive effort to appear interested as Wilfred Woolsey waxed nostalgic about the better days Salem had seen, before the preponderance of the "damned automobile" had made the simple act of walking to work a treacherous risk. The old man spoke with didactic authority and the volume to match. He also sprayed a fine mist with each sibilant syllable; Dinah noticed that Kenny barely touched his food.

The lights had begun to glimmer in the dusk as the waiters delivered the soup course; by the time the chocolate mousse was served it was almost impossible to tell the twinkling ceiling of the canopy from the starry night sky. Throughout the meal, Dinah craned her neck, peering over the crowded tables to see if her mother and Tom were in place, seated with Coco at the table of honor. It was hard to tell through the bustle of waiters and the rows of towering centerpieces, but she was fairly certain that there were two empty places front and center. Halfway through dessert, she recognized Coco's tall, angular profile moving toward the stage, engrossed in discussion with a fellow board member. Even from a distance, Dinah could tell that Coco was upset—she was literally wringing her hands. Stopping at the stage risers, the pair seemed to be deliberating about something.

Just then, Dinah noticed two figures coming in from the garlanded entrance path. Tom was moving at a reasonably hurried pace, given that he needed to use the cane. He reached his sister as she was turning to mount the steps, and then he did something unusual: Dinah watched with baffled curiosity as Tom threw his arms around Coco and lifted her off the floor, his cane toppling over but his balance holding steady. Then a waiter stepped in front of the table, blocking her view.

Tom and Caroline took their seats as Coco took the stage, a chorus of forks tapping on the crystal to quiet the crowd. After a moderately lengthy speech about the success of the Friends of the Library fundraising campaign and the significance of the centennial landmark, she moved on to the award recognition, heralding the recipients with all the pomp and fanfare of a royal coronation. Not surprisingly, Tom's presentation was saved for last. Coco's voice resonated with satisfaction as she pronounced her brother's name. He stood, and Dinah saw that Caroline stood with him, accompanying him to the risers and holding his elbow firmly as she ushered him up the stairs. She stepped back into the wings as Tom crossed the stage. He was smiling broadly despite the sway of his step, and he fairly beamed as he accepted the honor, looking over the crowd with undisguised pleasure. Dinah was surprised by his evident delight—she hadn't thought Tom enjoyed that kind of recognition. But his happiness was contagious, even across the span of the canopies, and she found herself smiling along with him.

The orchestra struck up as the applause died down, and there was a busy rush as the guests rearranged themselves, fanning out to the cocktail tables on the perimeter and the dance floor at the front. Dinah felt a nudge under the table; Kenny was looking sideways at her, darting his eyes toward the parking lot. She grinned, knowing that he was desperate to get away from Mr. Woolsey. Mischievously, she played her advantage: "Are you asking me to dance?" Her innocent expression was contrived—she knew full well that Kenny hated dancing. "I'd be delighted!" She stood, holding out her hand expectantly.

Helplessly, Kenny stood, taking her arm as she headed toward the bandstand. "This isn't exactly what I had in mind," he grumbled. "I was thinking more along the lines of finding an escape route."

"Come on—it won't be that bad. Dancing is easy; you just have to feel the rhythm." The phrase brought a piercing stab as she remembered her first dance with Tru, when he had cupped his hand under her chin, pulling her into his eyes, saying "Look here. Look at me." She closed her eyes, waiting for the sharp pang of longing to subside.

The orchestra was playing "Stardust." As Dinah looked around her, she couldn't help admiring Coco's achievement—the trees twinkled against the black velvet of the night, the stars sparkled in the sky, and the party glittered as if it had been sprinkled with fairy dust. The only thing that didn't shine was Kenny's expression, as he awkwardly grasped her hand, laying an arm stiffly across her back. She had to suppress a smile at his ungainly shuffling—he was even worse than Bill. As the song came to an end, she teased him coyly. "Would you care to stay for another, or would you prefer to go back and get the weather report from Wilfred?"

Defeated, Kenny once again took her hand. A sweet, haunting melody floated through the air—"I'll be Seeing You"—one of Dinah's favorite songs. With the poignant lyrics running through her mind, Dinah's eyes played a trick on her. As Kenny turned mechanically in a small circle, she thought she saw a ghost—the manifestation of her subconscious yearning—standing alone, just outside the ambient glow of the tiny lights, watching her. Knowing it was nothing but a hallucination, she turned back, wistfully looking to the space where Tru had been, anticipating the disappointment, understanding she would find no one but a stranger.

But she was wrong. From the shadows, the dark eyes she knew like the beating of her own heart—the same eyes that held her in her dreams—now held her in their gaze, rooting her to the spot as the rest of the world disappeared.

Confused by the abrupt halt in her step, Kenny was defensive. "I told you I couldn't dance." He was looking at her sheepishly, waiting for reassurance, but it didn't come. In fact, she didn't seem to have heard him. It was then that he noticed a tall, vaguely familiar-looking guy crossing the floor, moving toward Dinah like a slow and deliberate arrow, straight to its mark.

Without taking his eyes off Dinah, Tru addressed Kenny. "Mind if I cut in?"

Kenny looked curiously at Dinah, and then at Tru. And then he understood. With resigned acceptance, he answered with a question of his own: "Let me guess—you speak Latin, right?"

Without responding, Tru took Dinah in his arms. It was clear that, for them, Kenny didn't exist—nor did anyone else.

Shaking his head, Kenny walked away, turning back briefly to see them fused together, alone in the crowd. He also saw something he had never seen before: It was the look on Dinah's face. Though he knew they couldn't hear him, he said it anyway—a muttered reproof to whoever it was that held her now, putting the light back in Dinah's eyes: "It's about time."

CHAPTER THIRTY
Deliverance

MOVING AWAY FROM THE CROWD, they gravitated toward the darkness—toward the privacy of the night. Tru held her hand, and they walked across the grass of the park. Although it seemed surreal, Dinah also had the feeling that the earth was finally fully under her feet. Beneath the curtain of an ancient willow, his eyes fell on the tiny sailboat glinting below the hollow of her throat. Softly, he ran his finger over her collar bone, looking wonderingly at the necklace. "It's still there." His voice held an awed disbelief—a witnessing of a miracle.

Dinah couldn't speak; she was afraid that he was a mirage, terrified that he would disappear. Finally, she risked finding out: "How . . . when . . .?"

Slowly, he drew something from his jacket pocket. It was dog-eared and rumpled, but Dinah recognized the pale blue velum. Proffering it as explanation, he closed his eyes and pulled her to him, his voice a hoarse whisper as he buried his face in her hair: "What took you so long?"

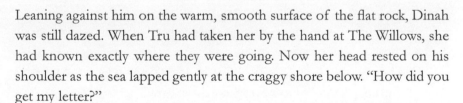

Leaning against him on the warm, smooth surface of the flat rock, Dinah was still dazed. When Tru had taken her by the hand at The Willows, she had known exactly where they were going. Now her head rested on his shoulder as the sea lapped gently at the craggy shore below. "How did you get my letter?"

"It came with a letter from Coco, along with an airline ticket home." He sounded exhausted—a tattered, war-weary refugee who had finally been given asylum. "Why didn't you send it?"

Coco had sent him her letter? Dinah was floored—the woman had never given any indication she found it. And then she sent it to Tru? How could that be possible? Dinah could understand his confusion—she could understand the hurt in it, as well; it made her weak with regret. Why hadn't she seen it sooner? Why had it taken her dear, wise old aunt to tell her what she should have known?

"I did . . . it got lost. All the time, I thought you knew, and then I didn't know what to do . . . " She realized she wasn't making sense, but there were so many things to explain—she didn't know how to begin. And so she told him everything—how she had misunderstood, how she had suffered, how she had continued to love him, even though she believed she had lost him. She reiterated everything she had written and more.

Resting against the sheltering wall of granite, they slowly filled in the blanks, saying all the things that had needed to be said for a very long time. Finally, Dinah explained how Coco came to have her letter. Tru explained that he had arrived just as Tom and Caroline were leaving for the gala—that they hadn't known he was coming home. "There was something I had to talk to my dad about—it was the reason Coco wrote to me. I'll explain it later."

So that was why Tom and Caroline had been so late to the Gala, and why Tom had looked so happy. Now Dinah understood why he had embraced Coco that way, and why he couldn't contain the smile on his face. She ran her hand along the pleats of Tru's shirt front—his jacket was slung over his shoulder. "Where did you get the tuxedo?" The idea that he was here with her, that she could touch him, talk to him, after all the days and weeks and months—a year and a half—was still confounding her. It seemed like a dream.

"Harley had it in the car when he picked me up at the airport. Coco knew I was trying to get home in time to be there for my dad—I guess she must have known that my flight was delayed."

"Harley's here?" Dinah was surprised—she had half-believed that Coco had left him.

"He's here. Just in time for Coco's big moment. I guess he's still jumping through her hoops." He stood up, reaching down to pull her to her feet. "Come here." Dinah noticed that he winced as he used his right arm. They walked to the water's edge, holding hands and looking out over the dark waves, where Jacob's ladder climbed to the moon. Dinah noticed a thin white scar that ran from his right temple to just below his cheekbone. Impossibly, it made him even more attractive.

After a few minutes, Tru pulled something else out of the pocket of his jacket. In the moonlight, Dinah recognized the holly pattern of the wrapping paper—it was the small box from the hall closet shelf. Silently, he handed it to her, the tag from Christmas past still attached. It simply said: *Dinah*. Slowly, she opened it, revealing a small velvet box. Inside was the most exquisitely beautiful thing she had ever seen—a fulgent, square-cut emerald, set in a gleaming platinum ring. She stared at it, speechless.

"It was my mother's—my dad gave it to her when I was born. After she died, he gave it to me." He was looking at her steadily.

She was motionless. It had been in the closet all this time, with her name on it. He had intended to give this to her long, long ago.

"There's something I . . . need you to do." Tru was hesitant, as though afraid he was asking too much.

Dinah couldn't imagine what he could possibly think she wouldn't do for him. She would walk right across the harbor if he asked her to. "What is it?"

He took a deep breath. "I can't . . ." He paused, a haunted expression crossing his features. "I won't . . . go back to school, or anywhere else, without you. I can't ever do that again. So . . ." He looked into her eyes, speaking very softly. "So it looks like you have to marry me." And then, like a child in prayer, he added a word, fervent and hushed: "Please."

When Caroline realized that Dinah and Tru were gone, she smiled. She was glad they had left; she knew they needed time alone. She was still overcome with relief—on behalf of both her daughter and her husband. When Tru had walked up the driveway, she could actually feel Tom's happiness, shimmering like a mirage over a warm, sandy desert.

At first, when Coco had come to her with her plan, Caroline had been hesitant. She had written her own letter to Tru not long after the accident. In it, she had insisted that he wasn't to blame, imploring him to come home. But her words had failed to stanch the bleeding; her essay couldn't heal the wound. She read the letter that her sister-in-law had written, wondering if it could be possible that Coco was actually offering it up for Caroline's approval. It explained everything about Whit and Margaret. Coco told Tru that his father had borne the burden of the secret for too long, and she had decided to take the matter into her own hands, releasing Tom from the crushing responsibility of the decision. And then she told him about the change in Tom's condition—the worsening of the symptoms. Subtly, she implied that it was time to take the weight off of his father's shoulders, to relieve the worry and the relentless anxiety of finding a way to tell his son the truth. She asked him to come home.

Her letter was beautiful—Caroline was struck by the delicacy and grace of her words. It was truly, she realized, an act of love. But as much as she approved of the letter—as much as she could see that it was, above all, a gift to Tom—she still wasn't sure. She worried that Coco's revelations, instead of calling him home, could drive Tru even further away. And then Coco had shown her Dinah's letter, and suddenly it was clear: If Coco's letter couldn't bring him home, this one would. She knew with empirical certainty: This was what he had been waiting for.

Her sister-in-law hadn't told her about the cabled response from Tru. It wasn't until Harley pulled up in the driveway as they were leaving the house and a young man stepped out of the passenger side that her instincts were confirmed. Tru immediately went to Tom, who held onto his son like a life preserver in a stormy sea. When Tru asked to speak to his father alone, Caroline didn't wonder why. The two men were shuttered in the library for nearly an hour. When they came out, Tom was transformed. It was clear that they both knew the identity of Tru's father: It was the man with his arm around his son's shoulders.

Now, looking over at the woman accepting congratulations from a trail of exiting guests, Caroline tried to reconcile the implausibility of Coco as savior. From a stranger's perspective, her asperity continued to give off a cowing formidability, but Caroline could no longer feel the chilling draft. Instead, she felt warmth—the warmth of sincere gratitude for the woman she was glad to call family.

Standing to Coco's left, Harley wore his signature bored countenance, but he, too, had turned out to be a surprise. Just when Caroline had decided the marriage was over, Harley arrived to celebrate Coco's efforts—revealing a supportive loyalty that proved a real devotion to his wife. He had also proven that he wasn't a total loss when it came to hard work and diligence. Evidently, it simply took the right combination of recreational passion and vocational opportunity for Harley's light to shine. After Tom and Tru had come out of the library, Harley asked for a moment with Tom, in which he presented him with a check for full repayment of all monies advanced. Tom seemed as proud as a new father of Harley's success.

Turning toward her husband, Caroline thought he seemed stronger than he had in a long time. Relaxed and leaning back in his chair, he was surveying the scene with a distant, dreamy expression on his face. She knew he was miles away, relishing his son's return, basking in the relief of the truth told. He looked contented. Although the disease continued to press forward on its relentless march, there was no longer a shadow behind her husband's eyes. Caroline knew that as long as his son was shining, Tom's sun would shine.

As she gazed at him, she caught a movement over his shoulder, in the branches of a tree. Not one of the willows, but a delicate Pagoda dogwood that stood just outside the canopy. There was a fluttering sound, and then a soft cooing. In the twinkling light, Caroline saw something rarer than snow in June: It was a pure white dove, perched on a swaying bough, watching them steadily with tiny, bright eyes. For a long, marvelous moment she looked back at the luminous creature, allowing its calm gaze to suffuse her heart with transcendent hope. She felt the warmth of Jemima's spirit just as though her daughter's small arms were wrapped around her neck—a solid presence snuggled against her, tucked to her breast. And then, with one last lingering look, the dove lifted its wings to the breeze and flew away. Turning her face to the sky, Caroline followed its flight, wondrous at the deliverance of hope, and the grace that allowed her to look ahead.

EPILOGUE
How to Sail

THE LITTLE BOY COULD HEAR his name—a duet of voices, frantically calling to him from just beyond the crepe myrtle. He hadn't meant to cause alarm; he just wanted to put his new boat in the water. "I'm over here," he called back. Watching his wooden sailboat bobbing along on the water, he carefully pulled it by a string, wandering along the river's edge. Suddenly his grandmother burst through the foliage, shaking her head and her finger at him.

"Naughty boy—you know you can't come down to the river by yourself." Caroline scooped him up and hugged him tightly, as the owner of the other voice hurried through a thicket of kudzu with her hand over her heart.

"Lordy! You nearly gave me apoplexy, little boy. I swear—you will be the death of me yet!" Batty's drawl was breathless. Each of the women took him by a hand, leading him back to the yard beyond the trees. "We'd better get you home, so your momma can get you cleaned up before bed." His great-great aunt looked askance at his dirty hands and knees.

He loved all the women in his life—they were a constant, nurturing presence that enveloped him in kisses and caresses and love. He clutched his sailboat, carrying it back to his own doorstep, where his mother waited on the front porch swing.

"The little scoundrel got away from us today!" Batty smiled, her exasperation tempered by affection. "He scooted down to the water before his grandma could catch up with him."

His mother stood to take his hand, leaning toward him in consternation. "When Nana is looking after you, it's very important that you listen to what she tells you." She scolded him gently as she led him inside.

In the bathtub he played with his toy boats while his mother scrubbed his hands and face. She grabbed a fluffy towel and wrapped him up, hugging him tightly and kissing his cheeks. He rested his head on her shoulder: "Were you a good 'brarian today?"

"I certainly did try to be. Were you a good boy today?"

"I certly did try to be," he said solemnly. "I'm sorry I scared Nana and Batty."

His words were sweet and sincere—she felt a familiar helplessness against them. He had clearly inherited his father's disarming charm. Carrying him to his bedroom, she plopped him down on the bed, lying by his side with her arms still around him. She looked at him seriously. "You know that you can never go to the water by yourself, don't you?"

He gazed back at her, and then reached up a small hand, gently fingering the silver sailboat that dangled from a chain around her neck. "I went with Nana and Batty," he insisted quietly. Squinting his eyes, he held his bottom lip between tiny teeth, as if trying to remember something: "But the little scowdrels got away from me!" His small voice resonated with self-righteous justification.

His mother laughed, discerning a subtle pattern in what was revealing itself to be a rather defiant nature. She helped him pull on his soft, cotton pajamas with the sailboats on them. She was tucking the blankets around him when his grandmother came in.

"I thought I'd just peek in before I leave." She leaned down for their special goodnight—a kiss on each cheek, one on the nose, butterfly eyelashes, and the last on the lips.

After his grandmother left, his mother sat on the bed and stroked his hair, streaked from the sun and falling in feathery disarray—like a bird's wing, she thought. Looking into deep, coffee-colored eyes, she kissed him gently, holding his face in her hands. And then, as she did every night, she recited their prayer: "The moon watches over the boy that I love, one perfect angel, sent from above."

Running her own bath, she stepped into the deep, copper tub. These days she worked at the Beaufort public library only on Saturday afternoons, but it had been a long day, and she felt a little tired. Earlier in the year she had taken a sabbatical, turning the head librarian position over to someone else. But she found that she missed being surrounded by books, and so she managed to carve out a tiny slice of time on the weekend to immerse herself in the milieu that was as natural to her as breathing. Now she immersed herself in the warm, fragrant bath, squeezing the sponge to let the water run over her face, washing away the traces of the day.

Rising, she wrapped a towel around her and went into the bedroom, pulling her nightgown from the closet. A low voice stopped her in her tracks. "Stay right where you are."

She froze, one hand holding the towel around her chest, the other holding the negligee.

"Turn around."

She did as she was told, turning toward the voice.

"Now walk over here . . . slowly."

She moved forward, stopping at the side of the bed.

"Drop it."

Smiling, she shook her head, looking down at the supine figure on the blanket. He was wearing only a pair of worn chinos—the ones he usually wore to go sailing.

"What about her?" she asked.

"Who, her? She's asleep—she won't mind. She's seen it before, anyway."

Reaching down, she picked up the tiny form sleeping on his bare chest. She held her tightly for a moment, inhaling the lovely baby scent before laying her gently in the bassinet by the window. As she moved back to the bed, her husband put down the brief he had been reading and snapped off the lamp on the nightstand. In the darkness a pair of hands grabbed her, whisking the towel away as they pulled her down onto the bed.

She put a finger to her lips. "Shhhh. If we wake her . . ." She gasped, whispering through a giggle: "What are you doing?"

"Res ipsa loquitur, baby." His voice was muffled.

"You lawyer-types are all alike . . ." Her words had taken on a breathless quality. "You think you can just throw around a little Latin and all the girls will swoon." She couldn't deny that the thing *did* speak for itself.

"Daddy?" A small voice came from the doorway.

A groan floated out of the darkness. "Hey, Buddy. What's up?"

"You didn't say goodnight."

"Sorry, pal. Your sister was holding me captive. Come here."

The little boy padded over to the bed, and his father pulled him into his arms. "Goodnight, Tommy. Tomorrow we're going out on the cat, so you get right to sleep now, OK?"

"Is Momma coming?"

His mother leaned over to smooth her hand over his cheek. "I need to stay here with Jemima—you boys can go ahead without me."

He turned to his father, looking serious. "You should take Momma sailing, Daddy."

A familiar, oblique grin spread across his father's face. "I was just thinking that very thing." He kissed his son goodnight. As the little boy scampered back to his room, Tru took Dinah into his arms, and once again, he showed her how to sail.